To Josh,

# BLACK HALLOWS

Blappy reading!

Tom G.H. Adry.

# BLACK HALLOWS

## TOM G.H. ADAMS AND ANDREW NAISBITT

Writing in Starlight

Published by Writing In Starlight, Brampton, Cumbria, UK

# Contents

    ix

Acknowledgements     xii

Tayem     xv

1.   A black rain falls     1

2.   On majestic wings     17

3.   Evil comes to call     24

4.   Rumblings from beneath     36

5.   While the laughing moon bleeds     44

6.   Seven sewn and seven split     52

7.   Waiting for the nail     66

8.   Ambush at the crossing     75

9.   Under the mask     82

10.   Silver spoons and golden chains     92

| 11. | Lord of dreams | 104 |
| 12. | The temptation of Wobas | 111 |
| 13. | Time for tea and treachery | 125 |
| 14. | Colour me darkly | 141 |
| 15. | One eye above, one below | 148 |
| 16. | Unusual appetites | 160 |
| 17. | The burning of yesterday | 170 |
| 18. | Trysts and collusions | 180 |
| 19. | Of fire and blood | 191 |
| 20. | Soul grinder | 210 |
| 21. | All flags fall | 220 |
| 22. | One blasphemy too many | 228 |
| 23. | A thunderstorm in the heart | 240 |
| 24. | A change of fortunes | 263 |
| 25. | A maelstrom of deceit | 275 |
| 26. | A city falls | 290 |
| 27. | The angry mountains cry | 298 |
| 28. | Blood on the Dragon Talon Gates | 316 |
| 29. | Tir ti rinov wurunwa di loreatis (Don't ever dream of dying) | 336 |

| 30. | Benevolent malevolence | 346 |
| 31. | Bereft of a kingdom | 358 |
| 32. | Shadow of shame | 371 |
| 33. | Path of the Gigantes | 382 |
| 34. | At water's end | 390 |
| 35. | The anger within | 399 |
| 36. | Amongst the mist and shadows | 416 |
| 37. | Dreamer deceiver | 432 |
| 38. | The culture of hidden means | 447 |
| 39. | Tunnel of torment | 463 |
| 40. | A Queen's messenger | 477 |
| 41. | For want of a soul | 491 |
| 42. | Sojourn in the sanctuary | 512 |
| 43. | Holy outlaw | 530 |
| 44. | Hiding from the light | 539 |
| 45. | Choices of the damned | 554 |
| 46. | Keeper of evil | 561 |
| 47. | A gathering storm | 570 |
| 48. | The Earthshaker's gift | 582 |

49.  Shout at the wind                              589

50.  Busted souls                                   601

51.  'Til all is gone                               613

52.  Aftermaths                                     635

Oga                                                 651
Characters                                          652
About Tom Adams                                     658
About Andrew Naisbitt                               660
Can't get enough of the Black Hallows?              662

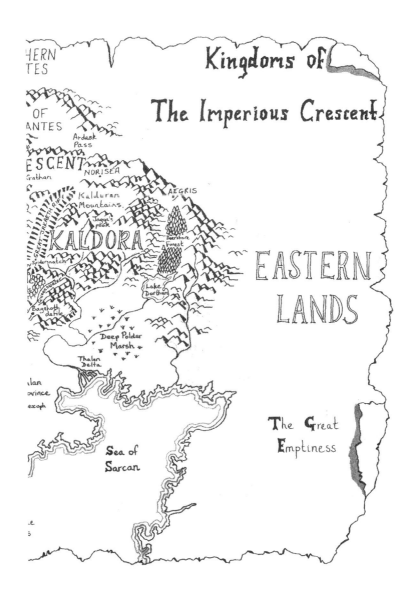

Kingdoms of

The Imperious Crescent

HERN
TES

OF
ANTES

Ardask
Pass

ESCENT
Grathan

NORISEA

AEGRIS

Kulduran
Mountains

Jagra's
peak

KALDORA

Spidernatch

Queensbolt

Deershore
Forest

Lake
Dorthan

EASTERN

LANDS

Bagshott
dattle

Deep Polder
Marsh

Thalan
Delta

llan
ovince

exoph

Sea of
Sarcan

The Great
Emptiness

e
s

# Acknowledgements

Writing a novel of this length, let alone a trilogy, is a daunting task. It was eased along by the constant support and contributions of many.

First and foremost, we would like to thank all those who pledged on the Black Hallows Kickstarter campaign and expressed their confidence in the Cradle of Darkness project by signing up. They are:

Joranth, Richard Orbain, Adam da Silva, Anthony Dauphin, Jose Perez, Craig G, David Stockford, Carlo Striebel, Alucard, John Duxbury, Kyle Watters, Ben Wicka, Knockman, Gavin Brown, George, Ishaelle, Enzo Maini, Chris Allen, Dominique Locatelli, Flying Explosive Monkey, Francesco, Kent Reinbold, Patrick Melvin, Jimmy Segrist, Brian Hum, Matthew Ferry, Lhunaira, Luis Mari, Jonathan West, Rhel, Luke Styer, Jerry Betti, James Lynch, Cristalios, Brandon Ames, Tadgh Pound, Nathan Swift, Mark — Poet Laureate of Valoria, Christian Kirchberg, Sergi Martinez Vilaboa, Christopher

W. Kowalski, Robin Mayenfels, Ols Jonas Petter Olsson, Kehlenschnitt (Miremarsh Stumpy), Roland, Graham Rymer, Tim Noble, Alexander Brethouwer, Marco Solleveld, Alexandre Boisgard, Mark, Helen R. Harkness, Joshua Mobley, Adrián Merino Martínez, Tammy Wyatt-Johnson, William Creighton, Russell Love, Thimo Wilke, Boyd Atkinson, Alucard, Robert Fanelli, Raymond Saunders, Nestor Pumilio, Craig Welsh, Brenan Flinders, Paul D. Jarman, Michael Stump, J. Dean Strohm, Derek R Boudreaux, Leokii, Andrew Hauptman, Finlay Smith, Peter Mitchell, Maggi D, Max, Benjamin, Martin Carrick, Andrew Parker, Hellcat, Ethan Malloy, Rubin Bryant, Jimmy Segrist, Doug Eckhoff, Frank Blau, T.J. Mathews, Matthew Ferry, Robert, Iain Smith, Patrick Mastrobuono, A. Hardy, David Franklin, Paul M. Reynolds, Martin Håkansson, Elijah Hanson, Jean Adams, Alexander Olney, Gary Johnson, M. Zottmann, Christopher Farrington, Mark of the Raging Blood Clan, Marcos, Violet Fermin, Benjamin, Robert, Bubba MacPherson, Luke Styer, Mick McArt

Special mention must go to our illustrious team of beta readers – Helen Harkness, Karen Brown, Natalie Naisbitt, and Natalie Hedley, Peter Moore, Paul Raistrick, Nick Carbonaro, Victoria Adams, Brenda Wintle and Dave Wharton. Your feedback really helped shape the novel at a crucial stage.

Many thanks to our essential grammarian and editor,

Karen Brown, for the meticulous work she carried out on line editing and proof-reading.

Our sincere thanks go to Charlotte, who acted as model for Tayem, and posed for many a photo-shoot in woods, castles and the general wilderness. It was these sessions that initiated the whole writing project. Thanks also to Jon Stynes for his expert photographic skills that produced such stunning shots.

Tom would like to thank Helen, his ever-patient wife, for putting up with him being locked in the Dragon Cave for months on end. It was particularly taxing for her to keep quiet while recording the audio book.

Andrew would like to thank all those who talked through plot ideas when visiting Hadrian's Hobbies and of course Natalie, his long suffering wife for her patience and support...And last but not least the Ozzy (Oswald) the ginger tomcat.

The authors would also like to acknowledge the wonderful hospitality afforded by a number of coffee shops where much of the first draft writing took place: Off The Wall, Mr Brown's, Dunelm, Meg's Tea Room, Costa, Cakes and Ale.

I

# A BLACK RAIN FALLS

———

Veils of darkness shrouded Queen Tayem Fyreglance as she sat brooding on the grey powdered earth — residue of a hundred shattered dragon wings from aeons past. The first heavy drops of rain fell from an overburdened sky, wetting her scalp and forming beads on the iron pauldrons of her armour. Beyond this sanctified ground lay a meadow of poisoned grass, together with the occasional contorted, blackened tree clawing its way through sickly greenery, as if drawn upward by some unseen energy. Leaves shed from these arboreal travesties formed a mouldering carpet of death. Yet this inhospitable setting had a special place in her royal heart. A single tear streaked her cheek as her eyes came to rest on her father's grave. Although it had been five sols since his passing, she had found herself drawn back here daily, the place of his final resting. The shrine seemed to beckon her.

Beside the Queen lay her royal shield. The dragon's eye boss at its centre seemed to blink as if in mute sympathy with her grief. A dull purple light emanated from the eye and reflected off a small pool of water lying at the bottom of a deep depression in the ground. As Tayem watched, the unearthly crater sent out a wisp of etheric energy, tracing its way upwards to caress the polished stone resting on her father's tomb.

Tayem had heard the mythos of these hallows from her father, a man whose lasting achievement was to die too soon, a victim of his failure to summon the potential from these myriad fissures in the earth.

She followed the purple finger's path back to its source, noticing how the pool's surface bubbled. There was something feeding the energy there in the depths — a subterranean rupture, perhaps? Had she finally stumbled on the very phenomenon her father had quested for all his life?

Her gaze turned to the skies once more, and she viewed the descending cataract of indigo darkness heralding the genesis of the long night.

"I care not for this change in the weather," Cistre said. The head of the Royal Guard stood on a small mound of earth. She grasped the hilt of her sheathed sword, always ready for unseen attacks. Tayem swore she was the living embodiment of a tightly wound spring, apt to uncoil in an instant.

"This is not weather," Tayem replied.

"Then what?" Cistre did little to disguise her frustration at the Queen's growing obsession.

*Something auspicious,* Tayem thought. "Perhaps an event we should have seen coming a long time ago."

"You spend too much time here. These persistent daily vigils have yielded nothing." Cistre's diminutive stature belied the strident opinions she vocalised, often without consent. It was an annoyance Tayem tolerated given the compensations of the orphan's unique talents and loyalty. "Why must you brood over a myth your father could never fathom?"

"You cannot deny that this change in the air is significant."

"Whatever it is, I sense it will not help us."

"Our writings tell of a great flux of power to be released when Sol-Ar is in the ascendency."

"You also said they warned against becoming seduced by this outpouring."

"Our people need something to empower them," Tayem retorted. "The Cuscosians exact a toll that becomes more unbearable by the week. This day has seen ten more exactments taken from us under the guise of apprenticeship."

"That much is true," Cistre said. "They do little to hide

the fact that our youngest are but slaves to their expanding dominion."

"Little Celemon was amongst their number. Barely fourteen sols old and destined to become a chattel in some Cuscosian noble's household."

The exactment was something the Dragon Riders had become used to. Indeed, Tayem's grand parents had signed the treaty that required it — an exchange for Cuscosian 'protection.' But Celemon had been close to Tayem, bursting with enthusiasm and a teenager's curiosity at the world that promised to unfold. And yes ... innocence. How long would that innocence last in the place they had taken her to?

"I have said many times that we should bear this no longer," Cistre said, a steel underlying her naturally husky voice. "Yet, this augury you were called to see, this ... hallow ... fills me with foreboding. I fear no good will come of you accepting its enticement."

"Is that what you think it is doing? Tempting me?"

Cistre stepped down from her elevated position, cautiously approaching the lip of the crater where Tayem crouched. "You know it does. We both feel it; a promise of empowerment, the wind at our backs in the battle's charge, a guiding strategy over our plans and the unstoppable might of a higher power, but what am I to believe when you are obsessed with your father's legacy?"

Cistre's admission took Tayem by surprise. Not that it was a revelation, but that it echoed what the Hallows had communicated to her. "If this is from a higher power," she said, "then it should confirm itself to be true."

She stood to her feet, the frustrations and trauma of the day's events boiling over in a cry to the heavens: "How much longer must I wait. Give me a sign!"

But though the rain grew heavier, no answer came from above or below.

After minutes of unearthly silence she said, "No matter. It is as ever before. I must determine the fate of my people alone. Come. We will return tomorrow."

She turned on her booted heel to leave, yet as she did so she felt a tremor from beneath the ground send vibrations through her legs. Without warning, the earth shook violently as a fissure erupted in the hollow, vaporising the surface water into a violet vapour. When Tayem spun round, she observed purple energy billowing out of the crater, sending wisps of Hallows energy outward, engulfing her father's tomb. As she watched in horror the stone statue collapsed and toppled towards her.

*Is this my sign?* The thought flashed through her mind yet she remained immobile, as if resigned to the impact of her father's falling monument. Yet before the masonry could crush her, she was shoved to one side as Cistre barrelled into her, sending them both sprawling to the floor.

As the dust settled, Cistre said, "My Queen, are you hurt?" She pushed a crumbled piece of marble aside as she scrambled to Tayem's side.

Tayem muttered a muffled groan. "I will live," she said,

and stood up, her legs still shaking. Then, with a mesmerising movement, wisps of Hallows energy reached out and enveloped the Dragon Queen. The vapour's touch energised her, sending something akin to dark fire up her spine, filling her being with a tumultuous purpose.

This then was her sign.

She turned to Cistre, who observed her with mouth open.

"My Queen, what is it?" Cistre finally said.

"Call the Donnephon," Tayem declared.

"At this hour?"

"The full Fyreclave. At once."

Cistre bowed, jogging into the darkness and leaving Tayem to bathe in the infusion of power that now energised every cell of her body.

Minutes later she heard the beating of drums like a heartbeat in the night. It marked the turning of the tide. The Dragonians had suffered long enough. Her legions would shake off the yoke that enslaved them and rise to claim their freedom.

~ ~ ~

No matter how many times she invoked the ritual, Etezora — Queen of the Cuscosians — never failed to receive a tangible jolt, like electricity running through her wiry frame. Yet today was different. She stood, arms outstretched, absorbing a resurgent dark force rising from a jagged scar in the earth, a bleak rupture lying in the shadow of the disused Edenbract temple.

The Cuscosians had lived peacefully with the peoples of the Imperious Crescent for generations. Now, the prophesied turning of the Hallows energised a change in this balance, a shift she knew would pit the Ruling Council of brothers and sisters against the very people who had brought about this uneasy truce.

Standing next to her trusted consort, Etezora grew stronger with each moment. She gasped as purple-hued regenerative energy from the fissure surged through her body. It seduced her, like a living consciousness whispering promises of domination and a future where she ruled with unopposed force.

"See how the Hallows is initiated, Tuh-Ma," she said to the hulking warty creature in the shadows.

"Beautiful," he replied, the distorted words dribbling from cracked lips.

"You are privileged to witness this, my maladroit servant. It has arisen earlier than expected, but this can only mean the realisation of my plans all the sooner."

"Shall I tell Eétor and Zodarin?"

"Gorram, of course not. I need to absorb the import of this bestowal before revealing my hand. Eétor would only take advantage of the situation."

The blue-skin looked puzzled for a second, then shrugged. "As you wish, Mistress."

"Now stand back, I feel the power surging within me."

Almost involuntarily, she pointed her outstretched fingers to the sky. A crescendo of static built up in the air, followed by the release of etheric fury. With a deafening sound that cracked the night, jagged shards of light shot up to the clouds, seeming to tip the natural order into chaos, freeing an overwhelming darkness and vaporising the still falling rain.

A sound from the undergrowth startled her, footfalls crunching on garbeech nuts. "Tuh-Ma, there was one who saw. Seek them out!"

The blue-skin looked at her with obeisant, slit-eyes and grunted an acknowledgement.

"Now, you knuckle-crawler, or they will escape."

Tuh-Ma might be faithful, but he was not quick-witted. No doubt he would sulk at her admonishment later, but he recognised the rising of his mistress's ire and bolted from the clearing. Etezora would have accompanied him but the Hallows demanded her attention at that moment.

The electric aura from moments before had subsided, but she knew it had formed a reservoir within. "At last," she said with unbounded malice, "I will see the fruition of all I have planned." She revelled in the euphoria for a time, making the most of it while she could. She knew that tomorrow would be a day of freneticism unparalleled.

Tuh-Ma's return was heralded by a swishing of branches. He stopped, head hung in shame.

"They got away, didn't they?" Etezora said.

The creature nodded. "Tuh-Ma sorry, Mistress. He was

fleet-footed. But Tuh-Ma recognised him. Tuh-Ma knows where he lives."

Etezora smiled, an expression mutated into a sneer from the dark energy she had just absorbed. "Then our friend will receive visitors tomorrow."

"Tuh-Ma will crush his skull into powder," the blue-skin said, his tone conveying the need to appease her.

"That you will," she said, "that you will."

~ ~ ~

*To fly, to soar through silent canopies of the night and feel exhilaration from the air passing over one's wings.*

This was the dream of so many, yet something Wobas experienced repeatedly on his forays into the Dreamworld. On this occasion, however, he did not venture to sate an appetite for pleasure. In fact, there were dangers if he remained in this state. Oft times he found himself longing to become distilled into the night, to have nothing remain of himself, not even a shadow. Such an elevation would be enlightenment supreme, but the shaman of the Gigantes had a higher purpose in mind. The keen, nocturnal eyesight of his dream avatar picked out the quarry ahead, acute hearing confirming that the beast stepped majestically through dense undergrowth.

Wobas smiled inwardly. *Quarry?* He was no hunter, despite the feathered predatory form his avatar took.

Besides, that which he sought was entirely aware of his presence.

He swooped lower, tilting his body to avoid burred trunks and prickly branches. He perceived the thicker drapery of chasquite bushes ahead, recognising the potential for the spirit-beast to vanish. Alarm gripped his fluttering heart at the prospect of a convocation denied — as had happened so many times before. This was where the Spirit Guide — part horse, part reptile, part bird — would disappear into the ether, diminishing the hope of a meeting he suspected death would finally extinguish.

However, this was not to be a normal play of events. Wobas sensed the creature stop, turning on its hooves, waiting.

He stalled his flight, alighting on a garpine branch, allowing his talons to grip the gnarled bark. The Spirit Guide stood on a floor of leaf litter, observing him with avian eyes, cold, ancient and unblinking.

At last, the venerated one was to grant him an audience. Yet Wobas dared not speak, despite sols rehearsing his entreaties.

*You take the form of a wise bird,* it eventually communicated in dream-speak, breaking the silence, *yet you seek greater enlightenment. You think yourself worthy?*

Wobas remained speechless. What words could he utter to impress the guide? The beast stamped on the ground, snorting — a sign of impatience, or of offence?

*Are you insulted that I have sought you all this time?* Wobas sent.

*Insulted!* The Spirit Guide replied. *You are a seeker a persistent one at that. I respect those that dream the inconceivable then make it a reality.*

Wobas forgot his pre-planned overtures and blurted out the burden on his heart. *I seek these things not for myself, but for the good of my people. I know there are those who enter this realm to realise the fulfilment of their own desires, but I have learned the folly of such selfishness.*

The Spirit Guide nodded its eagle-like head. *I sense your sincerity, and have observed the refinement of your quest over the sols, like a precious metal purified in the crucible of perseverance.*

*Why, may I ask, have you now acquiesced to address me?* Wobas sent.

The Spirit Guide's beak could not form a smile, yet Wobas sensed it humoured him. *Time is short. I know you seek the interpretation of your dreams, that you have detected the onset of the Great Darkness, and yet you are not aware how the scales are tipping even as we speak.*

*The Black Hallows?* Wobas said, *they are upon us?*

*Varchal enters the influence of Sol-Ar tonight. It has tracked through the heavens and passed across the last few megiarchs in the blinking of an eye.*

*So soon?* Wobas said. *I ... we are not prepared.*

*It is as it ever was. The peoples persist with their petty concerns and ignore portents, the lessons of history.*

Wobas protested, *I have not turned my eyes from that which was foretold. I simply lack insight. My dreams are without form, allowing me only the opportunity to use them for malign purposes.*

*The physical manifestation is so often the grotesque result of the unworthy dreamer's desire.*

*You know that is not my intent.*

*No. But I cannot grant you the knowledge you seek. It is beyond even my authority and abilities.*

*Then what?*

*Advice,* The Spirit Guide sent. *Your dreams and visions will coalesce once you have an unburdened heart.*

*I have reached a plane of enlightenment unprecedented amongst my people!*

*And yet there is enmity between you and your seed.*

*Milissandia?*

The Spirit Guide nodded again.

*But I have no influence over her,* Wobas continued. *She is a renegade, estranged from me.*

The creature inclined its head. *You must make reparations. Yours is the greater responsibility.*

*But —*

*We have no more time. You must witness the unfolding of events. There are acts you must perform.*

*Surely there is more you can —*

But the creature had already turned and galloped off into the night at a speed even Wobas could not match. He was tired, the intensity of his audience with the Spirit

Guide having sapped him of energy. His vision clouded, and he sensed his form returning to the corporeal world.

He blinked, and when his eyes reopened, he was once more seated cross-legged on the bare floor of his cave. Outside, the heavy patter of rain struck limestone boulders.

Something was different, a smell of ozone in the air and the sound of crackling energy.

He rose to his feet, ancient bones and muscles protesting at the exertion, and stumbled outside.

Below the crag which served as his retreat, a rupture in the mountainside drew his eye, a site of archaic and holy significance. It glowed purple, shadow-hued like venom-vapour reaching out from the rock scar.

"By the spirits," he said. "The Black Hallows rise from their cradle."

~ ~ ~

"It ees beyond a joke!" Gribthore said, saliva dripping from a mouth rendered slack on one side by a childhood disease.

"You see me laughing?" Magthrum said and raised a pewter tankard to his cracked lips. He quaffed the root-ale, throwing the potent liquid to the back of his throat. There was a time when its pungency tasted rich and satisfying to his tongue, but that time was long past. All that remained was the mule kick it gave him. It was enough. It helped him forget, albeit for an hour or two.

"Are we going to let the Cuscosians get away with it?" said a squat stonegrabe. Bilespit was his name, and Magthrum trusted him about as much as he did a stone scorpion not to sting the hand that grasped it. However, he had talents, skills Magthrum could use. Once they were exhausted, he could consign Bilespit to the slag pits, or better still — slit his throat.

"How much, exactly, have they got away with?" Magthrum demanded.

"Our spies observed cartloads of ore moving out from Bagshot Defile this morning," put in Gorespike.

"A new mine? On our side of the divide!" Magthrum picked up an axe and hurled it across the room. It thunked into an ironwood pillar, narrowly missing Gribthore who ducked just in time. "I could chew on that Cuscosian schjek's throat. If they undercut our price on cryonite we'll be eating our toenails within a month." The thought of eating Etezora's flesh filled Magthrum with a yearning that eclipsed the memory of the hermit's leg meat he'd just finished.

"Surely da time for skulkeeng and bideeng our time ees past," Gribthore said, warily lifting his head above bench height again.

Magthrum growled in response. He was thinking. The rusty cogs in his former gin-trap mind turned ever so slowly these days, but that did not mean he was beyond resourcefulness. "How have the Dragon Riders responded to the sabotage of their latest construct?" he said, when a strategy did not present itself.

"The bridge? As expected," Gorespike replied. "They blame the Cuscosians."

"Do they plan retaliation?"

Gorespike shook his turnip-like head. "In time perhaps. But Nalin did not report any outriding today."

Magthrum grunted again. His Kaldoran Rockclave remained silent, knowing better than to interrupt their Fellchief's thoughts. After several minutes Magthrum cocked his head, listening. "The rain falls heavy above," he said.

"It ees a storm that will pass," Gribthore replied.

"No. The thunder cracks louder than Belthraim's hammer and the air seems ... electrified." Even though hundreds of metres of limestone separated Magthrum's hordes from the open air, his preternatural Kaldoran hearing detected the sounds acutely.

"To the surface," he said. "Something is afoot."

The sound of tankards slamming down accompanied the Rockclave's departure from Magthrum's chamber. They moved as a pack, like rats scurrying through the upwardly sloping tunnels.

By the time they reached the entrance to their stronghold, a black rain was pounding the rocks with the fury of a stallion herd.

"See the sky," Gribthore said in awe.

Magthrum observed anvil clouds roiling across a moon turned violet. Sheet lightning flashed across the blackness, illuminating Jagga's Peak in the distance, and beneath it all he heard a drone-like hum emanating from a gash in the opposite side of the valley.

"What is it that rises from Spidersnatch Cavern?" Gorespike said, his toothless mouth hanging open.

As he watched, Magthrum regarded a raisin-coloured vapour reach across the valley towards them. Fear clutched his entrails along with something else — a lust for what that vapour's tendril seemed to offer. It closed the distance with unnatural speed, permeating the air around the Kaldorans.

"Retreat below," yelled Gorespike.

"Too late," Magthrum said, breathing in the energised cloud. As he did so, a sensation like that of an irrepressible fist closed over his mind, followed by the lifting of confusion. For the first time in many sols he could think clearly again, yet his cognition seemed tinged by a mischief and cunning beyond anything he'd imagined before, a diabolism even.

There, on that mountainside, Magthrum imagined at last how his desires could be realised. Kaldora could be great once more. Etezora could crush the Dragon Riders if she wanted, then he would strike at the distracted Cuscosians, and their haujen-queen would become succulent meat for his table.

# 2

# ON MAJESTIC WINGS

---

*Heart beats so loud, in my ears,*
*Wind blasts my face, cools cheeks,*
*Cruel crags loom large, so near,*
*Beast's heat so warm, my thighs,*
*Harness so tight, no fears.*

These familiar sensations pulsed through Mahren's frame, immersive and exhilarating, a charge to her otherwise wearied existence. As Jaestrum approached the knife-edged arête, she applied gentle pressure to the beast's flank, signalling it to adjust trajectory and bank away from the rock hurtling to greet them. It was a practised manoeuvre, but Mahren loved to see how long she could leave it until Jaestrum pulled out of the dive. It was an unspoken agreement between them. She knew the dragon was aware of its capabilities, and would communicate its alarm if it sensed she pushed them too far.

The folded, fractured bluestone slid to the side of Mahren's view as Jaestrum almost grazed its surface. He swept parallel to the cliff face then rolled his body to follow the line of the arête. Mahren shrieked in delight; adrenaline causing a buzz in her brain. This next manoeuvre was in fact more perilous than the hair-raising dive she'd just executed. One rogue air current could cause the dragon to strike the toothed basalt scrolling beneath them and end their aerial exploits forever. It was such moments that made life worth living to Mahren.

"Are you ready to attempt the lion's mouth, Jaestrum?" she shouted to her mount.

She saw the natural arch fast approaching at the foot of the arête, a hole in the rock measuring mere hand spans in diameter. Mahren speculated oft times if it was wide enough to accommodate Jaestrum's bulk, but she believed if they were to accomplish the feat, they would have to attempt it before he grew too large. The beast hesitated and then lifted his head in affirmation. Mahren's pulse quickened. A moment of doubt, then she committed them both.

"Just like we practised," she said to him.

They were ten seconds away from a portal to death — or a life enriched by the experience. The outcome rode on Jaestrum's ability to hold his course unswervingly.

When Mahren calculated there to be five seconds before reaching the target, a squall gusted over the arête and hit them without warning. It was enough to alter their course and result in disaster. The decision came easily, and she dug her heels into the dragon's flanks. It responded in an instant and pulled upwards, climbing out of the dive, its claws flicking off fragments of rock from the apex of the arch. Mahren gasped in shock but Jaestrum was not perturbed and compensated for the impact.

They were soaring above the vale now, rising into a sky turned purple by Sol-Ar, and, despite the breath-taking view, Mahren couldn't help but feel deflated. The emerald foliage of the Dragon Vale appeared below, and Jaestrum uttered a heaving sigh, resonating with Mahren's despondency.

"No regrets," she said. "There will be another day, another attempt. Tomorrow we will succeed."

"Mmmm — Gragh!" the dragon responded.

"That's the spirit. It is enough for today. We should return and see to your brothers. They need their exercise too."

With a further bellow, Jaestrum beat his wings forcibly, accelerating until Mahren's back pressed into the saddle. She reached down and patted the beast, its scales rough and powdery to her touch. Jaestrum owed his ancestry to the rock dragons of Aegris. They lacked the preening iridescence of the ayku but were more obedient and manoeuvrable — perfectly suited to the Dragon Rider's needs. Although the fyreblood coursed through his veins, Jaestrum was still too immature to expel fire from his mouth. This phenomenon might never materialise — it was a matter of luck, ancestry and time. One could hope.

She checked his harness and tightened a buckle. The apparatus was essential for the aerobatics she executed, and although she often wondered if Jaestrum relished the possibility of her dispensing with it, it was recklessness beyond even her daring mindset. Besides, Jaestrum did not mind. He accepted his duty and restrictions not as servitude but as a calling. It was a bond Mahren had nurtured since the dragon's hatching. Five sols of coaxing and coaching had brought them to such a pinnacle of trust that they would die for each other — without question.

She glanced up again, noting once more the disturbing hue of the sky. Its appearance sent a ripple of disquiet through her. Instead of the usual azure glaze she was accustomed to at this altitude; it was as if a blanket of rolling, slate-coloured cloud covered the firmament, creating a sense of claustrophobia in the atmosphere. She suspected it was something to do with the previous night's events. Mahren had obeyed Tayem's call to arms despite her reluctance. To see the royal household and guard of the Donnephon assembled at that unearthly hour, the torchlight reflecting off their leather armour, made her feel both proud and scared. Tayem formally declared the Teshwan, and Mahren understood the significance of this. She had so many questions. Foremost was why Tayem's eyes stared at the multitude with a blackness that was both uncharacteristic and baleful. There was more to be said on the matter. Perhaps her sister would reveal all later.

Her thoughts drifted to the 'Sanctity of the Dragon,' an oath repeated upon the occasion of every Air-Sworn rider and their claiming of a mount. She had taken the oath many times, yet the number willing to dedicate themselves in this way was dwindling. If this continued, it would mean the loss of a lineage that extended back centuries; the effective extinction of the Air-Sworn. Such a loss embittered her more and more, compounded as it was with a despondency that afflicted the Donnephon as a whole. Her people seemed to accept the yoke laid upon them by the Cuscosians, as if they were doomed to a servitude impossible to shake off.

It was not always so, as the relationship with the Cuscosians had always been fragile. Yet matters were not so one-sided before Etezora's accession to leadership.

*Etezora.* The very name left a taste as bitter as gall in Mahren's mouth — to think Tayem once counted her as a friend. That all ended at the feast of Shaptari, when Etezora had committed an act that would define her for sols to come. Mahren remembered that day with an abhorrence that still sent a hot shaft of loathing through her core.

She shook her head, unwilling to let such memories further sully her already bleak day. The canopy of bachar trees loomed, and she spied the clearing that identified the draconest ahead. Figures stepping like ants busied themselves in the yard, dragons led from their pens appeared as miniatures feeding on the carcases of boar and deer lobbed to them by the dragon hands.

Mahren did not need to instruct Jaestrum as they closed in. He intuitively stalled his approach to the landing ground, wings stretched, and beating with increased frequency, sending clouds of dust into the air. The dragon grunted as he alighted, then lowered his frame to allow Mahren to dismount.

She hardly set foot on the sand when Gostrek, a member of the Underguard appeared at her side.

"My Lady," he said, thumping an arm to his chest in salute, "The Queen requests your presence straight away."

"At this hour?" she said. "Does she not know I have the stud to attend to?"

"She said it could not wait. The entire Royal Court is in attendance."

"Do you know the reason?"

"No, my Lady. It is beyond my station."

She thanked him, taking time only to heave a deer thigh over the fence to Jaestrum.

*It seems I am to learn of last night's events earlier than I thought,* she pondered. *The full complement of the Court, though? Surely this is an over-reaction?* But as she passed through the fortress corridors and up the steps to the Great Hall, a twist of anxiety and anticipation took hold. She had no doubt that matters of great significance were about to unfold.

## 3

# EVIL COMES TO CALL

---

Sometimes Tuh-Ma wallowed in a mood so dark he felt he was drowning in the black sludge of abyssal tar pits. These were times when he would pick up his keen edged flint-blade and place it against his neck. He would stare at his reflection in the seeing glass — a present from his precious Queen — and despair at what he saw there. Tombstone teeth set in a mouth disfigured by a jutting lower jaw, porcupine bristles erupting haphazardly from a skin covering that held more resemblance to a lunar landscape than biological tissue. He was ugly — he knew this.

His Queen didn't employ him for his looks, however. He had other redeeming characteristics. He would scan downward to his hands, shaped like spades and tipped with yellow, chipped nails. *Instruments of death,* Etezora called them. This would bring a smile to his grotesque face. If she valued this talent, then maybe she could one day come to appreciate other qualities about him. He could hope.

This morning found him in a lighter mood. He chose not to stare at himself overly long and confined himself to washing from the basin of water he'd drawn from a spring outside his ramshackle log dwelling. It was a matter of pride that he look his best for the Queen, and she had made it clear he should attend at the rise of Sol-Ar.

He swivelled his muddy eyes to the heavens and nodded his head. Heavily moving masses of cloud continually passed before Sol-Ar's face. It was an unprecedented skyscape, tinged with a violet hue that seemed to emanate from Sol's twin.

"Tuh-Ma sees you, Darkenfall," he said. He spoke to the spirits often, sometimes believing they spoke back, but he could never be sure. God-speak was the poetry of whispers after all, not something you could directly testify to. Not without inviting ridicule. "Tuh-Ma thanks you for empowering our Queen last night, and he asks that he play a part in her designs."

A tolling bell broke his meditations, and he viewed the tower from which the dull clanging emanated, a judgemental minaret jutting from the incubus-purple of the Cuscosian Castle. It was a signal, telling him he was already late. Etezora was not pleased, or perhaps she was impatient. The reason was immaterial — he would be scolded whatever the source of her frustrations.

"Yes, yes. Tuh-Ma comes," he muttered, the normal sibilance of his words distorted into a raspberry-like sound from his disobedient lips.

He shambled away from the shadowy hollow he called home and scaled the stone steps that led to the Castle proper. The Hallows-rain had stopped falling an hour earlier, but dampness still glazed the rock surface creating slippery footholds for a standard tread. Tuh-Ma's bare feet could hardly be termed humanoid. They could adhere to glass if required as they possessed minute hooks on the pads, a characteristic causing others to speculate that his mother might have been a gecko. Tuh-Mah never spoke of his true lineage. As a squat but overtly muscular blue-skin he was reviled by most, even his own kin. For him to elaborate on where he came from was only to invite further mocking.

The steps terminated in a courtyard. A single guard stood next to the entranceway on the opposite side. As Tuh-Ma approached, the man curled his lip in distaste. He was a new recruit, and should have been better drilled by the Captain.

"What is your business, troll?" he said, lowering his spear and pointing the tip at Tuh-Mah's chest.

The blue-skin looked at the weapon and slowly

extended one finger to feel the point. "Weapon is sharp, fecalspawn. But is it as sharp as your wits?"

"I don't know what you are saying, but I like not your tone."

"Then maybe this makes it clear." With one swift motion, Tuh-Ma snatched the briar elm haft from the guard's grip, spun the spear over and brought the storm-iron tip up to his throat.

The guard simply looked at the blue-skin with incredulity, his mouth moving but words failing to come.

"Now get out of Tuh-Ma's way or I'll cut off your robang," Tuh-Ma said.

The man stepped aside obediently, and Tuh-Ma lumbered past without a backward glance.

He found Etezora in her antechamber, dressed in journeying apparel and pacing the floor. Tuh-Ma took a few furtive seconds to regard her lithe form. Even in these drab clothes she carried herself like one possessing royal blood in her veins. *She is beautiful,* he thought for the thousandth time, taking in her high cheekbones and upwardly tipped nose. Others thought her skin to be deathly pale, but he likened it to the finest porcelain. This morning, however, there was something else about her demeanour, an infusion of something both diabolical and mesmerising.

"What are you staring at?" she said, noticing him. "I hate it when you skulk in the shadows."

"But, my Queen," he replied, "skulking is one of the things Tuh-Ma does best."

"Never mind," she said. "We must away and remove that problem you created last night."

"Tuh-Ma will be glad to make good his mistake," he replied. "No need to dirty your royal hands with this simple act."

Etezora smiled, full lips exposing a mercurial impression. "I would see the fruits of my baptism," she said, "first hand."

"Tuh-Ma not understand, my Queen."

"You observed the Black Hallows emerge, did you not? How the power entered my body?"

"Why, yes." Tuh-Ma's mind clicked like an abacus trying to calculate a sum that incessantly evaded him.

"Then I need to assess its extent. I feel the power of the Hallows, and it promises much. But will it deliver what I seek?"

"Ah — Tuh-Ma see," he said as the gear wheels of his brain finally clicked into place. "So, *you* wish to carry out the deed?"

Etezora nodded. "You say you know where this interloper dwells?"

"Yes."

"Is he likely to be there?"

"If not, Tuh-Ma can trace him."

The smile returned to Etezora's face. "Then we should hurry. I cannot remain under the gaze of the sun for long."

"Man lives on outskirts of Hallows Creek, about two periarchs hence."

"Then we will run. Well ... " she hesitated, regarding Tuh-Ma's hunched frame, "at least, I will. Your movement could not be described exactly thus."

"Tuh-Ma *rumbles*!" He said with glee.

"Rumbling and skulking," Etezora laughed. "I'm not sure the two can be accomplished at once."

Tuh-Ma wasn't certain if the Queen mocked him, or offered one of her rare compliments. Either way, he didn't mind. That he would spend the next two hours with her was enough.

"Well?" she said. "What are we waiting for? Lead the way."

Tuh-Ma offered a salute and lolloped from the antechamber. They left by the West Gate, an unpretentious portal, and one that would attract little attention. Hallow's Creek lay in a clearing surrounded by thick woodland, and the unlikely pair of Cuscosians progressed along the winding trail at a rapid pace. Tuh-Ma's keen hearing picked out the sounds of the township long before it came into view.

"We should go in woods," he said, pausing on the muddy trail for a second. "Someone might see us coming."

Etezora frowned. "If we must, but I hope the thorns do not snag me over-much."

"Tuh-Ma clear our way," the blue-skin replied, his manner apologetic.

"Very well — but *quietly*, Tuh-Ma."

The blue-skin bowed his bulky head and paced into the undergrowth.

He was true to his word, and ripped up any briars that snared their passage, snapping off intervening branches and creepers too. This left a swathe of destruction, but he had no fear of anyone discovering their pathway. By the time they had done their work, his crude woodland highway would be a moot point.

The shade grew lighter as they approached the man's house, although scar birch leaves still provided some concealment as they surveyed the cottage before them.

"There is no smoke from the chimney," Etezora said, "I doubt if anyone is home. If he has any sense, he will have run for the border already."

"Tuh-Ma not think man knew he was followed." The blue-skin said.

"You told me he escaped. To evade your persistence and speed, he must have known."

Tuh-Ma looked sheepish. "Tuh-Ma did not ... did not pursue for long," he said.

"What do you mean?"

"A gnarl-root caught my foot before I had run even half a periarch."

"You are a clumsy krut,"

"Tuh-Ma sorry, my Queen."

"Enough. Your blunder has presented me with this

opportunity — if he still resides in that house. What is his name?"

"Does it matter?"

Etezora's cool gaze answered him.

"Rawkin is his name," Tuh-Ma continued. "Man well known in Hallows Creek."

"What led him to spy on us?"

Tuh-Ma furrowed his brow, thinking. "He is nosy grosbeak. Likes to know everything that's going on."

"Then perhaps we should question him. Others might know what he saw."

Tuh-Ma nodded then cocked his head. "I hear footfalls behind the cottage."

"Then let us close in on the quarry," Etezora replied.

They sprinted across the sward of grass separating them from the housestead, and edged around the corner of its rough-hewn walls.

Rawkin had his back to them, sifting through a small, rickety shed, looking for unspecified items to stash in a bulging backpack.

"Looks like he's preparing to go on a journey," Etezora whispered in Tuh-Mah's elephantine ear. He could not deny her closeness thrilled him, but resolved to concentrate on the task at hand.

"We should act now," he replied.

In answer, Etezora emerged from the shadow of the building. Rawkin must have heard her because he spun round, surprise turning to shock as he recognised the unwelcome guests. He cast his eyes around for an escape route or some unlikely means of salvation.

Etezora stopped, placing her hands on her hips. "Rawkin, isn't it?"

The greasy-haired man nodded.

Etezora glanced at Tuh-Ma, who had hauled his intimidating bulk up next to her. "Is this the interfering peasant who watched what transpired last night?"

Tuh-Ma smiled. He knew it exposed his misshapen teeth but he couldn't help himself. "It is, my Queen."

"Inquisitiveness can be a boon to the common man," she said, turning back to Rawkin. "Sadly, in your case, it is an irritation."

"I did not mean to spy," Rawkin said, taking a step backwards.

"Of course you didn't," the Cuscosian Queen replied. "I'm sure you just *happened* upon the site of our most sacred and forbidden temple. What I need to know is, did you tell others what you saw?"

"I told no one, because I did not see anything," he said, a nervous smile playing across his face. "Or, if I did, I have forgotten. I do not remember well these days." He winked conspiratorially.

"Is that why you are hastily packing to leave?"

Rawkin looked at his backpack as if it had placed itself in his hand without his awareness or permission. "I am simply preparing for my weekly visit to Milhaven. I have a cart load of logs to deliver."

"There was no cart at the front of your ..." Etezora looked disdainfully at Rawkin's abode, "... hovel."

Rawkin swallowed, his eyes blinking rapidly.

"Are you sure you did not speak to anyone about last night?" Etezora stepped closer, backing Rawkin against the shed wall.

"No," he said, "I told you before."

"He lies," Tuh-Mah said.

"I know," Etezora said, "but I forgive him. After all, everyone lies. It shouldn't surprise us."

Tuh-Ma felt a charge in the air, causing his hair-quills to stand on end. He looked at the Queen and marvelled at the motes of energy that now floated around her frame. He also noted that her eyes had turned blacker than darkwood. She reached out her hand into the air and clenched it into a fist.

Rawkin's eyes bulged while a gurgle escaped from his constricted throat. Tuh-Ma wondered later whether what he saw next actually happened, or if he just imagined it. Rawkin's body rose slowly up the side of the shed, propelled by an invisible force, his legs flailing beneath him as the strangulated sounds increased from his throat.

"I have a degree of patience, and a modicum of mercy at my disposal," Etezora said, "but they tend to run fast, like sand through an open hand. So answer me, peasant, and perhaps you will convince me to spare your life."

Rawkin choked, and then managed to utter, "You would?"

"Of course," Etezora said, "and I'm true to my word."

"Then ... I will tell ... you," he said. The man's face was now turning dark red.

Etezora's concentration relaxed and Rawkin dropped to the ground. After clearing his throat he looked up into Etezora's determined face. "I spoke to my friend, Brethis."

"Brethis?" Tuh-Ma said. "Who is this man?"

"The blacksmith's son."

"What did you tell him?" Etezora interjected.

Rawkin hesitated, but with a crackle of Hallows energy, Etezora's invisible grip tightened on his throat again.

"No, no more," Rawkin spluttered, his voice but a croak.

She released him again then hissed, "My patience wears thin."

"I ... I said that I saw a great evil rise from the pit and enter your body. I did not understand what happened, but I was sorely afraid. That's why I ran."

"You did not tell anyone else?"

"No, I swear."

Etezora nodded. "I believe you." She stood up straight and signalled to Tuh-Ma. The troll understood his Queen's unspoken command and leant over the ragged doll of a man.

"Make it quick," Etezora said.

He reached down, grabbing the man's head in both hands. He looked into his eyes, saw the abject terror there and smiled. "Tuh-Ma crush," he said with glee. He applied his brute force and felt the skull crack in his grip. A straw-coloured fluid issued from Rawkin's ears and one eyeball popped from its socket. Still Tuh-Ma continued to squeeze until his fingers broke through Rawkin's temples and sank into the brain tissue beneath. In his final seconds, Rawkin issued a rattle of death from his lungs and went limp in Tuh-Ma's hands.

The blue-skin wished he might have lasted a few seconds longer, but recognised the man's spirit passing and wiped his gore-soaked hands on the grass.

He joined Etezora at the front of the house, and they made their way back into the undergrowth. A dismal drizzle had begun to fall, loading the air with dampness.

The blue-skin chuckled as he walked side by side with his Queen. "Tuh-Ma worried you would let Rawkin live," he said after a while.

Etezora blessed him with one of her cruel smiles. "It's like I said before," she replied, "everybody lies."

# 4

# RUMBLINGS FROM BENEATH

---

It was a mistake that Magthrum had ignored often enough, but this day saw an end to his patience. The occasion was Nalin's return to the Rockclave, and the stonegrabe was not empty-handed. He had come with sackfuls of jarva-leaf, a prototype model and, best of all — information. But whether it was a loss of patience or an outflowing of the malefic energy he had inhaled from the Hallows, Magthrum could not contain his anger when Gorespike overstepped the mark.

The exchange within the Rockclave had begun amiably enough. "This leaf is easily the finest you have harvested," he had said to Nalin. The Kaldoran chief puffed on the long-stemmed pipe, inhaling russet smoke deep into his lungs. He'd expected the usual headiness that accompanied this first draw, but nearly fell off his stool when something like a finger prodded his brain and sent his nerve endings frizzling with intoxication. When he later reflected on the scene that ensued, he concluded that Nalin's narcotic might have been responsible for tipping him over the edge.

"I confess, Fellchief, that the soil has been especially fruitful this last month," Nalin said. "It is as if something has entered the very earth. I swear that the jarva bushes have grown at least three spans in this time."

Nalin was prone to exaggeration, but given recent events Magthrum was less inclined to dismiss the stonegrabe's observation. "Why, this leaf could stone a dragon," Magthrum said. "Indeed, it could drop the cursed beast from the sky."

Most of the Rockclave had confined themselves to sycophantic laughter at their Fellchief's jest, but Gorespike had let his mouth run off.

"Hah," the underling said, "mayhap that was the excuse given by the wyrm that crushed your late wife!" Gorespike had continued laughing long after silence descended on the Rockclave's cavern, sending the temperature down an extra couple of degrees.

"What was that you said?" Magthrum growled.

The penny had still not dropped for Gorespike. "Why, it explains how the beast was so clumsy as to ... well ...

you know ... do what it did." It was only then that the hapless stonegrabe had stuttered, looking around him at faces grave and pitying. "I did not think ..."

Magthrum's face turned from red to purple, the eyes smouldering beneath brows ridged high to match the hackles rising like a fury within. "You would make jest of Hetherin's demise?"

"I meant nothing by it," Gorespike said, edging away from the table, "I just thought — "

"You thought to humiliate me further by your insinuations?"

"I apologise, Fellchief," Gorespike uttered too late, his fellow stonegrabes moving further away from him, creating a circle of contempt. Magthrum sprang up, his body swaying from the jarva still coursing through his veins, elevating him beyond usual heights of anger. He launched himself at the turnip-headed stonegrabe with a speed defying his girth and weight, slamming his frame into the flinty pillar behind.

A gurgling grunt issued from Gorespike, silenced abruptly when Magthrum brought his war-axe down in an arc, cleaving Gorespike's skull. Such was its force that his head fell into two parts, spliced unevenly and peeling aside like an overripe fruit.

Magthrum released the stonegrabe's body that had, up to this point, been held in the vice-grip of his left hand. It slumped to the floor, blood guttering down from Gorespike's disfigured head to pool on the granite floor.

The Fellchief's chest heaved with exertion and rage, fuelled by Hallows energy. He could not forget his wife's untimely end when a Dragon Rider's steed had dumped itself on her dumpy form as she washed clothes next to Lake Dorthun. The Dragon-Lord had not even been aware of the mishap. Her beast had simply taken its fill of water then flown off into the blue, leaving a pulped body on the shoreline.

The awkward silence was finally broken by an embarrassed tittering from Pitchbass, a wrinkly stonegrabe. "Another clean-up job for you, Ropetail," he said, nudging a friend next to him.

Magthrum waited for the fury to subside, and then ordered his attendant, "I need a drink. Fetch me a flagon of ale." His retainer scuttled off while the remainder of the Rockclave seated themselves back at the table and pretended nothing had occurred.

"So, what's this I hear about a new Cuscosian mine at Bagshot?" he said to Nalin.

The stonegrabe smoothed his plaited beard and spread his hands on the table. "It is true, Fellchief. I overheard Etezora receive reports from her mining foreman. They extracted a bovicaur's weight of cryonite this last month. They are using it to supply tool workshops in the capital."

"It is as I thought," Magthrum said. "Their snivelling merchant renegotiated our deal on his last visit — downwards. I knew there was something he wasn't telling me. We had no choice but to accept, as they know we have no other trading partners. Now I can see they are looking to exploit a resource that is our birthright to mine. I should have caved his skull in." Thinking about it now, Magthrum reflected that, had this encounter occurred since the advent of the purple vapour, that is precisely what he would have done.

As if reading his thoughts, Nalin said, "It will pay us to tread carefully, Fellchief. The Cuscosians grow in strength, and it would only take one diplomatic incident like that for them to exact swift retribution."

Magthrum accepted the advice. Nalin was not only an invaluable source of intelligence but also a trusted adviser. Since he had inveigled himself as head engineer in the Cuscosian Keep he had earned his weight in gold providing a steady trickle of confidential information. "Mmm, and they would no doubt cut off our trade altogether," the Fellchief mused.

His retainer returned with a hefty tankard of ale, and Magthrum seized it from him, downing half of it in one gulp. "So, you advise biding our time?"

Nalin picked up his own drink and supped it warily. He looked around at the Rockclave, a conspiratorial look on his face. He needn't have worried. They were engaged in games of Bakkadol or recounting inane stories and jokes. They were obviously happy to let their Fellchief's anger subside at arm's length. "Indeed I do," Nalin said. "I know you are itching to hatch your cunning plot, but there are many pieces to put in place first. We will achieve more by subterfuge than outright confrontation."

"It is the Kaldoran way. This is why we must set the Dragonians and House of Cuscosa against each other if we are to achieve our aims."

Nalin tweaked an iron bead twisted into the warp of his red beard. The stonegrabe was clearly mustering the courage to say something. "You know, our late friend, Gorespike, may have planted a seed to provide a means to such unrest, despite his extreme impertinence of course."

Magthrum's ridged forehead wrinkled. "I doubt whether anything that gob-vomit said or did would help us."

Nalin took the opportunity to swerve the subject away from Gorespike's insult. "There is only one thing more precious to the Dragon Riders than their accursed woodcraft."

"The dragons themselves?"

Nalin nodded. "What if their beasts were to suffer an illness? Something that set them back?"

Magthrum shook his head. "Their wyrms are impregnable. We cannot bring them down, nor even get close to them. Those scaled creatures hate us."

"There might be a way. What if we dealt them a blow and pinned the blame firmly on the Cuscosians?"

"I would hear more."

So Nalin elaborated on his plan while Magthrum

nodded, his smile increasing all the more until he was laughing with glee at Nalin's inventiveness.

"We will put this plot into action next week," Magthrum said. "I know just the place and occasion."

They toasted the plan, finishing the contents of their tankards. Magthrum ordered two more and invited Nalin to show him the prototype he had referred to upon arrival.

The stonegrabe reached down and took what looked like a toy from his pack, placing it on the stone table.

"What is this?" Magthrum said, brow knotted. "A child's plaything?"

"It started as that," Nalin said. "But then I got thinking."

"That's always a good sign when it comes to you." Magthrum picked up the toy with both hands and inspected it more closely. It was a construction made of wood and iron, comprising a rugged fuselage complete with cockpit overlooking a rotating cutting disc. This rested on an undercarriage mobilised by a series of six bogies housed inside surrounding tracks. "Is it a design for my new chariot? I could do with something more fitting to my station."

"Not so," Nalin said, a mischievous wink in his eye. "Look." He grasped the model and pushed it forward. Metal joints articulated and gears meshed, enabling a fluid motion. He then gripped a handle between forefinger and thumb, turning it in minute circles. As he did so, the disc rotated.

Nalin's demonstration had drawn the attention of the

inquisitive Rockclave. They gathered around in rapt attention. "Hah," Magthrum declared. "It looks like a rock-mole before it burrows into the earth."

"Exactly," Nalin said. "Now imagine this one hundred times larger, with the proportionate increase in power."

"A fanciful idea," Magthrum said, "but I can imagine it excavating a tunnel taller than a fabled Cyclopes."

Nalin scanned the surrounding stonegrabes, pausing for effect. "What if I said I could construct such a machine?"

Magthrum slapped Nalin on the back. "Nalin, my friend, you have been smoking too much of your jarva-leaf. But I admire your imagination."

Nalin stared intently at his Fellchief. "I do not jest, Magthrum. A full-size working prototype already exists in my hidden workshop."

# 5

# WHILE THE LAUGHING
# MOON BLEEDS

———————

Wobas hesitated before knocking on the weathered door. He could hear movement and voices inside. Two people, his daughter, her tinkling laughter like a summer rain, and another, walking the floorboards.

It had been so long since the sound of Milissandia Moonwatcher's laughter had graced his ears. She was always a joyful child; up to the day he finally abandoned the home he and his wife had built together. Now, hearing this precious sound again, he almost turned away. *Surely,* he thought, *this is a memory to treasure, something to hold on to during the lonely nights of my existence.* But the mission drove him on. There were higher objectives at stake here.

His swarthy hand rapped three times on the wood bringing the conversation inside abruptly to a stop. He braced himself as someone drew up on the other side of the wood. The door had long since given up its ability to open easily, but after a couple of tugs a man with bovine eyes loitering under a mono brow met Wobas's without a trace of recognition.

"What do you want?" the muscled man said, accentuating his insolence with a wide yawn. He was barely clothed; his only garment being a hemp loincloth.

"I wish to speak to my daughter," Wobas replied, his expression neutral despite the raging in his breast.

Bull-face turned and shouted over his shoulder. "There's an old dodderer here reckons he's your father."

Wobas heard a groan and then muttered words. He could tell that his presence wasn't welcome.

After listening, the man looked back at him and stepped to one side without a word.

Wobas entered, placing his gnarlwood staff against a cupboard and let his eyes accustom themselves to the gloom. He lived an austere existence himself, but had retained a certain self-respect regarding his environment. His daughter's one-room cottage however was little more than a midden. Dirty pots, most of them chipped or cracked, lay abandoned in a grimy sink. The floor was littered with a mixture of clothes, household utensils and indeterminate knick-knacks. He stepped as carefully as he could, but his foot still crushed two items on his journey into the depths of the abode.

"Over here," a disembodied voice said, all trace of humour gone.

He stepped through a crudely fashioned archway to find Milissandia still in bed, a hastily donned shift over her top. He didn't need to speculate on how she had spent that morning. She swung her naked legs over the side of the cot and he observed the twisted tapestry of an extensive skink-oil tattoo snaking up the calf and thigh.

She rose and lit a bunch of incense sticks with a tinder box, still saying nothing. When the trail of smoke reached Wobas's nostrils, he identified the rich sandalwood fragrance as the opening invocation for a warding spell.

*Is this how she sees me — an evil spirit to be exorcised from her home?*

He was her father, and it was his responsibility to make the first overture as politely as possible. "I apologise for my unannounced visit," he said.

"Make it quick," she replied. "I have much to attend to this morning."

"I noticed," he said, not able to help himself.

Bull-face was clanking around in the kitchen area preparing a morning brew. Wobas had little doubt about his chances of being offered refreshment. He cast his eyes around for somewhere to sit, thinking it would make him appear less domineering, but couldn't spy a surface uncovered by clutter.

She stood with arms folded, eyes glaring at him, waiting. He cleared his throat and formulated the words. "I traversed in the Dreamworld last night."

Milissandia blew air through pursed lips. "So, nothing changes there."

"No, no. Let me explain," he said, holding up his hand. "This time it was different. I met the Spirit Guide — at last."

Although she didn't express surprise, her eyes widened then narrowed again. "You're deluded, father of mine. Even if this were true, why should it concern me?"

Wobas turned to view the skyline through the rotting window frame behind. "Have you noticed the heavens this morning?

"I've hardly even risen from bed — as you can see."

"Look," he said, making his way back into the main atrium. Milissandia rolled her eyes and traipsed toward the window, squinting at the relative glare. *She prefers her blessed moonlight*, he perceived.

"What am I looking for?" she said, petulantly.

"Do you not see the hue of the sky?"

"I suppose it to be little more violet than usual."

"A little — " he bit his lip. "This is a sign, an omen above to herald the start of the cycle."

"I imagine you think it so."

"Don't tell me you didn't perceive what befell the land

last night." His voice was raised, and he told himself to calm down. But it was hard, so hard. He knew she was playing with him, point-scoring in the only way she knew how.

Bull-face stepped up, handing her a steaming earthenware cup, then retreated into the kitchen. *Gods, I wish he'd put some clothes on,* Wobas thought.

Milissandia sighed. "All right. I was abroad last night and, yes, I witnessed the change. But unlike you, I don't attach the same importance to it. There are some events that have magical significance, and others that simply mark a change in the alignment of heavenly bodies. You would know this if you weren't wrapped up so much in prophecies and demented hallucinations."

"Hallucinations? You know that the Dreamworld is real. How can you deny it?"

She smiled, not with warmth, but more the suggestion of a smirk. "I make use of altered states of consciousness but, as always Father, you read too much into these things."

This was going nowhere fast. He took a deep breath and tried another tack. "You know I have sought many sols for an audience with the Spirit Guide."

"How can I forget? You sacrificed your wife and daughter's affections for this 'noble quest.'

Wobas swallowed. It was true; he obsessed about his mission, his destiny. He had been fixated with a desire to obtain the knowledge his race thirsted for, secrets that would release the Cyclopes from the curse that afflicted them — amongst other things. Such a commitment required sacrifice. Why couldn't Carys and Milissandia understand that? "Will you at least hear what it said to me?"

His daughter glanced at the moon-clock on the wall. "I'll give you another three minutes, then you must leave. There's only so much time I can devote to your ramblings. I thought you'd realised that sols ago."

The seer knew she would hold to this promise and wasted no more time. He recounted the audience he'd been granted, the words of the eagle-headed beast, and the evil scar spewing forth its purple emission. There was a moment when her expression shifted, a look he'd seen last on her thirteenth birthday when the gift had been bestowed on his moon-child, a lambent flickering in her eyes. But it subsided as soon as it began.

"So you must understand it is imperative we make amends," he concluded, "despite all that separates us. These omens are larger than our rift."

Milissandia folded her arms again, eyes turning steel. "And here was I thinking you desired to heal the wounds of the past, to recognise the folly of what you did. But nothing changes. You still chase your phantasms, looking for what? Meaning in your bleak existence?" She balled her delicate hands into fists. "You had the best reason to live — your family. But you cast us off. Why is it not enough that we should be reconciled for its own sake?"

Wobas realised his mistake too late. "But of course I want this on its own merits. I — "

"Don't lie to yourself. Now go. Pursue your Dreamworld, but I will have no part of this madness."

"Milissandia, don't — "

"Go!"

Bull-face appeared at her shoulder. "You should leave, old man. You have said enough."

Wobas might have tried to stare him down if he was younger, but the shaman was spent. He grasped his staff and moved towards the door. He took one hopeful look back, saw the expressions on Milissandia and her paramour's faces, and passed out of his daughter's life.


Milissandia watched her father's shuffling form retreat towards the mountain. Despite her harsh words, the emotions that battled within left her desolate, mournful even. *He is but a shadow of who he once was,* she thought. *A man who has sacrificed everything for a dream made of straw.*

She brushed moisture from her cheek and convinced herself this was the pronouncement she would adhere to. But as her father became a pinprick on the horizon, she looked upward again. The skyscape seemed to her a lurid indigo, as if shades of malignancy hung over the Imperious Crescent. One part of her insisted this was a projection of her emotion onto the landscape, but another — the part that had emerged breathless from her trance last night — argued differently. She hoped to forget her vivid dream, consign it to a shelf of experience labelled *nightmare*. But she had been unable to, and her father's unexpected appearance served to underscore her disquiet.

He had not mentioned it, but she now mouthed the words — *Black Hallows.*

# 6

# SEVEN SEWN AND SEVEN SPLIT

---

Tayem tapped her fingers on the arm of the royal throne. Its hard, ironwood seat dug into her behind, and for one more suited to spending life on her feet it was a discomfort that only served to aggravate her irritation. There was little conversation amongst the six Fyreclave members present, and that which occurred was conducted in hushed whispers. She tried not to be annoyed with Mahren for taking her time; after all her sister had a duty to the dragons, and Tayem *had* called the Fyreclave at short notice after an eventful night. Still, the girl was a dreamer with a tendency to drag her heels when it came to official matters, and she had to get a grip. Riding the air currents wasn't the only priority of a Dragon Rider, after all.

There was something else acting as fuel for the ire she harboured in her breast. Her father had called it the *Hallows Light*, but the purple vapour she had inhaled, even *absorbed* last night, could not be described in those illuminate terms. Cistre had observed it, and she sensed others were aware of what transpired, barely masking their disquiet at the event. But to her, it represented the key to free her people. As yet she hadn't fathomed *how* it would help, she only knew that something now resided within, energising her mind and body. Something had to explain the remains of the yarra tree she'd hacked to pieces during her practice earlier, the uncanny accuracy with which she'd loosed her arrows at the target. If the Hallows had blessed her with this strength, these abilities — perhaps others could benefit.

*No, this is for you,* a voice seemed to say in her mind. It wasn't quite alien, more a fog of intuition, a wraith of dead matter, fallen in the rain, bound in the wind. She shook her head. There was something she didn't like about the voice.

"You look tired, my Queen," Cistre said. "The night's events exacted a toll on you. Please rest after this meeting."

Tayem looked at her faithful bodyguard. She meant well by her words, but they only annoyed her further. "We'll see," was all she said. Any more would abash Cistre unnecessarily.

"Your Majesty," an aged courtier, Disconsolin, spoke up. "Might I suggest we adjourn this meeting until your sister returns?"

"Or, we could simply proceed without her," added Merdreth, his wife. They rarely contributed anything constructive, and their presence in the Fyreclave owed more to privilege than merit.

"There are decisions to be made," Tayem replied. "They require full quorum." Her tone was typically imperious, but it was also tinged with an uncharacteristic venom, caustic even for her. It brought the room to silence however, and Tayem told herself she'd give Mahren five more minutes only. The Hallows murmurings rose within once more, and she sought to find a worthy target for her fury.

Etezora.

How could such a friendship have been dashed on the rocks so suddenly, so completely, and so irrevocably?

The Festival of Shaptari meant 'bringing'. A time purportedly to bring the peoples of the Crescent together, to celebrate unity, forge links and cool any rivalry with fresh treaties and trade of goods. Varchal's axis tilt did not permit a changing of seasons. In truth, the peoples would not understand such a concept, but the Festival of Shaptari was the closest one could imagine to a celebration of harvest and fruitfulness.

But Etezora had put paid to that. Tayem remembered the shattered egg with a bitterness that burrowed in her gut even to this day. She saw through the lens of memory a dragon embryo lying twisted in the dust, splashed with the viscous remains of its yolk sac. This bitterness was exceeded only by her eventual loathing at the expression she had seen on Etezora's face: A sadistic joy at the desecration she'd just committed, a look of conspiracy inviting Tayem to join her.

As these memories flooded back, Tayem felt something like acid burning behind her eyes. Her fists clenched and every muscle in her body tensed.

"My Queen?" Cistre detected the change in Tayem. She had an uncanny sensitivity to her moods, some would say empathic. Ignoring her Chief Guard, Tayem stood up abruptly and strode to the window. She had to engage in some activity that would break this turmoil within. Through the dragonglass she saw Mahren pacing up the main concourse of the palace. Her form disappeared beneath the canopy of a garbeech, and she estimated her sister would arrive in the next minute or two.

Tayem's troubled heart was stilled again, and she exhaled her relief.

*What is wrong with me?*

Turning round, she waved her hand, signalling a call to order. "Be seated everyone. Mahren comes."

The clave-members took up their positions in the horseshoe of high-backed, heavy chairs surrounding the royal throne, and settled themselves attentively by the time two guardsmen opened the main doors for the Queen's sister.

"Sorry for the delay," Mahren said and jogged the last few yards to take her seat.

Tayem neither rebuked nor offered forgiveness to her. "Now the Fyreclave is complete, I would put to you the matter that has troubled me since yesterday's exactment." She looked around the six members of the Fyreclave judging their reactions. When nothing conclusive was apparent she continued. "In the last three sols the Cuscosians' annual exactment has risen from thirty to sixty of our youngest age-comings. Not only does this stunt our people's growth in stature, but it is also designed to cow us into submission. They teach our young to mistrust their heritage, and they return to us unruly and resentful."

Gemain, an overly cautious but trustworthy administrator spoke up. "Your Majesty. This burden on our people troubles me too, but we accepted it at our last assembly with the Cuscosians. We deemed it a lesser of evils compared with the withdrawal of our food supply."

Tayem had prepared for this. "I thought this too. But they have included a greater proportion of maidens in their quota of late, and some less than sixteen sols old. This is unprecedented and unacceptable." Her recounting of the matter brought the itching back behind her eyes.

"This has preyed on my mind since yesterday's

exactment too," Ascomb, a mature matriarch said. "If we allow it to continue, the Cuscosians will not stop here. They are testing us. Indeed, I fear they will weaken our bloodstock to the point where we can resist no longer. It is no secret that the Cuscosians covet our dragon broods, and I have no doubt they will be targeted if we allow this to go unchecked."

Ascomb had it only half-right, Tayem mused. Etezora didn't so much desire the dragons — she longed for their complete destruction. "Something else to consider," Tayem said. "Increasing numbers of our age-comings marry into the Cuscosian populace and never come back. What they have failed to accomplish by outright conquest, they hope to achieve by a slow undermining of our ancient society. I will not permit that."

"And what of the sabotage that occurred to our bridge over the Halivern River?" Merdreth added.

"We don't know for sure that was the Cuscosians," Gemain said.

"Can there be any doubt?" Merdreth shot back. "They take us for fools."

Gemain shifted uncomfortably. "What do you propose, My Queen?"

Resolve burned in Tayem's eyes. "We should demand our age-comings back." Gemain looked horrified. "And suspend further exactments," Tayem added.

Gemain's disquiet turned to horror. "Your Majesty, this is reckless. The Cuscosians — "

"What is our battle strength, Cistre?" Tayem interrupted him.

Her bodyguard and Battle Commander stepped forward. "With the current number of recruits, freshly trained, four thousand two hundred and twenty three."

Cistre's attention to detail and knowledge of her troops never ceased to amaze Tayem. "And how many dragons?" Tayem asked.

"Battle ready?"

"Of course."

Cistre didn't flinch at the Queen's impatience. "Forty nine."

"I wouldn't say forty nine were battle ready," Mahren chose her moment to contribute. Tayem noted her guarded expression. It could mean many things. "At least a quarter have only flown a handful of practice sorties, and five are unruly — kicking against their rider's goads."

"So, essentially some thirty five? It is enough."

"Enough for what?" Gemain's complexion had turned from its natural tan hue to something more pallid.

"We cannot make demands without the force to back it up," Tayem said.

"But the Cuscosians number ten thousand or more!"

"Most of which are garrisoned at the borders defending them against Outlanders."

"A further contingent guard the new mines at Bagshot," Cistre added.

"You would mount an assault on Castle Cuscosa?" Gemain exclaimed.

"A show of force only. Dragons can be very intimidating." The itching behind Tayem's eyes increased. A perverse notion surfaced in her mind. If the Cuscosians did not comply she would not baulk at unleashing the fury of her dragon hordes. She dismissed the suggestion but sensed it only retreating to a corner of her mind to sulk. "We need to bring Etezora to the negotiating table with a credible threat. After sols of compliance she will not be expecting this."

"The Cuscosian Queen will call our bluff." This came from Darer, Tayem's most trusted adviser. He rarely spoke in the clave, saving the most sage advice for private audiences with the Queen. The man's age was written into features that resembled cracked leather, his wisdom commensurate with his demeanour.

"Then they will see it is no bluff," Tayem said.

This drew murmurings and a gasp from amongst the Fyreclave.

"Your Majesty," Gemain said, "this would be an act of outright war. We are not ready for such a conflict."

"You have a counter proposal?" Tayem tilted her head upwards, looking at the man with flared nostrils.

"Diplomacy must always be the first option. Do not forget, we depend on the Cuscosians for food. Our forests do not yield enough nuts, seeds and roots to feed our impoverished people. We should call them to an extraordinary conference, threaten to withhold our supply of ironwood and garbeech."

"That would take months to bite. Time we do not have," Tayem replied.

"What do you mean?" Disconsolin said. The man looked flustered, obviously dreading a disruption to his passive, ordered existence.

"You have all heard of the stirrings in the Dragon Ash Hallow. You have seen the skies turn violet. Varchal's child rises from its cradle. I saw this first hand, but we all know that similar awakenings will occur across the length of the Crescent. Magister Reganum?"

The remaining Fyreclave member rose to his feet. Silent up to now, always the one for drama, he spread his hands as if revealing an exquisite work of art. Such was the gravity he lent to his pronouncements. "It is true. I have predicted the beginning of the cycle of darkness for many months now, but it has come sooner than expected. We need only look at history to know that great upheavals in the Crescent Kingdoms will ensue. We cannot predict how these will play out, but the Hallows will exert its influence and only the strong and the shrewd will prevail."

"You think the Cuscosians are plotting more than a punitive exactment?" Gemain questioned the Magister.

"Again, history is our guide. The Black Hallows influence will cause unpredictable consequences. We should be prepared for anything. We can't be caught unawares."

"Surely you exaggerate," Gemain said.

"You forget the massacre at Lyn-Harath?" Reganum said, "A defeat resulting in the withdrawal of the Gigantes from the Lowlands? The Reiver ancestors of the Cuscosians decimated their people."

This silenced Gemain. He could not deny the reality of the account Reganum spoke of.

"The Black Hallows will also influence the vs' shtak," Darer said. "Do you think our resources will be strengthened?"

Tayem sensed there were undercurrents to Darer's statement. "We should expect an empowerment in some form. But, as the Magister has said, these matters are ... unpredictable." Tayem understood this would not satisfy the councillor, but it was substantial enough for her to move toward a conclusion. "Very well, I sense the Fyreclave's reluctance to overstep the mark, but the time for weak-willed diplomacy is past. Our discussions with the Cuscosians this last sol have been useless porticoes, empty predictions of prophecies, abandoned castles waiting to become finally deserted. I would break our indolence. Therefore my decision is this."

She paused, aware that she had lapsed into grand-speaking as her father used to counsel her. It was a habit that came from reading about vs' shtak ancestry and legends recorded in the many tomes lining the Grand Library's shelves. It *did* add to her powers of persuasion however, and the turmoil behind her eyes seemed to augment this ability — she could see it on the faces of all but Darer.

"Mahren, the Cuscosians will deliver tonight's Dragon food as usual?"

"Yes, My Queen," Mahren said.

"You will ride to the meeting point early and apprehend the carriers."

"Apprehend? You mean take them hostage?"

"We will not call it so. Consider it our own exactment."

"The delivery will be overseen by Etezora's nephew, Setaeor. We should apprehend him too?"

"Him especially. As I said, we need to bring Etezora to the point of realistic negotiation."

The Fyreclave knew the time for consultation was past. Tayem had made her decision, and she detected her command had been accepted. "I bring this meeting to a close. We will gather at the same time tomorrow. By then, Mahren's sortie will be accomplished."

The Fyreclave members exited, accompanied by no little murmuring and discussion. Only Darer hung back, wiry arms folded and bald head tipped downwards in contemplation.

Sharp exchanges between Mahren and Cistre drew Tayem's attention.

"You questioned my assessment of the dragon host?" Cistre said to Tayem's sister. She was prodding Mahren in the chest, a gesture Mahren would respond to in kind unless Tayem intervened.

"You assume too much, Cistre. The royal brood is my domain. You should have deferred to me." Mahren had taken hold of Cistre's wrist, forcing it downwards. Cistre's expression was thunder.

"Enough!" Tayem said. "You both have important tasks to perform, and I demand you are not distracted."

Cistre wrenched her hand from Mahren's grip. She was a full span shorter than Mahren, but her prowess in combat more than made up for this. Tayem was adamant this rivalry should not spill over in the Royal Hall — or indeed anywhere. "Cistre!" she said.

The bodyguard turned to Tayem and saluted. "My Queen?"

"You are to draw up a strategic plan according to a series of contingencies I have in mind. I will need up-to-date appraisal of troops, weapons and supply lines. There is much to discuss. Mahren?"

Her sister turned to her and also saluted. "Ready the Dragon Riders and brief them. Tonight must see an effective operation. In addition, make ready secure accommodation for our Cuscosian guests."

"Of course, my Queen," Mahren replied, striding away with a scolded expression clouding her face.

"Cistre — you have something to say?" Tayem said.

Cistre's forehead furrowed. "I ... no, My Queen. I will attend to your wishes."

Tayem nodded and watched her leave. Mahren could be read like a tome, but Cistre's demeanour often left Tayem perplexed. There was loyalty there, devotion even. But sometimes she sensed there was a hidden impulse.

Darer approached, a gentle smile playing on his face.

"Decisive as ever," he said.

"You hold reservations?" she replied.

Darer shrugged. "You have weighed up options, I am sure. But is there something I should be aware of?"

"Such as?"

The councillor's lips stretched thin. "The rising of the Black Hallows is a matter of great import. I gather you had a rather special encounter last night?"

"Special? In what way?"

"You were especially persuasive just now. You are also well read in the legends of the Black Hallows."

"I learned much from my father."

"He was a seeker, but was denied the baptism he sought."

"He might have succeeded if he had been given time." Tayem recognised the melancholy rising but quelled it instinctively.

"The traditional Hallows lacked potency, but I visited the Dragon Ash site after your summoning."

"Did you ..?"

Darer shook his head. "It reached out to me, but I denied its overtures."

Tayem felt a strange relief. But why should she? Darer had as much right of access to the Dragon Ash site as she did. "Do you think I was mistaken to accept?"

"I will simply say this," he said, looking out at the burgeoning clouds in the sky. "Proceed with great caution. The Hallows draws some more than others. You possess a steel will and may use the Hallows to your advantage. But many fall foul of its influence."

"I understand the risks," she said.

Darer nodded. "I am here should you need further counsel." It was a natural close to the conservation and Tayem knew they had an understanding. But as Darer left, the entity skulked out of the shadows of her mind again.

*You should tread carefully with him,* it whispered. *He is not free from envy — watch him well.*

# 7

# WAITING FOR THE NAIL

———

Wobas had another meeting to attend after the unsuccessful liaison with his daughter. He hoped it had a better outcome. His destination was the Gigantes' village and, though it occupied a lower elevation than his cave dwelling, it left one with a sense of loftiness, as if perched on the roof of the world.

He passed through a stand of colossus pines lining a promontory of sandstone shrouded in mist. It was a treacherous path for the unwary, to those who sought to breach this realm. One mis-step could send a trespasser plummeting over the bluff to be dashed on the unforgiving shards below, and Wobas wondered how many broken bodies had found their final resting place down there since the Decimation.

*Three turns left and one turn right,* he said to himself, finding the hidden trail that only a rock goat would find easy to traverse. It led him down in a zigzag fashion to the hidden settlement nestled amongst the crags.

Sol-Ar approached its zenith, and the village bustled with activity. These dwellings were where the Minutae lived, the diminutive kindred of the Cyclopes who dwelt in the higher reaches of the village. A woodsman brought his axe down outside one house, whilst the smell of freshly baked sour-bread drifted from another. The turf-covered roofs of these simple dwellings concealed them from above, and also served as homes to dormice, squirrels and an astounding flora of fungi and mountain flowers. As Wobas observed this familiar bustle of life it struck him that, to an outsider, the two races making up the Gigantes were an incongruous mix. Even more perplexing to think they had all sprung from the same ancestors, if the volumes in Ebar's library were true.

He skirted around Ginnie the sooth-sayer's diminutive house and prepared himself for the exertion ahead. Ebar's house, supported on four great rowspen trunks formed an imposing construction, although this was not the Cyclopes' intent. The Hill-Warden would like nothing better than to retreat into complete obscurity, yet his duties prevented such indulgencies. White smoke billowed from a single chimney pot crowning the pitched roof, and Wobas hauled his aged frame up the large wooden staircase surrounding the property.

Ebar waited on a blackwood platform, his towering form casting a long shadow across the worm-holed surface. Wobas made to greet the giant but a guttural belch stopped him short. A nar pushed its way between Ebar's legs, slaver dripping from its fangs, tongue lolling from the side of a cavernous maw. It burped again as it lolloped towards the dream-sage.

"Barabas!" Ebar admonished, "get back." The bear-thing snivelled but lumbered obediently over to a basket large as a beer vat, slumping itself down in a huff.

"Don't worry, he's eaten already," Ebar said, a parabolic smile creasing his weathered face. His voice never failed to remind Wobas of a bough sighing in the breeze, lazily sounding its poems to an unseen audience. Long, ratty-grey braids hung over Ebar's wizened face, the centre of which housed a single, rapidly blinking eye.

"That does little to reassure me," Wobas replied, "I've seen that nar devour three deer in one sitting. He has a peckish look in his eye."

Ebar let out a guffaw, creating an air current Wobas felt even though a matter of yards separated them. "There's not enough meat on you to satisfy him," he said. "Now come, take a seat."

The giant beckoned Wobas over to a log bench, fully fifteen spans in length and five high. The dream-seer looked at the Cyclopes sceptically. "Here," Ebar said, and pulled up a stool enabling Wobas to perch himself on the over-sized seat. Once up, he took a moment to gaze over the Hill People's land. They chose not to refer to it as a Kingdom. The Gigantes had dispensed with these terms since the Decimation. Such dominions were anathema, and only reminded these gentle people of a tumultuous past, together with unending strife. Although the Hallows violet added a baleful glow to the horizon, it couldn't dispel the beauty of this land. White fleecy clouds blanketed purple stacks of rock that peeked through like columns in a vast cathedral. The view encouraged a body to worship this land, yet Wobas knew Ebar held his reverence for the spirits of the Dreamworld, not physical idols.

"Refreshment?" Ebar intoned.

"That would be welcome," Wobas said. "My last host was less than hospitable."

Ebar avoided commenting and shouted through to his wife inside the house proper. "Shamfis? Do me a favour and pour some of that figberry juice for us, would you?"

"On its way," came the reply.

Ebar reached into his well-tailored garbeast robes and pulled out a pouch, opened it and offered the contents to Wobas. The shredded jarva-leaf was a potent herb, and Wobas declined. "Thank you Great Ebar, but I need a clear head to find my way back over Camber Crag without tripping into its cloudy embrace.

Ebar nodded and withdrew a pinch that, in his

gargantuan fingers, constituted a handful to Wobas. The giant chewed on it, closed his eye and savoured the heady cocktail of chemicals it released in his mouth. Wobas knew better than to interrupt the giant's pleasure and waited patiently.

Before long, Shamfis appeared with a tray upon which stood a wooden jug and two different sized goblets. "I brought you Djabi's baby cup," she said to Wobas. He thanked her, noting, as always, her cheerful expression framed by dreadlocks tied back in a bun. She left them to their conversation and busied herself preparing the family meal. He heard the clatter of pots and the shriek of children, loud as bear cubs, sounding from the interior.

"You understand why I signalled to you?" Ebar said at last.

"I can guess."

"The cycle begins early."

"Indeed."

"You know what this means."

"I know very little. That's the problem."

Wobas and Ebar's friendship, if it could be called that, spanned many decades and although their words were sparsely issued, a lot of meaning lodged between them — much like wallets of insight in a coat of many pockets.

"What are the portents from the Dreamworld?" Ebar enquired.

Wobas exhaled heavily. "The Spirit Guide granted me an audience."

The giant turned to him, his eye blinking twice in rapid succession. "That is significant."

"The most important turn of events to emerge in my humble lifetime."

"Dare I ask what it said?"

"It was evasive, said I had to make peace with my daughter before I could gain the knowledge I seek."

Ebar's mouth turned down. "Well that's that, then."

"Alas, yes. But not for want of trying."

"You paid her a visit?"

"I did."

"The Spirit Guide might as well have asked you to sew a garment made of sand."

"I'm sorry I have reached an impasse. I share your burden in the Cyclopes' search for release from this curse."

A smile returned to Ebar's face. "We all have our burdens to bear. Things could be worse."

"How long?" Wobas asked, sadness creeping into his tone.

"Sixteen hundred and twenty-two days. Thankfully, Shamfis has much longer. But who knows of the children? Our eldest is still seven sols from her revelation."

"Revelation? That seems a wrong word for it. It must be akin to observing your coffin and the number of nails to be hammered into the lid."

"It is an apt thought. Yet we are denied the knowledge of what transpires beforehand."

"Have the predictions always held true?"

"You know they have."

"Then, there must be a way to lift this unbearable curse."

"There might be. But it seems your daughter holds the key." Wobas sighed, and the giant gently patted his back. "Don't take that as an accusation. It's not my place to apportion blame."

"It is a paradox, though, is it not? My devotion to seeking an answer to your plight has cost me the means by which to achieve it."

Ebar laughed loud enough to stir his dozing nar. "Sometimes I think we are playthings of the spirits."

It was Wobas's turn to smile. "Still, there is yet more wisdom I seek. This change in the depths and the southern sky brings challenges all of its own."

Ebar grew sombre once more. "I have had my ear to the ground and my eyes in the air."

Wobas looked up and regarded two circling raptors, the sun reflecting off their tawny undersides. They looked innocuous enough, but how many were aware they reported to the Hill People. "And ..?"

"And the news is not good. There is activity in the Kaldoran mines."

Wobas's brow furrowed. "They're always digging — seeking richer deposits of cryonite or jewels of even greater value."

"This is different. The sounds are more like rumblings.

They cause landslips in the valleys, and this is not all; Brownbeak saw a large sortie of dragons take to the air just now."

"Where were they headed?"

"They circled the Dragonian Vale and soared on the heights for an hour. Then they returned."

"A flexing of muscles, or a show of strength?"

"No one else was observed. The nearest Cuscosian regiment is barracked at Fort Gorriund."

"Sounds to me they were rehearsing for something. What of the Cuscosians themselves?"

"Nothing obvious, but purple vapours hang over the Edenbract knoll."

"There is a Hallows there is there not?"

"Yes — very similar to the one south of your hermitage." The giant turned and stared intently at him. The eye was bloodshot at the perimeter — probably a result of the jarva-leaf he was chewing, but the pupil fixed Wobas with a clarity he found perturbing.

Wobas nodded. "You are right to enquire of my dealings with the Hallows. I have not ventured close to the Scar, you can rest assured of that."

Ebar sat back and placed his hands behind his head, looking more relaxed. "I thought as much, but I had to ask. Still, the Black Hallows may impinge on the Dreamworld too — they seem to be having an effect everywhere else."

"You think the activity your emissaries have witnessed are connected to the Hallows?"

"Co-incidences happen, I suppose."

Wobas took a sip of figberry juice. The treacly liquid invigorated him considerably. "The Spirit Guide did not say, but I have not returned since last night, so I do not know for sure."

"You don't need me to tell you that it pays to be be watchful. Other factions might entertain what the Hallows have to offer, but there is always a price to pay."

"What do the rest of the council think? Have you met?"

"We will — this afternoon, and I am going to counsel caution, a waiting game. Our people had a heavy toll exacted on them as a result of the previous Hallows cycle."

Ebar's speech was growing slurred and his voice took on a droning quality, and Wobas knew he would get no further cogent insight from the giant. He only hoped Ebar would sleep off the jarva haze before his meeting with the rest of the council. He took his leave, saying a quick good bye to Shamfis and the children, then made his way back up to the bluff.

Just before entering the mist corridor, Wobas took one last look at the purpling sky on the far horizon. "Do you also inhabit the Dreamworld?" he asked, as if the Black Hallows was some entity that could be addressed. Although the risks were great, he would fly through the sacred realm this night. If he could not reconcile himself to Milissandia, then he had no choice but to embark on the forbidden way and seek an audience with the Augur. Perhaps in this there might be a way to tame the Hallows.

# 8

# AMBUSH AT THE CROSSING

—————

Bilespit held the scryer to his jaundiced eye and adjusted the focus. "Ten wagons," he said, "they've upped their production even more." Above the usual stench of unwashed Kaldoran flesh, he detected the subtle smell of anticipation and — yes — fear. Like all the stonegrabes, Bilespit abhorred natural light. His warband were swaddled in thick, drab-brown wrappings that covered them from head to toe. This afforded them some protection from Sol-Ar's harmful rays but, despite the recent Hallows darkening, Bilespit could barely tolerate the brightness above ground.

"How many guard the train?" A dumpy Kaldoran said, leaning on his maul.

Bilespit lowered the scryer and regarded the foot soldier. "Don't you mean 'How many guard the train, *Sir?*"

"You are only captain for this one mission," the other replied, "we all know you're operating on a trial basis. So don't get ideas beyond your station."

Bilespit considered his next words carefully and then decided to dispense with them. Quick as a stone-serpent, he caught the stonegrabe on the side of his head with a granite fist. It wasn't enough to cave in his skull, but still struck with enough force to send him sprawling into the dust. "You mentioned my ideas? Well, that's what I think," Bilespit said, looking through the scryer again.

The wagon train rolled along a hard-packed road, flicking clouds of graphite-coloured powder into the air. Bilespit counted fifteen foot soldiers and five horsemen, a goodly number, but unlikely to consist of Cuscosian elite. His warband could take them, not least because they had the element of surprise.

"Someone give that little krut a slap," he said, nodding at the unconscious figure. "We'll need every stonegrabe battle-ready if we're to overpower the Cuscosian scum."

While two burly stonegrabes brought their comrade back from sleepland, Bilespit assessed his warband's strength: twenty-five in number, armed with mauls, axes, slings and bows. The archers weren't particularly adept, but then the arrows were only there for effect, to lead the

Cuscosians up the garden path as it were. Bilespit barked his commands and the stonegrabes obediently took up their positions, eager to avoid the fate of the recovering Kaldoran.

The wagons would soon reach the ford below, where the shallow waters of the Queenswater River tumbled loudly over a jutting line of rocks that marked the shallows. The depth of the water, though diminished, would still slow the wagons down, and the Cuscosians would be exposed in the middle of the waterway. *Odds I like,* Bilespit thought. He observed the stonegrabes bearing slingshots together with a number of archers climb to higher ground, while the axemen and hammer-weld took cover in willows bordering the riverbank. Now, as long as the motley bunch of rock scuttlers followed orders, the operation should proceed smoothly enough. Hopefully it would all be over in a few minutes. Then again, the chaos god could always fart in your face and upset the most carefully laid plans. Bilespit had come to learn this.

The Cuscosians were close enough for the stonegrabes to see their features now. The gar oxen harnessed four at a time, plodded a steady rhythm as they pulled heavy wagons laden with cryonite ore. As well as sowing mischief, this raid would garner the Kaldorans some valuable resources. The first wagon entered the water without missing a hoof-fall, and it wasn't long before half the train were up to the oxes' knees in water.

*Just a couple of moments more.*

Bilespit cupped his rock-encrusted hands over his mouth and made a sound part way between a squawk and a rattle, the call of the pied wrathwing. A signal his stonegrabes understood.

A whipping sound accompanied the release of a volley of pebbles loosed from Kaldoran slingshots. Each found its mark, striking a Cuscosian horseman full in the face, despite their protective helmets. Four riders fell from their mounts, either unconscious or dead. The Kaldorans loosed several arrows also, although most struck the water. A lucky pair pierced the hides of two oxen — to little effect. It would take more than longbows to bring these beasts down, and the Kaldorans would need them to cart the cryonite away in any case.

To his credit, the mounted Cuscosian leader responded quickly and rallied his remaining soldiers behind the wagons. The wagon drivers were armed only with shortswords and would not pose that great a threat, Bilespit assumed.

"Fire the second volley," he shouted. Another hail of stones and arrows came at the Cuscosians, but bounced uselessly off the wagons or stuck into the tarpaulins covering them. They would not pick off any more without a drawn-out siege, and the Kaldorans didn't have time for that.

"Break cover," Bilespit cried. "Charge!"

Those stonegrabes concealed beneath the weeping willow boughs exploded forth with a battle-cry on their lips, jogging with high steps through the water. Two fell, skewered in the chest by javelins thrown from the spearmen. Bilespit had set up the ambush to catch the Cuscosians in a pincer movement. While the defenders gave their attention to the first onslaught, Bilespit's second wave caught them by surprise when they closed in from further down the bank, thus flanking the Cuscosians. Two more fell beneath mauls wielded by the second Kaldoran wave, their long shafts making up for the stonegrabe's shortness of stature. The remainder met the stonegrabes bravely, bringing spears and swords to bear with practised precision. The Cuscosian captain alone had decapitated two of Bilespit's horde.

"Krut — the tide could turn in the Cuscosians' favour at this rate," Bilespit cursed. The captain had to be brought down. The honourable course of action would have been to engage the captain in one-to-one combat, but Bilespit wasn't honourable. Still in his position of concealment, he tapped the stonegrabe standing next to him and pointed at the captain. He raised the slingshot, took aim and loosed a specially forged iron ball, moulded with cruel spikes. The vengeful sphere found its target and passed through the captain's cheekbone, spinning the man round and exposing his flank. The missile didn't kill him, but the blow from a Kaldoran axe did. Bilespit recognised the stonegrabe that had insulted him and decided not to throw him into the slag pits upon their return to the Kaldoran stronghold. His slaying of the captain was a turning point. Three minutes later the Cuscosians fell back, some tripping into the water as Kaldorans swarmed over them, hacking and beating them with their weapons.

Bilespit chose this moment to join the fray. He hopped down the hillside, jumped on top of a wagon and swung his maul down upon an unarmed wagon driver. The men were easy pickings and, once dispensed, left him time to assess the rest of the melee. "Take them all," he yelled, "gut every last one of them. Leave no survivors."

One minute later, the last Cuscosian had fallen in the water, his skull caved in by a Kaldoran mace.

Hakrish, Bilespit's second in command, waded over to him, blood dripping from both ends of his warhammer. He panted and perspired with exertion.

"How many stonegrabes did we lose?" Bilespit enquired.

"By the looks of it, seven. Eight wounded, but not mortally," Hakrish replied.

Bilespit nodded with satisfaction. "Right, the job's not finished. Have the archers loose more arrows into the corpses from further back, and unload those sacks of dragon mord on the far bank. Make it look natural.

Hakrish shook his head. "I doubt if the Cuscosians will fall for it. Since when have the Dragonians coveted cryonite?"

"Since now," Bilespit replied. "Look at Sol-Ar and the sky. See how even now the heavens grow darker — and it's only early afternoon. The Black Hallows puts things in the minds of men they wouldn't usually consider. All we need to do is nudge the Cuscosians in the right direction."

Hakrish shrugged. He was a footsoldier not a tactician and was happy to follow orders. It wasn't his place to question.

"Colon. Akath," Bilespit shouted. "Take eight others and drive these wagons back up the Eastern Road. We must cover fifteen periarchs before nightfall, and we don't want a Cuscosian counter attack to befall us."

The stonegrabes carried out their duties, loading their wounded and dead onto the wagons before setting off. Bilespit considered taking one of the whinnying horses to make the journey back more comfortable, but he wasn't a horseman and didn't want to risk a broken collarbone. *No*, he contemplated, *there are things Kaldorans do well, and others not so well*. Killing and treachery were their stock in trade. Elegant pursuits such as equestrianism were just unseemly — and Bilespit would be cursed if he was going to appear unseemly.

# 9

# UNDER THE MASK

———

Eétor glanced impatiently at the water clock. This was not a characteristic state of mind for him, but then events could wear away at a lifetime's virtue, he reflected, and the advent of the Black Hallows was such an event.

He needed to talk to Zodarin, consult with the man. Man? Zodarin was many things: magician, sorcerer, wizard, and soulsearcher. To describe him merely as a man was to underestimate him, and Eétor suspected he hid many of his talents. It was therefore prudent to weigh the man's capabilities carefully.

Could he be trusted? Up to a point. The House of Cuscosa was a nest of writhing vipers, so to give anyone your total confidence was a mistake. Yet the sorcerer had aided him in Eétor's most nefarious of atrocities — the murder of his parents.

Sometimes the Praetor of House Cuscosa imagined it was some other that perpetrated this deed. He wasn't proud of it, but to say he was full of guilt or remorse would misrepresent him. The justification was a way of distancing himself from the distasteful but necessary machinations of statesmanship. Yet sometimes he wondered whether his seemingly impervious shell was all he had constructed it to be. It was at moments like this, when he was on his own, that spectres of the past would sometimes haunt him. He circled his small, spartan anteroom looking for a distraction to pass the time. As a result of his searching he came upon the decorated dragon wood jewellery box his mother gave him.

It had been the occasion of his twentieth natum day. Eétor was a frustrated man even then, his father having ruled nine sols of his allotted tenure. Eétor would assume the throne in a sol's time according to Cuscosa's accession rules. Not a long period to wait, but too long if he was to enact his bold plans.

"I know you are discontented with your father, my dear Eétor," his mother said, "but your time will come."

"It's not just the matter of the throne," he replied. "It's his condescension, his dismissiveness. Father is putting decrees into place contrary to my wishes. He knows this, yet persists."

His mother gave a tight smile. "I know." She paused, and Eétor knew in that moment she would always favour her husband, even condone him manipulating events in the background once Eétor accessed the throne. "Perhaps this might be a consolation," she continued, opening a drawer in her dressing table. "I know we gave you your official gift, but I wanted to give this as something special — just from me."

She lifted out the oblong engraved case and Eétor caught his breath despite himself.

"The heartwood box? Are you sure? This is normally handed down to the Queen's eldest daughter."

He accepted the small casket from her and regarded its surface. The finest Dragonian craftsmanship, inlaid with delicate flakes of garbeech and spalted herry. The sides were encrusted with azure and emerald coloured jewels, mined and selected from Kaldora's most precious hoard. It was beautiful — and so disappointing. He knew it was symbolic. But he had no use for such an heirloom, and it would only drive a wedge between him and Etezora. Something his mother had either not seen, or unwittingly accepted as part of his father's schemings.

*Gorram them both.*

Zodarin had detected Eétor's ambitions and the Praetor took the wizard into his confidence. To have such a longstanding advisor and powerful ally was a boon, and Zodarin shared Eétor's ambitions for aggressive expansion. He was also willing to carry out baser acts when required.

That night, Zodarin pledged to deal with the 'parental problem' in his own inimitable way. Eétor was aware of the Dreamworld via tales passed down from mystics, but he considered it a legend. That was until Zodarin showed him its wonders through administration of various concoctions and muttered incantations. The wizard seemed to pass into this fantastical realm at will, but Eétor required extraordinary means — methods that Zodarin was well versed in.

"I would see the moment that they die," he told the sorcerer.

"There will be little to see," Zodarin replied. "Some simply have a seizure and die in their sleep. Others scream as if in the grip of a nightmare, and then come to rest."

Eétor looked crestfallen.

Zodarin fixed him with eyes tinted yellow in the sclera and snake-slit pupils. "But in the Dreamworld ..."

Eétor was eager to learn more, to partake, and with a little persuasion Zodarin complied, although he said it would be a difficult thing to enable Eétor's access to the realm.

Nevertheless, Zodarin was successful, and they entered a trance state during the early hours. Eétor remembered hearing the night scops hoot, sounding a death knell as their incorporeal forms drifted across ethereal boundaries.

*Are you sure they will be here?* Eétor asked the wizard.

*All who walk the lands of Varchal have their spirit form —
except those of the Dragonian race.* Zodarin replied. *The hard
part is detecting and recognising them amongst the billions that
exist here.*

The dread-scapes they traversed through were enough
to bring Eétor to the brink of madness, but he was strong-
willed and resisted their infiltrations. He himself ran on
multiple legs, his body a chitinous mass of articulations
that moved like a clockwork mechanism. He asked
Zodarin to contrive a more seemly form, but the wizard
related that there were laws governing such things,
precepts beyond his ability to manipulate. Eétor had his
doubts about this, but accepted the mage's explanation.

Zodarin adopted the form of a ginger tomcat, overly
large with tufted ears, yet the Praetor identified the same
serpentine eyes and gait of the man. Similarly, when
Zodarin homed in on his parents, he recognised them for
what they were. His father, a squat rat-like mammal,
crouched on a tree stump, while his mother curled up in
the form of a miniature cur, coated in long wispy fur and
snoring in a snivelling fashion. When he observed them
in that state, their spirit forms revealing more of their
character than he could ever have divined in the world of
the Near To, his distaste for them turned to revulsion.

*Do it,* he sent to the cat-wizard.

*I need to assume a different guise,* the wizard said. *Do not
relate what you see next to another soul — ever.*

One look at the cat's piercing eyes convinced Eétor that this was wise counsel. *You have my word*, he replied.

If there were any regrets about that night's fateful decisions, then choosing to watch what transpired next would be the only one to repeatedly surface in Eétor's mind.

Zodarin turned to face Eétor's reposed parents and then collapsed in upon himself. The feline form was replaced by something much larger and infinitely more horrific. To this day, Eétor could not find words to describe the monstrosity; indeed he tried to blot it from his mind. Yet he had found that only a hefty dose of jarva-leaf could even begin to achieve this.

To compensate, the Praetor could savour the expression of fear on his mother and father's faces. The wizard's transformation was not silent, and they awoke with alarm at the disturbance. His father had defecated at the sight of Zodarin's nightmare form, while his mother simply shook, unable to muster the will to flee.

The Zodarin-monster fell upon them with an avalanche of grotesque limbs and tentacles — ripping and shredding with an abandon that to Eétor appeared ecstatic in its energy. In the end, the son turned away from the savagery that the monster exacted on his parents.

Yet the Zodarin-beast was not finished. *You must partake*, it sent in a voice that echoed eternal corruption.

*What?* Eétor replied.

*Kill.*

I cannot —

*You must take ownership,* it sent, and the voice was so compelling that Eétor could not refuse, though the prospect reviled him. His father's rodent visage was mutilated almost beyond recognition, yet Eétor saw the flickering light of life still kindled there — just. He snuffed it out with a rain of blows to the rat's head. The bloody pulp that remained was unrecognisable.

Then he turned to his mother, the almond shaped cur-eyes staring at him with incredulity.

*Why?* she uttered through blood-encrusted lips.

Eétor answered by breaking her neck with a single bite from his mandibles. She deserved a quick death, after all.

Eétor pushed the memory from his mind and focused on the jewellery box again. He repaid her seeming generosity with an act of unspeakable treachery. It represented a waymark in his life and, though he'd been responsible for countless deaths since, none could equal what he perpetrated that night.

"You are ruminating again," an oleaginous voice said. Zodarin was at the door, as if he had just materialised. He slunk into the room, ducking under the lintel, a lop-sided smile on his face. *Why does it always seem he is stalking something — or someone?* Eétor thought.

"It is my wont to consider all things," Eétor said.

The sorcerer's smile broadened. "Indeed it is."

It irked Eétor that Zodarin offered no apology for his tardiness. More so that he suspected the wizard sensed his thoughts — if not in their entirety then at least in essence. He drew a cloak over his musings and thought he sensed a withdrawal of something impinging.

"I summoned you here to discuss my sister's recent empowerment," Eétor said. "This enhancement of Etezora's, it has shifted the balance, and she continues to confound the plans we agreed to put into place together ten sols ago."

Zodarin folded his slender arms; the elongated fingers splaying around his elbows unnaturally. Not for the first time, Eétor speculated as to the man's origins. "You had hoped the Hallows would bestow similar gifts upon you," the wizard said.

"I returned to Edenbract just before dawn and — "

"And you were disappointed." Zodarin inclined his head. "I warned you that an existing reserve within a body is required to — "

"Yes, yes. I know what you said." Eétor was keen to show Zodarin that interruption was not only the wizard's preserve. The wizard had to be handled carefully, true, but the Praetor held greater authority. Eétor pressed home the initiative. "Have you yourself visited the Hallows?" It was more than a question.

Zodarin hesitated long enough for the man's evasion to be confirmed. "The temple site is forbidden to all but the royal family. It would be a serious violation for me to even step within its boundaries."

"That is not an answer," Eétor said.

Zodarin took one step forward, ostensibly a shifting of weight, but Eétor felt threatened nonetheless. "Tell me, what punishment would you exact on such a trespasser?"

Eétor drew himself up to full height, yet was still two spans shorter than the wizard's towering form. "It is Etezora's prerogative to decree such things. I was simply warning you, as she placed a heavy guard on the temple this morning."

Zodarin nodded. "Thank you for the warning, Your Excellency. But, as a humble servant of the crown, I would not even think of overstepping my station."

There it was again. The man was an expert at deflection. *How long can I continue to trust him?*

"Sit down," Eétor said, "we have much to talk about. Can I offer you a drink?"

It was a hospitable act, but also a device to reduce the wizard's commanding presence. Zodarin accepted the invitation, requesting a goblet of red wine and, as they discussed their next moves, Eétor felt a little more comforted at the wizard's assessments and suggestions.

Half an hour later, they had agreed on a course of action.

"So, I should bide my time for the present, and allow you to put these matters into place?" Eétor said.

"That would be prudent. Etezora is fixated on her new talents and suspects nothing of our intentions. Best to keep it that way until the final pieces of our ... I mean *your* plan are in place."

Eétor was satisfied at the outcome and dismissed Zodarin. He was sure the wizard had other machinations in mind, but Eétor had plenty of his own. It was time to talk to Grizdoth. The Praetor might be lacking in magical talents but he had influence over others who could compensate for this deficiency — and Grizdoth owed him a debt or two.

10

# SILVER SPOONS AND
# GOLDEN CHAINS

---

The dragon was only ten sols old, little more than a fledgling, but already attempting to exert its dominance. Cistre had carried out Tayem's duties and had a short time to do something more relaxing, more frivolous.

Hours ago, Mahren had taken off with five Dragon Riders. The bodyguard had no doubt that Mahren would accomplish her mission, and this was all well and good for Tayem's plans, but it irritated Cistre that the kirith-a was entrusted with such a responsibility. She, on the other hand, was stuck here carrying out more menial tasks. She knew she ought not to harbour such thoughts. After all, carrying the mantle of personal bodyguard to the Queen was not a humble position, and it did mean she could spend many hours in Tayem's presence.

"Don't be fooled by his tender age," Sheldar said, "Kutan's gained a habit for tipping his opponent this last week, and your mind doesn't seem to be quite on task — if you don't mind me saying so."

The dragon-hand was overly fond of giving out advice, particularly to Cistre, and she wasn't sure she was in the mood for receiving the benefits of his wisdom this afternoon. "Still your tongue, Sheldar. I know what I'm doing," she said, circling around to the dragon's flank.

Kutan responded by shifting his six-span body from side to side, looking for an opening. Dragons didn't smile, but it didn't stop Cistre from wondering at times. This wyrm seemed to enjoy himself as he feinted first one way then another.

*Cistre — Dragon Wrestler* was not a title she relished, but the sport *was* a welcome distraction — and she certainly had a talent for it. The initial strike or 'embrace' was a crucial moment in the match. The opponent who gained the upper hand in those first thirty seconds or so put themselves at a considerable advantage, and she was determined this would be her. Sol-Ar's rays beamed through a gap in the garbeech canopy and reflected off Kutan's scales, the laminations creating a blue-green iridescence that struck her with their beauty.

The moment of appreciation was her undoing. Kutan's posture and expression gave no indication of its intent, and the strike came swift as lightning. He came in low, his snout buffeting her leg and tipping her onto her back. Immediately he was upon her. He knew better than to bare his teeth, and his claws had been clipped to prevent them inflicting excessive damage. Nonetheless it knocked the wind out of her, and within the space of two seconds she was staring into the face of the mischievous dragon, smelling its fresh meat-breath.

"I told you," Sheldar said, "he's a sneaky diggod, and it looks like he's caught you napping."

Cistre wished that Sheldar would krut off, but she blotted him out and considered her counter move.

*Krut, he's strong.* The dragon, unlike most, seemed to put on weight faster than a typical wyrm, and it was all muscle. She attempted to roll him with a swift forearm smash to his neck but his weight was impossible to shift, and he brushed the blow off, swinging his head around to nuzzle into her chest, pinning her to the ground. The beast had caught her between the breasts — an almost intimate affront, and Cistre could tell by the glint in his eyes that he knew what he was doing. It was playful rather than malicious.

"Now *that's* a low move, even for you," she said. *Well, I'm not above trying an underhand manoeuvre myself.*

Stilling her inner spirit so as not to give away her intentions, she clapped her hands over the beast's ears — a sensitive part of any dragon's anatomy. Kutan shrieked in pain, caught off guard. Cistre pressed home the advantage, using her strong thighs to twist his body and roll him off her. The ruse worked, and she executed a practised move that brought her up behind him, locking arms under his wings, clinging on like a limpet.

Try as he might, Kutan could not shake her off and he bellowed in frustration. Sheldar began the count, and by the time he reached three she'd won the bout.

"Hey, hey, hey," Sheldar exclaimed, "you gave him a dose of his own potion."

Cistre released the dragon, stroking his nose and feeding him a chunk of squarra meat, letting him know she meant him no malice. This was sport after all.

The beast sighed in submission, glad of the morsel. He shook his head, tossing the fillet to the back of his jaws, and with three closings had swallowed it gratefully.

Sheldar held out his hand to help Cistre up, and without thinking she accepted it out of politeness. It was the only overture Sheldar needed.

"Say, would you accept a humble dragon-hand's invitation to share a flagon or two in the Willow Tavern tonight?"

Cistre pursed her lips and regarded his expectant face for a moment. She supposed he was handsome, for a man. His long sable locks formed an attractive surround to his overly boned features, and he could make her laugh with his quips and anecdotes. But he stirred nothing within her.

She pinched his nose mischievously. "Save yourself for someone who's less likely to break your arm," she said.

"Oh, go on," he continued, unpersuaded, "you need more fun in your life, Cistre. Why not — "

"I need to relieve Coren on guard duty," she said, "then I have my evening duties to perform." Her demeanour turned stony and officious. She didn't mean to hurt his feelings, but he needed to be left in no doubt. "See that you secure the dragons well. They're restless due to their brothers and sisters' absence."

"Mahren's sortie? Why did so many ride out this afternoon?"

"It's not your concern. Now, you have your responsibilities and I have mine. See to the dragons, Sheldar."

With that, she strode away, not giving him a chance to reply. Her thoughts turned to Tayem. Cistre's heart was troubled at the Queen's outburst during the council meeting, disturbed by the shadows behind her fierce gaze. She had hung back at the grand chamber's doorway, overheard Darer's conversation with Tayem as they had discussed the Black Hallows. Cistre was charged with the duty of guarding the Queen with her life, but might she now have to save her from herself?

She marched through the Dragonian courtyard, tendrils from the giant tisthorn trees forming a curtain of greenery lining the hardwood walkway. The main acropolis was marvellous in its design. When first she had come to Dragonia, it had stolen the breath from her mouth with its towering ironwood spires. In the failing light, the creepers that draped the edifice came alive with chirping crickets and singing night-warblers. Tayem's father had welcomed her to the royal household — an orphan with forgotten origins. He had taken her in and bestowed an education and security she knew she was immensely lucky to have received. Yes, her allegiance to the royal house came from a sense of indebtedness, but her devotion to Tayem somehow went beyond this.

The Queen might be strong-willed, but Cistre was prepared to step in should her resistance to the Hallows break her down. Perhaps tonight would allow her the opportunity.

~ ~ ~

Tayem sat cross-legged on a dais in her small chamber. She would normally have been relaxed, surrounded by her bards and the inner circle of attendants. But her stomach churned, waiting to hear the outcome of her sister's mission.

She held a small, carved figurine depicting her dragon, Quassu. Her father had carved it, his last gift to her. As such, it represented a lost security, a symbol of comfort and her father's protection. When she handled it this way, passing it from hand to hand, it helped soothe her anxieties. She held onto it, much as a child would cling to a soft toy.

Growing irritated by the tone of the music, she called for Vanya to change her tune and sing the lay of the Dragon Riders.

"It is a melancholy song, Your Majesty. Perhaps something more light-hearted might —"

"Do as I ask," Tayem replied.

The bard saw her expression and bowed her head in obedience. The charazon she held was a beautiful instrument. Its exquisitely crafted gourd-shaped sound box was joined to a long neck-piece that extended a full ten spans. It was pegged with fourteen cat-gut strings, the bottom five of which were plucked as bass notes to complement the melody played on the remaining nine.

Vanya began the piece by striking the bottom string once. The resonant note rose in the air and echoed off the ironwood vaulted ceiling, acting as a prelude to the song that followed. Her voice was a soothing alto, fitting for the subject matter of the lyrics. As she began, the courtiers suspended their conversation, anticipating delight at hearing a masterful performance.

*Daughters of Dragonia weep,*
*Let your lamentations wail upon the wind.*
*For our people are enslaved,*

Cowed under the foot of the conqueror.

Our chains were forged with links of treachery,
Cast in the moulds of dark Hallows magic.
A conspiracy woven with spider and worm,
To grind proud Dragonia into dust.

Many sorrows and dismal throes
Marked the passing of the age.

The enemy's assaults defeated not our brave warriors.
Tho' blood poured from the mountains,
And strong limbs fatigued in the heat of battle,
Still we prevailed.

From whence did the rains cease?
No one could comprehend.
Starving children, fathers cried,
Mother's hearts did rend.

Recorded in a book of brass
At the passing of the age.

They cleaved the heartwood of our kingdom,
By censor of the heavens.
Thus the Cuscosians brought us low,
In a tide of clashings and groans.

TOM G.H. ADAMS AND ANDREW NAISBITT

*We worked the fields from long ago,*
*Let the soil bring forth its yield.*
*Land of plenty, reaped and sown,*
*Become chaff cast into the dismal deep.*

*Shrill was the trumpet*
*At the passing of the age.*

*Cold flesh of clay,*
*Lying on bones heaped high.*
*This was our legacy —*
*Confiscated lands and a people indebted.*

*Our lathes and chisels now create their adornments,*
*Our looms erected for their benefit,*
*Shuttles pipe shrill thro' the listing threads,*
*Their bounty handed to the Overlords.*

*Pneumafire suffered to decay,*
*In the passing of the age.*

*We sing our silver-throated songs,*
*And play our many-corded lyres,*
*Declaring that our day will come.*
*A day when Cuscosia's deadly black will disperse.*

*They reign amongst tarnished jewels and unseemly titles,*
*Sapping our people with their exactments.*

*So fill their flagons with mandrake,*
*Team the salvers with wormwood.*

*Bring in the coming of the age.*

*The dragon will wake from slumber,*
*And the heavens will crack open.*
*We will tear the spider web apart,*
*And divide their city asunder.*

*May their monarchs dine with death,*
*And their catafalque procession fill the streets.*
*We will shout with vindication in our hearts,*
*And thus will behold them no more.*

*So begins the coming of the age.*

Vanya allowed the final bass note to sound for several moments before damping the strings gently. Applause would be inappropriate, but a nod from Tayem told the bard she appreciated her offering. As she encouraged the other musicians to strike up a more rousing piece, Tayem reflected on the content of the song. It summed up the history of her people, laid bare the reasons for their enmity with the Cuscosians. Its rendition roused her, and increased the resolve to carry through her edicts. The now familiar voice within roused itself, muttering its accord.

Cistre's appearance in the room stilled its susurrations,

however. The head guard conferred with Coren, no doubt sharing anything of pertinence to the hand-over of duty. After she had dismissed the sergeant, Tayem beckoned to Cistre.

"What news of Mahren?" she asked.

"I have heard nothing," Cistre replied.

"It is taking too long. Something has happened."

Cistre offered no words of consolation. She knew Tayem was not one for platitudes. "There is one matter to report," she said instead.

"Speak."

"The town guard apprehended a villager named Singarin. They said he was raving and out of his mind, causing a disturbance of the peace."

"Why are you troubling me with this?" Tayem said.

"It seems he trespassed on the Dragon Ash grounds."

Tayem's face clouded. "What other symptoms did he present?"

Cistre looked puzzled. "Why, nothing My Queen. Except that where once was a respected weaver, there now remains nothing but a lunatic."

"That is ... sad for him and his family. We should place guards around the perimeter."

"Already done, my Queen. But it raises the question of ..."

"What, Cistre? Speak your mind."

"You drank a strong draught from the Hallows last night. Are you sure you have suffered no ill effects?"

"Do I look like I am deranged?"

"Why no. I did not mean to suggest — "

Cistre's response was cut short by a commotion outside the chamber. Mahren appeared at the door, a sheen of sweat and grime streaked on her skin. She saluted and stepped toward the dais.

"What has transpired?" Tayem demanded.

"My Queen," Mahren said, breath coming in heavy gasps. "Disaster — our dragons have been poisoned."

## II

# LORD OF DREAMS

———

The meeting with Eétor had been successful as far as Zodarin was concerned. The man made for a formidable conspirator, but at the same time he possessed malleability — a perfect tool for the wizard's uses. He had no doubt the Praetor was capable of his own machinations, but these were nothing Zodarin could not anticipate or handle.

He slunk along the battlements of Castle Cuscosa, conscious that any errant gaze from soldiers he passed were quickly turned away by his mere appearance. Small wonder. His sunken eyes and sheer stature were enough to dissuade any mortal from staring, let alone lingering too long in his presence.

He could not claim immortality. In truth, his lifespan was not indefinite, but it dwarfed those that surrounded him. Only one had ever come close to guessing his origins. That man had called him 'Off-worlder.' Such knowledge should have exacted a swift end to his life, but circumstances had intervened; events that Zodarin was too humiliated to dwell on — even now, after so many sols.

He arrived at the foot of his tower. It could not claim to be the tallest turret adorning the edifice of Castle Cuscosa, but it was the most imposing — and the most shunned. None save Etezora and Eétor had ever set foot in it, and even they had not dwelt long. Before entering, he took one more look around at the sprawling structure that the Cuscosians had constructed barely two hundred years ago. The limestone blocks had been imported from Kaldora, an economy that had served them well in the short term, but the stone had weathered poorly and already showed signs of crumbling. It was like everything accomplished by Cuscosa, born from expediency and the desire to impress; but compared with Wyverneth, for example, it marred the plains of Cuscosia like a carbuncle.

He climbed the helical staircase, the loose grit crunching under his doe-skin boots. Ephemeral phantasms guarding the sole entrance recognised his presence and receded in obeisance. They would exude themselves from the stonework again within moments, forming a haunting security more robust than any physical defence.

The circular chamber topping his tower had become

overly cramped with the passing of sols as his library and collection of artefacts and potions expanded in size.

*One day the royal chambers will be at my disposal,* he thought. That day was still distant, but it would come.

In the meantime he had to attend to matters of import. He stoked the fire and threw on another two logs, then sat himself down on an elaborately carved dais, preparing to meditate.

Of late, he had engaged in shape-shifting to accomplish his ends. No one knew of this talent — not even Eétor. As Oswald the cat he walked undetected by the local populace. His feline form became a regular visitor to Hallow's Creek where he witnessed conversations and interactions that the unwitting townsfolk thought veiled in secrecy. Yet nothing could be kept secret from Zodarin.

Reflecting while he stilled his mind, a broad smile creased his face as he contemplated the simplicity of life his feline alter-ego enjoyed. Tonight was not a time for simplicity, however. He needed to pass through to the Dreamworld. Indeed, he craved its embrace.

These contemplations were a restless sea, not compatible with the state he required. He reached over and dropped a pinch of odiferous powder into the censer lit specifically for this purpose. As peacefulness descended, he closed his eyes, slowed his pulse and breathing, and then succumbed to the night.

He was harroc ini thurkear — hunter by night. More than this he had become harroc persvek wurunwi,' a hunter in dreams. As a matter of necessity, as well as pleasure, Zodarin awaited the thrill of wurunwa vargachic,' the dream battles.

He flew astrally through the boundary that separated the Near To world from that of the Far Beyond, experiencing sensations familiar but nonetheless immersive. Tonight he would kill, not man or woman — that particular ecstasy he would deny himself for now. Instead, he would content himself by tracking down animals or perhaps birds, singling out any beast that brought uncertainty to the Dreamworld. That was his intention, anyway.

The trance deepened, and he transformed to wolvern form, a harroc on the scent of a small calf. He quietly stalked the unsuspecting bovine, staying downwind so as not to betray his position. There was no compulsion to hasten the attack as he had the ability to hold himself motionless for hours if necessary. On this occasion he did not need to wait overly long, however. Recognising his opportunity when the beast turned away, he struck, rolling the calf onto its back and staring into its startled eyes. *What is this? Someone I recognise?* He looked more closely at the calf's features and identified the face of a creature known to him. It belonged to one of the infuriating Kaldorans. They annoyed him more than any other species as they had a habit of interfering with his carefully laid plans. This one would interfere no more.

In reality, the Kaldoran would be asleep or caught in

a moment of nightmare reverie. But here in the Dreamworld, the seeds of death were sown. He could not determine the time of the Kaldoran's death. It might be days, weeks or, more rarely, a whole sol — yet always within an uneven number of days. Recognition of the victim occurred by a variety of means. It might be revealed in the cry of the prey as it died, or perhaps the way the animal walked. More often it resulted from a purely intuitive process that Zodarin was not able to fathom.

If the harroc only wounded its dream-prey, then the person it represented would meet with an accident rather than death. But this prey would not escape so easily. The wolf regarded the quarry one last time then sank his teeth into the calf's throat, a killing frenzy taking over until the animal fell limp in Zodarin's jaws.

He released the animal and contemplated eating its flesh, but killing by the harroc was a symbolic act, perpetrated in the realm of dreams. The spirit had now been severed from the body. In due course the corporeal form would inevitably follow. The levethix di wurunwi — wizard of dreams — recognised that tasting the calf's flesh would only satisfy some prurient instinct, and Zodarin considered it beneath him. His only regret was the likelihood he would never hear of the Kaldoran's death in the Near To. The thrill of this Dreamworld hunt would be enough for now.

He scanned the surroundings and recognised the rolling downs surrounding Hallow's Creek — familiar territory.

He knew every pasture, mountain slope, cave, pool and stream.

Hunting near water came naturally, it being the haunt of dangerous spirits, those belonging to the dead who had not atoned for their sins. These invariably conspired with other harroc di wurunwi — potential rivals. It paid to be aware of these entities, even to eliminate them whenever possible.

He determined to venture over the next rise where he knew such a stream existed, tumbling its way from the foothills of Dragonia. It could have been restlessness, but he sensed a disturbance in the ether, and he needed to set his mind at rest. The Dreamworld usually gave him peace from the irritation of petty Cuscosian politics. Yet there it was again — a ripple in the air. Another was abroad tonight, one whose essence touched the periphery of his memory, a kindred intellect that reached out inquisitively toward him. It resided over the hill his paws now trod, down by the water, the source of iniquity. Did it recognise *him?* The presence of the interloper found him unprepared, and it was imperative he marshall his resources.

Zodarin's eyes opened, and he rapidly emerged from his trance-like state. Thirst assaulted his mouth and gizzard, and sweat beaded his face. He looked at his hands. They trembled.

Was this fear? He stood up, unsure if his legs would support him and stumbled towards the turret window.

Outside, the Hallows purple appeared as a haze, tinged with a hint of carmine on the horizon. It spoke to him of blood, *but whose?*

The Dragonian Vale drew his gaze, which then moved towards the mountains of the Imperious Crescent. Peaks towered like a bulwark of mystery, hiding their secrets in darkness, concealing the presence he had detected in the Dreamworld.

"Wobas," he said. "Is that you I sense, old friend?"

No answer. Not that he expected one. *Does the shaman still live?*

Zodarin wiped sweat from his brow and stepped towards the embers in the hearth, thinking, always plotting.

Perhaps this would not be the only foray he undertook tonight. Perhaps he should confront the Augur before the other harroc found it. This was forbidden, but he needed to glean from the entity what he could. Perhaps the Augur might give him what he wanted.

*But, if not ...*

# 12

# THE TEMPTATION OF WOBAS

————————

Wobas woke with a suddenness that wrenched him from the Dreamworld and left his spirit worn and ragged. Mere seconds ago he had been soaring over a brook as the night scops in search of the Spirit Guide. He had come to rest on a knotted tree stump and immediately become aware of another. He'd rotated his head a full half-turn and seen bright, blood-red canine eyes glaring in his direction from the nether-darkness of the hillside. The malice implicit in that gaze was palpable, yet he couldn't be sure the wolf — or whatever it was — had seen him or not. It seemed to scan the copse in which Wobas was perched; then just as quickly as the eyes appeared, the wolf was gone.

Was the levethix di wurunwi's appearance significant in terms of the Hallows, or had it always existed here? The latter was hard to believe given Wobas's perpetual sojourns in the Dreamworld. Whichever was true, the intrusion had jolted Wobas so severely it displaced him from the Dreamworld and left his physical form shaking with fear and apprehension. He waited for his breathing to return to a steady pace, but struggled to find a point of equilibrium. Every time he attempted to pacify his mind, the image of the wolf's eyes burned into his consciousness. He could not even move his leaden limbs.

After what seemed like half an hour of torment, Wobas twisted his body with a surge of effort, forcing himself off his meditation dais and onto the floor. The activity was enough to break whatever spell had bewitched him. With a gasp he rose to his feet and wobbled to the cave mouth, desperate to drink in the cool evening air.

The rain still fell. It had begun at dusk as heavy droplets, and continued unrelenting, swelling streams and coursing over the rocks surrounding Wobas's home. He regarded again the Hallows scar, a periarch distance on the opposite side of the valley. It spewed its purple energy into the night, the vapours meeting with overburdened clouds as if entreating them to release their load.

Gigantes lore was vague regarding the Hallows, as were indeed all scripts in any tongue. Yet Wobas had an increasing sense they exerted their influence far across the Imperious Crescent. Four sites existed that he knew of;

but there might be more, and after this last venture into the Dreamworld he was certain they had touched even that sacred realm. How else to explain the presence of the wolf?

An involuntary trembling began in his legs at the memory. Fear of such harrocs was his enemy, but he couldn't let it stop him from finding answers. Now more than ever, he needed to acquire the requisite knowledge. The Spirit Guide had warned him about the Hallows and then dismissed Wobas from his presence. Now he had failed to make reparations with Milissandia, he had a duty to extract the wisdom to restore the Cyclopes by other means, bypassing the Spirit Guide perhaps. However, with this 'other' now skulking in the Far Beyond, the task was more perilous.

Rest. He needed it desperately. Afterwards he would try again.

Knowing malicious entities roamed abroad at least put him on his guard, and he would be doubly cautious.

He slept, and when he awoke the water clock revealed three hours had elapsed. It was still dark, and though he was far from ready he stirred himself, adopting the nwosu position with legs crossed and hands clasped upon his knees.

Despite a gripping apprehension he allowed his inner spirit to transcend to a state of Wurunwa Ith — Dream Lord. The dislocation of transition lasted only a moment, and once more he flew with the wings of the scops. His keen hearing detected nothing but denizens of the night, crawling under leaf litter and scuttling amongst the tangled undergrowth of the forest. A habitual foray would have seen him aspire to harroc ini thurkear, a hunter of the night, but his goal now was more exigent. It would require a long flight, longer than he had ever attempted in the Dreamworld. It would take him beyond the forest, his natural habitat, and through the swampland known as Nish. If he had the ability, he would have transformed into a buzzard or an eagle, but such a capability was beyond him. He had known only one who had such accomplishment — and he was long gone.

Within the glades and mangroves of his destination lay the Shrine of Knowing, or so it was told. From Wobas's study of Ebar's books, he knew the sacrarium was forbidden to all wurunwa ith, but how well was this enforced?

His eyes and ears remained in a high state of alert. The Spirit Guide was nowhere in the vicinity. Neither was the wolf.

He emerged from the forest, his wings beating more rapidly now he was traversing across open grassland. In the Near To world he had walked the plains only once. Here in the Dreamworld, the terrain was totally unfamiliar. He had only the references and landmarks he had read about in Ebar's tome — and that was over ten sols ago.

*Seek out the Trignal Rock.*

His route brought him to skirt the Barrow Mounds, and a fell wind whistled through their passes, buffeting his flightpath. He compensated, and in so doing recognised the beginnings of fatigue.

*Two more periarchs and then I can rest.*

He concentrated on the sky to take his mind off how slow his progress was. It did not rain in the Dreamworld, but the clouds and mists were of an alien hue — browns, russets and umbers. This was something he had grown accustomed to, but tonight there was a heliotrope tinge on the horizon. With a creeping dread he recognised the encroaching of the Hallows' *rekthi*.

*The Dreamworld resists it, but for how long?*

Glancing downwards he saw moonlight reflected off sporadic ponds and lagoons. Grassland gave way to moss groves and marsh reeds, then up ahead, silhouetted against the purple glow, a rock outcrop appeared, split into three as if a claw reached for the heavens.

*The Trignal. I am close.*

He beat his wings down more forcibly, and cleared the formation, swooping down onto a lower elevation. The wall of mangrove trees took him by surprise, and he had to bank his flight to avoid a battering by gnarled trunks and tangled branches. He expected an oppressive gloom, but found that here under the drooping canopy an uncanny luminescence lit his way. The source of this light seemed to be an exudation on the bark of the trees, but he also observed dancing fireflies and what seemed like airborne medusae billowing in clusters.

He was now completely at the mercy of his instincts. Ebar's tome had not described the shrine, other than that the Augur inhabited it at the centre of the grove.

As the scops, he exercised an unerring sense of direction and topography, so he knew the bearing he took should take him across the midpoint of this swampy abode. Yet would he recognise the place if he saw it? Would he even be permitted to lay eyes on it? If entering the shrine was forbidden, then it would hardly be prominent amidst the landscape.

Fatigue overtook him now, and he alighted in a cleft between two entangled sterrath trunks. As his avian heart subsided to a steady beat, he thought he heard a whisper on the night. It was an enticing sound, reminiscent of long forgotten childhood memories; intense feelings of innocence, yet expectations of possibility. He often yearned for such an existence again — free from responsibility and the burdens of the world. To have this again would be such bliss. The promise now appeared to him like a cascade of water over garden stones, its appreciation lying in the crevices where the water flowed.

The whispering intensified, and he took to his wings again, following the beckoning call.

*You will find a bridge between a place that no one ever leaves and another that no one ever approaches.*

The message was a riddle written in the tome, but as

Wobas wove his way deeper into the grove, he thought he saw a construction ahead. As he glided closer on silent wings, he made out a single wooden arch rising from the rooted tangle of mangroves, spanning a murky fissure. Then he understood it was not so much constructed by the hands of men but a living thing, having germinated and grown across the chasm. He darted across it, fearing to gaze into the shifting shadows below and quested deeper into what lay beyond.

Then he was upon it. A mossy hollow, at the centre of which grew a bulbous tree with a bole that must have measured at least fifty spans diameter. A narrow vertical fissure extended from the base of the tree up to where the first lichen-covered branches began. From the crack in the bark, luminescence intensified, and Wobas had an irresistible urge to enter. He looked upwards. The hollow nestled below a break in the mangrove canopy and the sky above was clearly visible. The usual Dreamworld fog mixed with Hallows purple from above and formed a smoky column extending upwards from the higher branches of the tree.

*Is this what I sought? Why have I not met with resistance? And why does it beckon me so?*

There was a sense of impending downfall when Wobas saw the Hallows invasion of that place, but the silent evocation was impossible to resist now. He had to enter.

The crack was just wide enough in the middle to admit

his flying form and he entered, the tips of his wings just grazing the grey bark of the aperture's edges.

Inside he found himself in a home of sorts. He had little time to absorb much detail, except for a table with chairs and a dresser against one wall.

It was a challenge to remain aloft in this enclosed space and he had to find somewhere to perch.

*Over there on the pedestal,* something said in silent communication.

The mind-voice came from a ginger cat, sat in bread-loaf fashion on a rough-hewn table in the centre of the room. Startled, Wobas considered flying straight back the way he had come. No good could come from encountering a harroc di wurunwi such as this.

*Settle yourself,* the tom said. *Have you come this far simply to turn tail and run? I pose no threat to you.*

Wobas was weary, and the harroc had offered him a resting place. He chose to trust the creature — for now.

With a clattering of wings he reluctantly landed on the pedestal with little grace. *You are he who dwells here?* He sent to the cat.

It looked around, almost lazily, and communicated to Wobas in thought-speak. *It is a humble abode, but serves me well.*

*I had expected an augur to take a different form,* Wobas sent.

*Expectations — such things can undo a man.*

Wobas scrutinised the cat. He owed the Augur reverence, *and yet ...*

*You had more expectations in seeking me out, did you not?* The cat continued.

*I ... I seek answers, true,* Wobas sent. *But I am wary of the atmosphere that surrounds this place. It seems to speak to the darkness.*

*You mistrust the Hallows? What if I told you it is the only way to receive what you desire?*

*The Spirit Guide told me —*

*A spirit guide? What is this?* The cat looked genuinely puzzled.

*You do not know of Memek-Tal?*

The tom lifted a paw and licked between the toes. *Not all who inhabit the Dreamworld converse with each other. Not unless our paths are destined to converge. But, never mind. What did he tell you?*

*That I must make amends with a certain person before I received the key to unlocking the curse of the Cyclopes.*

*Ah — so that is your desire. A noble one. But there are so many other things the Hallows could bestow.*

*I am sure. But —*

*Let me show you.*

The cat pointed with its paw at a looking glass on the wall. *Tell me what you see.*

Wobas looked where the cat pointed and viewed a small reflective surface surrounded by a frame of witch-hazel branches. *I see my reflection, of course.*

*Anything else?*

As Wobas gazed longer, his feathery features seemed to blur at the edges. As he watched, the beak gradually morphed into a nose and the feathers became skin. Soon the transformation was complete, and he viewed his wrinkled human visage.

*What is this?* He sent.

*Keep watching.*

Wobas looked again. The view zoomed out to a position where he saw himself standing and looking to the skies. His features had lost their aged form, and he appeared middle-aged again. Yet the wonder did not stop there. As he continued to watch, the face filled out a little. It lost its wrinkles and his frame became more muscular. In addition, he felt his aches subside and a new vitality fill him.

*Do you feel it?* The cat sent.

*Yes. I had forgotten the vigour that comes with such a tender age.*

*This could be yours if you invite the Hallows in.*

The temptation was significant. Wobas felt a pull that was difficult to resist, yet his extended lifespan had given him wisdom and he gave a considered reply to the cat. *Such a thing must carry a great price.*

The cat narrowed its eyes and nodded. *Of course it does, but it is not a price beyond your means.*

*Whatever it is, the treasure is unworthy.*

The cat's pupils dilated. *You desire something more honourable.*

*I have told you what I seek.*

*The Cyclopes?*

*That, and a way to protect the Gigantes people.*

*The Hallows can only augment gifts already present in the supplicant.*

Wobas shifted his position on the perch and blinked several times. *I have often felt on the brink of discovery in the Dreamworld, yet answers have always eluded me, seemed to be just out of reach.*

*The Hallows will give.*

*Then why did the Spirit Guide warn me about them?* Wobas asked.

*Perhaps he was speaking from his own place of fear and ignorance. I cannot say.*

Wobas was not convinced. Something still held him back.

*I can tell you are vacillating. There is no compulsion to receive, but remember, it was you who sought me out.*

*I cannot deny this but ...*

*Let me show you one more thing,* the cat sent. It lifted its paw and pointed at the mirror.

Out of the shimmering, Wobas saw his daughter. She approached a man, and Wobas thought it to be one of her many lovers, but as he looked more closely, he realised it was himself. She was holding out her hands, embracing him. The sight of such a thing would have been wonderful enough but, as before, it was enhanced by an intense stirring of emotion in his heart.

*How did you know this troubled me?* He asked the cat.

*I did not. The sacred augur mirror simply reveals what the observer wishes to see.*

Wobas found himself on the cusp of a decision. *Surely, this is what I have sought all this time,* he pondered, his thoughts veiled from the cat. *Yet I cannot help feel there is something I am not being told.*

He turned to the harroc once more. *I take it you have drunk of the Hallows yourself?*

*Indeed I have,* it said, *and I have had no reason to look back.*

*What if I refuse?*

The cat lowered its head. *Alas, the Hallows does not take kindly to rebuttal. You will suffer no harm, but the opportunity will be gone — and you may never know the fulfilment of your desires.*

Wobas stared at the cat, weighing up the options. *I have one more question.*

*Ask.*

*What price did the Hallows exact from you, Augur?*

It narrowed its eyes again, and for the first time Wobas noticed the yellow of the cat's sclera and the snake-like pupils. Behind those eyes he also glimpsed something else. Something the cat was trying very hard to conceal. It was as if it held back its true spirit form, a shape redolent of crimson orbs, of tentacles and of a vast leviathan body. It sent a shudder down Wobas's spine and broke him out of his trance.

*That I cannot tell you,* the cat sent.

It was Wobas' turn to lower his head, feeling all of a sudden as if the chamber of the Augur was closing in on him, asphyxiating and smothering.

*There are too many unknowns,* Wobas sent. *I must take my leave.* He did not wait for a reply, did not even look back, fearing what he might see. And as he fluttered out from the Augur's tree it was as if some gravity pulled at his dream-body. Looking at his wings he observed purple vapour clinging there.

He beat down with greater force and, with every muscle straining, willed himself forward. For a moment he feared he would succumb, but then the vapour lost its grip and he accelerated into the night, leaving behind the faint groan of an entity denied its quarry.

~ ~ ~

Zodarin, in the form of the ginger tom, jumped down from the table and entered an adjoining chamber to the main living space. On the floor lay the blasted form of the Augur. A blackened crater in its torso still dripped with fresh, green blood, the expression on its gnarled face frozen in anger.

"I give you this," Zodarin said, "you showed me no fear.

A pity you also showed me little of what I sought. You were stubborn — much like Wobas."

Had it been a mistake not to put an end to the shaman here and now? Zodarin rose and stretched himself, arching his back and yawning in feline fashion. He was more than weary, and the transformation back to wolf form would require still more reserves of energy. To have attempted an outright attack on the scops would have carried great risk, and perhaps Wobas might yet have his uses.

He kicked the corpse with contempt. "Still, one thing was proved tonight. I can remain concealed even from a wurunwa ith, and that is to my advantage. I bid you farewell, Augur. The centipedes and worms of this place will consume you, and I doubt whether any will mourn your passing."

It would be a long journey back in wolf form; he had not yet mastered transformation to that of a bird, but he anticipated it would not be long before he could. What he had learned tonight, what he had extracted from the Augur, would ensure that.

# 13

# TIME FOR TEA AND TREACHERY

———————

'To be of use' — that was Nalin's father's motto. It was his single most valuable contribution to Kaldoran culture and the family legacy. He'd devoted the rest of his short life to consuming ale and beating seven hells out of his disappointing son.

"Krut his soul," Nalin muttered as he waded through a bank of reeds shielding a small plantation of jarva shrubs. He had cultivated the crop carefully under the Cuscosian's noses for several sols now, the merchants assuming he imported the intoxicating weed from the desert lands of the East — a myth he did nothing to dispel. After all, it ensured the price stayed high if they imagined it was grown in exotic lands and transported over two hundred periarchs.

It wasn't only narcotics he provided for his adopted people, however. Etezora's father had enthusiastically acquired his engineering and technological skills, and within his first sol of employment, Nalin had overseen the construction of an aqueduct system to provide fresh water from the nearby Queenswater for the royal household. As was their wont, the Cuscosians had not extended this benefit to the great unwashed of the wider city and surrounding villages, but that was their affair.

After hailing this project a success, he had been given leave to design and build a regiment of chariots and fleets of carts employing a unique wheel mount containing rings of tiny steel balls lubricated with shale oil. These extended the times between servicing and provided smoother running without the joints glueing up with mud and dust. From there he had built two new war machine prototypes and advised on the development of further fortifications surrounding Castle Cuscosa.

Of course, each device he was responsible for had inbuilt design flaws an enemy could exploit if they had access to the knowledge. Nalin kept records of these weaknesses locked away in a chest hidden in his underground workshop. Usefulness brought him privileges from the Cuscosians, whereas his position made him an invaluable source of intelligence to his true Lord and Master — Magthrum.

Such progress and standing had come with a price, however. His constant industry and attendance to the Cuscosians' every whim meant he rarely enjoyed more than three hours of sleep. Such a lifestyle required chemical stimulants to sustain it, and jarva pods fulfilled this need.

At first, his horticultural accident had provided a welcome source of income to feather his increasingly expensive nest, but a fateful 'quality control' sample had led to him overindulging one evening — and from that time on he was hooked.

Nalin was an addict. Something he would not articulate in words, even to himself. But like any dependency, shame fostered denial, and it became his best-kept secret.

The going was boggy in this stretch of unwelcoming terrain — a useful deterrent to trespassers but a nuisance for gaining access. *I must consider building a concealed walkway,* he told himself, but he knew such a fabrication would risk drawing attention to his plantation. He would have to put up with it for now.

Beyond the reeds lay a band of alders, clogged with treaclegrass and grosbriar. Nalin had established a narrow clearway from his regular forays along this route, but he still emerged from it with sticky-seed bobbles clinging to his breeches and the faint foxy smell of forest weeds hanging in his nostrils.

A final screen of underbrush concealed the plantation beyond, and Nalin paused to drink in the sight of some fifty or so prime jarva bushes of the rare *Skillia* variety. They sprouted through the fertile, dragon manure-enriched soil in regimented lines. They could accurately be termed his pride and joy, representing as they did the only pocket of such highly sought after specimens. Most notably, they possessed both stimulant and depressant narcotics within the same plant. *Leaves for bringing you down; roots for lifting you up*, he thought with a smile.

Nalin kneaded one of the tan-coloured leaves between his fingers. Sniffing it, connoisseur-like, he determined the crop was ready for picking and drying. Smoke released from the shredded leaf contained a potent mix of thallocybin and maratoxin, sure to induce feelings of mellowness and euphoria in the partaker. Nalin would carefully select two sacks of leaves and hang them out to dry later that morning.

In the meantime, he had a more pressing matter. Sweeping past a line of jarva plants in full bloom, he approached a wooden hut and pulled open the sedge-mat door. In a drawer below a rough wooden bench he found what he sought — a box of nut-size gummy balls. These spheroids were rolled out of the milky exudation from dried jarva-flower heads, and when heated produced a vapour that charged the user's brain with renewed vigour. They also had the additional benefit of fuelling Nalin's imagination with fresh ideas for further ingenious designs.

This morning, however, he would content himself with the immediate sizzle of rapture released from the drug.

With a trembling hand he cut a few choice flakes into a porcelain crucible, and struck a flintlock device, lighting a candle beneath it. He had heard the Easterners experimented with eye drops. Such an extreme practice sent a shudder through Nalin, however. He may be an addict but he wasn't *that* far gone.

He inhaled the potent vapours, which immediately filled him with a sense of well-being and euphoria.

"Aaah," he said out loud, "this must be what Exthallos is like." He was evoking the ancient Kaldoran belief in a utopian afterlife. He himself doubted its existence, but if one could experience a little paradise on Varchal then what was the harm? The fact that he now partook of his narcotic at least three times a day lay at the back of his mind like a lurking ogre. Yet here in the privacy of his little sanctuary the ogre slept and presented only a dim, latent threat.

Following a period of time that might have been half an hour or more — Nalin couldn't tell as he lost track of time — he picked the ripe jarva leaves and hung them on racks facing the twin suns. Sol-Ar was suspended prominently in a violet sky while his sister Sol drifted, detained and diminished further to the west. The advent of the Black Hallows had wrought many changes in the last few days, and Nalin wondered if Sol-Ar might irradiate his leaves with some unpredictable determinant too. Such a thing was a concern, and he would have to monitor his product closely over the next few weeks. There were a handful of expendable stonegrabes grateful for a free supply who would jump at the chance of acting as subjects for his trials. That said, his most sensitive guinea pig had recently succumbed to a mysterious illness; a symptom of Sol-Ar's influence — who could tell? Yet even by a Kaldoran's grim standards his end was particularly traumatic. "Neck constricted and choked as if by some invisible beast," Jashkin the physician had pronounced. The stonegrabe had been given a hasty but dignified cremation during Nalin's recent visit to Regev, but his passing was not easily forgotten.

The suns were still only at the start of their daily journey when Nalin returned to Castle Cuscosa. He had a tolerance to their light peculiar amongst the Kaldorans. Nonetheless he found their intense rays as they rose to their zenith quite irritating. His agenda for the afternoon was to visit the subterranean workshops and inspect his minions' progress with a spear-throwing machine. First, however, he intended to eavesdrop on a planned meeting between Etezora and her council. This was a regular function of his and was his main source of intelligence when reporting back to Magthrum.

He entered his chamber on the first floor of the castle and locked the door behind him. A bookcase lined the far wall, and he removed a dusty book entitled 'History of the embattled kingdoms.' It was a thorough, scholarly work but incredibly dry and boring, therefore very unlikely to be inspected. Behind the volume was a lever, which he depressed. The adjacent bookcase slid aside smoothly on counterweights to reveal a passage beyond.

He lit a torch and proceeded up the constricted tunnel. There were advantages to being responsible for building the castle extensions, and such clandestine conduits were but one. A shame he had to arrange the untimely deaths of his builder-collaborators, but secrecy carried its consequences. A few minutes later he came to a cul-de-sac. On the dead-end wall was a metal plate, which he silently swung to the side to reveal a peephole. On the other side of the wall hung an antiquated gargoyle, the eyes of which gave a commanding view of the Cuscosian throne room. In addition, its ears funnelled and amplified the sound from the chamber giving Nalin complete surveillance of all that occurred in that privileged place. If his espionage activities were discovered it would mean certain death. But if nothing else, Nalin was exemplary at covering his tracks.

~ ~ ~

Etezora sat on the imperial throne grooming her pet salix, Cuticous, with a thistle-brush. The creature had little by way of hair, but the brush served to stimulate its carapace and elicited a purring that all but Etezora found revolting. Its three-span segmented body curled around her left forearm while its fifteen-eyed, bulbous head lifted in response to the Queen's affectations.

"Must you pet that beast during our meetings?" Eétor said, a look of distaste on his face.

"Listen to what my brother is saying about you," Etezora said in a fawning voice. "Beast indeed. You're just an adorable little bundle, aren't you?" She puckered her lips at Cuticous, but there was a purple fire in her eyes as she observed Eétor.

"It's distracting, that's all, and we have important matters to discuss," her brother continued.

"I find his presence clarifies my thinking," Etezora said and picked up a sliver of cured dragon meat, chewing on the succulent morsel with relish.

Zodarin stood to one side in the shadows. Etezora had ordered the blinds to be drawn as the sunlight irritated her sensitive eyes. But even the gloom could not hide the fact that Zodarin looked drawn, the grey crescents under his eyes more pronounced than usual.

*What keeps you up at night, sorcerer?* She thought.

The wizard's presence, as always, was indispensable. He had a way of seeing through the fog of politics that dominated the Cuscosan council meetings and offered sage advice — albeit on a limited basis. Etezora suspected he could offer more, but for some reason remained mute on all but the most serious of considerations. Perhaps he considered certain matters beneath him. Whatever, he came across as aloof and Etezora found her respect for him had diminished with time. *He spends too long in his precious Dreamworld*, she thought. *Still, best not to ignore him. Eétor seems to value his company, and that in itself is reason to keep him under close observation. I must ask Tuh-Ma to post one of his creature informants on the wizard.*

"This attack by the Dragon Riders is a disturbing development," Tratis spoke up. As third in line to the throne, Etezora's younger brother was keen to exert his authority and contributed more vigorously to the councils of late.

*A pity he may never see the day he ascends to the throne,* Etezora reflected. *But let him flex his muscles for the time being.* She remained quiet, waiting for others amongst the council to air their views.

"I suspect Tayem has reached her breaking point," Eétor said. "It was only a matter of time, and the latest exactment was especially punitive."

"You object to our change of policy, Eétor?" Phindrath, the youngest sibling said. "I seem to remember you gave your consent to the increase in numbers." Her squeaky voice grated on Etezora but she bore it with stoicism. She had to at least give the impression she was consulting with the council. Then she would act according to her will, anyway.

"Indeed I did." Eétor responded. "I'm simply observing an eventuality we should have prepared for."

"I understand surveillance of the Dragonians' activity

is *your* domain, brother," Etezora said, feeding Cuticous a piece of dragon meat.

Eétor shifted uncomfortably. "Tayem has stepped up the guard on her palace, and my usual spies have found it hard to gain entry."

"You're always good at offering excuses," Etezora said. "Still, what has transpired has occurred, and I believe it is time to scale up our response accordingly."

"What are you thinking of?" Tratis asked.

Etezora smiled, her eyes glinting. She paused before replying, noting how her view of the world had become tinged with different colours since her absorption of the Hallows energy. People seemed to carry different auras according to their mood. As yet, she couldn't fully decipher their meaning, but perhaps Zodarin could help. Tratis's aura was an emerald colour. *Jealousy perhaps? A sense of wanting to control events yet being impotent to do so?*

"Our troops are at a strength that far exceeds anything we have built up in the last hundred sols," she said, "and our armouries are bolstered with an unprecedented stockpile of weapons and engines. It is time to remove the briar-thorn of the Dragon Riders once and for all."

Zodarin coughed. "If I may venture an opinion," the sorcerer said.

*At last, the lanky pale-face contributes*, Etezora thought.

"The reports we received of the attack. There are aspects I would question."

"It was a blatant assault on our people and our authority," Tratis said. "What is there to question?"

Zodarin gave the man one of his lop-sided smiles. "It just seems a bit ... clumsy."

"The Dragon Riders are not known for their subtlety," Phindrath said.

"But they're not stupid," Zodarin replied." What would they hope to gain from such an attack?"

"Why, revenge of course." Phindrath said.

Zodarin winced. "It's too haphazard and, as Eétor said, we had no forewarning from our intelligence sources."

"But the evidence at the Crossings — "

"Easily manufactured."

"You think the Dragon Riders were set up? Who would gain from such subterfuge?"

"You only need look to the Kaldoran Mountains," Eétor said.

"The Kaldorans?" Tratis interjected. "Those stone encrusted imbeciles couldn't mount a chicken fight, never mind a full-on ambush."

"We know very little of their capabilities, actually," Eétor said.

"Nalin tells me they are pre-occupied with internal strife and finding provisions to feed their starving population," Etezora put in.

"I don't trust that stonegrabe," Tratis said.

"You ought not to be so prejudiced," Etezora responded.

"That's rich, coming from you."

"Tratis, Tratis," Eétor said, "our sister is playing with you."

Tratis scowled. "Your behaviour is unbecoming, Sister. What has come over you this last week?"

"Still your tongue!" Etezora's eyes flared again, and she had to make a conscious effort to restrain that which surged within. "It is a full sol before you accede to the throne. Until then, you will refer to me as your Majesty."

Tratis accepted the scolding and growled an apology.

"It is irrelevant anyway," Etezora said. "We have planned an invasion for many months now. I see no need to delay any longer."

"You wish for Dieol to mobilise the troops?" Eétor asked.

"I have already told him to make preparations."

"You did what?" Phindrath blurted out. "You presume too much."

"Am I not Queen?" Etezora said, and this time an audible crackle of energy sparked like a halo around her head.

"What is that ..?" Phindrath said, her squeak elevating to a higher pitch. She held her hand to her throat and wheezed in her next breath of air.

"Majesty, please," Zodarin said, staring at his Queen with an inscrutable smile.

With great effort, the baleful purple ire in Etezora's eyes subsided. Phindrath leaned forward, gasping and choking.

"Is this what comes of your baptism in the Hallows?" Tratis said, rising to his feet. "You would exert this uncontrolled power on members of your own family?"

Zodarin placed a placating hand on Tratis's arm. "Settle yourself, Tratis. I'm sure our Queen meant no affront. Did you?" He turned to face Etezora again.

Despite herself, Etezora sat back on her throne. The wizard had a way of disconcerting even the most powerful. *His days are still numbered,* she thought. *The Hallows power grows daily within me. Soon, even he will fall under my will.*

Eétor chose that moment to lead the discussion. "If you are determined to invoke war, your Majesty ... then so be it; but in view of this attack, we must prioritise securing the north-eastern route. Nothing should interrupt the flow of ore from Bagshot Defile. Nor should it prevent our opening the new mine."

"I agree. Order your Praetorian Guard to take charge of the supply routes. We need to treble the numbers given the threat level."

"Use my own elite soldiers? It is a frivolous use of this resource!" Eétor was about to press the point further, but then saw the intensifying of colour in the Queen's eyes and appeared to think better of it. "I would suggest ... oh, very well. But only until the latest conscripts become available."

Etezora placed Cuticous on a cushion, clapped her hands and stood. "It is decided, then. My brothers and sisters, the time has come. House Cuscosa may be very recent in its ascent, but the kingdom we are building will last through the ages. It is time to expand our empire and bring the primitive hordes to heel. Within weeks we will be celebrating a new era."

Etezora was impressed with her pronouncement and saw that it stirred a resolve amongst the council — albeit a reluctant one. *They do not grasp my vision for greatness,* she thought. *Which is why I must extend my reign — once the expansion is complete and my rivals subdued.*

She watched with satisfaction as the council members stood in deference to her authority. They each had their duties to perform and, though the decision to embark on a war came sooner than they expected, they would welcome the rewards coming their way.

~ ~ ~

Nalin slid the cover back over his peephole and drew in a deep breath.

*War? This is an unexpected development. Magthrum wanted to stir up trouble between the Dragonians and Cuscosians, but it sounds like Etezora's expansionist plans know no bounds. This could mean the downfall of Kaldora itself.*

He hurried down the tunnel back to his room, resolved to inform Magthrum. Etezora's appearance and conduct in the meeting dominated his thoughts. She had always been an imposing leader, but what he had seen terrified him. *She wields a power most fell,* he thought. *Are there other*

*Cuscosians under this influence?* He also remembered Magthrum's demeanour when he had visited Regev — the Fellchief possessed a dark resolve and fire he hadn't witnessed before. This too frightened him.

There wasn't time to travel to the mountains again. He would have to use swifter means. Taking a small sheaf of parchment and a quill, he scribbled a note, blew on the ink and rolled it up. Beyond the main courtyard was the Royal Aviary. It took only a few minutes to reach the squat building, and he quickly found the cage he sought.

"Speedwill," he said to the imposing bird behind the wooden bars, "I have need of your wings." The bird resembled a swift, only twice the size and jet-black in colour. It uttered a high-pitched 'tseep' noise and shuffled along its perch, accepting Nalin's hand.

"Here," he continued, "take this straight to Magthrum. Do not dally on the way. He must receive it by nightfall."

Nalin looked over his shoulder, ensuring no prying eyes observed his activity, then took the bird outside and released it. The mountain swift was the fastest beast in the air, more fleet than a falcon on a horizontal flightpath. He was confident Speedwill would deliver his explosive news promptly. Magthrum would need to call his war council. In the meantime, Nalin resolved to step up his own plans.

He returned to his chamber and brewed himself a pot of sweetleaf tea. He needed something to calm his nerves. As he supped the soporific brew, the next course of action coalesced in his mind. *Time for my minions to knuckle down,* he thought.

It would be a long day and night, and only the jarva would see him through.

# 14

# COLOUR ME DARKLY

———————

"Tell me again," Tayem said to Mahren.

"I already explained as fully as I can," her sister replied.

They were stood in the dragon pens, Tayem watching morosely as the dragons that returned from the ill-fated sortie writhed and groaned in torment. Cistre as ever, had placed herself in close proximity — within sight but beyond earshot of the sisters.

"I need you to speak from the dragons' point of view," Tayem continued. "It is one thing to recount a military report, but you possess the confidence of the kirith-a, they tell you their secrets. I would hear their pain."

Mahren regarded her Queen and noted her voice did

not carry the Black Hallows invective so prevalent in the previous evening's emergency council meeting. That had seen her raging at the affront reported to her, calling for Cuscosian heads to roll.

"Very well," she said. "We arrived at the appointed place ahead of time. I should have noticed matters were awry when our dragons grew restless on the approach. It was as if they sensed something was amiss."

"You said the Cuscosians were nowhere in sight?"

"Yes. It was as if they had abandoned the wagons and left in haste."

"This lends weight to what Disconsolin said last night. Word must have got out to the Cuscosians, forewarning them. It can be the only explanation. I hope his investigations yield the identity of our spy. But I interrupted you. Please continue."

Mahren was distracted for a moment by Jaestrum rolling over on his side again. His scales were raised, and dust covered him as a result of his contortions, as if he found it impossible to adopt a comfortable position. "We reconnoitred the area, suspicious there might be hostile presences close at hand; but we did not find any. There weren't even any travellers on the main highway save for a couple of farmers carrying hay."

"Was it you who allowed the dragons to feed?" Tayem said.

"No. I was the one who spied out the road. It was Aedrellipe who gave permission. You must understand the meat-trade was three days late. Our beasts were starved from the Cuscosian's tardiness and they devoured the Cuscosian cattle in a matter of minutes."

"And you let Jaestrum join the feeding upon your return?"

"How could I not?"

"Despite your suspicions?"

"If you are looking for blame, sister, then understand that I accept full responsibility. But there is such a thing as over-stating the case."

Tayem reached out and stroked Jaestrum's neck. The beast groaned his appreciation, but his breath continued to come heavy and Mahren saw that his neck artery pulsed rapidly. "I am sorry. I know you feel their pain more than most," Tayem said.

"I am not the only one. At least Quassu was spared this indignity." Mahren nodded in the direction of the adjacent pen where Tayem's royal mount stood alert, confused by his brothers' and sister's suffering.

Tayem twitched her nose, a sign she was thinking. "What is Rusior's opinion? I understand he examined each of the dragons last night and administered his potions. Will they survive?"

"He thinks so," Mahren said, "although how long it will take is uncertain."

"Has he ascertained the nature of the poison?"

"He was surprised," Mahren said, leading the way out

of Jaestrum's pen. "He said it wasn't so much poison as an intoxicating drug."

"Which one?"

"Jarva leaf."

Tayem raised one eyebrow. "Isn't that the hash Easterners smoke in their long pipes?"

"Yes, but it would seem it does nothing for dragons — quite the opposite."

"So, are the Cuscosians forging links with those from the Exotic Lands?"

Mahren shrugged. "One thing's for sure, this was deliberate. Whoever dosed the cattle carcases with this drug knew exactly what would happen if the dragons consumed the meat."

"It is unforgiveable," Tayem said, and for the first time that morning Mahren saw Hallows fire spark in her eyes.

"There is something more," Mahren said in the hope she could distract Tayem from another outburst.

"Surely there is enough bad news already," Tayem replied.

"Would that it was the case. Come — see."

Mahren led the way to an internal enclosure, Cistre taking the cue and following on behind Tayem. At the door, Mahren picked up some clean cloths from a basket and handed one each to the others. "You need to tie these over your mouths and noses."

Cistre and Tayem looked at each other quizzically but followed Mahren's instruction. She walked apprehensively past several empty pens. Then, towards the end of the enclosure she stopped. "Do not go any further," she said and pointed at the pygmy dragon sleeping in the corner.

"Does Gathel suffer from the same drug?" Tayem asked.

Mahren shook her head. "Look at the skin under her shoulder."

Tayem leaned forward and then gasped. "Those scales, blackened and gangrenous. Is it ...?"

"Rusior confirmed it this morning. Dragon blight."

Tayem reached up to the cloth covering her face and tied it more securely in place.

"Where could she have picked it up from?"

"It's impossible to say. Gathel roots around a lot when out exercising. She may have contracted it from a dead lizard or snake, but we know so little about this terrible disease to be sure."

"Is she suffering much?"

"Just a mild itch, but the disease will spread over the next weeks. Then her torment will increase as blood poisoning takes hold. Human victims tell of an endless crawling sensation beneath the skin — as if a thousand ants are burrowing."

"And a cure?"

Mahren shook her head. "Poor Gathel is doomed. It is just a question of how long."

"Then perhaps we should end her suffering before the disease fully takes hold."

"You know the statutes of vs' shtak — none may slay a dragon. For any reason."

Tayem remained motionless, a tear forming in one eye. She was not prone to showing emotion in this way, and Mahren saw that the dragon's plight weighed heavy on her heart. "I wish I didn't have to share this news with you, but we will need to put in place certain practices to ensure the disease is contained. If it should spread to the people — "

"Then it will accomplish more than any Cuscosian treachery," Tayem finished her sentence for her. "Quarantine this compound and restrict Gathel's care to one dragon-hand."

Mahren nodded, and then considered carefully what she was to say next. "Are you still minded to put in place a reprisal for this Cuscosian mischief?"

"I would mount an attack today if I thought it would accomplish something, but we need to gather more intelligence."

"Disconsolin?"

"He has appointed a coterie of spies to infiltrate Hallow's Creek at my request. In the meantime I sent an official dispatch to Etezora demanding a meeting."

Mahren pursed her lips. "Etezora does not take kindly to demands."

"Indeed she does not, but it will be interesting to see how she responds. We must exhaust diplomatic channels, to satisfy Gemain if nothing else."

Mahren sighed inwardly. At least her sister would not

initiate something rash. She shared her sister's ire towards House Cuscosa, but she had other reasons leading her to counsel restraint regarding outright war. The Cuscosian populace were as much victims as the Dragonians and when it came to conflict, it was always the innocent who suffered most.

"I suppose it will give us time to prepare for the worst," Mahren said.

"Yes, and I will increase patrols along the outskirts of the Vale. Cistre is already drawing up plans for a possible offensive should the diplomacy fail — as I fear it will."

Mahren's previous relief turned to apprehension again, but she held her tongue. However, she resolved to visit Hallow's Creek herself. There was one she needed to confide in, and it had been a whole week since they last met. It would be difficult slipping away with the heightened security, but she would find a means.

15

# ONE EYE ABOVE, ONE BELOW

———

*Davof Calti.* That was what they would have called him in Oldspeak. *Sounds so much better than 'tomcat,'* Zodarin thought as he stole amongst the alleyways of Hallow's Creek. It was one thing to inhabit the Dreamworld in another creature's body, but to achieve this in the real world — well; he had the Hallows to thank for that.

Having the heightened senses of Oswald the cat was at first exhilarating, but here in this rat-infested back street he began to wonder. A cocktail of refuse, rotting food and human excrement wasn't the most inviting of scents, and to think he was stepping in the stuff!

*Gorram! How do these people live like this?*

A sucking of air through pursed lips drew his attention to a doorway. "Here little puss, you on the prowl for a fine juicy mouse — or even a rat?" It was Petter Proudson, the Innkeeper. He stood at the back door of his tavern, The Boar's Head, stooped over a keg of ale.

Oswald looked up at him. *Common Diggod!* Zodarin formed the words in his mind but they came out as a *Miaow*, uttered in a rather pathetic tone.

"Ah, so you *are* hungry then? Not having much luck with the rodents tonight, eh? I'll get you something, don't you worry."

Proudson rolled the wooden keg effortlessly back inside and emerged a minute later with something silvery on a plate. "Here," he said, throwing the leftovers at Oswald, "put yourself round that."

Oswald sniffed at what turned out to be the remains of an undercooked trout and, despite his human sensitivities, he licked the tasteless flesh with apparent relish.

"Thought you'd like that," Proudson said, "but I mustn't dally. There are thirsty throats to quench in the tavern, and hungry bellies to fill. An Innkeeper's work is never done."

*Peasant,* Zodarin thought. *Miaow,* Oswald said. *I suppose the locals think him to be a charitable soul,* the wizard mused, all the time wishing he was in his wolvern form; then he could show the Innkeeper where his charity got him.

*You're either predator or prey in this world — or indeed any world.*

The thought brought up echoes of his past; a time of great travail and cataclysm. His species, the amioid had been old before Varchal's races had even emerged from the primordial swamps of the South. They had travelled from beyond the heavens in a fantastical winged ship, a vessel that had come to rest in the vaults of the Everscorch Mountains, far beyond the Southern Wastelands. He remembered very little of this time as a young amioid, other than long treks through inhospitable lands, being hunted by the races they encountered ... and the hunger — always the hunger. In the end it was just his birther and he who remained. Somehow she had wrought a great magic to transform his physical body from what it was, a form that he only inhabited now (if he chose) in the Dreamworld. Their pursuers had slain his birther, found him — a mere youngster — unconscious in the hollow where she made her final stand. The hunter tribe assumed the monstrous beast had abducted him, and adopted him as their own, little knowing the nature of the creature in their midst.

Many sols had passed since those formative events, and Zodarin had witnessed the previous manifestation of the Black Hallows. It had taught him much in terms of who he was, who to trust, and who not to trust. At first he had found the Dragonians a welcoming people. They had made use of his talents and he had almost traced what one might call a 'righteous path.' But events have a way of turning even the most deep-seated of beliefs, and events amongst the Dragonians had overtaken him. He didn't like to dwell on the humiliation of those times, but suffice it to say, he had been let down, disappointed — by one in particular.

Spurned by the people who had once welcomed him, he inveigled himself amongst the Cuscosians — a fitting, duplicitous people he could infiltrate and influence. Now he was reaping the harvest of three hundred sols' patience, and it filled him with unbridled exaltation.

This sally into the township was more than just a mere frolic in the wilds, however. True, he wanted to test the bounds of his new abilities, but there was a greater purpose. He had heard rumours of discontent in Hallow's Creek. For sols now he had advised Etezora to moderate the burdens she placed on the Cuscosian populace at large. One could satisfy one's lust for power and delight in coercion while, at the same time, ensuring the commoners saw fruit from their labours. It was a matter of simple politics he had observed in the more successful civilisations he had dwelt amongst during his long lifespan. To deny the people a means to progress or even the ability to exist beyond a state of subsistence was to court the possibility of dissent and even revolution. But Etezora had not listened.

The denizens of Hallow's Creek were suspicious of strangers, and this had limited the intelligence House

Cuscosa could glean from conventional espionage. But Oswald was not human, and his presence would not be questioned — as long as he could gain access to the tavern. This proved to be a simple thing. An open window on the ground floor provided an entry point. He left the skeleton of the stinking fish in the alleyway and leapt up on to the windowsill. Inside, the warmth of a log fire beckoned and the hubbub of a dozen conversations filled the room. The smell of ale soaked into softwood tables filled his nostrils as he sniffed the warm air. The odours mingled with pipe smoke and a rather peculiar human scent that was somehow indefinable.

He leapt down to the sawdust floor and wove his way between the carousers, inviting the odd stroke and fuss from those who noticed. He rubbed himself against legs both human and wooden, acting out the part of the perfect domesticated feline. It made him want to retch, but he calculated such behaviour would help him blend in. All the time, he kept his ears open.

"... and we've hardly enough food to feed our own families, let alone deliver wagon-loads of crops to the Dragonians ..." a farmer said, while sat at an oak bench.

"... problem with rats? I'll deal with them for a mere twenty silbet," a leather-hatted, wiry individual boasted. His appearance was reminiscent of the animals he professed to exterminate.

"Let me sing you a quaint melody, good Sir; a tale from

the Kaldoran legends that'll leave you wondering and awestruck," a rather comely bard was saying.

These were all fascinating conversations, but not what Zodarin sought. It was amongst a group of young men ensconced at a corner table that he finally overheard a more likely exchange. They spoke in whispers while quaffing the contents of their tankards.

One of them, clearly the leader, spoke. "If we are to organise and collectivise, we must capture the hearts and imaginations of the people. Only then will our numbers grow large enough to overthrow the tyrants."

"But Brethis, how can we achieve such a thing?" a red-haired man asked. "The people complain, but they're not willing to step out of line or raise their heads in protest. Small wonder, did you see how they treated Ragenthorp and his family last week — just for holding back one sheaf of corn from the tithe so he could feed his family? Now they have no home and beg on the streets."

"Aye, who would want to protest if that's the punishment you get?" said another.

"But, don't you see?" Brethis continued. "This austerity will only get worse if we take no action. House Cuscosa may have the weapons and the authority that comes with a company of soldiers, but we the people have the numbers."

"That may be true," said an older, weatherworn countryman, "but we are dispersed and demoralised. Who is to lead the kind of uprising you speak of?"

Brethis looked down. "If no other will arise, then I will do what I can to rally the people."

This remark was greeted with considered expressions from Brethis's drinking partners. Not exactly disapproval, but a heightened sense of doubt.

It fell to the countryman to speak for the others. "No offence, Brethis, but you have very little influence and your — shall we say — idealism tends to rub some people up the wrong way."

Brethis sighed. "I'm aware of people's opinions. I'm also aware there is no other who would take on the role, none to my knowledge anyway. But why do we have to think in terms of a single leader? That's exactly what's wrong with Cuscosia and all the other kingdoms. Power lies in the hands of just a few of the privileged. What if our movement made use of everyone's talents?"

The red-haired one, a man named Oathair, posed a question. "That's a strange way of thinking, Brethis. How would it work?"

The bard had struck up her song and a small but boisterous contingent of the tavern joined in the chorus, making it difficult for Oswald to hear. So he jumped up onto the bench next to an unassuming young woman who had, up to this point, said nothing. He proceeded to wash his paws, inviting a rub under the chin from her. It was a risk, but no one bade him any attention, and it meant he could take in the entirety of the conversation — something he did with increasing interest and alarm.

Brethis, obviously a zealous individual, was waxing lyrical about his imagined new order. A utopia in which people voted in their leaders and wealth was distributed equally amongst the peoples. He was pragmatic enough to understand that such a re-balancing required a revolution, an uprising — and blood would inevitably be shed.

Oswald was about to dismiss the rantings of this idealistic rabble when something Brethis said made him prick his ears up.

" ... it will take careful planning and a co-ordinated effort, but I have gathered the resources we need, and enlisted help from men trained in siege warfare."

"Who?" the countryman asked.

Brethis looked around and lowered his voice. "I have a Dragonian friend who has access to certain men."

"Dragonians?" said Oathair, "you've been consorting with — "

"Shush!" Brethis said. "Keep your voice down. You don't know who might overhear."

The girl next to Oswald spoke up. "Can we trust outsiders, Brethis? This could be just a ruse to allow the Dragonians to usurp power. We might end up with that she-tyrant, Tayem Fyreglance ruling over us instead."

"I trust my friend completely," Brethis said.

"So," Oathair said, "*if* we can depend on these allies, and *if* we can come up with a good plan, then what's the target for your plot, and what will it achieve?"

"There are some matters I have to put in place first

before I reveal that. But you can be sure it'll be something to make Etezora take notice. We'll strike right at the heart of her regime. In the meantime, we need to find more allies, enlist the people. They've had enough of Etezora's harsh rule. They just need a movement to unite behind. What I'm planning will show that they can be overcome."

"It won't be enough to just strike once," the girl said, "we need to plan a campaign of attacks."

"And there will be reprisals, you can be sure of that," Oathair added.

"That's why you need to give me time to put more of my plan into place." Brethis looked around the table with earnestness in his eyes. Oswald thought it was more than earnestness — it was zeal. He'd seen it in the eyes of religious fanatics before. "What I need to know is — are you with me? Can I count on you?"

Hesitantly, the girl nodded. "I have reason to hate Etezora more than most. I haven't got anything else to lose, so I'll gladly lend myself to the cause."

One by one, the others grunted or nodded their approval.

"One thing I would say before we leave tonight," continued Brethis. "What we are about to begin will involve sacrifice, perhaps even our lives. So, if you have any doubts, it is best you say so now." He met the solemn gaze of all present but none spoke against what he proposed. "I must away. I have a lot to do. We should meet again at the same time tomorrow night, when I will have tasks for each of you."

"Here again?" the countryman said.

"It served our purposes for tonight," Brethis replied, "but we need somewhere more secure. Our numbers will grow and this will attract attention." He went on to relate an out-of-town meeting place, and Oswald made a mental note of where it was.

The group lifted themselves off the bench, the cat jumping off with them and disappearing through the window he had entered. He waited a few minutes outside the front door and watched as the conspirators left one by one. He chose to follow Brethis and before long learned where the young agitator lived. The man was the eldest brother in a family of five. He greeted them and settled down to an extended conversation. Oswald couldn't ascertain the details of what they said, but soon decided it was of no consequence. He had learned enough for now, and this intelligence would help put him in Etezora's favour. Perhaps get her to trust him more.

He left the town behind and padded the most direct route back to the castle, avoiding the feline temptation to chase mice or mark his unlikely territory. He considered changing shape back to human form outside the castle, but he didn't know how he would be affected, and calculated he'd be safer within the sanctuary of his tower.

The decision proved to be wise, because as he gathered his will and his appearance morphed back, a sapping weariness overcame him. During the transformation he could not focus on his surroundings; he felt vulnerable, weak, and exposed. When full awareness returned, he was shocked to find himself lying on the floor, a thumping pain between his temples.

He stirred himself, feeling an almost poisonous cramp in every muscle conspiring against the simplest of movements. "By the stars, this ability may not be worth the cost," he said out loud. "Entering the Dreamworld has its consequences, but this is ... almost intolerable." With a considerable effort he lurched over to a seat and poured himself a goblet of water from a nearby jug. After a time, feeling returned to his numbed frame, and he felt able to think again. The thoughts that formed in his mind moved about like tessellating pieces of a mosaic until they formed a new and improved scheme, a pathway that would lead to the dominion he had yearned for during the decades of standing in the shadows. The realisation caused a twitching smile to spread on his face. He would sleep for now, but come the morning an audience with the Cuscosian Queen would be the order of the day, then a meeting with Eétor and finally another sojourn in the Dreamworld.

He was about to close his eyes when a shifting rustle in the opposite tower caught his attention. Grizdoth's feint padding would have escaped the attention of most, but to Zodarin with his off-worlder ears the spy's footfall was all too easy to detect. This was despite the two hundred strides or so that separated Zodarin's tower from that of the main library. The wizard heaved his frame to the window and observed Eétor's spy emerge from the foot of the tower and creep furtively along the battlements.

*Where do you return to, you sneaky rodent?* Zodarin's patience was rewarded minutes later when Grizdoth appeared outside Eétor's quarters, fully visible even at this distance.

*So Eétor has his own insecurities,* Zodarin thought. *Well that was to be expected. Anyone poised for rulership would be a fool not to have extra eyes and ears in his service. The question is — how much has Grizdoth observed? And how has he circumvented my magical defences? Perhaps the spy has seen enough to warrant an abrupt end to his treacherous life? Perhaps — but there are other ways to make use of the situation apart from crude dispatchment. More to ponder.*

The weariness from his earlier exertions afflicted him again, and he staggered to his bed. *There may be conspiracies and counter-conspiracies,* he thought as he laid his head down, *but I am in control. All is well, all is well.* Then he drifted off into a dreamless exhausted sleep.

## 16

# UNUSUAL APPETITES

---

"This is the bestest toy you've made for me yet, Papa. What was it called again — a Charry-at?" Palimin crawled in the sandpit Nalin had made him earlier that week, pushing a sturdy but expertly carved chariot along a track swept out in the sand from Palimin's primitive excavations.

"That's right, son. But what's that lump of rock over there?" Nalin pointed at a knobbled lump of limestone that the grabeling had heaved in from the castle courtyard.

"It's the cave-stable for the horses," Palimin said enthusiastically.

"But how do they get in? There are no entrances."

"I've got to chiz ... chisel them out."

"You'll need some tools for that, then."

"Can you give me some, Papa?"

"Chisels and hammers? They're sharp and hefty, son. You're likely to mash and cut a few fingers before you're done."

"Won't," Palimin said. "I'll very, very careful."

Nalin smiled. Here in the depths of the Cuscosian castle, the grabeling was safe and secure. A place where a distinguished father could keep an eye on his wandering son and make sure he didn't get up to any mischief.

*Mischief?* Nalin laughed at the thought. *Isn't it in Kaldoran nature to be up to no good?* If there were awards for roguery, then Nalin would be sure to receive first prize, so he supposed this burden was well deserved. Ellotte, his wife, was enjoying a night spent knitting and sharing the latest hearsay with her circle of friends, so it fell to him to look after the little burrower. Not that he resented the duty. Palimin was one of only a select few Nalin placed before himself in order of importance. Looking at him crawling about in the box of sand, his heart swelled with a father's love and pride. Kaldorans were no different to any other race in this respect. Already the characteristic plates of hardened skin were forming on the grabeling's legs, back and arms. Soon, the natural protective armour of the Kaldorans would cover him. He would grow of course, moulting every eighteen months to make way for his developing frame. *Five sols,* Nalin thought, philosophical about how quickly time went. *Reckon he'll be taller than his father, hopefully cleverer too.*

As his son played in the sand, making neighing noises and shouting the commands of his imaginary charioteers, Nalin pondered the engineering problem that had perplexed him all day. He had visited his hideaway, the secret location of an invention he had come to call the 'cave-crawler.' The machine had performed reasonably well in trials. It ate through rock with its cutting head, burrowing a tunnel twenty spans wide at a rate of ten spans per minute; a distance far too slow for his ambitions. How could he increase its efficiency? The solution eluded him, despite hours of pondering and looking at the problem from different angles.

*Perhaps replacing the drill cutters with higher-grade diamond? No, that would be costly and add little to the excavating power. Construct a triple nose-cone with replaceable carbind implants? No, that would take months to develop, and carbind is not hard enough. The nose-cones would have to be replaced far too often.*

When he next looked at the water clock, he was surprised to find half an hour had passed. Sometimes, when pondering his designs, he entered what his wife called a 'muse-state'. More often than not, this was an effect of the jarva-leaf, but he hadn't indulged since mid-afternoon. *I need to put the problem aside,* he thought, *return to it with a fresh mind in the morning.*

"Time to go to bed," Nalin said, bringing his attention

back to his son. Palimin turned, sand covering his face and hands. "Oh, already? Can't I finish this one last channel?"

Nalin chortled, "Always one for digging, aren't you little burrower? But I think it's time you lay your head to rest. You've had enough for one night."

"Then maybe a story?"

Nalin narrowed his eyes. The grabeling was playing for time, of that he had no doubt. But Ellotte wouldn't be home for another couple of hours, and he was partial himself to a little recounting of tales and legends. "All right," he said, "which story would you like?"

Palimin's face lit up. "Tell the one about Gatdroul and the Brabagant."

"That's a favourite of mine too," Nalin said, "now come and sit on Papa's knee and I'll tell it."

And so, Nalin did. He told the legend precisely in the words of the stone fablers, as was the custom amongst the Kaldorans. Legends were passed down by word of mouth, the language unchanged, and Nalin did not depart from this custom.

Many hundreds of moons ago, before the rise of the Cuscosians, there lived a tribe of humans called Dorwin in the valley of Limneth, just south of the Dragon Vale. They were a hardy people, colonisers who threw up their wooden settlements rapidly, spreading across the plains like an infestation.

One day, an ancient behemoth from the clan of

Brabagants descended from the hills. His name was Yauthlorgh, and he stood ten centiarchs tall, bearing a spiked ironwood club and a sack in which he placed his victims. His feet shook the earth as he thundered across the plain and the Dorwin cowered in their huts, trembling in fear. A few brave souls confronted the giant with spears and pikes, but they were no match for him. Yauthlorgh beat them to a meaty mush and placed them in his sack.

But he did not stop there. He broke down the villagers' hastily-constructed dwellings and lifted the bodies up, handfuls at a time, squeezing the life out of them with fingers the size of pythons. They fled before him, hiding in the woods until he had finished decimating their township.

Once he had left, they sent out search parties but could not find the Brabagant's lair. Their mourning was great, and many considered leaving for the Southern Lands from which they had come. However, after a month with no further appearance, they thought the beast gone, and started to rebuild. It was untimely, though. The Brabagant returned and slew a handful of the villagers, not exacting as great a toll this time as the Dorwin fled as soon as they heard his approach.

One foolhardy soul attempted to parley with the Brabagant and — some would say to his credit, others not — he struck a deal, agreeing that the villagers would offer up five children every month for the beast to devour. In return, he would allow the villagers to live in peace and raise their township again. Some could not stomach this and left for their homeland, despite the meagre living they knew awaited them, far from the lush plains they had come to inhabit. Most stayed however, believing this Brabagant's burden acceptable to bear.

Yet after several months, during which they argued over which children they should offer up, the people grew wearied at this harsh imposition and sought another way.

Now Gatdroul was a famous stonegrabe — a mighty warrior, skilled rocksmith and expert diplomat. The only thing preventing him from becoming Fellchief of the Kaldorans was his dislike of administration and the petty concerns he perceived to be part of running a kingdom. He much preferred inhabiting his workroom, dreaming up new architectural works — for which he was highly renowned.

One day, the Fellchief summoned Gatdroul to his Rockclave and introduced him to a delegation of the Dorwin. They had approached the Kaldorans with an offer of three sacks of gold pieces and fifty head of cattle to rid them of their monster. They had heard how the Kaldorans overthrew the Brabagants and established their kingdom hundreds of sols ago.

The offer was acceptable to the Fellchief, and he commanded Gatdroul to deal with it. Gatdroul was loath to follow this instruction, knowing that Brabagants were fearsome behemoths and could only be defeated by a combination of guile, specialised weapons and great loss of life. Yet the Fellchief compelled him, and he took a company of stonegrabes to the Brabagant's lair.

They spied on the creature, waiting until it had eaten its latest meal. Then, in a moment of great boldness, Gatdroul approached the satiated Brabagant and parleyed with it, offering a settlement far in the north where it could feed off the North-Eastern enclave of Norisea. They were known to breed like rabbits, and though they dwelt in a secret location, Gatdroul promised to show the Brabagant where they were, and so ensure a plentiful supply of food.

However, the Brabagant refused, as he had come to like the taste of the Dorwin. He particularly enjoyed the tender flesh of their infants, which it likened to sweetmeat.

"You should try some," the Brabagant offered, Gatdroul having ingratiated himself at Yauthlorgh's fireside. The Brabagant assured the stonegrabe he was safe from his claws as he didn't like Kaldoran flesh. "Too rocky and acidic. Lies heavy on my stomach," the creature growled. "But this," it said, lifting a piece of warm leg meat. "This is much more pleasant to the tongue. Taste it. I insist."

Gatdroul was compelled to take the morsel, not wishing to offend the Brabagant. He took it in his hand and sprinkled a little nutmeg and onion powder on it from a sprinkler in his pack, hoping it would take away the flavour of something he anticipated would be abhorrent. To his surprise, the flavour of the cooked child sent his taste buds wild. He salivated uncontrollably and asked, meekly, for a little more.

"What is that dust?" asked the Brabagant.

"Just a little seasoning," Gatdroul replied innocently.

"It seems to add something to the dish," Yauthlorgh said, "give it here.

But Gatdroul was a duplicitous soul and, by sleight of hand, substituted the condiment pot with an identical one. This one, however, contained a poison extracted from the tail of a rock scorpion.

The poison was quick acting, and the Brabagant was thrown to the floor, writhing in pain. The behemoth lashed out at Gatdroul and his cohort, killing ten and wrenching Gatdroul's right arm from its socket. Seconds later, though, the Brabagant fell dead with an almighty crash before it could exert a heftier toll.

Despite the pain wracking his body, brave Gatdroul chopped the thing's head off and returned it to the Dorwin. The villagers celebrated and paid their dues, despite the cost leaving them destitute for a sol afterward.

As for Gatdroul, his severe wound healed quickly — a trait possessed by all Kaldoran stonegrabes great and small. The arm grew back but not as it was before, earning him the title, 'Gatdroul Withered-Arm.'

He returned to Kaldora, concealing some of the cooked human meat on his person. That very night he shared it with honoured guests who also took an instant liking to the succulent meat.

Days later, their appetites got the better of them and they conspired an attack on an unwary Dorwin wanderer.

It wasn't long before they were abducting humans more and more to feed their newly-found savage appetites. All the while, their secretive acquisitions remained undetected, the Dorwin assuming there were other fell beasts come to prey upon them. So, their people never established themselves and were easily conquered when the Cuscosian avalanche invaded in later times.

It was from Gatdroul Withered-Arm's exploits that the seeds of Kaldorans' specialised tastes were sown. To this day, we enjoy the feasts of Echthorim, where this rare meat is indulged and we eat our fill.

Nalin finished his story, studying Palimin's expression. It was one of wonder and transport. "When can I eat human-flesh, Papa?"

Nalin tweaked his son's nose. "Soon enough, my little grabeling, when your stomach is ready — and when we can stock our larders again. Such food has been scarce in the last sol since Cuscosian patrols have thwarted our raids. But this will change soon. Magthrum will see to that. Now, what do you think the moral of this story is?"

Palimin considered for a moment, then said, "Be brave and you will defeat all of your monsters?"

Nalin laughed. "Perhaps. But more importantly — extend the hand of friendship to a stranger and then stab him with the other. That is the Kaldoran way."

Palimin nodded and then furrowed his brow. "Or …

maybe — extend the hand of friendship to a stranger, then eat his flesh with the other?"

Nalin laughed even louder at this. "You may become a Rockclave poet yet! Now, tidy your toys up and I'll get you a cup of milk."

It was as Nalin rose that a frustrating but ultimately happy accident occurred. He'd left a vial of rare dragon saliva — also called fyredrench — on the edge of the bench, and his elbow clipped it as he brought himself to his weary feet. The vial tipped over, tumbling in the air. Nalin scrabbled to catch it but to no avail. The green glass shattered as it struck Palimin's cave-stable.

"Stand back." He shouted at his son. He knew that one drop of the stuff could eat its way through even a stonegrabe's flesh in a matter of seconds. Indeed, as they both watched, wide-eyed, the viscous fluid caused the limestone to seethe and bubble, weathering the rock away until it was a flowing trickle of goo in the sandpit. The liquid continued to eat its way downwards until a small crater had formed in the floor — and still the hole grew deeper!

"Chikohk! Who would have thought?" Nalin exclaimed, realising he'd just wasted a month's wages in that one vial. But, his frustration turned to glee as he contemplated the implications of this discovery.

*Perhaps,* he thought, *I may have stumbled on the solution to my problem.*

# 17

# THE BURNING OF
# YESTERDAY

---

The Dragonians came to call it the Dead Zone. The Gigantes had another name — the Ever-forgotten Fields. Before the rise of Cuscosa and the swarming of the Kaldorans it was known as Lyn-Harath — the translation from Oldspeak meaning 'soul rest.' Encircled by the Black Mountains, this disc of land spanned seven periarchs in diameter, carpeted with lush meadows and rolling downs, home to a luxuriant myriad of creatures and flora. To those who made their pilgrimage there it was paradise. To the Gigantes it was home.

This vision of teeming beauty is what Ebar liked to remember. He recalled how his people would pick luscious fruit from the trees throughout the sol to sustain them, and how the heavens blessed that pocket of landscape with even winds and light, warm rain. They would sit in their circles by the light of glow-lamps — for the wood of the forests was sacred — and invoke ancient magics. Their shamanism blessed the surrounding realms with bountiful crops and benevolent weather. They were sought out for their ability to heal the sick and bring comfort to the dying. They were a venerated people, though this was not their aim. Gigantes soothsayers wandered the lands from Escatar to Drumlig, applying their lore, donating herbal gifts and administering wisdom to grateful recipients. The thanks of the people were enough for them. The land gave its bounty freely, and they in turn passed on their blessings to all in need.

But like anything precious, this pocket of paradise became coveted by the unenlightened eyes of others. Forces that wanted to claim it as their own plotted to acquire Lyn-Harath for their own ends. Thus came the time of the Decimation.

Ebar was old, even in Gigantean terms, the sols of his existence seeming like the passing of seconds. Yet he was unable to erase the Decimation from his memory, despite the intended talisman of *Ever-forgotten*. How could he forget? He had been there, witnessed the fields drenched in blood, the burning of the forests and the lamentation of the bereft.

So despite every effort to cast the memories aside, Ebar's mind wound back like a coil to that night ...

The Hillman who came to be known as Ebar the Great stood motionless in the dark, moss-lined entrance to his abode, located on the edge of Mereshan, the Gigantes' sacred grove. Something had awoken him from his meditations. *But what?* He thought. *A premonition or a warning perhaps?* He spent seconds like that, transfixed in horror at what he now detected on the wind. A faint stench of burning flesh, distant screams of terror, portents of a doom that should have been foreseen.

A shout from nearby broke his stillness. "Ebar, we are under attack. Narchen has summoned the gifted to his house. He says we must combine our individual strength to resist the invaders." It was Scorfleet, a Gigantes three spans taller than himself and imposing in girth.

"Under attack? Who?" Ebar's senses reeled.

"We do not know, but the West Reach has already fallen and a vast army approaches. It is the barbarous Cuscosians. No time for further words now, accompany me."

The youthful Ebar followed Scorfleet, racing through the sweeping mallowdrift fronds until they came upon the elders, circled around Narchen — the Gigantes they considered their leader. It was a title he only reluctantly accepted.

"Brothers and sisters," Narchen said to the assembled, settling them with a natural authority. The leader stood tall in the night, face lined with concern yet possessing an undercurrent of stoicism. "We have little time, and we must save our people. The Cuscosians have formed an alliance with the Kaldorans and invaded the borders of Lyn-Harath. Already they have destroyed Waithros and trodden down the Rayhan meadows. They advance upon our sacred grove and will be upon us within the hour.

"Those who have survived are fleeing this way, and we have only one hope of redemption. We must combine our strength and summon the Mists of Confusion. It is a feat never attempted on this scale, but it might buy us enough time to gather our populace and escape."

"To where. Narchen? Where will we go?" It was Torthen, wise-woman of the Gigantes and mother to Ginnie.

"Through the Whispering Hills to the north. We must take to the mountains, disperse, and lose the desecrators in the passes. We will regroup at Herethorn — those of us who can survive."

The pronouncement carried a bleakness uncharacteristic of their leader, and there were some who baulked. "We should strike back," said one. "We are stronger than they," shouted another.

Narchen raised his weathered hands and calmed the

dissent. "The path of Carnos is alien to us. We are not a war-like people, and though these invaders are like rats beneath our feet, even vermin can overcome us with sheer weight of numbers — and their count is thousands.

"Now, will you join with me and take part in the summoning? We must act now or we shall be overrun."

*So it has come to this,* Ebar thought. Would that his friend, Wobas was here. Instead, he had been sequestered in the Dragon Vale, aiding them in their plight. Yet what peril loomed greater than this? How the Gigantes might have benefitted with help from Thorshil Fyreglance's dragons. But there was no time to enlist their aid.

Ebar had little in the way of *Sygist* energy at his disposal. His talents lay elsewhere, but what he had he would freely give. He could only hope it was enough. Already he heard Cuscosian drums in the distance, and the rattling of Kaldoran mauls on their shields.

"Link hands," Narchen exhorted them.

Ebar felt Scorfleet take his hand, the Sygist flow already apparent in the Gigantes' touch. Another to his right, followed suit and the circle was complete. Narchen began the incantation, and within seconds the Sygist crescendoed. Experiencing this infusion of power was a wonder to Ebar, yet it was accompanied by a sense of disquiet. At once, he knew he would never be a worthy vessel. Perhaps Wobas could live with the strangeness of this remarkable conduit of power — the desideratum of his sallies in the Dreamworld. But to Ebar, it seemed there must be a cost to this agency, and it was one he sensed he would not be willing to pay.

"Túl ana us — este leir lumenn' o maure," Narchen's voice rose in volume, the Oldspeak impelling and elevating his speech with gravitas. The Gigantes added their mantras to the invocation and to Ebar it was as if the earth and the trees resonated in harmony with this unprecedented benediction.

"Meneth i holui ensorcel tob — ammen," the head Gigantes intoned, and as he uttered the last words, hairline cracks opened in the forest floor beneath them. As these lengthened, a silver mist emanated forth to form a dense blanket that swirled around them.

"Flee, my brothers and sisters," Narchen cried. "The enemy are at our door and they will show no mercy. Hide yourselves and your families in the mists. Let the light of the Sygist be your guide and, with grace, we may meet again at our destination."

Those were the last words Ebar ever heard from Narchen. Of the Gigantes who stood in that circle, barely ten survived and only a few dozen from without made it through the Whispering Hills.

Ebar never fathomed why he was chosen to survive what followed. Perhaps no reason existed. He had no family, and so was not encumbered as some were, so he helped those that needed aid. Yet to this day, he felt it was a meagre effort. One whom he aided was a young girl called Shamfis. He saw the Cuscosians bring down the rest of her family, young and old alike with their heavy iron crossbow bolts. As they fled through the Northreach they passed the fallen, looks of horror contorting features that all their lifetime had been pictures of peacefulness.

The mists had simply bought them a little time. There was one amongst the Cuscosians, one whose cloaked appearance sent dread through the Gigantes' souls, an off-worlder, dread Harrowbane shapeshifter. He ... it had guided the enemy alliance through the enchanted shrouds, called down a hail of arrows on the fleeing Gigantes, exhorting the troops to slaughter and mutilating the fallen. Ebar remembered looking over his shoulder as he lumbered into the lower slopes of the mountains, all the time thinking he was a coward for not turning back. He remembered seeing a dark shape silhouetted against the torchlight, a shape invisible to its own minions. It was indescribable, perverse, an entity that invaded his dreams even to this day.

As far as anyone knew, the bones of the Gigantes still lay in those desolate fields. Their blood soaked deep in the earth still cried out to him. *But for what? Vengeance?*

*Revenge was not a path the Gigantes trod.*

Ebar shook his head. *Yes, to forget must be a blessing, but it is not one granted to me.*

Ironic that, apart from the lost scrolls, the razing of Lyn-Harath had not benefitted the Cuscosian-Kaldoran alliance in the way they lusted for. With the destruction of that sacred habitat and the murder of its inhabitants, the inherent lore and blessings disappeared like thistledown on the wind.

And so they had come after many days to Herethorn, a cold and uninviting place, yet one that few knew existed. Though young, the dishevelled remnants of the Gigantes had looked to Ebar for leadership, and he had known at once that this place would not harbour them long without protection. He had summoned Wobas using Brownbeak's mother to seek him out, and though he had been reluctant at first, the shaman had entreated the denizens of the Dreamworld, the spirit guides, to grant them magical aegis. Wobas' request was heard, and over the decades the Gigantes had enjoyed the sanctuary of the hidden realm.

Perhaps the Cuscosians thought them completely annihilated, for that was their aim. Yet Ebar had his doubts.

The price they had paid to the spirit guides for concealment was great. Why they exacted the penalty seemed cruel beyond words, but the Gigantes had accepted it, for the sake of survival. For what price was too high to avoid extinction? Yet to know the date of one's death was a heavy burden.

Ebar removed carefully selected scrolls from the wooden cylinders that occupied the shelves of his meagre library — all that remained of a once voluminous archive. The rest had been stolen by the Cuscosians or destroyed by Magthrum's vulgar horde.

They should have foreseen the Decimation, just as they should have predicted the early advent of the Black Hallows. The judgement of the Council meant a delay, yet could they afford such a thing? Though it was not the primary consideration, he was also cognisant of sands slipping through the hourglass. As a Cyclopes, he was acutely aware of the sixteen hundred and eighteen days left for him to walk this land. Was it vain of him to think of his contribution to these events in such elevated terms? Perhaps. Yet the converse argument weighed heavy on his heart. He was responsible. The Gigantes looked to him for leadership, and Wobas relied on him as a friend.

Ebar emerged into the light and unrolled the first of his scrolls. *What was it Wobas had asked for on his return visit? Knowledge of the Augur? That had been one thing, but there was also lore relating to the 'relinkur' — changeling. Why did the mention of that name bring back such dark memories?*

Brownbeak's arrival interrupted his reverie. With a screech and a fluttering of staunch flight feathers, Brownbeak grasped the perch bar on Ebar's platform with his talons and squawked again.

"What is it, Lordling of the Skies?"

The raptor communicated with a blinking of its eyes, almost imperceptible gestures and changes in body position. After a few minutes of the exchange, Ebar's already melancholy mood had turned grim.

Questions arose in his mind. *Cuscosian troops massing on*

*the borders of Kaldora? Platoons marching to the North-West also?*

The council had voted for a cautionary approach. The kingdoms of the South were not their concern. Survival *was*. Yet as Ebar pondered Brownbeak's report, he wondered if the time for waiting was past. Maybe if they held back too long they would be overwhelmed when they least expected it — just like at Lyn-Harath.

Although he tried to resist it, once more the memory of a dark, slithering, shifting shape invaded again. Whatever it was, Ebar had become increasingly anxious it was still out there — even after all this time. Waiting, anticipating.

# 18

# TRYSTS AND COLLUSIONS

———

Mahren pulled the hood over her head, looked both ways at the exit to the alleyway, and then hurried into the main street towards her rendezvous. She had only walked five paces when a sound from beyond the town outskirts brought her up short. It was a curious blend of mewling and rumbling that travelled across the intervening distance.

*Krut — Jaestrum. Can you not keep quiet for a second?*

She'd tied the beast up in a briar copse to the north of Hallow's Creek, hopeful that he'd stay restful until her return.

*Perhaps he's not as well trained as I thought. Or maybe he's upset at what happened with the poisoning.* He'd certainly been more than a little sluggish on the flight down from the Vale, and Mahren had felt a certain amount of guilt about riding him so soon after his affliction. But the pull of Hallow's Creek was too great to resist.

She considered returning to the dragon and settling him down. He had flown only a couple of periarchs short of Castle Cuscosa after all, right under Etezora's nose, and the Queen had her surveillance methods. But Mahren had been sure her low-level approach to the township had gone unnoticed under cover of the dark, and she yearned for this meeting.

She looked to the moon as it peeked its head out from behind a cloud. It was tinged with Hallows Purple, matching the now familiar indigo shades of Sol-Ar. Indeed a malaise seemed to have crept over her since the events of a week ago, an oppressiveness that created an itching in her brain and a perpetual dull headache. Did the others feel it too? It was as if no one dared mention it, yet the Dragonians had become restless as a people, constantly looking over their shoulders, bickering at the slightest provocation. Even Sheldar had refrained from cracking as many of his jokes in the Dragon Keep.

*A leviathan has awoken in the land,*
*A monster that moves invisibly among us.*

She remembered the lyrics from one of Vanya's songs.

She forgot the name of the ballad and had not appreciated the significance of the words. But now, they seemed to ring true of this malign intrusion — and to think this might last for decades! *How will we bear it?*

*Are all kingdoms of Varchal affected in the same way?*

*Keep focused on the now,* she told herself. *You must not be caught trespassing in this place. Tensions are rising high enough already.*

She began to walk again, mindful there were few on the streets. Those that were present tended to consist of the city guard. She kept to the shadows and was relieved when she entered the suburbs, the traffic of pedestrians and the occasional horse-drawn cart easing off as she did so.

"Psst!" she heard from a ramshackle outbuilding. "Over here." Although the tone was sharp, she recognised the voice, and a tingling passed over her skin bringing it out in goose bumps.

She stepped closer to the rotting structure, caution still preventing her getting too close. "Brethis, is that you?"

"No, it's the Emperor of Nettlebroth," the voice came back.

"Oh," she exclaimed, suddenly fearful.

"Of course it's me, silly," Brethis said, his head appearing in the sole window.

Mahren puffed out her cheeks and exhaled, meeting him as he opened a door that hung from one hinge. Inside, a candle provided limited illumination, and what it revealed made her wish it was even more limited. A dankness hung in the air, consistent with the decaying logs and rough-cut timber leaning against the walls.

"I'm sorry about the decor," Brethis said, "I haven't had time to furnish the place yet."

"You live here?" she asked.

A wink from Brethis told her he'd caught her twice already, one of several traits that attracted her to him in the first place.

"Are you sure it's — " Her words were cut off when Brethis pressed his lips against hers. Not for one instant did she consider resisting, although in the courts of the Dragon Riders such an affront was punishable with incarceration. Instead, she surrendered to the moment, enjoying the sense of abandonment, of not caring about responsibilities. Gone was any notion of royal etiquette or decorum. She found her muscles losing tension, the irritation behind her eyes soothed and her headache seemed to evaporate. As Brethis's kiss lingered, she noticed her heartbeat. It pulsed in her ears, drumming out the rhythm of her desire.

Then all of a sudden, he pulled away. "I needed that," he said, "now, we have much to talk about."

"But, I thought ...?"

"There'll be time for that," he said with a smile that dimpled his face. "Business first."

He brushed down a rickety, three-legged stool and pulled it up for her, turning round another one so they sat face to face. "I met with the others last night, and they have agreed to mobilise support. We are getting together at the twenty-first hour, where I will lay out details of my plan."

"Hold on, Brethis," Mahren said. "You're speaking too quickly." It was true. Mahren saw the fire in his eyes and understood he was in a state of hyperactivity. "You can tell me everything. But you need to relax — so do I, and I have just the remedy."

She rose from the stool and leaned over him, tilting his face upward and meeting his open mouth with hers. This time, he didn't interrupt and soon they were laid out on the ground, a rough horsehair blanket their only comfort against the woodcutter's floor. Neither noticed the time pass as they explored each other, his lips blazing a trail of liquid fire across her smooth skin, she returning his attentions as if drugged. It was a spell of time to be savoured, made all the more precious because of its transitory nature. She wished that it would never end.

They spent further moments lying side by side, a cool breeze entering through the open window and caressing their naked skin.

"What do you imagine will happen to us?" she said after a while.

"What do you mean?" he replied, raising himself on one elbow.

"It all seems so unlikely, doesn't it? I mean here we are, you a Cuscosian — "

"I hate that word, and I refuse to be associated with it," he said rather curtly.

"However you wish to be known," she said, "I am a member of the Dragonian royals. If my family were to know about this — well ..."

Brethis laughed. "I know. It would turn that poe-faced expression of your sister's to a look more sour than lemon."

Mahren shoved him over playfully. "Don't make fun of her. She has the weight of the kingdom on her shoulders."

"Then if it is too heavy a burden to bear, she should give over the reins of power to the common people."

It was Mahren's turn to laugh. "There you go with your idealism again. And how long do you think it would be before the kingdom was bankrupt, and the people left starving as they squabbled amongst themselves over who should have their say? Nothing would get done."

"It would seem both royal houses have made a good job of achieving that already."

"You paint my sister with the same brush as that schjek, Etezora?"

Brethis held up his hands. "Of course not. Etezora is a tyrant, and all the more so since this change has come about in the skies. Your people may be arrogant, but they are not intent on oppressing all who inhabit the Imperious Crescent."

Mahren looked at him with an inscrutable smile.

"What?" he said.

"Dragonians and Cuscosians? Maybe our troubles would be over if we could find a way to agree. Perhaps only a union of the two houses could force the issue."

"A union? You mean ..." He pointed a finger at her then back at himself. "Ha! You think I am royalty? More than this — you think I could father your children?"

Mahren put her tunic back on, putting her arms through the vents of the light leather armour. "No to the first. You are but a common peasant."

"Hey, who are you — "

"But as to the second ..."

Brethis's eyes widened. "It's only been a month since we came to know each other, and you are already talking about offspring?"

"Does the idea appal you?"

Brethis eased himself to his feet, and Mahren couldn't help but admire his muscled torso and strong, bronzed arms. He put his hands on his hips. "Well, now you mention it, the thought is not unattractive. A fine brace of blacksmith's sons to carry on the family business, and a couple of daughters to marry a rich nobleman or two."

"For a revolutionary, you project very patriarchal sentiments."

Brethis blushed. "I suppose you are right."

"We may be authoritarian, but you can't say the Dragonians are guilty of holding their women back from a leading role."

"You know, we could bring our children up in a new

way. Let them break free of the mental chains that enslave our people."

"I'd still want them to learn the art of vs' shtak, and even the kirith-a."

Brethis looked puzzled.

"Vs' shtak is dragon riding and the ancient lore that encompasses everything connected with it. There are few who are ready to take up the sacred mantle, and none who understand the dragon's language as I do. This is the essence of kirith-a, rare empathy and communication with dragons."

"Cuscosian Dragon Riders?" Brethis said. "Who could imagine such a thing?"

"I dare to imagine," she replied. Then her visage turned dark. "But there is much that would stand in our way. Perhaps too much."

"It's just outdated rules and customs. Why should we let others dictate to us?"

"It's not just that. The Hallows wax black. Have you seen it in the skies? You understand the meaning of this, don't you?"

"We've been told nothing — other than what the likes of Vanya the bard pass on — and she embellishes things somewhat."

"The Black Hallows are no embellishment. I've seen what they can do."

"Really? Tell me."

Mahren rose and shook her head. "I don't want to talk

about it now, but we must watch our backs. If what I read in our library contains only half the truth, then we can expect great upheaval."

"Well, that's good isn't it? We need a revolution — at least on this side of the border. We can't suffer like this any longer. Do I need to describe Etezora's latest atrocities?"

She could see Brethis had grown animated again and no amount of soothing would ease his burden. He had things to get off his chest, so she let him speak.

He continued talking, rapid-fire as he donned his clothes again. "Like I said before, the Brotherhood meet later and I promised we could expect help from the Dragonians."

"You did? I hope you didn't say too much. I've only spoken to Sashaim and Aibrator from my own dragon host, and my sister seems to be holding off a direct attack at present. She has agreed to persuade Etezora to attend a summit."

Brethis swatted at the air. "A meeting will achieve nothing. In fact you need to be careful you're not walking into a trap. Have you noticed the mobilisation of troops from the garrisons?"

"I was curious as to the number of guards on the streets of Hallow's Creek. Still, it's one thing to show strength of arms, quite another to make threats while staring down the mouth of a dragon. What is happening with the troops, anyway?"

"It's hard to say, but movement of soldiers on this scale usually means only one thing."

Mahren's expression clouded. "Tayem must hear of this. How long since the activity increased?"

"The day before yesterday. The captains recruit from the striplings of our families too. It is only a matter of time before they come knocking on my family's door."

"What will you do?"

Brethis's eyes lit up. "The Brotherhood aim to strike before then, and with the Dragon Rider's help we can deal a mighty blow to Cuscosa."

"You can't expect too much, Brethis. Tayem would not countenance an all-out attack with dragons — "

"I'm not asking for that," he replied, "simply weapons and guidance. We possess but axes and staves. Properly crafted weapons would be far more useful — and the expertise of true warriors. Our brotherhood can supply the cunning and subtlety of a well-planned attack."

"Where?"

Brethis didn't answer but glanced through the window at the moon. "We should be away, the brothers meet within a half hour."

"You want me to go with you?"

"Of course. You can give us weapons and a helping hand, can't you?"

Mahren resigned herself. "Yes, I think so. Although if Tayem hears of it, there will be a reckoning."

"No one in your royal palace need ever know."

"Very well, lead the way, then. But don't expect me to speak publically. That's Tayem's skill, not mine."

It was enough for Brethis. He blew out the candle, which had burned low, and they stepped furtively through the night to another rendezvous. On the way, Brethis related his plan to Mahren, and despite a few flaws she became increasingly impressed with its daring and ingenuity.

No human eye detected their movement through the suburbs and out to the surrounding woods. But a pair of amber feline orbs observed them with curiosity, padding after them languidly.

*A union of Cuscosa and the Donnephon?* Thought the off-worlder with amusement. *This night has already provided much entertainment, and there is more to come!*

19

# OF FIRE AND BLOOD

_____

Etezora closed the blinds of her bedroom window more securely, darkening the room but not blotting out the light as completely as she would like. With Sol-Ar's influence diminished through her actions, she sensed the Hallows infusion decrease in sympathy, and her mood become more reflective. The anticipation that Tayem would soon be humiliated, defeated or completely vanquished filled her with satisfaction; yet this was tinged with a mote of regret. Their relationship had not always been thus. *When had the rift occurred?* She could point to many incremental incidents, but it would have to be the celebration at the last Feast of Shaptari that marked the turning point.

She found her mind transported back to that day, and the fateful events that transpired.

There is an ancient game played in the Eastern lands called Heryx. It consists of coloured tiles of four suits. The object is for a player to build one's tiles upwards in a connected manner so one gains control of the upper tiers. A skilled strategist will use the foundations built by other players to dominate a given level. But it is a fragile construct that is produced, and a rogue opponent can sabotage a leading player by toppling whole tiers as a result of removing a single tile.

The Feast of Shaptari exemplified this kind of fragility in a profound way. However, for Etezora, having only just celebrated her thirteenth natum day, these things floated far beyond her sphere of understanding like distant concussions from a far-off volcano. Four kingdoms held together by tentative bonds of commerce and hastily written treaties agreed to this occasion of pomp and pageantry in the interests of diplomacy. However, even a tender shoot like Etezora could detect undercurrents beneath the veneer of pleasantries and etiquette: a 'bending' of rules in a wrestling match; favouritism shown in the awarding of trophies or an affront concealed in a flattering compliment at the high table.

Etezora played with her helping of goat's cream pie at such a table during the afternoon celebrations. Of late she had little appetite for conventional food; not since she had tasted darastrix rhyaex — the cured dragon meat procured by her brother from illicit sources. If the Dragon Riders knew the Cuscosians farmed dragons in underground pits purely as a source of exotic and expensive meat, then it was certain the precarious alliance would break down. So far the puritanical Donnephon had not detected this abhorrent practice, yet Etezora had heard Tayem relate how her parents viewed the uncultured Cuscosian appetites. *You indulge too much in the sensual pleasures,* Tayem had communicated in an overly educated diatribe. Etezora was not quite sure what this meant, but was under no illusion that it was not complimentary.

That sol, the Donnephon hosted the Shaptari festival. They had spared no expense despite the fact their coffers were all but empty, having been drained by unequal trade agreements and the punitive exactment system enforced by the Cuscosians. They were a warrior breed after all, not well versed in commerce and unable to capitalise on their obvious talents. Their ornate furniture and carvings made from the exotic woods of the Dragon Vale would have commanded a price four times that which Cuscosa offered. If only they were not so inward looking and perhaps sought agreements with other races beyond their borders. In many ways they were victims of their own insularity. Yet these economic shortcomings were not to be an obstacle as far as the Dragonians were concerned. Appearances and one-upmanship had to be maintained above all else.

Against both their parents' wishes, Etezora had engineered a place next to her friend, Tayem, at the dining table. In a Cuscosan court dominated by males, to consort with other young girls of like mind was a rare treat. Her unorthodox seating arrangement had been permitted, as Etezora was always able to get her way, despite Eétor's protestations.

"I am bored beyond words," Etezora said to Tayem, "hurry up and finish your pie. You promised to show me the palace grounds, and there will only be tedious speeches for the next hour."

Tayem shovelled a large spoonful of pie into her mouth and spoke between every chomp of her jaws. Seemingly, the chance to partake of such hearty food was an occasion oft denied her. "Mother and Father will not be pleased," she said.

"They won't notice," Etezora replied. "Grown-ups get caught up in these feasts, and the wine is flowing. Come on, we won't be missed." She eyed her compatriot, noting with a flush of jealousy how Tayem already had a regal bearing. Her golden locks fell over shoulders already well honed from hour upon hour spent in the company of dragons, tending them and taking to the air on their backs. Unlike the daubed artificiality of Cuscosian make-up that adorned Etezora's face, the daughter of the Dragon Queen possessed a beauty as natural as a mountain stream. Although the thought had not yet crystallised into conscious thought, she longed for such comeliness, and in that moment Etezora's envy seemed to focus on the object of Tayem's devotion. *What a waste to commit all your attention on such ungainly and repugnant beasts.*

"Well, if we're to get away," Tayem said, "now would be a good time. Look — Mother is rising to speak."

They made the most of the moment and stealthily climbed down from their high seats, slipping between folds in the thick velvet curtains behind the high table. As they descended the wooden steps behind the temporary stage, Etezora heard Queen Jezethorn start her opening address.

"Fellow citizens of the Imperious Crescent ..."

*Fellow? Didn't the high-minded schjek realise that her family were far from friends? Even the name 'Imperious Crescent' had been imposed to emphasise Cuscosian dominance.* For all their high-minded pretensions, the Dragonians would ever be serfs to the House of Cuscosa.

She was reeling off well-learned tropes from her father's pronouncements. It is in this way that young minds are shaped by the incessant inculcation of their upbringing, and the Cuscosians had their own dynastic pretensions. Yet Etezora could not be blamed for this — unlike the actions she was to perpetrate in the next hour.

The two of them slunk away from the freshly clipped lawns of the palace frontage, giggling at shared imitations of the most pompous characters at the high table. Now, as Queen of Cuscosa, Etezora could reflect how circumstances had removed that carefree joy from them.

In fact, as she dwelt on those moments, it dawned on her that she had not laughed with anything approaching that degree of unaffectedness since. These days her laughter was elicited from the glee at seeing others suffer. The seeds of this perverse joy were sown later that day.

Etezora smelt the reptilian odour even before they laid eyes on the dragon enclosures. She could see by the wonder on Tayem's face that she revelled in the sight and smell of what she appreciated as magnificent creatures; whereas for Etezora, it was the *taste* of dragons she savoured most.

"I've wanted to show you the dragon pens for ages," Tayem said. "The royal mounts are riding the clouds at the moment. They will fly in formation over the palace once the speeches are finished."

Etezora nodded, feigning a look of eagerness, all the while harbouring a smouldering resentment towards the wyrms.

"But the youngsters are penned up still," Tayem continued. "Come, I'll show you Quassu. He's my dragon. You'll like him."

*I doubt it.*

"He has this way of winking, as if he's sharing a joke with you."

*How delightful.*

The pens were screened from the palace by a line of bachar trees. Constructed as a latticework of willow woven between uprights of living tisthorn trees, even this functional enclosure carried the hallmarks of ornate craftsmanship reminiscent of all Dragonian endeavours. They passed enclosures containing smaller beasts of varying sizes, while Tayem took great pleasure in explaining the taxonomy of the regal reptiles.

"These dull-coloured ones," she said, "may not be much to look at, but they are the best flyers and the most teachable. They form the backbone of our host. Here, this one is Jaestrum, my sister's mount. Already he can fly higher than Mount Gathan and perform the looping manoeuvre."

"Doesn't Mahren fall when he's upside down?"

Tayem laughed, the sound having a tinkling quality. "She's strapped into the dragon harness, so she comes to no harm."

"It must be frightening. How is she not terrified?"

"My sister trusts Jaestrum more than she does a human. She has this way of talking to the dragons — my father tells me she's a natural *kirith-a*. Now this bright blue beauty is the daughter of Teshgazzadar from the ayku host. When she flies close to Sol, the light glitters off her scales and blinds the onlooker. Be careful to avert your gaze if she ever flies past."

The dragon was laid on its side, sleeping, and Etezora appreciated the handsomeness of the beast despite herself. Yet she couldn't help visualising the belly, cut into strips and cooked slowly over a charcoal fire. "I heard these wyrms breathe fire," she said, saliva bursting over her taste buds.

"Some do," Tayem said. "This ability is found only amongst the Agnarim."

"Do you own any?"

"Only two, and they are not old enough to have shown signs of the pneuma-fyre."

"They are still young?"

"Ensutharr is two hundred and twenty one sols — our oldest dragon."

"And he is young?" Etezora's mouth dropped open in disbelief.

"It's a 'she', and dragons live many thousands of sols. I myself have never seen one produce a full gout of flame. Our pygmy breed can sputter a little smoke — but it's a little like a burp — quite funny to watch! Now here is Ensutharr's enclosure. Don't get too close, she's rather tetchy."

Under a thatched canopy, the two girls came upon a deep pit, excavated out of the shale. The bottom was impossible to make out after being in the bright sunshine, but as Etezora's eyes adapted to the gloom, she detected a serpentine movement in the depths. A shifting in the shadows revealed itself to be the tilting of a gargantuan, elongated head. The aged wyrm blinked a rhombus eye at her, and it was as if it sensed Etezora's enmity because a deep rumble as of tumbling boulders emanated from its massive chest. The Cuscosian stripling took a step back, holding her hand over her mouth.

"It's so ..."

"Magnificent, isn't she?" Tayem finished Etezora's sentence.

*Loathesome.*

"Oga, her mate is in the next pit. You'll like him, he's —"

"All of a sudden, I feel a bit faint," Etezora said. In truth she was close to spewing up the little food she'd eaten. Such was her revulsion of the beast she'd seen. Reflecting on her reaction now, she wondered how this instinctive dislike could have sprung in her. After all, she liked what others would consider more detestable animals such as the salyx. Perhaps, it was the sense of exclusion, the notion she wasn't part of Tayem's world, and could never be.

"Can we go back outside? I don't know quite what's come over me."

Tayem looked at her with concern, touching her arm, and the gesture warmed Etezora, restoring her sense of companionship and of being wanted. "Of course. Our dragons are a shock when you first lay eyes on them. I will show you something that you will stomach better."

*She imagines I am frightened of her wyrms? Does she think I am such a trembling flower?*

Tayem clasped her by the hand and led her out the other side of the enclosure to another building. Inside, the temperature was considerably greater, and sweat broke out on Etezora's skin.

"It is so hot in here," she said, wiping her brow.

"The braziers are kept burning all day and all night."

"Why?"

"The dragon eggs need to be kept warm."

"Eggs? Don't the mothers brood them like a chicken would?"

"That happens in the wild, but we have need of the dragons continually, so we remove the eggs and place them in these brood boxes."

"I'll wager the mothers are not too happy with that."

Tayem sighed. "No, they are not. But they get over it." She pointed at a series of wooden arks stacked like shelves. "Here they are. Would you like to see them?"

In truth, Etezora had had her fill of dragons and wished to play a different game where she could engineer a necessary victory over the Dragonian girl. She had held court for too long already, and Etezora was driven to monopolise the situation again.

"Here, this one is close to hatching." Tayem unclipped a wire-mesh door at head height and opened it. "Here it is."

"It is smaller than I thought," Etezora said. In fact the light arctic-blue egg was twice the size of a plains-fowl but compared to the beast Etezora had just seen, it was difficult to believe these wyrms could grow from such a miniature genesis. She looked again at Tayem, observing the wonder and devotion on her face; and if jealousy could be likened to an animal, then at that moment it had become a cobra in Etezora's heart.

"Let me hold it," Etezora said.

"No, it is not allowed," Tayem responded, disapproval written on her face — and it was this expression that goaded Etezora to do what she did next. With mischief playing on her painted face, she reached in before Tayem could stop her and grasped the egg with both hands. The warmth of it conducted into her hands, and she swore she detected the movements of the wyrmling within.

"Etezora," Tayem exclaimed. "Put it back before you harm it."

The daughter of Cuscosa ignored the Dragonian princess and turned with the prized possession cupped in her hands. "Tell me, Tayem," she said, "our friendship is special is not?"

"I ... yes, of course. You know I enjoy your visits."

"But surely it's more than that? I'm always excited when we spend time together. It's so boring in our castle listening to my teachers drone on all day, being forced to learn how the court is ruled. The rare hours we spend together are such a blessing. It's the same for you, isn't it?"

"Umm. Yes," Tayem said, sounding far from convinced. "But you must put the egg back. No one is allowed to touch them, let alone a — "

"A what?" Etezora exclaimed, the rage building within. "You were about to say *commoner* weren't you?"

"No. You are from the Royal House of Cuscosa. You are as much a royal as I."

"That's what you're taught to say. But we know that you think yourselves above us."

"That is not true. I respect you, Etezora."

"Do you respect me more than your dragons?"

Tayem's face fell, and Etezora knew from her expression that she would never be held in Tayem's affections as much as these precious wyrms. A cruel smile cracked Etezora's face as she held the egg up then let it go.

She remembered how Tayem's expression turned from incredulity to horror as the egg fell through the air and smashed on the hard rock floor. The shell shattered into a dozen pieces to reveal the remains of a yolk sac and the struggling, embryonic form of a pale dragon. Not a word was said as they watched its premature form wriggle and writhe, its mouth opening in silent agony.

Tayem found her voice first. "Etezora, what have you done?"

The Cuscosian wasn't quite sure. She couldn't articulate her motives at the time, but she did remember feeling in control, a sense of being able to manipulate events and the pleasure derived from seeing a living thing in torment. It was not so much the dragon — that was satisfying enough — but the look on Tayem's face was exquisite. In many ways, mental suffering could be more satisfying than witnessing physical pain.

"What I have done," Etezora said, "is shown you how pathetic your dragons really are."

She did not see the blow come, but the force and speed of Tayem's punch felled her like a tree. The humiliation endured while sprawling in the dust of that hated sweltering enclosure remained with her to this day.

Events followed in rapid succession. Tayem made no attempt to cover for Etezora. The Cuscosian princess was stunned for several minutes, and when she came to she was surrounded by the Dragonian Royal Guard and the concerned faces of her parents.

"What is the meaning of this?" she heard her father saying. "I demand an explanation!" He addressed his comments to Tayem's father, forgetting all decorum that it was Jezethorn who ruled. She soon disabused him of this notion.

"Is this how the House of Cuscosa honours our patronage? By killing a royal dragon?"

The wyrmling lay dead in the dust. Etezora supposed it had not survived long, exposed and vulnerable, unable to breathe with its underdeveloped lungs.

"It is simply a paltry egg," her father said, turning to the matriarch, "but your daughter has assaulted a member of the royal household."

Jezethorn might have been but a woman in the Cuscosian king's eyes, she was a force he would come to regret provoking. "You do not realise the seriousness of the crime *your* daughter has committed here. The dragon eggs are sacred, offspring of the gods that fly. You would try to make small of this?"

The King was taken aback by Jezethorn's effrontery and his eyes widened. It only took him a moment to recover, however. "I'm sure it was just an accident. You can't expect —"

"That's not what Tayem told us!"

"Can we honestly believe the word of a thug?"

"What did you call her?" Jezethorn's eyes flashed, and she took a step toward the King, her imposing frame offering an unquestionable threat. The Cuscosian Guard responded immediately by unsheathing their swords and pointing them at Jezethorn. Things escalated from there as the Dragonians lowered spears at the entire entourage, their faces grim and determined.

"Jezethorn, Cotarth, please. This is no way for royalty to behave." Zodarin stepped forward, raising a placating hand. "Lower your arms, this matter should be resolved responsibly."

The wizard seemed to have a calming presence, despite his bizarre appearance. It was as if a wave of lassitude emanated from him. "May I suggest we refrain from accusations and harsh words?" he said. "Your Majesty, please deliver your complaint by official transcript to the House of Cuscosa." He spoke directly to Jezethorn, his amber eyes mesmerising in their regard. "We will consider this ... affront with due gravity. Equally, there are counter-claims that should be borne in mind. But I'm sure some form of compensation or agreement can be made.

Jezethorn looked as if she had been caught in a moment of trance as she stared, wide-eyed at the man. Then she shook her head. "How can we have any confidence you will not cover this matter with the dust of speculation and delay? We demand justice."

"And it shall be given," Zodarin said, "but we will gain nothing from a brandishing of weapons. Tempers are running high. Let us resolve this in an amicable manner."

He didn't give Jezethorn a chance to respond but turned to Cotarth, the Cuscosian King. "We should decamp back to Castle Cuscosa. Let the noble Donnephon come to terms with their loss. There is also the matter of Etezora's wound."

Such was the wizard's mesmerism that Cotarth acquiesced, albeit with some token bluster and protestation.

Etezora nursed her split lip, accepting a cloth from her mother and noting the expression of smouldering disgust on Tayem's face as she was guided away from the confrontation.

Twelve sols later and here she was, the events of that day having determined the fate of their two nations in the intervening time. She stared at her reflection again in the looking glass on the wall, noting the scar on her lip inflicted by Tayem's cowardly blow. As she touched it, the impact from the punch seemed to impinge itself on her again as if it had only occurred yesterday.

*Soon there will be a reckoning, dragon schjek, and no amount of appeal to your wyrm's so called godhood will do you any good.* She reached for a sliver of darastrix rhyaex and chewed on it slowly. As she did, she imagined it was the belly flesh of Tayem's wyrm and a frisson of pleasure spread from her tongue to her stomach.

"My Queen," said a guttural voice from behind. "The sorceror wishes to speak with you."

She turned to see Tuh-Ma's hunched form loitering at the door. Behind him, the stork-like wizard loomed.

"What now?" she retorted.

Zodarin pushed by the blue-skin as if he was inconsequential. "My Queen, I have credible reports of a plot from my sources, it is important that you hear."

"A plot — against me?"

"Against the whole House of Cuscosa."

"The Dragon Riders? They have only just perpetrated an attack on our food supply, and now this? How laughable that they have requested a meeting to discuss a diplomatic way forward."

"Strictly speaking, the threat comes from your own people."

"What?"

"An underground movement of dissidents. They plan to strike tomorrow evening."

"Where?"

"The royal store rooms and repository. They have discovered a secret way in and conspire to set light to the buildings."

"Pah! They lack the resourcefulness. It is just talk."

"Not so, they have enlisted the help of a contingent of Dragon Riders."

"Tayem's doing! Does her effrontery know no bounds?"

"I believe she knows nothing about it. The conspiracy is aided by her sister, Mahren."

Etezora considered Zodarin's statement, weighing up its import. "So, Tayem has lost control of her close family."

"Indeed. But I know who our plotters are, it will be a simple matter to apprehend them."

"Then we should do so right away. I will have Eétor take the matter in hand."

"Very good, my Queen."

The wizard made to leave but Etezora had another question. "I trust our troops' movements are going ahead as planned?"

"They are," Zodarin replied.

"What word from your spies? Has there been any suspicion raised amongst the Kaldorans and Dragon Riders?"

"A little. But word will not get back before our planned strike. We will have caught them unawares. But once again, I ask if you are sure you want to provoke the Donnephon at this stage?"

The Hallows rage crescendoed within. "Do not

question my strategy, Zodarin. I have spoken." As she uttered the words, she felt a compulsion descend, and the crackling of energy in her brain. The wizard's eyes widened and she sensed an immediate invisible push-back from the man. *He dares!*

"My Queen?" He asked, his amber eyes turning a shade of crimson.

Caught by surprise, Etezora could not answer.

"Will there be anything else, my Queen?" The wizard invited.

"I — no. That will be all."

The wizard left, leaving a puzzled Tuh-Ma standing in his place. For a creature of limited intelligence, the blue-skin was remarkably perceptive of his Queen's shifting emotions.

"You should let Tuh-Ma crush his skull, Mistress. Does he not know his place?"

Etezora looked benevolently at her loyal servant. "That is very helpful of you Tuh-Ma, but Zodarin is a useful asset at present. I am curious nonetheless. How does he get his information?"

~ ~ ~

A few buildings away, the answer to Etezora's question was discussed between Eétor and his spy, Grizdoth.

"The cat has been on the prowl again?" the Praetor asked.

"Yes," replied Grizdoth. "The wizard's powers have clearly gone beyond that of walking in the Dreamworld."

"And you say the condition leaves him weakened?"

"Only temporarily. But the lessening of his power is great. He is vulnerable while recovering."

Eétor smiled. "I thought he looked a little peaky this morning. You have done well, Grizdoth. Here, take your payment and keep a close eye on him. Meanwhile I must speak to Etezora about our battle plans."

Grizdoth looked out of the window and saw the Queen's messenger approaching. "It looks like she wants to speak to you too," he said.

"Always at her beck and call," he said with irritation.

"Your time will come again, Master," the obsequious man replied.

"Not soon enough," Eétor said, "not soon enough."

## 20

# SOUL GRINDER

---

There it stood, fully twenty spans high, a gleaming machine made from steel and precious hard woods felled from the flanks of the Dragonian Vale. It barely made clearance against the roof of the reverberant limestone cavern, deep in the heart of Magthrum's Rockclave chamber.

It had not been easy transporting such a massive contraption from Cuscosia. Nalin had employed ten of his loyal workmen, and under cover of night, hauled the separate pieces of the tunnelling machine onto carts pulled by mighty rockbulls. These huge woolly beasts, supported by strong backs and legs trekked at a ponderously slow rate, but they could carry ten times their own weight. Nonetheless, five day's journey was a long time and they were confined to travelling by starlight to avoid detection. Cuscosian troop-movements meant they had to be constantly vigilant for fear of discovery. There was also the risk that Nalin's absence would be noticed. This was diminished somewhat by the war preparations that seemed to preoccupy the Royal Family; yet even Nalin's privileged position would not protect him if he had to explain this peculiar train of beast, stonegrabe and machine. Perhaps his days at Castle Cuscosa were numbered given the open hostility Etezora was showing towards Magthrum's regime. How long before her ambitions moved beyond that of defeating the Donnephon?

Despite all this, they had arrived safely within the borders of Kaldora, and for days now Nalin's stonegrabes had meticulously followed the detailed plans the engineer had drawn up. They assembled the large cylindrical body within this cavernous vault, mounting it securely on a chassis of six wheels.

Now, on this demonstration day, the engineer proudly looked on at his masterpiece. He did not hesitate in naming it his greatest invention. All the more impressive that it had been designed, built and shipped to Kaldora right under the noses of the arrogant Cuscosians, a race too preoccupied with lust for conquest to detect the Kaldoran's mischief.

Magthrum had called the machine the 'cave-crawler', but in his heart, Nalin had named it after his son, Palimin. Indeed, the name could be found etched discreetly onto the fuselage, just below the conveyer mechanism. It was a fitting tribute. After all, it was during that fortuitous moment, distracted by his son as he spilt the fyredrench, that the crowning moment of his design had been realised.

"Nalin, we're waiting," Magthrum bellowed.

"Very good, Fellchief," the startled Nalin said. He observed the throng of stonegrabes assembled in the cavern and realised they extended back fifteen ranks or more — if indeed 'rank' was the correct term for such a motley collection of monstrosities. *Krut, all of the Regev stronghold must be here.* The thought inflated the balloon of his pride still further.

Nalin cleared his throat and began his lecture. *Keep it short and to the point,* he reminded himself. *These stonegrabes have the attention spans of gnats.* "Behold the cave-crawler," he began. "A noble grinding machine designed to cut a circular tunnel through the Imperious Crescent limestone. Such mining is normally an arduous task for our esteemed regiments of stonegrabes." He paused at this point and indicated the grime-covered troglodytes shuffling around the machine's wheels. "I'm sure you will welcome an easing of your hammering and chiselling won't you?" This was greeted with affirmative grunts and whoops from the mob. Nalin speculated as to their fate. If the unpredictable sub-class could no longer be usefully employed in the mines then what future did they have? *I guess they would taste nice served up with a hearty helping of root vegetables.*

Nalin turned his attention back to his overview, stepping up to the front of the cave-crawler. Towering above him, a good twenty spans in diameter was a cutting disc. "This impressive rotating tool is where machine meets native rock, so to speak," he said, estimating that one could fit three Kaldorans across its width. "As you can see, it is strengthened by these eight steel spokes set into a central hub. But their function isn't just that of support. Diamond-cutting heads are set in each spoke at regular intervals. As it turns and grinds against the rock-face, the collapsing rubble falls through the disc spokes into this large funnel. This in turn channels the material onto a conveyer belt turned by cables which carry the rock to the rear of the machine here." Nalin was walking alongside the huge length of the cave-crawler as he explained how it worked. He was warming to the task, unable to contain his enthusiasm for the creation. He finished his stroll along the side of the machine pointing out a series of gears and pulleys that were turned by a massive central crank attached to a flywheel.

"Very good," Magthrum said, "but what is that device containing the hoses strapped behind the cutting disc?"

"This," Nalin replied "is what makes the cave-crawler truly revolutionary. These tanks contain fyredrench!"

This announcement drew gasps of surprise and awe from the crowd.

"Dragon-spit?" Magthrum said, his eyes narrowing. "You would make use of such a vile fluid?"

Nalin realised he'd touched on a raw nerve of his Fellchief. The stonegrabe hated anything to do with the wyrms. "Wait until you see what it does," he interjected quickly. "Efficient excavation is best achieved through a combination of mechanical and chemical attrition. I have diluted the concentrated fyredrench into a thin corrosive liquid that can be sprayed from two hoses mounted within the central hub of the cutting disc. As the disc-turning crank rotates, a series of gears drives two pumps which spray corrosive dragon-spit onto the rock in front of the machine. The effect is to weaken the rock sufficiently, allowing the grinding disc to easily progress through the rock strata."

"Mmm," Magthrum said, sounding far from convinced, "fyredrench is expensive stuff. Is there enough of a supply for our needs?"

"That's where having access to Etezora's illicit dragon pens pays off."

Magthrum looked genuinely surprised. "I wasn't aware the Cuscosians bred the wyrms."

Nalin laughed. "They cannot master their behaviour, but apparently dragon meat is a delicacy."

Magthrum nodded. "Perhaps we needn't have drugged

Tayem's wyrms after all — not when exposing the Cuscosians' appetites was all we needed to do."

A loud farting noise cut across Magthrum's observation. It emanated from four squat hairy bipeds built as wide as they were high. They were *Kalti*, a sub-race of Kaldorans that lived deep in the catacombs of Regev, and their manners left a lot to be desired. Several troglodyte miners shuffled away from the creatures, holding their noses. The wretched albino creatures were immensely strong and obedient, but lacked intellect and language, only able to communicate their primitive desires by grunts and snarls. But they were the power-house of the cave-crawler.

The scene was set and Nalin was ready to reveal the full extent of what he had created. He walked around the machine one final time and checked each gearbox. Once satisfied, he signalled to Kalor the lead Kalti to turn the crank.

"*Urah urah!*" Kalor signalled to his team of hulks.

Nalin smiled. He knew the Kaltis would be rewarded well with a feast of stray human flesh from the unfortunates captured while entering the upper tunnel system. They groaned as they took the strain and started to turn their individual cranks. The flywheel engaged and the giant machine edged towards the wall at the back of the cavern. It inched forward and, as it came within a pikiarch of the wall, Nalin pulled a lever engaging the cutting disc drive gear. As the massive disc started to rotate, Nalin stepped across the bridge of the machine and set the sequential pumps in motion. He watched with trepidation as the refined fyredrench sprayed onto the wall ahead. Unperturbed by the scream of a stonegrabe who had strayed too close to the spray, Nalin held his breath as the cutting wheel ground into the rock. Acrid smoke and vapours rose from the front of the machine, causing the crowd to stumble backwards to avoid inhaling the noxious cloud. Several were trampled in the process.

Then, from the midst of the cacophony, there appeared the first signs of smoking carbonate crumbling, and Nalin heaved a relieved sigh.

"More power, more power," he shouted to Kalor. The Kaltis responded and the cave-crawler's speed increased to the cheers of the assembled Kaldorans. To Nalin's surprise, the machine made even quicker progress than his previous test runs, and after it had cut to a depth of twenty spans, he signalled the Kaltis to stop. The flywheel slowly came to a standstill and Nalin dropped the cutting disc out of gear. He then signalled Kalor to turn the crank in the opposite direction, and the cave-crawler reversed back into the main cavern.

When he descended from the machine, the cheering mass of stonegrabes greeted Nalin. Magthrum stood at their head with his hands aloft, applauding the engineer. "Magnificent, magnificent, you have succeeded in revolutionising the way we dig. Break out the flagons and feed the Kaltis. This demands a celebration."

Nalin's pride knew no bounds and a broad smile spread

across his swarthy face. Several stongrabes scuttled off to fetch ale and a supply of jarva-leaf pipes, while Magthrum slapped Nalin on the back as they inspected the circular cut in the cavern wall.

"You are indeed a magician Nalin my friend, your machine cuts rock like an axe through flesh."

After sharing a couple of pipefulls of jarva, Magthrum changed the subject of the conversation to the Cuscosians. "So Nalin, what news of the Cuscosian kruts?"

Dragging himself back to reality Nalin focussed his mind, took a swig of ale and turned to Magthrum. "Speedwill delivered my last message, yes?"

"He did indeed. The Rock Council discussed the developments, and concluded we should play a waiting game. Let the Cuscosians and Dragonians fight each other. It will be a short-lived battle as we all know the Dragon Riders are no match for the might of Cuscosia." Magthrum swallowed over half a tankard of ale in one gulp and ordered more. "From what you report," he continued, "only that interfering wizard suspects our involvement. You should keep watch on him. He has a reputation for deceit."

"He is a strange one, yes. Not to be trusted. He sides with Eétor, and there is clearly an understanding between them. I even think they may be plotting against Etezora. But I suspect there is something deeper going on. It is as if the sorcerer has eyes everywhere. I fear I must take care in this, as the mistrust within the ruling house means I am not above suspicion despite my privileged position. In fact I should hasten my return or my absence might raise further concern." Nalin lowered his tankard and met his Fellchief's gaze. "You should also beware. I have no direct evidence, but the Cuscosians are massing troops on the north-west road. Could they have desires beyond acquiring new mines in Kaldora?"

"An invasion? It would be madness for them."

"Yet a madness *has* taken hold of Etezora. You should see the purple fire burn in her eyes when she is roused."

"You have given me food for thought, and by putting heart and soul into your work have proved yourself to be a great servant of Kaldora, Nalin my friend. But before you leave, another question: could the rock grinder help us burrow a way beneath the Cuscosian Castle? Could it be used as a weapon of war?"

Nalin took another long drag from his jarva pipe and closed his eyes. "I feel you ask too much. We would have to start digging near to the castle. It might be possible on the western side where the underlying strata are calcareous, but we could well be detected."

Magthrum's eyes flared with the same purple hue Nalin had observed in Etezora's, and a dark crackling energy seemed to fill the air causing the engineer to stop swigging his beer and stare dumbfounded at his FellChief.

"I ask too much, do I?" Magthrum said.

"Fellchief, I meant no — "

"Hah! I know I ask a lot of you, but this is your next mission, my friend." As quickly as it came, the darkness shrouding Magthrum's countenance disappeared and Nalin exhaled with relief. Magthrum took a considered sip of his ale, and then said, "Find a weakness in the Cuscosian defences so the Rockclave can plan our next move. Perhaps we will need to strike before the Cuscosians breach decades of treaties. I sense things are changing, and we must act if we are to avoid oblivion."

Nalin nodded. The day had started with so much promise, but now he felt a twinge of fear that even his jarva-leaf would not assuage. He looked at Magthrum one more time, and then gazed ahead into space. The engineer could sense changes that spread far beyond the impositions of the Cuscosians. Fear for his hard-won position bloomed, but more importantly, fear for his family and future.

# 21

# ALL FLAGS FALL

————

Brethis woke soon after dawn; sleep proving impossible after the previous evening's events. The tryst with Mahren would have been enough to lighten up his existence, but the dissidents' assembly exceeded all expectations. He'd been amazed at the commitment and determination shown by his fellow conspirators. Not only had they rounded up a dozen or more capable men and women, but each had made the preparations required of them — even taking the initiative when encountering obstacles. The only reservation was Mahren's hesitation in providing exact details of the personnel she could provide. But Brethis wasn't downcast by this. He understood he was asking a great deal from her, but the Dragon Riders' presence was more of a morale boost than a requirement for the success of their operation.

The previous get-together of the dissidents had seen him striving to convince the group their cause had a chance of gathering momentum, but last night's gathering had seen such an eagerness for action that they had determined to bring forward their strike to the next evening — tonight! It was an audacious move, but Brethis had planned the attack for months: observing watches of the guard, checking that the Ravager's entrance to the castle was undiscovered; gathering torches and portable combustible materials. He had shared the plan, apportioned roles and ensured that everyone knew the part they had to play. Most importantly, he had prepared notices and communiqués that would follow the attack, letting all in Hallow's Creek and the city of Cuscosa know that the dawn of rebellion was upon them. Cuscosa was pre-occupied with its preparations for war and the summit with the Dragon Riders. This was the ideal time to strike.

He quietly exited the simple cottage he had called home all his life and surveyed the awakening township. Sol-Ar had just cleared the Wareshall foothills to the north-west, and not even the violet Hallows haze could darken his mood. He heard marketeers setting up stalls in the town centre, and the knocking of a cobbler's hammer. It was the ensuing hive of activity that would provide cover for storing weapons and materials for tonight's roguery.

He paused for one more moment and an unbidden image of Mahren entered his mind. He saw her rich fawn-like beauty as he remembered it, lit by candle flame from the previous evening. Her face was bronzed by wind and sun, and he recalled the touch of her close-cropped, honey-coloured hair. Now, in the light of morning he dared to think they *did* have a future together — once Cuscosa was overthrown. Their union would be the first of many, a forging of alliances and families building a just and prosperous society.

These notions added speed to his step, and he was so focused on his goals for the day that at first he did not notice the commotion from the suburbs he had just left. Shouts in the distance could easily have been the early morning continuance of a local family feud, the shriek of a child the result of a simple physical admonishment from a tested parent. But when Brethis caught the clash of steel on the wind, he spun round.

Black smoke over in the Lutek quarter — the district in which he lived. *Is Hallow's Creek under attack?*

He sprinted back the way he had come, passing astonished townsfolk paused in their mundane duties. As Brethis rounded the corner where his family's abode was located he stopped in his tracks.

*This is no attack from without. Those are members of the Praetorian Guard.*

He recognised Eétor's Captain, Chalmon ordering his soldiers to drag villagers from their houses. Some instinct made him retreat behind the wall of the cottage next to him.

"Take them to the town centre," Chalmon growled, "Eétor wants a public spectacle made of them."

Before Brethis's horrified eyes he saw his own mother, father and sister thrown to the floor and their home put to the torch.

*Where were Eryx and little Jeramin?*

The answer to his question came when he saw Eryx appear at a bedroom window, thick smoke already billowing past his petrified form. "Momma, Papa," he cried, "the stairs are afire. We can't get out!"

Brethis's father rose to his feet. "I must save them," he said. "They're trapped." His plea was answered by a cruel swipe to the head from a guard, sending him sprawling to the floor.

"Your children are forfeit, as is your house, peasant. They will burn as an example to all who would seek to rise against Cuscosa."

"No, you monster," cried his mother. "My baby is still inside. Let us rescue her."

Chalmon considered this for a moment. "I will let you, if you tell me where your cur, Brethis has gone."

Brethis's mother greeted this demand with a dismayed look. "If I tell you, will you spare his life?"

"Of course. Are not the Cuscosan Guard known for their mercy?" The Captain said with a sneer.

His mother hesitated, but then the cry of a tormented infant rose from the house.

"Momma," Eryx shouted in desperation, "I've got Jeramin but I can't get to the bottom floor." He held up the screaming child in his arms, both of them edged with amber from the flickering flames behind.

"Drop her to me," shouted the mother, scrambling to her feet.

Chalmon responded by placing his booted heel on her back, pushing her face into the dirt. "Your eldest," he breathed menacingly, "where is he?"

The mother was beyond discretion. Brethis could see the sheer panic born of a mother's protectiveness written across her face. "He set off for the market twenty minutes ago, said he was helping Jan with his stall."

Chalmon nodded and then removed his boot from the woman's back.

As Brethis watched, he attempted to gauge his options. His parents were doomed to certain death, of that he was sure, and by the looks of the neighbouring houses and palls of smoke beyond, his fellow dissidents were heading for a similar fate. Reason left him and he made to run at the nearest guard. Perhaps he could surprise him, wrest the sword from his hand. But a strong grip on his upper arm held him back. He turned to see Oathair, his face grim but determined.

"You can't save them," he said, "there are too many guards. We must flee and re-group."

"Krut off!" Brethis snarled. "They will butcher my family."

Oathair held his gaze, pathos and anger in his eyes. "I know. They have already put my wife and bairn to the sword."

"I'm not going to stand by and — "

A blood-curdling scream snapped his attention back to the dreadful scene playing out in the street. He observed with abject horror how Chalmon withdrew a broadsword from his mother's torso. He'd impaled her where she lay. Another guard swung his mace at the helpless father, dashing in his skull with a sickening crunch.

Shock and anger immobilised Brethis, numbing every muscle and chilling his bones. *This cannot be. It must not be.* Yet the morning had not had its fill of tragedy.

Up above, desperation smeared Eryx's face. He took a final look behind and then climbed on to the window sill. His clambering was all the more difficult as he tried to keep hold of Jeramin in his arms, and it was this that doomed his escape bid. Brethis's gaze was drawn away from the brutal murder of his parents to his brother, Eryx, as he launched himself from the window, the infant in his arms. Eryx's trailing leg caught on a creeper, pitching him forward, sending him head first toward the unforgiving ground. The baby, torn free from his grasp sailed to the ground, bouncing once then lying still.

Brethis turned his head away, tears streaking his face. He shook with rage and grief, but Oathair held on to him firmly. "We must go. They are lost; but if Chalmon finds us, then their deaths will mean nothing. Your loved ones have bought us time. We must use it."

Brethis felt bereft of any powers of decision, the shock still leaving him transfixed. So Oathair imposed his own choice. He dragged his disconsolate friend away from the building and headed towards the woods.

"If we can make it to the forest, then we have a chance," Oathair said. "My life as a woodsman has blessed me with knowledge of the secret trails, and we can take shelter in the place we set aside for this purpose."

Brethis succumbed to Oathair physically removing him from the scene. His limbs possessed no volition of their own, and it wasn't until he had been dragged to the next street that his senses returned, albeit in a surreal swim of emotions.

"What of the others?" Brethis said in a cracked voice.

"They know the back-up plan. Those that survive will make their way there."

A greater horror impinged itself now. "The planned attack — Mahren will be walking into a trap," Brethis exclaimed.

"The plan is in ruins," Oathair replied. "She will have to take her chances."

"No. I will not lose her too."

Oathair pulled him up behind a hay cart, gripped him by his shoulders and locked him with a stare of steel. "We have suffered a rout. Return if you want, but you face certain death. You saw what they did. Our best chance is to get away and try to get word to the Dragon Riders." He released Brethis, indicating he was free to choose. "I'm heading for the woods now. Stay if you must, but recognise that I have lost much today too. You said our cause would require sacrifice. Now you see how immense that can be."

He glanced back at the burning houses and then jogged off into the woods.

Brethis looked back also, realising that his decision would determine whether he died now or simply postponed his demise. Either way, his was a path of suffering. With a sheer act of will he uttered a raw, agonised cry, and sprinted after Oathair.

## 22

# ONE BLASPHEMY TOO MANY

———————

"This is ill-advised," Cistre said.

"It is a formality," Tayem replied, "I am under no illusion as to the outcome of this farce."

"Then why undertake it? We know what the Cuscosians have done, and they obviously have no intention of honouring the treaties. We should crush them while we have the chance."

They had secured their dragons in the shade of the garbeeches a mile hence, a condition of the Cuscosians. The Donnephon had in turn demanded their own conditions: no troops within a mile radius and a maximum of five representatives from each faction.

Tayem scanned the blasted plain, site of the Gigantes Decimation and focused on the approaching Cuscosians. Even at this distance she recognised Etezora's haughty gait. Flanking her was the unmistakeable form of her wizard and the shambling form of the troll. *No Eétor?* That was only sensible. To put all members of the royal family in a potentially treacherous situation was foolhardy — which was why she'd insisted Mahren remained at the Vale despite her protests. Her sister seemed preoccupied in any case, although what could weigh more heavily on her sister's mind than this meeting was beyond Tayem.

Tayem felt the Hallows light burn behind her eyes at the sight of the approaching Cuscosians. Here on the exposed plain, site of the Cuscosians ultimate blasphemy, the scorching rays of Sol-Ar seemed to augment the stirrings within. It was like a cauldron, driving her to a boldness and concomitant rashness that was difficult to contain. She was also aware of other enhancements: her arrows flew with an unerring accuracy on the practice range; the Hallows influence increased her strength and dexterity with the glaive tenfold. Most of all, the Hallows seemed to transfer to Quassu. He was swifter in the air, more easily stirred by an aggressiveness that threatened his usual bounds of discipline. This would have disturbed the Tayem that ruled before her baptism at Dragon Ash, but now it filled her with a confidence that spurred her toward whatever consequence followed this meeting.

She stepped forward, striding across the charcoal

coloured dust of the plain under which was buried the charred remains of a thousand Gigantes. Cistre, Darer and two of her most adroit guard followed, surprised at her sudden action.

"Tayem, tread carefully," Cistre said. "We should let them come to us. Show them it is they who should be subservient."

Tayem didn't answer; the Hallows compelled her. It was all she could do not to raise her glaive and charge at her most hated of enemies.

"My Queen," Darer said, his breath already coming in short gasps from their sudden activity, "remember the strategy we discussed. We will gain nothing from defiant accusations. If they are guilty of this affront, they are unlikely to accept responsibility — even if they admit it. They must think they can gain something from this negotiation. We must play on this."

"Yes, you told me," Tayem said, impatient at the man's interference.

*He was your father's recommendation for chief advisor,* the voice of reason said in her head.

*Be decisive,* said another whose voice echoed from a darker place in her mind, *bleating sheep will not command deference from the Cuscosians.*

When they were ten paces from each other, both parties stopped. A hot wind gusted from the east, whipping up swirls of dust from the ash-black plain prompting Etezora to secure a scarf across the lower half of her face. Tayem noted how an abaya swathed the Cuscosian Queen from head to foot, as if the sun was abhorrent to her. All that could be seen were her eyes, glowing like purple coals. Tayem's own inner flame ignited in unholy recognition of its counterpart.

*Perhaps the schjek burns in sunlight,* she thought with amusement. Her attire made it impossible to read Etezora's features, and although her wizard's pallid face was fully exposed, he was equally impossible to gauge.

"You called this meeting," Etezora said, Tayem allowing her to open the discourse, "but I must admit had you not, I would have demanded it."

Tayem placed one foot further away from the other, adopting a confrontational stance. "You are used to making demands," she said, Hallows energy sizzling behind her eyes. As she uttered the words, she thought she caught a sisterly response in Etezora's own visage.

Etezora cast her eyes around. "I find this location oppressive. Tuh-Ma, erect the parasols and seats. If the Dragon Riders are intent on meeting in this wretched basin of land, then at least we can afford ourselves some comfort."

Tuh-Ma dropped a heavy pack to the floor. Three large screens were strapped to its sides. Her guards helped him erect the sun-shields and seats while she stepped closer to the Donnephon representatives.

Tuh-Ma had laid out garishly coloured cotton blankets on the floor for the Dragon Riders to sit on, but Tayem knew what the Cuscosian Queen had in mind. Seated as they were, it would put the Cuscosians on an elevated platform. Appearances and posture were everything. Tayem considered stating she would remain standing, but this would make her appear awkward. Instead, she approached a seated Cuscosian official.

"Would you mind?" she said, feeling her Hallows stare fix him. He was caught unprepared, and the influence stirred him to respond without thinking. Before Etezora could interfere, he rose and offered Tayem his place. She lowered herself into the seat and indicated her entourage to kneel in the traditional Donnephon pose. Cistre, as usual, stood behind her, sword held loosely to her side.

Etezora was clearly ruffled at the switching of power, but brushed it off. "It has been three sols since we last met, Tayem, more than ten since the last Feast of Shaptari. A shame it is no longer honoured by our peoples."

"It was an expensive veneer," Tayem replied, "and your cowardly actions on the last occasion still remain unforgiven."

Darer leaned towards Tayem. "Diplomacy, my Queen," he whispered with earnestness in his tone.

Etezora sniggered; a childish response, but Tayem suspected it was designed to irk her for circumventing the seating ploy. "But I don't suppose you requested this meeting just to bring up past trivialities."

"No," Tayem replied, quelling the Hallows-lust and its admonishments to slit the schjek's throat where she sat.

She remembered Darer's words and decided to go through the motions of the Dragon Rider's strategy. "There are greater matters that have transpired. I imagine you know of what I speak."

"Indeed there are," Etezora said, "but state your case. This should be amusing."

Tayem sat upright. Up to now she had refused to face Etezora directly, but she now turned so the Cuscosian Queen couldn't ignore her. "Very well. It is not enough that we endure your exorbitant costs for grain and the imposition of your exactments, but we now have to suffer an outright attack on our royal mounts."

It was Etezora's turn to sit up straight. "What are you prattling about?

*What was this?* Tayem had expected a cool, snide response alluding to Etezora's complicity but giving nothing away. Yet she seemed genuinely surprised.

"The poisoning of our dragons, of course. Don't pretend you know nothing of it."

Etezora let out a patronising laugh. "You are deluded. This 'poisoning,' did it occur before or after you attacked our wagon train at the Queenswater Ford?"

"And you accuse me of delusion?"

Etezora's upper lip curled. "Was it a delusion that found twenty dead, skewered by Dragonian glaives or pierced with your arrows?"

"You play games with me. Is your purpose simply to fabricate stories as a pretext for further acts of savagery?"

"Your Majesty," Zodarin interrupted. "We seek an explanation for the attack, that is all."

Tayem scowled at the wizard. His mesmerising eyes shifted with amber sorcery, and she felt again — as on that final Shaptari Feast — his power of persuasion coming to the fore. Only this time it was reinforced by something else, a more subtle, underlying yet familiar enchantment.

*Gods, are we all being used by the Hallows?* But Tayem had her own powerful defences now, and this sorcerer's subterfuges would not work.

"Well?" Etezora said. "Has guilt silenced your tongue?"

Tayem recovered herself. "I'm choosing my words carefully," she replied. "Darer here, thinks I should be diplomatic and allow you to state your case. Well, you've done that, and all I've heard is fabricated allegations. I am here to tell you the Dragonians have had enough." She stood abruptly, Hallows motivation spurring her beyond any pretence of statecraft. The rise to her feet was immediately met with a drawing of arms from Etezora's guard. The escalation was quick. Cistre brought her sword to bear, holding the gleaming point against the nearest guard's neck.

"Hold!" Darer said. "This serves no purpose. Lower your arms — everyone." He stared at each combatant one by one and although advanced in sols his manner and voice carried an unexpected authority.

Etezora smiled and nodded at her guards, who obediently stepped back and sheathed their swords.

"Speak, old man," Etezora said, removing the muslin veil from her face, "what path do you offer through this impasse?"

Darer looked at Tayem who was still smouldering with fury. He raised his eyebrows, and she reluctantly took her seat again. Clearing his throat, he continued. "Both of us have our grievances, yet so far we have heard little evidence. Perhaps if we all related the reports we have received?" He inclined his head and looked at the Cuscosian Queen. "Your Majesty, if you would like to start?"

Etezora offered a practised, half-genial scowl and there was something in that expression that alarmed Tayem. Now that she could see her full visage, it was as if the Hallows bond communicated a shared understanding. But this was no communion of kindred spirits, more an oppositional firing of contempt, and Tayem detected a current of triumph in Etezora's mask.

*Why would she feel elation in this morass of argument? Unless ...*

"You ..." Tayem uttered in dismay. "This has all been a ruse, hasn't it?"

Then they all heard it, the rumble of approaching cavalry. It seemed to arise from the east, the west and the south.

"Treachery!" Tayem cried and sprang up, grabbing her glaive and turning to face the Cuscosian entourage. Cistre adopted a defensive stance while the opposing guards similarly readied their weapons.

"You're too late," Etezora sneered. "This is the last day of Dragonia's insufferable impudence. Prepare for defeat."

All along the horizon, above the shimmering heat haze, hordes of mounted spearmen galloped, appearing like a swarm of desert scorpions. "Take them," Tayem said, but the Dragonians had no opportunity to press home their attack. Zodarin raised his arms, an other-worldly smile on his face, and the sand released what appeared to be vents of magenta-coloured vapours. Tayem found her vision obscured such that she couldn't even make out anyone other than Cistre at her side.

"Battle formation," she ordered. "Be prepared for their strike from the mists."

Yet an attack never came. It seemed the Cuscosian guard were as blind as they were.

"My Queen," Cistre said, "we must retreat. The horsemen will be upon us in minutes."

Tayem raised the garbeech horn to her lips. She carried it at her side at all times, strung by its leather strap. The instrument declared the alarm with three shrill blasts. "Our guard will be with us in minutes. Darer, Gundin, Staithrop are you there?"

There was no answer from them. The thunder of hooves was deafening and Tayem guessed they would be surrounded soon. Thankfully, the vapours were dispersing as the plains wind gusted with greater ferocity.

Through a hole in the purple cloud above, Tayem saw the welcome sight of two dragons descending, their defiant roars carrying across the air and filling her with strength. This mixed with the white hot fury of Etezora's betrayal and the magma of Hallows energy.

Then, as the final wisps of Zodarin's cursed vapours disappeared she saw an alarming sight. Darer and her two guards lay face down in the sand, blood sinking into its hot blackness to mingle with that of the long-dead Gigantes.

"No" she cried, her anger that of a raging beast. "They will pay," she said to Cistre.

"A thousandfold, my Queen," Cistre said, her back to Tayem's. "But I fear two against a thousand is not favourable odds."

Etezora and her guard had vanished, subsumed in the multitude that now bore down on them. Clouds of ash billowed around so that only the front two ranks of horsemen were visible. The dust swirled with greater fury as a great down-sweep of wings was heard overhead.

"Tayem," Mahren's call came from above.

*What was she doing here? Was following orders beyond her?*

Yet, despite this irritation, Tayem welcomed the sight of Jaestrum's regal form and Quassu, ridden by Elohaim, following closely behind.

A cowled horseman broke ranks from the approaching horde and bore down on them. He lowered his spear and aimed it at the vulnerable Dragonian Queen. Tayem wished she'd brought her bow, but she had other means at her disposal. She eyed her attacker, blinking rapidly to remove the grains of sand that conspired to obscure her vision.

*Just a few more seconds.*

The rider was accomplished, the spear hardly wavering despite the jolting of the galloping armoured horse, but he was unprepared for Tayem's manoeuvre. She ran at the horse, leaping to the side at the last moment and then launching herself upwards on the rider's unprotected flank. Hallows fury powered the thrust of her glaive into the rider's abdomen, gutting him before he could swing his own weapon from the opposite side. With inhuman strength she pulled the glaive back and spun in mid-air to land back on her feet, ready for the next attack. Cistre had dispatched two further riders before the dragons were upon them, their forelimbs raised in defiance at the oncoming Cuscosians.

The Cuscosian riders circled them, and in the maelstrom of stamping hooves and sweeping reptilian wings Tayem found it impossible to pick out a suitable target. What she *did* see was several of them raise crossbows and aim at the Dragonians.

"Up here," Mahren shouted from Jaestrum's back, holding out her hand to Tayem. She did not hesitate, jumping upward and clasping her sister's hand as a hail of arrows shot through the air. Several rebounded from the dragon's hide while others embedded themselves in Mahren's protective shield. Cistre had joined Elohaim on

Quassu's back and Tayem felt a momentary pang at not being able to ride her own mount, but it was of no consequence. They had to retreat. Elohaim directed Quassu to sweep his claws through the innermost circle of horsemen. The bludgeoning might of the blows raked through their ranks, felling ten or more of them.

The horsemen reacted with skill and moved further away out of the dragon's range, although the task was difficult given the swarm that accumulated behind.

"To the skies," Mahren cried, "we must fly while they are on the defensive."

Jaestrum roared and the Cuscosian horses whinnied in terror, several of them rearing, sending their riders to the floor to be trampled in the dust. With a mighty down-sweep, the dragon rose, and within seconds both beasts were aloft. Arrows arced from below but bounced harmlessly of the dragon's bellies, and as the Cuscosian army became pinpricks on the ground Tayem tried to pick out Etezora's form — to no avail.

"I will find you, Cuscosian haujen," she swore out loud, "and even your wizard will not shield you from my wrath."

# 23

# A THUNDERSTORM IN THE HEART

---

"You promised me that schjek's head on a pole," Etezora screamed, her fury directed at Zodarin and her guard. She stormed from one side of her tent to the other, sweeping a myriad of objects from every horizontal surface and kicking at any furniture within range of her petulant feet.

Zodarin winced but appeared unruffled. "Your Majesty, it is a temporary setback. Already our troops march on their paltry army. It is only a matter of time before she is in your hands.

"But she was exposed on the plain. We had the

advantage; and what of you chizbaxes?" She turned to the two hapless guards who weren't sure how to react. "Was it too much to ask that you bring down those schjeks when the mists rose?"

"We did not see, your Majesty," one protested, "her adviser and guard remained stationary and it was easy to pick them off, but the Queen and her bodyguard were as swift as leopards and disappeared from our eyes."

"Aarh!" Etezora screamed again, and this time she grabbed the one who had spoken by the throat. The man gurgled as he tried to draw air into his lungs, shocked at his Queen's uncanny strength.

"Etezora," Zodarin said, "forgive me ... your Majesty, have mercy on these would-be assassins. To be fair to them, they did well to cover our retreat from the Dragonians. Tayem and her bodyguard might well have posed an immediate threat once the mists dispersed."

Etezora's eyes blazed purple for a second, then she released the guard who stumbled back and fell against a table.

"What news of the battlefield? Did our simultaneous assault catch the main body of Dragonians off-guard?"

"A messenger has just returned from the Pelethan slopes," Zodarin replied. "The Dragonians were indeed taken by surprise, but they melted into the forest once they realised they were outnumbered. Fifty were slain but they will now re-group."

"Imbeciles," Etezora cried. "Can I not count on anyone?"

Zodarin pursed his lips. "I did council against this course of action. The Dragonians are renowned warriors, and they are on their home-ground. If we are to win this conquest, then we need to employ cunning and strategy. They are not easy pickings like the Gigantes your fathers eradicated."

"Do not presume to question my decision," Etezora said, "I have told you before."

"Your Majesty," Zodarin said, his eyes shifting from amber to magenta again, "this setback does not affect our overall strategy. We prepared for this, remember?" He lifted a tumbled goblet, poured some red wine from a skin and handed it to Etezora. "You could use this," he said. Etezora acquiesced to his calming influence despite herself, listening as he outlined once again how the next act would unfold.

~ ~ ~

Cistre wished she could offer something to bring solace to Tayem, but as usual found her comforting skills sadly lacking, and nothing seemed to bring a salve to the raging Queen. So as ever, she stood close, offering protection and a reassuring presence. She had seen Tayem's fury erupt before, but this was different. As she shouted orders to her captains and rallied the Dragon Riders to arms, she noticed how an indefinable darkness enveloped her, sending an icicle shower of foreboding down Cistre's spine. She wished she could embrace her, absorb the turmoil she was enduring, yet such actions were beyond her station and she dreaded the consequences of revealing the depth of her feelings. Yet she could dream ...

"Where are Sashaim and Aibrator?" Tayem shouted across the dragon pens. "They should be here, ready to lead the ayku host.

"Tayem," Mahren said, stepping forward with a sheepish look on her face. "There is something I must tell you."

"What? Make it quick, we have no time to waste." Without giving her chance to answer, she turned to Gemain and issued further orders regarding the defence of Palace Dragonia and the possible evacuation of the populace.

"Sister, please hear me," Mahren persisted.

"Yes, yes. Get to it."

"Sasheim and Aibrator. The reason they are not here is that I sent them to Hallow's Creek."

Tayem stopped her flurry of activity. "Why in Sesnath's name would you do that?"

"There was an uprising planned. I promised the dissidents our help."

"Help the Cuscosians? Are you mad?" Tayem swept the

hair back from her forehead, holding her fingers against her temples, trying to contain her exasperation.

"I ... I thought it was in our interest to aid them, given Etezora's recent deceit."

"*You* thought? Committing Royal troops is a matter for the Queen. You know this."

"Yes. And I'm sorry. But I couldn't leave Brethis without word or reason for our Donnephon's absence. He depends on us."

Tayem looked more carefully at her sister. "This Brethis. It sounds like you know him well."

"He leads the dissidents; gives them hope, and he is a natural leader. Everyone looks to him."

"He is more than that to you," Tayem said, the Black Hallows rising again, this time in response to a basic human emotion. Something she would not even admit to herself. "You have feelings for this Cuscosian, don't you?"

Mahren didn't know what to say and looked down.

"How could you allow yourself to be so foolish? No doubt he was leading both you and our guard into a trap. You have let emotion cloud your judgement, and this is quite apart from the vs' shtak ruling that forbids matches between our two houses."

"He is not allied to Cuscosa. He detests them. That's why he's leading a rebellion!"

Tayem strode across the room and picked up her bow and quiver. "I have no time for this. Our kingdom is on the brink of destruction and here you are love-struck and tongue-tied. You will join me in the Imperial Host. Cistre will lead the ayku. Now, to arms. Cast all thought of this Brethis from your mind, I need you fixed on the battle."

With that, Tayem closed down the conversation and jogged to the dragon pens where she found the dragon-hands tacking up the full contingent of beasts.

"Have you woken Ensutharr and Oga?" she said to Sheldar.

"My Queen, Mahren was able to rouse Enthusarr, but even her skills could not wake Oga. He rests in the bosom of Sunnuth, as he has done for the last ten sols. Who knows when he will awaken from deep sleep?"

Tayem sighed. They now had forty-eight dragons, eight of them still sluggish from their poisoning. *Will it be enough?* She prayed it would. Their only advantage was superiority in the skies. She turned to Mahren, who had followed her from the palace and was donning a bronze battle helmet. "I have changed my mind," Tayem said to her. "You shall ride Enthusarr. She has not flown in sols and will need an expert hand at the reins."

"But Jaestrum, he — "

"He will be safe in Beredere's hands," Tayem cut her off.

She mounted Quassu and addressed the throng of Dragon Riders. "Mount up," she said. "The armies mass at the western border, we must fly to them before they engage, otherwise there may be nothing to save." As she spoke, she was aware the Donnephon looked at her in awe, and not just a little fear. She had always commanded

245

respect, but this was something more. *What?* Then she noticed the surrounding air. It had turned deep purple, tinged with an abyssal blackness, and she was at once charged with great purpose and confidence. It quenched any remaining reservations concerning the Hallows. This was no time for faint-heartedness. Darer had counselled against embracing this power, but look what happened to him. The memory of the recent loss fired her rage still further, and she sensed it transmitted to Quassu, who opened his maw and uttered a deep roar that reverberated through her frame. The dragon call elicited a response from the other mounts, who joined in the magnificent bestial chorus. Above it all, the rumble of Enthusarr issued forth, so loud it shook the ground.

Mahren struggled to bring Enthusarr under control, but with a few gentle words in her ear she calmed the ancient beast and prepared for flight. This was the first time Tayem had seen Enthusarr in her full glory. She estimated the dragon measured eighty spans from snout to tail with a wingspan of some seventy-five spans. *A sight to cause the Cuscosians to fill their breeches with mord,* she thought. *If anything can turn this day, then she can — as long as she remains obedient to Mahren.*

"To the skies," Tayem cried and with a mighty unfurling of his wings, Quassu rose into the canopy of the violet heavens.

~ ~ ~

Zodarin sat cross-legged on his dais. The tent he occupied was located in a fissure just to the west of the Dead Zone, a half-periarch from the battle-front. It was vulnerable to attack if found. This was unlikely given its position, and the fact that one of his bewitchments concealed it further. He closed his eyes and immediately felt the draw of the Dreamworld. The transition was brief, the acceleration aided by Black Hallows energy, and as he materialised in etheric form, he rode a wave of unbridled ecstasy. This was like nothing he had experienced in his long existence before, as if the Hallows fed on his desire and swelled in influence from the very depths of Varchal. He wondered if Etezora felt this too as she rode on to the battlefield; and as he did so, he suspected her overthrow might have to come earlier than he'd originally planned.

*Enough*, he scolded himself. *There are more urgent matters to attend to this day.* He'd cautioned Etezora against marching on the Dragon Riders so soon, but despite its premature nature he was reasonably confident they could press home the victory.

The wolvern form he had so often taken would not suffice for the act he planned. No, he would adopt his undisguised true nature. If another entity observed him then what of it? He was supreme, and with the Augur's execution, he sensed his power elevated to yet greater heights. He would need every pebbleweight of energy at his disposal to accomplish this feat.

First he had to find his quarry. Perhaps that might not be too difficult given the circumstances. Today he was not merely the hunter, he would be a warrior in wurunwa vargachic, the dream battles — and he knew he was more than equal to the task.

~ ~ ~

Etezora stooped down and handed Cuticous to her courtier. "Feed him on the hour, and do not let him out of his cage," she instructed. The courtier acknowledged her, and removed the salix, successfully cloaking any disgust he may have felt at the creature's touch.

Etezora pulled herself upright in the saddle of her war stallion and surveyed the battlefield. The Donnephon foot-soldiers were arrayed in clumps on the edge of the forest, almost difficult to discern due to their sage and olive-green attire. Yet her scryers had determined they numbered no more than some fifteen hundred. She was in no doubt there were a similar number hidden amongst the trees and undergrowth behind, but this still left them at half the battle strength of her army. Strategy would dictate they draw the Cuscosians into the woods. Out on the plain, the Cuscosian cavalry and sheer weight of numbers would command the day, but under arboreal cover, the Dragonians would pick her soldiers off with their cursed arrows. Then there was the threat of the dragons. *Be that as it may,* she thought, *Tayem has not reckoned with what I have in store for them.*

In the meantime, Etezora would employ a battle-plan to confound the Donnephon defences. She ordered the advance of the cavalry at a slow trot, and then handed over command to Dieol, her general. She wanted freedom to immerse herself in the butchery with the blue-skin at her side. Together they had a unique banquet of slaughter to partake in, and she didn't want the distractions of commanding troops to interfere.

The Cuscosian dragoons advanced, the front rank trailing chasquite bushes behind them, raising black sand into the air to form a dense impenetrable cloud. Etezora spurred her mount on once they had gained five minutes on her Royal Host. Sandwiched between her and the cavalry trundled a score of Nalin's war machines, catapults capable of launching a deadly payload provided they were set up within range. A contingent of the stonegrabe's engineers accompanied the troops in order to operate the machines

The advance proceeded without event, Etezora's only concern being that, just as her katapultos were concealed, the Dragonians response to the attack could not be gauged. Once within five hundred strides of the treeline, the war machines halted and the gunnery engineers pegged them into the soil with spikes as tall as a man. At this distance she heard the winches creak as the katapultos arms were swung back to launch position. Spherical bundles coated with flammable tar-gum were quickly hoisted into the cups and set alight. The Cuscosian captains had debated whether they should wait until the dust had settled before launching the fire balls, but then they would lose the element of surprise. Instead, they would take the risk, and fire their flaming missiles at the positions noted before their advance.

The captain gave the order and Nalin's engineers loosed the first volley. The fireballs sailed above the dust cloud and arced down toward the tree line. Before they had landed, the catapults were rewound and loaded with freshly lit missiles. Beyond their battle-line, the sound of the first volley's impact was heard. Nalin had designed the fireballs to spew ground-oil from metal gourds upon impact, spreading fire amongst any unfortunate to be within range of the strike.

"They might simply burn up dry earth and wood," said Dieol. A traditional Cuscosian cryolin helmet hid his face, but Etezora pictured his scarred features screwed up as if he was chewing on a wasp.

"No need to be pessimistic," she said. "Let us wait until the dust clears."

The second volley had landed, and with the dust settled, Etezora saw gouts of flame licking the air some twenty spans high. Then, above the crackling of fire, Etezora detected a pleasing sound — the cries of pain and anguish from Dragonian mouths.

Etezora smiled. "One more volley, you said."

"Yes," Dieol stated with a lift in his tone. "Then we charge."

The general saw the katapultos cranked back, and the arms subsequently released. At least this was true for most of the machines. Three however seemed to have developed a fault. When the arms of these machines had clicked into their retaining position, they unexpectedly broke free before the bombardiers could load the tar-gum missiles. One struck a soldier, smashing his skull to pulp as it swept upwards.

*An acceptable mechanical failure?* Etezora thought, *I wonder.* She turned to face the silent blue-skin at her side. He was mounted on a giant boar, its tusks tipped with iron. "Are you ready for the play?" she said to him.

"Tuh-Ma is always ready for his Queen," he replied, and slurped a string of dripping saliva back into his mouth.

After another minute, Etezora could wait no longer, and she instructed Dieol to order the charge. The Hallows fire burned strong now, and the Queen felt like it would erupt from every pore. Indeed the air around her seemed to turn dark, shifting from violet to black in a shimmering halo about her form. *Perhaps the Hallows has appetites of its own,* she thought. *Well eat your fill,* she exhorted, *there will be enough spoils for all.*

She dug the spurs into her stallion's flanks and it sprang forward. As far as the eye could see to either side of her, the Cuscosian cavalry thundered forward as a fearsome wall of metal and pounding hooves. The only break in this galloping mass occurred where the war machines were bypassed; and as these were cleared, Etezora saw her first glimpses of carnage. The Dragonian vanguard had largely held their ground — to their detriment.

*Fools,* Etezora mused with glee. *The Dragon People's bravery and stoicism are ever their downfall.*

Scattered amongst the still flaming balls of death lay the twisted, burning bodies of her enemy. Hallows innervation heightened her senses, and despite the confusion of sensory information that abounded, the satisfying aroma of scorched flesh filled her nostrils. Still more pleasing were the cries of the wounded and dying. They would be put to the sword later, but for now Etezora's sights were set on the fleeing flock of foot soldiers.

"Cut them down," she shouted, "before they retreat into the woods."

The most fleet of foot reached the forest line, but the remainder were overtaken by an initial wave of Cuscosian cavalry. Some — the bravest — turned to face their pursuers, and although they brought down a handful of mounted Cuscosians, they were quickly overcome and shown no mercy. Scores of running warriors were speared and butchered within paces of the wooded sanctuary. Etezora herself skewered three of them and Tuh-Ma's boar gored a further five, trampling their eviscerated corpses underneath its trotters.

Yet it was not enough. Etezora yearned to be close to the

enemy as she drew life from them. The Hallows demanded it, and this had become akin to a sanctified undertaking, one she embraced with every malefic granule of her being.

It was not to be. Dieol shouted the warning before she was completely overcome with battle lust. "My Queen. No further. The Dragonian archers will be within range!" He signalled the trumpeter to sound her horn, which she did with a piercing blast that brought the cavalry to an ordered halt.

"Stand fast," a captain cried. "Foot soldiers — advance."

Between the stationary horseguard, a regimented advance of infantrymen ensued. Once they had threaded their way through, they reformed in orderly fashion. The troops bore heavy armour and held large rectangular shields above their heads, the front rank wielding theirs in a vertical position. The resulting formation resembled an armoured lizard marching forward. Such a defence tactic was not premature as within seconds they had become the target of Dragonian archers, whose arrows rained down by the hundred, clattering off the bronze screen the Cuscosians had erected.

Despite the close-knit formation, many shafts infiltrated the tessellated shields and found their mark through eye-slits and joints between armour.

"Curse their falcon-eyed archers," Dieol said, "at this rate they will wipe out our troops. We should re-group."

"No," Etezora said, "I have something else in mind." She was tantalisingly close to the prospect of slaughter, and such a lust was worth the risk of performing her next intention. "Get me into those woods and I will bring their archers to an end."

"How will you do this, Your Majesty?" Dieol replied, "I cannot countenance the risk."

"Do as I command!" Etezora turned to her general, Hallows energy flaring from baleful eyes leaving him with no will to gainsay her.

He quelled his astonishment and called for nine soldiers, who trotted up bearing shields edged in curled tyrannium steel. "Link shields round our Queen," he ordered. "You are under her command."

The section of shield-bearers closed around Etezora and Tuh-Ma clipping their custom-built carapace together so that the individual plates of steel overlapped. Any loosed arrow would simply strike the feet of the soldiers, and these were armoured with heavy greaves and sabatons.

Within the primitive armadillo, Etezora sniffed at the odour of battle-sweat and mannishness. The close proximity of Tuh-Ma just added to the miasma. "Advance on the woods," she said, "and do not stop once you have broken the tree line. I will tell you when it is safe to break ranks."

The armadillo moved forward, and within twenty strides it was met with a clattering of arrow heads. The sound was deafening to Etezora's over-sensitised ears, but she did her best to block out the cacophony. Before long she would bring their pathetic counter-attack to an end.

As the shuffling Cuscosians entered the tree canopy, Etezora saw the ground darken, and she relaxed inwardly from the relief at being out of the blazing sun's direct light. As commanded, the shield-bearers continued the advance, stepping more warily now as the ground was covered in all manner of roots and undergrowth. Etezora gauged the sound of the arrows overhead. They were less in number now, and she wondered if perhaps the Dragonians had realised their attempts were coming to naught. The Hallows augmented her hearing, and she detected the *thwang* sound of the longbow release, comparing it to the strike of the arrowhead on the shield.

*They are directly overhead, and what is that?* Underneath the sound of archers shifting their positions in the trees and the rattle of arrow strikes there rose the sound of feet sprinting over the forest floor some five hundred paces ahead.

*I must act now before we are engaged in a melee. We are close enough.*

At last she could unleash the full force of her power, and she commanded the sergeant at the front of the armadillo to stop. Overhead, her acute senses made out a swarm of Dragonian archers. She released etheric tendrils of Hallows energy that bypassed the armadillo roof and wrapped themselves around the bodies of the archers. Although Etezora could not see them with her physical eyes, their forms existed as signatures in the air, and the whips of Hallows fury pulled them from their perches. Ten

... twenty ... thirty of them were ripped from the branches and either dashed to the floor or slammed into tree trunks breaking multiple bones in their bodies. And still the body count rose. Etezora laughed with glee and orgiastic pleasure as more and more of the devilish tentacles launched themselves at the hapless enemy until their bodies were piling up on the forest floor.

She lost count of the number of slain when she sensed a fatigue encroach on her mind.

*There is a limit then to this wonderful talent. Still — it is enough.* She withdrew her tendrils and instructed the squad of soldiers to prepare for an imminent attack from enemy foot soldiers. "Tuh-Ma, signal to Dieol that he should advance. I have dealt with the archers."

It was true. No more arrows rained from above, and as the shields lowered, the carnage she had caused was all too apparent. Any remaining archers out of range of Etezora's anemone-like assault had fled into the canopy, while all around stricken victims lay in a tangled mass.

Tuh-Ma lifted his head upwards and let out a piercing shriek. It would carry to the waiting Dieol and give him leave to advance the Cuscosian infantry. He lowered his misshapen head and grunted, "You have vanquished them, My Queen. See how the dead stare at the sky, as if the very air betrayed them."

Etezora did not answer him, yet she shared the blue-skin's elation. *This power is incredible. Surely nothing can stand before me.*

The approaching Dragonian infantry had slowed their pace, and from the look on their faces it was obvious they were hesitating before launching an all-out attack. The sight of such havoc must have been enough to cause even the bravest warrior to pause.

Etezora's euphoria was tempered only by the thought she had passed the zenith of her energies — at least for today. Still, there was enough left in her to mount a defence.

The thrashing of foliage behind marked the entry of the Cuscosian dragoons and the sudden incursion goaded the Dragonians into action. They took cover behind trees or disappeared into the undergrowth, their remaining missiles occasionally shooting forth and downing selected targets. However, the loosing of missiles was the marksmen's undoing. It revealed their location and Etezora was clear to release Hallows tendrils, pulling them from cover and depositing them at her feet. Tuh-Ma was quick to take the initiative and picked up the stunned bodies, banging their skulls together or simply crushing the life from them with his gargantuan embrace.

Dieol joined them as his thunder-troops jogged past and advanced on their elusive quarry. "Stay close, Your Majesty. One stray bolt and you will fall. Let us press home the attack, and our soldiers can overwhelm them with weight of numbers now their archers are defeated." He stepped in front of Etezora, shielding her with his body and, seemingly for the first time, took in the poses of the dead Dragonians lying in their piles of mangled corpses. "By Phydon, what has happened here?"

Etezora's face broke out in a secret smile. "I told you I would deal with them. But rest assured, I haven't finished yet."

~ ~ ~

Tayem's hair whipped behind her as Quassu beat the air with his wings. Mahren flew close beside, her sullen face all too obvious to ignore. They had covered the thirty periarchs from Wyverneth at high altitude in only a half hour yet it seemed an age. Every minute that passed saw Tayem's fury increase. As her host of dragons approached the edges of the wasteland that was once Lyn-Harath, she grew dismayed at what she saw.

The Cuscosians were advancing like a swarm of loathsome arachnids, assaulting the western border of the Dragonian sacred forests. She saw fires burning on the plain and the dead and wounded littered like refuse over its surface. The closer they got, the more it became apparent that what they witnessed was fast becoming a rout — and her loyal troops were on the receiving end. It wasn't certain how they fared underneath the canopy of trees, but if the number of Dragonian slain was any indication, the prospect was not good.

*Time to change that,* she thought.

Cistre's ayku formed a separate squadron further to her

right while Beredere's dull-coloured contingent of skeredith made up the bulk of the force behind.

They could do little to aid their forces in the forest itself, but the hordes that still pressed on the forest border were quite another matter. She gestured with her hand in a downward motion, signalling the Imperial Host to lead the whole cohort into a dive.

Quassu pulled in his leathern wings and Tayem tightened her harness, leaning forward to lower the air resistance. To ride the wind like this was always a thrill beyond measure, but to understand that she was leading the largest mobilisation of dragons since the end of the Marrowbane war added a sense of gravity. The ancient maxim of vs' shtak, learnt in infancy, echoed in her mind:

*If a dragon you provoke, 'twil end in fire and smoke.*

The prospect of a firestorm was remote. Enthusarr had yet to breathe her first gout of fire, but they could still inflict untold damage. Their approach meant they would appear to the Cuscosians diving out of Sol-Ar's gare. The opportunity of surprise would be with them — so she hoped. As long as the dragons maintained discipline and did not shriek their rage.

As Quassu fell like a stone, the wind blew so strong in her face it caused Tayem's eyes to water. The Cuscosian figures blurred in their outlines and she gave her trust to Quassu and his protective transparent eyelids to guide them to the enemy. The noise of dragon-wake was too loud for him to hear anything she said, but a gentle tweak of the hair sprouting from a crevice in his hide would tell him the attack strategy.

When he was but one hundred spans above the heads of their quarry, Quassu spread his wings and he pulled from the dive, sweeping over the bewildered cavalry, legs extended. His bulk, smashing into their bodies threw many from their horses while his talons picked up half a dozen riders from their saddles. Tayem drew her bow as Quassu ploughed a furrow through the sea of Cuscosians. She loosed ten arrows before the dragon finished his sweep, each finding its mark, guided by Hallows witchery.

As Quassu rose to the heavens again, dropping the screaming Cuscosians to their deaths, she took a moment to glance back. The combined fury of forty-eight dragons was causing carnage amongst the Cuscosian troops. Particularly jaw-dropping was the impact of Enthusarr. Mahren had goaded her to carry a heavy, rounded boulder from the heights of the Whispering Mountains and she had released it to roll like an unshaped dice, crushing a dozen Cuscosians before it came to rest. Her massive bulk overwhelmed scores of soldiers, the abrasive hide flaying outer layers of human flesh to the bone as it brushed against man and horse alike. The impact of that one dragon was devastating.

Tayem knew the next sweep would not deal as much death. The Cuscosians would scatter or dig themselves into cover on the edge of the forest, but their strike had served its purpose. The onslaught of Cuscosian ranks on her ground troops in the forests had been stemmed, and they now had a chance to fight back on their own terms.

Quassu approached the enemy on a trajectory more perpendicular to the forest this time. His passage killed less of the Cuscosians but she brought down more with her bow, loosing arrows every second in a supernatural blur of motion.

*This is incredible. Something impels every muscle, every fibre. I feel invincible.* And as she emptied her second quiver, Tayem beheld the purple colouration that accompanied the flight of each shaft. One, she noticed, passed right through the chest of one victim and embedded itself in the neck of another.

*What bewitchment possesses my archery?*

But she knew the answer, deep in the marrow of her bones — and she was lost to its insidious influence.

Quassu stalled his motion and alighted in the ebony dust of the plain just shy of the forest border. If the Cuscosians thought they were safe in the woods, they had reckoned without the might of a dragon's tail. The skeredith were smaller, better employed in picking off further exposed soldiers on the plain, but the Imperial Host scuttled round and whipped their tails against the bachar trees and thisthorns, felling them and crushing the complacent troops dug in amongst the undergrowth.

That was not the end of it. Once the imperial dragons

had inflicted their carnage, they gave way to Cistre's ayku, more serpent-like in appearance with long, emerald snouts. They slunk forward, their riders sheltering behind the stunted legs of the beasts. Ignoring the pinprick strikes of Cuscosian crossbow bolts, they lifted their heads then brought them forward, opening their snouts and releasing jets of caustic saliva that showered the hapless bowmen.

*Fyredrench.* One drop of the corrosive liquid was enough to burn through the strongest armour and eat its way into the vulnerable flesh beneath. Many received a complete dousing by the effluvium, reducing their bodies to a heap of blackened, smoking sludge in seconds. To die in this way was not a good death.

A roar to Tayem's left indicated that Enthusarr had made good her gamble to rouse the dragon from her slumber. Her forelimbs, moving like colossal iron pistons, battered the trees, pushing the Cuscosians deeper into the forest and sandwiching them against the lithe, elusive Dragonian wood-warriors. Tayem knew her *forest-ghosts* would capitalise on the Cuscosian panic.

*This is turning the tide,* Tayem observed with grim satisfaction. She stepped out from Quassu's shadow, confident the Cuscosian archers were on the run and jogged forward to the woods, glaive in hand.

*If you're in there, Etezora, I am coming for you.*

## 24

# A CHANGE OF FORTUNES

---

The complete transformation to his true form was a moment of great magnitude for Zodarin. It might be his spirit-form, but he knew with prophetic certainty that it was also his core essence in the realm of the Near To. *There will be a time for transcendence,* he reflected, *but for now this is more than enough.* He gazed at his transformed body, marvelled at its strength and vitality. To mortals it would be grotesque, but they were limited in their vision and appreciation. To him this was beauty incarnate, bequeathed on him by his progenitor. His skin glistened in the Dreamworld glow, absorbing the air along with his alien lungs to oxygenate haemolymph that coursed through vessels as thick as pipes. All at once he understood his previous yearning to be bathed in water, to be submerged and to luxuriate in its cold embrace. This was his culmination — his *becoming*.

He strode forward, remarking that his steps were no longer those of the furtive wolf, but the regal stride of a lord — Ith di wurunwi. His heightened Hallows perception had located the quarry, and there was an urgency in his pursuance. He had a numinous sense that something was amiss in the battle waged on the plain of the Near To, and his workings in this realm would be pivotal.

He had sensed them on previous sojourns in this realm, always dispersed and unreachable due to their nature and lack of activity. But now they were gathered, concentrated in one place, performing their dance in a manner that sent ripples through the realm of dreams.

He ascended a small incline, and once he stood on the crest of the hill, he beheld them in their true glory. They moved gracefully, regally in this bowl between the hills. Their scales flashed blue, green and scarlet and for a moment they mesmerised him. He understood the ultimate obligation of the hunter completely now — to respect and dignify, even as one contemplated the death of one's quarry.

*Consider your actions*, came the voice next to him. He was surprised that it had taken this long, but at last he was confronted with the form of the Spirit Guide, astral yet imposing in its presence. The creature resembled some hooved animal, yet possessed scales and certain avian features. He had never encountered this being, yet knew of its existence from Wobas.

Zodarin smiled, knowing that the inward expression did not translate to his form's outward features. *I have planned my stratagems for many decades. Do you seek to avert what is to come?*

The Spirit Guide turned to him and fixed him with a gaze that would have challenged even the off-worlder's mesmerism. *There is a cost to every endeavour — whether high-minded or low,* it said.

*Indeed there is,* Zodarin replied, *but the Black Hallows changes everything, and we both know how it has swelled in influence these past days.*

*You cannot see everything, off-worlder.*

*I know what you are doing,* Zodarin said, *now stand aside. We both know you cannot stop me, and the time has come.*

The wizard didn't wait for a reply but surged forward down the hill toward the dragon troupe. He was the current, the swell of the tide, the irresistible essence of the *amioid.*

He projected his limbs as he closed the distance, and though it was an unusual sensation, it was also preternaturally familiar. Multiple tentacles uncoiled in a similar manner to Etezora's ethereal Hallows fronds and they whipped toward the nearest dragon, constricting around its neck and chest, asphyxiating it as it struggled to the floor.

The others turned to face the threat, bringing their senses to bear; but they were engaged in battle on another plane, distracted and therefore weakened. Even as the first dragon took its last gasps of air, further tentacles unwound and snared two other dragons. Zodarin could sense the life essence removed from the beasts as they died and wondered how soon their demise would translate to the Near To.

As he waded through the throng, listening and revelling in the roars of pain and anguish from his quarry, he rode a wave of exhilaration. It was augmented by purple Hallows energy such that he deemed himself invincible.

Then he noticed it. When the fourteenth dragon fell — the largest of the troupe — there was a diminution, a sapping of force. He staggered for a moment then recovered himself. *There must be enough to complete the execution,* he thought. He struck out at an iridescent dragon, but this time when he brought it down the fatigue caused him to stumble.

*No. I would slay my due!*

But he could not deny it. If he continued, then he risked the dissipation of his core. As he lifted himself up, he saw the Spirit Guide observed all that transpired and, though he couldn't be sure, there was a glistening on its cheeks, as if it wept.

*Curse your self-righteousness,* Zodarin said. *One more. Just one more,* he implored whatever higher gods there might be.

As if in answer, he saw a smaller dragon, limping and separated from the rest, rooting about on the periphery of the dance. *A runt?* It would have to suffice. He closed the distance and bore down on it, summoning the last of his energy into flailing tentacles. The diminutive beast looked up too late, yet where Zodarin expected to see shock and horror, he simply observed resignation and sadness. *Die then, pathetic wyrm,* he hissed, and wrapped his tentacles around the thing's neck.

But the wyrm-avatar was not to die this day. Zodarin felt it like an injection of malignancy — one touch that would change his destiny, an infusion of pestilence transmitting itself from the beast. He cried out in dismay and pain as he stared at the dragon-avatar's visage.

*What is this?*

An avalanche of fatigue then consumed him, draining his essence with a poison plague, and as he slumped to the floor, he heard again the words of the Spirit Guide.

*There is a cost to every endeavour.*

~ ~ ~

Blood drenched Tayem. It formed a slick glaze on her skin, penetrating into the crevices of her leather armour and coagulating on her cuirass and glaive-shaft. Yet still she did not desist. Her blade, edged with a crackling violet glow, hacked through arms, pierced bellies and sliced flesh. It seemed nothing could arrest her destructive swathe as the surge of power within her body buoyed her up. Cistre fought close by, slashing her victims with two-bladed efficiency, warding off attacks to Tayem's flanks and rear. At times they fought back to back, and Cistre's undying loyalty seemed to cement itself on that battlefield. It extended beyond the oath she had taken sols ago, becoming something even more solemn and transcendent. Through the flurry of flashing blades Tayem caught occasional glances from her bodyguard, glances that spoke of duty, sacrifice and ... and what?

Yet even as the Queen felled her victims, three others rose to take their place, protecting the one who was the object of her bloodthirsty reaping. The Cuscosian Queen was being spirited away by her guard, slumped against her troll as if wounded. *What has happened to her? I hope she is not mortally afflicted — it is I who should put an end to her.*

Tayem roared in anger, a bestial fury that erupted from her lungs — the cry of a berserker.

*Tayem,* spoke someone from some distant place — a voice familiar yet faint.

She withdrew her glaive from a corpse and thrust its vengeful tip into the abdomen of another combatant. The Cuscosians fielded both men and women on the battlefield — unlike the patriarchal Kaldorans — yet Tayem slew both without remorse. They were all but chaff to her reaper's blade.

"Tayem." This time the voice was closer. *Mahren.*

"There is something amiss with the dragons. Can you not hear it?"

Tayem steadied herself on the pile of bodies under her feet and looked back through the greenery.

It was true. Above the clamour of battle she heard gargantuan bodies thrashing in torment, and worse than that: roars of anguish, the like of which had never assailed her ears before.

"We must return to them. They need us," Mahren said. She too had slaughtered many. Cuscosian blood caked the sword she held loosely in her hand, and her shield was dented in numerous places, evidence of a bloody combat that had lasted a mere twenty minutes.

"But Etezora," Tayem said, "she flees the field. If she escapes, then the Cuscosian figurehead still remains."

"Do what you must," Mahren said, battering aside a half-hearted attack from an infantryman with her shield, "but I must go to the dragons." She didn't hesitate, bounding away from the arboreal battlefront and back to the blasted plain.

A sudden weariness came upon Tayem in that moment of pause, as if Hallows energy leaked into the earth from her. Whether it was this or a deeper sense of loyalties, she took one last look at the disappearing Cuscosian Queen and sped back to her dragons.

As she cleared the tree-line again, heart beating in her ears, she witnessed what would come to be known as

Sventar vs' shtak — the Massacre of the Dragons. Five beasts lay motionless in the dust; a further ten appeared to be in their death throes, including Enthusarr. Her torment exemplified the suffering of all the dragons. Her head thrashed from side to side, and a sound like that of a thousand screams rose from her throat.

The Dragon Riders in attendance made futile attempts to calm them. One had been crushed by an ayku, the only visible part of her being a tattooed arm protruding from beneath a scaly corpse.

Tayem rushed forward and grabbed Beredere by the arm. "What is this? How are they slain?"

The Donnephon lieutenant stared at her in shock. "I know not," he stuttered. "It started without announcement. None of the enemy were close, no missiles fired. The dragons simply recoiled as from an invisible attacker."

"It is some fell magic," she uttered, "and we have no defence."

Mahren appeared in front of Tayem, tears mixed with the battle-grime and blood that streaked her face. "Fifteen dragons dead or dying," she said, unable to contain her reactions. "It is an abomination. Who ... what?"

Tayem was not immune to battle-shock, but she was also Queen of the Donnephon, monarch supreme. It was occasions like this, although unprecedented, where it was incumbent upon her to rise above the dismay and panic — and lead. "The Cuscosians are re-grouping from both sides, and they still outnumber us. We must rally." She cast her eyes around and searched to see if Quassu had fallen, every nerve preparing her for a weight she might find impossible to endure. But there, over on the periphery of the annihilation, she spied her mount, valiantly confronting a host of Cuscosian spearmen.

She reached for her horn, wiped blood from the mouthpiece and raised it to her lips. It galled her to sound it, for this meant a recall from the battlefield, an ignominious defeat. But it was the correct strategic decision. She looked at Beredere, who nodded his agreement then sounded the horn — one short blast followed by a longer sustained note.

Dragon and Rider responded with equal immediate obedience, turning their attention from the rapidly reforming combatant groups and rallying to Tayem's side. "Carry what wounded you can," she instructed "and ride your mounts east to Wyverneth. We must consolidate our defence there."

For the most part, the Donnephon responded with cool, battle-hardened efficiency, but some wavered, looks of bewilderment on their faces.

*It is the shock of seeing the royal mounts fall,* she thought. Looking over at Enthusarr's corpse, she saw how her eyes were wide open, fixed in terror.

*What could make such a mighty creature fear for anything?*

She took a hold of herself, remembering her position. "What are you waiting for?" she shouted at those who hesitated. "Are you witless? Don't give me leave to be disappointed in you this day."

"You heard your Queen," Cistre added and pushed a young male toward his mount.

Tayem nodded her approval and helped another Dragon Rider to his feet. Blood streamed from a shoulder wound and his arm hung limply. His face was twisted in a rictus of pain, and Tayem knew that if he survived this day, he would never use the arm again.

Quassu returned to her side, and she boosted the man into the pillion saddle, rising to the pilot position just as a rain of Cuscosian bolts began to descend upon them. Crossbows did not have the range of Dragonian longbows, so the fact that they faced this renewed assault meant the enemy were close.

She surveyed the scene from her elevated position as she detached the large shield at Quassu's side. Jaestrum had survived, as had the majority of the dragons.

*What had caused the invisible assault to cease?*

She could read the shock evident in Quassu's demeanour, the way he looked warily from side to side, as if anticipating another attack from the ether.

"Be calm, my loyal steed," she spoke in his ear, "you shall be avenged. I swear this too — I shall protect you and all your remaining family."

They were comforting words she didn't know if she could fulfil, but it was enough to pacify the dragon, and he rose to the air without further misgiving.

As Quassu gained altitude, she saw the extent of the damage inflicted on her army. The regal dragons lay in unnaturally contorted positions, many half buried in the ground as if they had sought to excavate a way of escape from their unseen tormentors. She hated leaving them like that. They deserved an honourable funeral. Instead, they would become meat for Etezora's abhorrent table. Around them, stricken Donnephon bodies numbered in their dozens. Sesnath knew how many more lay within the woods. The Dragon Riders had lost almost their entire contingent of archers.

*The Cuscosians must not be permitted to take any more.*

She directed Quassu over the woods, sounding the retreat on her horn. Her forest-warriors would know what to do, and she was confident they could dissolve into the undergrowth and make their way back to Wyverneth. Would that she had time to form a robust defence against the advancing Cuscosians, for as she observed the enemies reformed ranks on the plain, they seemed to form a countless number.

*We are confronted with the prospect of our extinction.* The thought brought with it a deep dread in her psyche, and she sought to quell it by tapping into what remained of the Hallows energy. Yet it seemed the dark well's water was empty for now. At least, if not empty, then temporarily drained, awaiting resurgence from abyssal springs. And in that dormant condition, in a state of mind that saw it free from Hallows influence, she felt a revulsion that rocked her to her core.

*I have been fuelled by the same force that motivates Etezora and her accursed House,* she thought. *Was it this that drove my impetuous response during the meeting hours before? Am I somehow partly responsible for this atrocity?* Darer and Cistre had warned her, and she had chosen to ignore them.

Tayem shook in her saddle, the combination of grief, dismay and increasing guilt conspiring to overwhelm her.

*No — I shall endure!*

The command she directed at herself served to pacify the raging emotions for now. Yet the day had not yet seen the full depths of her sorrow. What awaited her and the House of Donnephon would flense their ragged souls to the bone.

# 25

# A MAELSTROM OF DECEIT

———

Like his sister, Eétor was not adept at containing his anger and frustration. So when Captain Torell read out the message conveyed by messenger dove regarding the failure of the katapultos on the Dead Zone plain, he could not restrain himself from smashing his fist down on the throne room table. "What you're saying," he fumed, "is that test firing of the katapultos has identified an *inherent* fault in the firing mechanism?"

"Yes M'lord, it is not what we would expect from usual wear and tear under these circumstances. According to General Dieol, the additional stresses of the repeated firing caused the spring retaining bolts to shear."

"That's all very well Captain but — "

"They fixed the problem, of course," interrupted the Captain.

Eétor glared at him, the man's arrogance at interrupting him adding to his ire.

Torell, realising his indiscretion, apologised. "No matter," the Praetor continued. "I applaud their swift action. But you said it was the same fault on each machine. That is suggestive, is it not?"

"In my opinion — yes, M'lord. After inspecting the remaining katapultos here at Cuscosa, it seems the bolts are constructed from standard steel-cryonite alloy, and should not have failed. However, closer inspection reveals small cracks in and around the fractures."

"You spoke with Chief Engineer Nalin?" questioned Eétor.

"He suggests that exposure to extremes of temperature may have caused the unexpected brittleness in the katapultos."

"But he knew we would use tar-gum grenades. Is he not aware of the engineering implications?"

"He blames our chemical technician. Says his new recipe burned hotter than the previous concoction."

"And you doubt him?"

"Yes, M'lord. The chemist was adamant the tar-gum should have burned at the same maximum temperature. His new recipe simply made the stuff easier to ignite."

Eétor pursed his lips and took a deep breath. "So, the

treacherous stonegrabe is not telling the truth. Is there any proof of sabotage?"

The Captain shook his head. "No, only a strong suspicion. Since my gunners replaced the original bolts, there haven't been any breakdowns."

Eétor signalled his adjutant to step forward.

"Yes Praetor?"

"Summon Grizdoth, I need to charge him with a task most suited to his talents. He is able to uncover things that others miss."

Eétor and Torell were still in conference when Grizdoth entered the chamber.

"You sent for me Lord Eétor?" Grizdoth said. The man slunk forward as if he were a shadow. Eétor would not normally have countenanced employing a southerner. He had an aversion, admittedly irrational, to those whose appearance bore the characteristic signs of those sun-scorched lands, but Grizdoth's skills were invaluable.

"Indeed Grizdoth," Eétor said. "What is your intelligence regarding the stonegrabes, particularly their leader, Nalin Ironhand? Are they to be trusted?"

Grizdoth paused for a moment and responded. "You mean beyond the normal caution we would exercise for such snivelling troglodytes?"

Eétor raised an eyebrow as Grizdoth continued in his inflected tone.

"They keep themselves to themselves," he said. "Nalin

runs the workshops efficiently, and they seem to work hard. I do however suspect subterfuge."

"What evidence?" asked Torell.

"Only circumstantial proof at this point. I am aware Nalin and his minions make more frequent visits to Kaldora Prime. Also, the increased goods we allowed Nalin to take have not resulted in a corresponding increase in profit. It could be the Kaldorans are scything off more than their usual commission. Moreover, the Kaldorans are known to deal in smuggled goods. I wouldn't be surprised if they are shortchanging us and smuggling the excess across the eastern border. In any case, I asked the Captain of the Castle Guard to pay closer attention to the stonegrabes' movements. As yet, however, there is nothing untoward to report."

Eétor raised his hand. "If we could incriminate Nalin in a conspiracy against the throne of Cuscosa, it would be cause enough to bring forward our move against that ale-swilling trog, Magthrum."

"But M'lord," interrupted Torell, "that would mean massing a sizeable army beyond that which bolsters the north-eastern trade route."

Eétor smiled. "Not necessarily. We could accomplish a Kaldoran defeat using a little subterfuge and a small but highly trained fighting unit. But I am getting ahead of myself. Grizdoth, find me evidence of this treachery, if treachery it is. I will need a little more than hearsay to invoke what I have in mind."

"Yes Praetor," Grizdoth said. "I believe Nalin is making a trip to Kaldora this evening. I will take the opportunity to search his workshops once he is gone. Perhaps the other stonegrabes will be more willing to talk without their master looking over their shoulders too."

"Go to it, then. Let me know as soon as you glean further information."

As Grizdoth departed Eétor turned to Torell. "Captain, gather a battalion of your best soldiers. We must prepare for a rapid, strategic strike against Kaldora Prime. If our so-called friend did indeed sabotage the katapultos, then imagine the sense of irony if the very weapons he damaged bring down complete destruction on his people." He picked up a garapple from the well-stocked fruit bowl on the table and took a large bite out of it. "I presume Nalin is unaware of our suspicions?"

"Nothing beyond our displeasure at the failed bolts, no," Torell replied. "But there is one thing I am unsure of."

"Yes?"

"The stonegrabe's reason for sabotaging the katapultos. I know these cave trogs are sometimes mischievous for mischief's sake, but why would he do such a thing? His relationship with us has stood strong for over ten sols."

Eétor pondered the Captain's question. "Maybe he knows more of our plans regarding Magthrum than he lets on. Perhaps he is a purveyor of information as well as goods — despite his oath of allegiance to Cuscosa."

Torell seemed to accept this hypothesis and excused

himself from the Praetor's presence, obviously eager to ready the battalion and machines required for Eétor's prospective plan.

Eétor was left alone in the throne room, and he took the opportunity to seat himself on Etezora's throne. His sister would have raged at this affront, yet she was not present, having engaged in a foolhardy quest to pursue Tayem and her remnants into the uncharted lands of the north. He stroked the gilded arm of the throne and imagined himself seated there as ruler once more. The prospect brought a smile to his face. *It could well be that circumstances conspire to remove her as an obstacle from my path,* he mused. *But now is the time to be patient. I will wait for Grizdoth to do his work, and for Etezora to succeed or fail in her insane revenge battle with the dragon Queen.*

The only random piece in this game of treachery and subterfuge was the wizard. Zodarin had outlived his usefulness, and it was time to make firm plans for his removal. Eétor knew just the characters to call upon for this service, and irony was being heaped upon irony as he contemplated using some of Nalin's fellow countrymen for the task.

~ ~ ~

Nalin discretely packed the last basket of disguised machine parts for the cave-crawler onto his small cart and pulled a tarpaulin over the load. He moved to the front where one of his loyal stonegrabes hitched up two bighorn striders to the yoke and reins.

"Is all ready?" Nalin asked Buzmith Oakstone, his trusted works foreman.

"Yes Master, we will divert the irrigation ducts and flood the workshops tomorrow. Everything will be destroyed. We will make it appear like an accident." A wisp of sadness crossed his face as he confirmed the plan, and it did not go unnoticed.

"You are very attached to the workshops, aren't you?"

Buzmith shifted his weight from foot to foot. He found it difficult to express himself at the best of times. "We've designed and built so much in this place — machines, weapons, wonderful new vehicles. I can't help but mourn its loss."

Nalin put one hand on his shoulder. "My heart weighs heavy too. But our time here comes to an end. Now be sure to make it look convincing. I still think you'd be better making yourself scarce after you've done it. We don't know how the Cuscosians will take this news, and once it becomes obvious my disappearance is permanent, you will be at great risk."

"I will not overstay my welcome. But it is best I remain for now and cover your tracks. It will give you time to complete your journey to Regev with your family."

Nalin looked at his wife and son who now approached, carrying the last of their belongings. They placed them underneath the cart's tarpaulin and seated themselves on the riding plate. "Ellotte hasn't seen the caves of home in many a season," he said to Buzmith, "and Palimin has never entered the gates of Kaldor Prime. It will be a momentous homecoming."

"You'd better be on your way," Buzmith said in a low voice, so Ellotte couldn't hear. "You'll be travelling much slower than usual. Best to put as much distance between yourselves and the castle as you can."

Nalin embraced the prime-charge hand and climbed up to join his family. "You have been a loyal employee, Buzmith," he said by way of farewell, "and I look forward to seeing you at Regev before the month is out."

"Make sure you leave a barrel of ale uncorked for when I arrive," Buzmith replied and lifted his hand in a wave.

Nalin shook the reins, and the striders ambled forwards with a purposeful yet ponderous gait.

"Buzmith will return eventually too?" Ellotte asked. "This holiday of ours is more than it seems, isn't it? We've packed most of our belongings."

"It is," Nalin replied. "Far too dangerous for us to remain here, and I will certainly feel better once you two are safely housed in Regev. Did you include the sealed wooden crates?"

"Yes, they were lighter than I thought. I expected machine parts to weigh more."

He knew she was fishing, but it wouldn't pay to tell her he'd packed them tight with jarva-leaf. His workshop wasn't the only thing he'd miss about this place. Still, he could start another plantation in Kaldora. He had plenty of seeds, and the rich ash north of Lake Dorthun would be an ideal site.

"Palimin is excited about seeing his Grandgrabe again," Ellotte said. She was a prattler, that was for sure.

When Nalin didn't respond, she looked at her husband, no doubt recognising his brooding scowl for what it was. He wasn't telling her everything, but she knew now was not the time to ask. It was also beyond doubt that she'd raise the subject once they were further on their way.

Sol was setting as the cart clattered over the castle cobbles to the maingate, Sol-Ar having disappeared over the horizon an hour earlier. They would make their way onto the main route north via Hallow's Creek to the great limestone gorge that was home of the Kaldorans. Nalin waved to the guard patrol returning to the castle and whipped up the striders more vigorously. The guards accepted his departure for now. He couldn't guarantee that would continue for long.

The journey continued in silence, but after travelling for about an hour Ellotte broached the subject of Nalin's melancholy.

"What is it Husband? Why do we leave so suddenly?"

Nalin looked at the mountains looming ahead but said nothing.

"What has happened to make you behave this way, you have hardly said a word all week, and Palimin thinks you are angry with him."

Nalin sighed. There'd be no stopping her questioning. Perhaps now was the time to reveal all. "I am no longer trusted in Castle Cuscosa," he said. "I overheard the Cuscosian Council conspiring against not only me, but our entire people. It seems their ambitions are not limited to overthrowing the dragon folk." He paused and took a deep breath. "I have, at the request of Magthrum, been gathering information on Cuscosian intentions."

An incredulous look crossed Ellotte's face. "You've been spying?"

Nalin ignored the question and continued. "I also sabotaged the mighty katapultos my stonegrabes constructed."

"But why?"

"I fear they will be used against our people."

The news was too much for Ellotte to absorb. "Oh Nalin," she sobbed. "Why couldn't you tell me?"

"I didn't want you worrying, I would have got you out of the castle sooner, but the Cuscosians' suspicions might have been raised. With Etezora and half her army gone, I needed to engineer our departure more carefully. Tonight should not arouse suspicion, but once I fail to return my stonegrabes may suffer."

"Surely they will leave too."

"I gave strict orders that they do so. I only hope they obey my commands."

~ ~ ~

Back in the castle courtyard, Grizdoth smiled inwardly as he watched Nalin's disappearing form. He'd not managed to hear every detail of Nalin's exchange with Buzmith, but the portion about destroying the workshops was incriminating enough. "At last," he said under his breath.

He left his vantage point and called into the guardroom on his way to Nalin's dungeon workshops. Traversing back to the castle proper took a good five minutes, long enough for Nalin to disappear into the darkness. *No matter*, Grizdoth thought.

He found the Captain with his feet up on a table. "The Praetor requests you accompany me to search the Kaldoran workshops," he said to the man.

The Captain nodded and summoned two guards. Together, they descended the wide spiral staircase to the Kaldoran workshop. Grizdoth was eager to prevent Buzmith's sabotage, and he already feared Eétor's wrath at not intervening in Nalin's escape. He needed to bring his master something substantial by way of mitigation. *Then again*, he thought, *I'm a spy, not a man at arms.*

Upon entering Nalin's workshop, they found it empty, and the darkness prompted Grizdoth to send for torches.

"What are we looking for Grizdoth?" the Captain said, his tone clearly conveying irritation at having to carry out the orders of an outlander.

"Evidence of treachery Captain. I believe Nalin is

conspiring against us, but we need proof to present to Eétor."

"What of the other stonegrabes?"

Grizdoth thought for a moment. "Send the nightwatch to seize them in their quarters. They are part of the conspiracy, and we need to know how they plan to destroy this place. Which gets me thinking; they may have set boobytraps. Search with care."

The Captain grudgingly carried out the spy's request, and his guards set about their task with vigour.

A whole hour passed before they found what they were looking for. One of the guards called out, "Over here."

"What is it?" asked Grizdoth.

The soldier held up a handful of bolts, which on closer examination revealed fatigue marks just below the head.

"What are they?" the Captain asked.

"Retaining bolts that hold the katapultos release mechanism in place," said the guard.

"Hah," Grizdoth said, picking one up. "See how the stonegrabes weakened them so as to fail after repeated use."

At that moment, the nightwatch arrived, holding a bewildered Buzmith.

"What is the meaning of this, Captain?" the stonegrabe demanded, "all engineers are under the House of Cuscosa's protection."

Grizdoth approached Buzmith, menace twisting his

face. "You have questions to answer, trog." He held up the incriminating bolts.

"Who are you?" the Kaldoran asked, but already a note of fear was evident in his words.

"Never mind who I am. Answer the question!" Grizdoth was much braver when he had armed might for company.

When Buzmith didn't answer, the Captain slapped him across the face with his gauntleted hand. "You can save us a lot of time if you tell us what Nalin has been scheming, stonegrabe," he shouted.

Buzmith continued to hold his counsel and a strong fist connected with his jaw, a prelude to further assault.

"Tell us what we wish to know and the pain will stop," Grizdoth said.

"I will not betray my people," Buzmith replied, struggling against the guard's grip.

"Ah, so you *are* hiding something," the spy said. "Admit it; you treacherous trogs have sabotaged our war machines. And that is not all. What is this I hear about an 'accident' that is to occur in this very dungeon?"

"You're too late Cuscosian scum," Buzmith said, spitting on the floor, "Nalin has already escaped, and he has taken the spare bolts. It will take you a month to fashion new ones — and you won't be getting any help from me."

Grizdoth sneered. "You really think we didn't suspect your conspiracy? Rest assured friend, the faulty mechanisms were detected this morning and made good.

We also know how you planned to flood the dungeons. With you and your fellow conspirators captured, that plan has come to naught too." He stepped closer to the now quivering stonegrabe and fixed him with a self-satisfied glare. "You have given us all the reason we need to wipe out your pitiful race of cave trogs."

Grizdoth took the bolts and left the room, while behind him, he heard a gurgle that signalled the slitting of Buzmith's throat.

Minutes later he had joined Eétor in the Great Hall and explained his findings. Grizdoth had been correct in deducing Eétor was annoyed at not having been alerted to the finality of Nalin's departure earlier. However, he was more than pleased with the uncovered evidence of Kaldoran sabotage and planned conspiracy to destroy the remainder of Nalin's work in the dungeons.

"We must not waste this opportunity to test the loyalty of the Kaldoran Fellchief," the Praetor said.

"Am I to understand he will fail the test?" Grizdoth said. "Why not simply exact vengeance?"

Eétor scoffed. "You are a talented spy, Grizdoth, but not a strategist. How easy do you think it would be to launch an all out attack on Kaldor Prime? No — this protocol gives us the ideal cover to approach Magthrum in all innocence. It does not matter that Nalin has escaped, I can manipulate this turn of events to our ends. If, as I suspect, the Kaldorans refuse to hand Nalin Ironhand over, then

Captain Torell will take them by surprise. Now, ask him to join us. I need to apprise him of the details."

Grizdoth left the Great Hall with a spring in his step. He would be paid handsomely for tonight's work, and who knows, might be given a more favoured position in Eétor's court. It was also reassuring to know he had enough information about Eétor's own conspiracy to make him useful to other parties — should things turn sour. *Kingdoms may rise and fall by the fickle changes of the wind,* he thought, *but a spy can always bend with the gale.*

# 26

## A CITY FALLS

---

Tayem thought she understood the meaning of devastation. This day she had witnessed the decimation of the larger part of her army, the slaying of fifteen royal dragons and the shame that came from a routing, the like of which had never been endured since the Marauders war. Most dreadful of all — this had all occurred under *her* rule. *Do I even deserve to be a queen anymore?*

These were self-serving thoughts, however, and as the remainder of her dragon host approached Wyverneth, she resolved to save her reflections, her licking of wounds, for a future time — should that occasion present itself.

She directed Quassu over the escarpment that marked

the outskirts of Wyverneth and was at once confronted with a foreboding that penetrated to the marrow.

From this vantage point she observed a scene of soul-withering carnage. The lower slopes of Wyverneth were aswarm with the insect-like ranks of a rampaging army.

*Cuscosian diggods,* she thought. *By Sesnath, their number is equal to those that assailed us at Lyn-Harath. Etezora has thrown her entire force at our kingdom!*

Despite its natural defences and placement of defending troops, Wyverneth had been taken by surprise and the signs of complete conquest were all too evident. The Cuscosians had breached the walls in numerous places, and their ladders had spread like spiders' webs over the battlements. Inevitably, the palace gates had fallen despite fierce resistance from the Dragonians.

"No, it cannot be," she said out loud.

Mahren, Cistre and Beredere had taken in the scene of devastation too and had positioned their dragons alongside Tayem's. They were close enough to be in earshot and were clearly awaiting her orders, looks of panic on their faces.

The choices were stark. Attack the Cuscosians with the rest of her dragons? What if their invisible attacker should devastate them again? It was all too obvious that her ground forces were overwhelmed and could not augment a counter-attack. Most had been directed toward Lyn-Harath and were still many periarchs distant. They would arrive several hours too late, wearied by the long journey and demoralised by their recent defeat.

She calculated the odds, sifted through strategies inculcated by the seasoned military tutors of Dragonia. She also heard the words of her father:

*If Dragonia should ever fall, remember that the spirit of Donnephon does not reside in the city of Wyverneth. It lives in the hearts of each Dragonian. We arose from the ageless mountains, and the ancient forests — we can do so again. Many are our enemies, but the vs' shtak runs deeper than any superficial tradition. If we are dispersed, our people will live on. Never make the mistake of defending buildings over preserving people.*

Her course of action, free from hazy Black Hallows confusion, was clear. "Descend on Wyverneth, but do not engage the enemy directly," she shouted. "Save whoever you can, instruct those who remain to flee the city and head north to Herethorn. Do you understand?"

Each of her commanders nodded and banked away to relay her commands to their respective squadrons.

With the suns behind them, the dragons' descent was not expected by the Cuscosians. Nonetheless, it didn't take long for them to respond with missile fire, and Tayem had to use every scintilla of skill to manoeuvre Quassu beyond the battlements and alight in the palace courtyard.

The Cuscosians were crawling over the outer walls, and all around the enemy beleaguered the Dragonian defenders. Tayem had left Uniro in charge and she spied him on the steps of the palace, bravely holding back a tide of Cuscosian elite troops. His own guard were down to their last seven and it was only a matter of time before they all fell. She directed Quassu toward the Cuscosians, Cistre landing behind her and following suit. The dragon's claws made short work of the enemy, slashing through armour and flesh alike as if the soldiers were made of mere parchment.

Tayem called to Uniro. "Who remains within?"

The captain drew himself up, nursing a wound to his side. "Most have fled," he said. "We sought to buy them time here, but Disconsolin, Merdreth and their servants are still in the palace. They are stubborn and say they will remain as a matter of duty."

"You decided aright," Tayem told him. "We must flee to the mountains, initiate the Vicrac."

She was referring to the edicts laid down at the establishment of Wyverneth. As a beleaguered people, the Dragonian matriarchy had recognised the precarious nature of their existence and made plans for such an exodus. Each household knew what was required of them. Word-of-mouth relayed in an ancient tongue, together with the sounding of an undeniable call was all it took to spread the command.

"Have you ordered the tolling of the bell?" She asked Uniro.

"Not yet, my Queen. Disconsolin will not countenance it. He thinks he can parley with the Cuscosians."

"Gorram fool," Tayem said, "We have learned today

that Etezora cannot be reasoned with. Cistre — go to the tower and ring the bell. All must know."

"My Queen. My place is at your side. Send another — "

"I will be safe," she replied. "I will not engage in unnecessary combat. Ring the bell for no more than five minutes, and then order your squadron north."

Cistre hesitated for only a second then saluted, instructing her mount into the air and toward the bell tower that lay on the west side of the palace. Two more dragons had alighted in the courtyard and arranged themselves at their master's command as a bulwark against the sea of Cuscosians washing over the palace walls.

After instructing Uniro to beat an ordered retreat through the north gate, she ran into the palace, shouting at any remaining courtiers to leave their belongings and flee the city.

She found Disconsolin and Merdreth in their quarters. Disconsolin was donning the last parts of an official state uniform, while his wife alternately fussed over him and looked out the window, noting the inexorable advance of the Cuscosians.

"If you go out there in that attire, you'll simply invite a Cuscosian crossbow bolt," Tayem said. As she uttered the words, the deep peal of the Vicrac bell began and it seemed that Cistre's action added a doom-laden quality to her words.

Disconsolin turned to face her, the colour drained from his face. "Who are — " It took a moment for recognition to dawn on his face, and Tayem realised she must appear as some blood-caked monstrosity charged with murderous intent.

"My Queen," he said, recovering himself. "You have returned. What news from the plains?"

"We are defeated," Tayem said, "Etezora has betrayed us and a large number of dragons are slain. I have ordered the Vicrac. All must depart — including you."

Disconsolin and his wife looked at each other, the woman displaying a pleading expression. "We are ... we are too far gone in sols to countenance leaving Dragonia," he said. "We have decided to take our chances with the Cuscosians."

Tayem tried to suppress a rising anger, borne on the back of the day's ravages on her emotions. "This is not a request, Disconsolin. Should the enemy take you alive they will extract the secrets of the Vicrac. I cannot allow that."

The Fyreclave elder bit his lip. "Then you must invoke the *Kutri* for refusing a royal decree. Our life is here in Dragonia. We would not survive the journey you embark on, nor the conditions in the Whispering Hills."

"You would have me strike you down? Is your attachment to the comforts of the palace so precious to you?"

"You do me a disservice, My Queen. This has nothing to do with our position or privileges. I know you think we cannot negotiate with the Cuscosians, but you reckon without my powers of statesmanship. I would gain concessions from them."

"Look out of the window," Tayem declared. "What sense of diplomacy do you see there? Our cause is doomed. Now come, before it's too late."

Disconsolin remained resolute, lifting his chin. "We have made up our minds. We are staying."

"Husband," Merdreth interjected. "Our Queen may speak the truth. Perhaps you could reconsider?"

"Enough," Disconsolin said with overweening pride, "the decision is made. Now carry out the execution or leave us to our fate. I swear I will reveal nothing — even if they torture me."

Tayem paused. She knew what she should do, yet without the Black Hallows girding her with its malefic influence she realised with despondency that she had seen enough Dragonian blood spilt today. She pursed her lips and made her pronouncement. "I do not have time for this. Neither do I understand your reasons, Disconsolin. But know that Etezora will show you no mercy. Better to die by your own hand than submit to their interrogation. I trust you will do the honourable thing if it comes to it?"

"Of course, my Queen," he replied.

"Merdreth, will you come?" Tayem said.

The woman drooped her head. "My place is at my husband's side."

"Very well," Tayem said, "Dixtrath semlessin." It was the Dragonian salute of high office. A respect the man didn't deserve, but Tayem uttered it anyway, and then left them.

Back in the courtyard, the Cuscosians were battering back the Dragon Rider's hastily formed defence. No doubt the dragons could hold back the tide a further hour, but Tayem was filled with dread concerning the possibility of a magical assault. All the while she anticipated the sight of her dragons suddenly writhing in pain, the result of unseen weapons brought to bear.

She called to Cistre, who had just returned from the bell tower. "We leave now," she said. "Are the grounds evacuated?"

"As far as I can tell," Cistre said.

"Then take to the skies."

Tayem mounted Quassu, noting the slumped form of the Dragon Rider in the pillion. She saw that he drew no breath and concluded that his spirit had gone to join Sesnath.

*I will bury him with full honours in the mountains,* she thought. *A dignity denied so many today;* and as Quassu took to the air a light-headedness filled her. It was at once a deep melancholy and at the same time a drawing of waters from a hitherto unbidden source. Not the Hallows. That corrupt source had poisoned everything today, and though it already stirred again within her, she resolved to rid herself of its influence. In declaring this to herself, she recognised she might have an even greater battle awaiting her.

27

# THE ANGRY MOUNTAINS CRY

―――――――

It was almost dusk when Nalin steered his four-wheeled cart into the entrance framing the Great Gorge. Its deep vertical chasm had a way of inspiring him in a way that tales and songs often failed to do. At over half a periarch wide, the limestone gorge was a deep incision cut into the Imperious Crescent, and had become a vital conduit for traders and travellers alike. The Kaldoran people had adopted this gash in the landscape and offered hospitality and safe passage to the myriad folks that sought a direct route across the mighty mountain range. If an occasional traveller mysteriously disappeared, only to end up in a stonegrabe's cooking pot, then that could not be helped. It didn't stop the flow of traffic that frequented the gorge.

Ellotte tugged on Nalin's sleeve. She'd espied her best friend, Kartasia Silverforge in her carriage heading southwards. They waved at each other from a distance, and once close to, exchanged greetings as they passed. Nalin could see his wife's relief at seeing a friendly face after their long journey. Three days and nights spent looking over their shoulders had left their nerves frazzled and their exchanges tetchy with irritation. Nalin had been forced to journey off-road to avoid frequent Cuscosian patrols, and they paid the price in lost hours. As they continued deeper into the gorge, bright sunlight gave way to an eerie dark shade as the tall sheer sides of the gorge all but excluded the early evening rays of Sol-Ar. They still had several periarchs to go before they reached Kaldora Prime, meaning it would be at least three more hours before the security of their home-cave and loved ones welcomed them.

Every periarch they traversed up the steep inclines left Nalin feeling more relaxed, every turn of the wheel filling him with a sense of closure on the past and a renewed acknowledgment of his belonging. As they crested a further pass, Ellotte took the reins, and he had a chance to gaze at the narrow strip of dark indigo sky overhead. Already, the brighter stars were glistening in the heavens.

*What does the future hold?* He wondered as he watched the dance of the insectoid fire dragons above his head.

What role would he have to play in Magthrum's empire now his usefulness as a foreign agent was at an end? And what of the Kaldoran's future as a people? The ruling house of Cuscosa was a pack of duplicitous kruts, and it was clear that a confrontation of some sort was on the horizon. Hopefully, his people would have the mettle to face that challenge when it inevitably arose. He poked around in a pack and withdrew his jarva pipe, stuffing it with a fresh leaf of the narcotic herb.

"Nalin," Ellotte sighed, "not in front of Palimin."

He waved his hand in dismissal. "Hush, Wife. This is a moment of celebration and a stonegrabe deserves his vices — especially after what I've endured on this long journey." Ellotte continued to scold him, but it became background noise as his trepidation concerning the future lifted at the first few puffs. His mood shifted still further when he saw the lights of home in the distance.

As the first of Varchal's moons rose, shedding its pallid light on the track to light their way, the cart rounded a sharp right-angled turn in the gorge. Here, the valley widened and ahead loomed the great cliff wall of Kaldora Prime, also known as Regev in the ancient tongue. It rose, gargantuan, draped in fern vines, dense leafy creepers and mountain wisteria whose florets descended on fronds some fifty spans in length. The greenery disguised a complex network of tunnels, caves and caverns behind. They formed a labyrinth of passageways that only a handful of stonegrabes knew the full extent of.

The Kaldoran race had occupied these caves for millennia and had excavated the naturally occurring tunnels into a massive catacomb of townships and satellite villages. The catacombs extended far into the massif and deep into the bowels of the heart rock. A hierarchy had evolved over the sols determining which levels different Kaldoran castes occupied. Nalin acknowledged the inequality inherent in this crude system, but he was fortunate enough to have been born into a higher echelon — so it didn't bother him overly much.

A Kaldoran with a conscience was a rare thing indeed.

Those lucky enough to own caves overlooking the gorge had become more accustomed to daylight. Yet still, most were grateful for the hanging vegetation that provided much needed shade. It was a sight to behold looking at the small candle lights twinkling behind the leafy covering like an imitation of the stars in the sky.

As they approached the main entrance, Nalin pointed out the newly built pumping machine he had designed the previous sol. It extracted water from the deep cavernous lakes and subterranean well-springs to feed an intricate system of aqueducts, thus providing the citizenship with a sustainable supply of clean water.

Moments later, they arrived in front of a huge gaping cavern named *Jennu Narod* or *Great Mouth* in Common-speak. It was set under a massive overhang of rock, forming the entrance proper to Kaldora Prime. The huge orifice was lined and decorated with a façade of ornate wooden carvings paying tribute to great Kaldoran leaders from antiquity. Purple Hallows light illuminated the craftsmanship and glimmered from Spidersnatch's fissure across the valley. Nalin shivered at the phenomenon, reminding himself it was this baleful influence that fired Etezora's psychopathic frenzy of destruction and, word had it, also held Magthrum in its sway.

*No good will come of this*, he thought.

They passed under this architectural wonder, a scaffold of retaining timbers reinforcing the cavern opening and the mighty overhang above. To gain access, visitors to the Kaldoran underworld had to pass through a gated stockage and courtyard, which was home to a thriving market. This was not the only way into the kingdom. There were also a series of tunnelled access-ways along the cliff face to allow the inhabitants to come and go as they pleased.

A holder of the revered position of Chief Engineer, Nalin and his family lived in a cliff-view suite of caves above the Great Hall. The magnificent chamber itself had been excavated in a smaller void adjacent to Jennu Narod. As Nalin parked the cart, a group of stonegrabes came running to help unload their belongings. Speedwill had clearly been successful in delivering his urgent message to Magthrum, and Nalin's heart swelled with pride as he took in the sight of the cave-crawler. It was on public display — no doubt at Magthrum's command — standing in the shadow of Jennu Narod for all to see.

Ellotte took Palimin straight to their home while stonegrabes unloaded their cart. He was just instructing them to put the new cutting heads with the cave-crawler when a loud voice boomed across the concourse.

"Nalin, my brother. Welcome home," bellowed Magthrum. "Come, a tankard awaits. What news do you bring from Cuscosia?"

Nalin walked side by side with the Fellchief into the Great Hall, and it wasn't long before he was downing his fifth tankard of ale. He eventually flopped on to his bed at midnight, Ellotte and Palimin having long since retired. He and Magthrum had talked long and hard about recent events unfolding at Castle Cuscosa, together with the threat Queen Etezora presented. Tomorrow the Rockclave were due to meet, and Nalin would be required to give a formal report. Until then, he was free to drift off into the bosom of the sleep god, Pandur, and Nalin welcomed her embrace with open arms.

The following two days saw Nalin applying himself to upgrades and maintenance on the cave-crawler. The new cutting heads were fitted to their bearings, and all mechanical joints and relevant surfaces were lubricated with mineral oil. He'd procured two flasks of concentrated fyredrench from the recently acquired dragon corpses plundered on the Dead Zone pan, and after dilution, the machine's reservoirs were filled to capacity. The hulking machine was ready for operation, and its maiden dig was scheduled for later that week. Until then his shining creation would stand testament to Kaldoran engineering.

A Cuscosian trade caravan was due to arrive later that afternoon. Buzmith had not materialised, and Nalin hoped there might be some news of the stonegrabes he had left behind in Castle Cuscosa. The Kaldoran market place buzzed in anticipation of the merchants' arrival, and stallholders cleared a space for the impending largesse. Kaldorans were famous for their engineering prowess, and they traded machined goods for essential foodstuffs grown on the Cuscosian plains, together with cloth and leather skins imported by rural artisans in the south.

Lookouts spotted the trade convoy approaching the great turn in the gorge and shouted their warning that an advance vanguard consisting of a Cuscosian emissary and Captain Torell preceded them. It wasn't long before two outriders galloped through Jennu Narod on horseback. After acknowledging the salutations of the Kaldoran heralds, the diplomatic party surrendered their horses and requested an audience with the Fellchief. Nalin watched this overture from afar, but decided to distance himself from the exchange. He sensed that prudence was called for and retired to his chambers to await news of the outcome.

~ ~ ~

Ambassador Urrel was of Volwin descent, a race few encountered in the Imperious Crescent as the Volwin kingdoms lay many thousands of periarchs across the Western sea. He boasted the reputation of an experienced negotiator who had previously represented the House of Cuscosa in their diplomacy. He withdrew the scrolls of office from a saddle bag, holding them tenuously in his pudgy hands. Today would be a difficult one, although he could not have imagined just how testing it would prove to be. For completeness sake, he had also brought along copies of the tri-kingdom treaty, which defined the terms for coexistence and trading relations between Cuscosia, Kaldora and Dragonia. All parties paid only lip service to it, of course, but it would serve as an opening for Urrel. After all, it had brought an end to tribal squabbles, and ushered in an era of co-operation and understanding which had kept relative peace until the recent conquest of Dragonia. However, Urrel was quite aware that today might well see the shattering of its glass-like bonds on the remaining two participants.

A scuttling Kaldoran consort came to the stockade gates to meet the Cuscosian delegation and escorted them to the Great Hall. Urrel flared his nostrils at this attempt at hospitality. He guessed the flea-infested trogs were doing their best, but their crusty-skinned representatives fell far short of the diplomatic welcome he was accustomed to. *Perhaps this race deserves to die out,* he pondered. *Then again, it's not my place to determine.*

"Please wait here Ambassador," said one. "I will advise Fellchief Magthrum of your arrival."

Urrel whispered to Captain Torell, "Please leave all negotiations to me during our audience with Magthrum. I also suggest that you remain at ease during our meeting."

"As you wish Ambassador," Torell replied, "I will defer to your expertise in this matter. However, I do have my orders should our request fall on deaf ears."

"Be that as it may, Kaldorans are unpredictable, and this Fellchief is no exception."

The consort returned with refreshment. "Magthrum will be with you shortly Ambassador."

"Thank you," said Urrel accepting a tankard of dubious-smelling ceremonial ale.

~ ~ ~

In Nalin's quarters, Magthrum slapped his friend on the back. "So I believe they have come for you my friend," he laughed out loud. "They will be disappointed. Treaty or no treaty, I cannot believe they will jeopardise the profitable trade they now enjoy. Let's not forget it is *they* who repeatedly violate the terms."

Nalin frowned. "I do not trust this show of diplomacy, Magthrum. Things are not as they once were, and there is an unhealthy lust for power causing conflict with Dragonia. I also fear for our loyal stonegrabes at Cuscosa."

"The conflict with Dragonia means they can ill afford to upset us. Look." Magthrum pointed out into the valley. "Their merchants arrive even now."

They both watched as the Cuscosian trade caravan made camp on the opposite side of the valley adjacent to Spidersnatch Cavern.

"Wait here my friend. This meeting will not take long, and then we can return to our business. The Rockclave is in no mood to accede to foolish demands from these humans."

With another reassuring slap, Magthrum departed and descended to the Great Hall. He entered alone, as was his way.

"Ambassador Urrel, how gratifying to see you again," he said, opening his arms magnanimously.

The Ambassador bowed, not quite sure whether Magthrum expected an embrace or not. He was thankful when he lowered his arms and walked towards the over-sized granite table standing in the centre of the room. "My Lord Magthrum, it is a pleasure, and I trust all is well. May I introduce Captain Torell of the Queen's Guard?"

Magthrum acknowledged the Captain's salute. "What troubles our Cuscosian friends, Ambassador?"

"I believe it is an established convention to read out the tri-nation treaty at meetings such as this, My Lord."

"Rockbull's guts, man. That'll take half an hour or more."

"But — "

"Just get on with it. We'll all feel the better for getting straight to the point."

Urrel sucked in air through pursed lips and responded.

"Very well. It is with great regret I must convey the request of the Praetor for Nalin Ironhand's extradition — for the crime of treason against the Royal House of Cuscosa."

Magthrum's brows knitted together as he walked to his high chair and sat down. "Tell me Ambassador, do you have evidence supporting this request?"

"I do M'lord. Captain Torell if you please."

The Captain stood and read the indictment from the royal scrolls. Magthrum raised his hand after a list of stonegrabes were cited as witnesses.

"Ambassador, am I to understand Nalin has carried out these alleged crimes on his own. Pray how? I wish to speak to Buzmith Oakstone."

The Ambassador looked at Torell. "Can you bring this Kaldoran forward?"

Torell remained silent for a moment and then admitted, "I'm sorry M'lord, that will not be possible. He has since met with ... an accident."

Urrel looked back at Magthrum, whose countenance had taken on the appearance of rolling thunderheads.

"What is that you say?" the Fellchief rumbled.

Torell's face twisted with discomfort. "His body was found at the sluice gates outside Castle Cuscosa. It appears he was trying to divert the flow of water and got caught in the gears."

"Most unfortunate," Urrel added quickly. "Still, accidents do happen."

"Accident indeed," Magthrum roared. "Do you take me for a fool Cuscosian scum?"

The bulky frame of Magthrum rose from his elevated seat with an expression hardening in rage. "Ambassador," he said through clenched teeth, "I am unwilling to comply with your request, and if you wish to avoid any diplomatic unpleasantness, I suggest you leave immediately. Tell that krut, Eétor that if harm comes to any more stonegrabes, I will have the great pleasure of visiting the same misfortune on him."

"M'lord, the Praetor is adamant that this Nalin be taken back for trial."

"I sense deception Ambassador, now take your leave peaceably before I have you thrown to the Narrogs." Without waiting for further reply, he clapped his hands and a dozen armed Kaldoran guards entered the hall. "Take these men to their horses," he commanded.

"Be warned," Torell said, his ire impossible to hide, "our ejection will result in severe reprisals. Are you sure you want to stoke the fires of our already considerable anger?"

"Krut off!" Magthrum bellowed his reply. "And if I ever see you two inside my chambers again, then you'll leave without your bizouis."

Urrel and Torell were roughly escorted from the Great Hall to the paddock where their horses waited. As they rode away, Torell steered towards the merchants' camp across the valley.

"Where are you going Torell?" Urrel said. "We should

return swiftly to Cuscosa and inform Eétor of this outrage."

"Ambassador, you had your orders, and now I'm following mine. Diplomacy was always bound to fail."

"What do you mean?"

As they approached the Cuscosian wagons, Urrel understood at last the grand deception. Soldiers had discarded their civilian garb and uncovered a bank of katapultos war machines.

"Prepare to fire," shouted Torell as he dismounted at the command tent.

Anyone who witnessed events that unfurled that afternoon and lived to tell the tale would wish they had been swallowed in the maelstrom that followed. The battalion of Cuscosian warriors could not have expected the cataclysm that was to befall them moments after the first burning tar-gum gourd launched from the katapultos.

Magthrum was briefing the Kaldoran Council in the Great Hall when the first ball of burning grenade smashed into the stockade. The ensuing rapid bombardment of spiralling flame ignited the ornate timber frontage of Kaldora Prime. Dry seasoned timber scaffolding caught fire and the resultant flames engulfed the great cavern opening. Fingers of flame snaked their way up the cliff face on either side of Jennu Narod, blackening everything in their grasp. Smoke engulfed the once wondrous structure shutting out the light.

As chaos descended, many Kaldorans were burned alive or crushed under falling timbers. These were the lucky ones. Plumes of dense smoke were sucked into the great cavern, depriving many of precious air and coating their lungs with acrid tar. The stonegrabes who could run, fled further down into the bowels of the fortress, grateful for avoiding the onslaught of Cuscosian fury.

Magthrum summoned his warbands from their barracks and charged them solemnly, "We are betrayed. Prepare to retaliate."

Any further words were swallowed in a cacophony of screams as a greater cataclysm unfolded. Intense heat from the burning wood and tar caused water in the grykes and cracks of the limestone to vaporise and the expanding steam weakened the integrity of the cliff face. It only took a matter of minutes for the cracks to widen and the massive cliff front to collapse in a monumental avalanche of stone. Thousands of tons of rock tumbled down, sweeping aside any remaining struts of scaffolding. Without the wooden structure to support it, the giant overhang groaned before it too collapsed like a toppling behemoth, creating a landslide of shattered rock and dust clouds that engulfed the entire valley floor.

At this spectacle, cheers erupted from the Cuscosian troops; shouts that quickly turned to screams of pain as sharp dust fragments from the collapse enveloped them, shredding their skin like razors. Those who had taken shelter from the rolling dust cloud enjoyed a short period of relief before the full consequence of the cliff's collapse became apparent. Tremors resulting from the rock fall triggered a surface ripple that spread through the strata until it reached the depths of Spidersnatch Cavern. Here in the abyssal fathoms of rock, once-healed fissures opened, releasing a discharge of Hallows energy unprecedented on Varchal.

Urrel and Torell watched as plumes of black-violet Hallows energy snaked across the valley, decimating all that stood before it. The two would-be diplomats simply disintegrated to dust, along with every last member of the mighty Cuscosian battalion. None survived.

Continuing earth tremors wreaked carnage within the Kaldoran kingdom. Limestone caverns crumbled, stalactites speared the ground, tunnel rooves collapsed and underground lakes burst their banks, flooding the surrounding caves. The lower castes of trogs and Kaltis didn't stand a chance. Only those in the upper levels, who had retreated away from Jennu Narod, stood any hope of survival. Eventually the aftershocks subsided, and the surviving Kaldorans regrouped. Incredibly, The Great Hall had survived almost intact, whereas Jennu Narod was no more. Magthrum displayed true leader's qualities by shaking off the dust that covered his royal jerkin and rallied the stonegrabes with a mixture of exhortations and threats.

The industrious Kaldorans were soon tending to the injured and recovering what could be found of the dead.

Those that weren't trapped deeper in the cave system started to make their way to the Great Hall.

Muffled cries emanated from underneath rock piles. Those near the surface were rescued, but many more were too deep to be reached without excavating equipment, all of which had been submerged in the lower catacombs.

"Where's Nalin?" shouted Magthrum. "Has anybody seen Nalin?"

"He was in his quarters when the roof came in," Gribthore spoke up.

Magthrum ran up the broken stairs, jumping over fallen masonry and gaining the fractured cave entrance of Nalin's chambers.

He found the engineer sprawled over a pile of fallen rock. "Nalin, are you all right? We need you at the Rockclave."

Nalin didn't respond. Magthrum grabbed him by the shoulder and pulled him back, but Nalin shook him off, screaming to be left alone.

"Pull yourself together, stonegrabe. Now's no time for sentimentality. You need to — "

Magthrum stopped mid-sentence as he took in something that had escaped his attention up to now. A look of horror painted his face as he observed the crushed limbs of Ellotte and Palimin protruding from under the mass of fallen limestone.

"Leave me alone," Nalin cried. "Would that I had died with them. Now I have nothing left to live for."

The Fellchief stood speechless for a time, and then gathered his resolve. He flung his arms around Nalin and wrenched him out of his cave. He too shared Nalin's pain, but now was not the time for grief; it was the time to fight — to survive.

"Nalin," Magthrum slapped his friend hard across the face. "Kaldora needs you. We are buried alive by the collapse of Jennu Narod, and our air supply is running short." He dragged Nalin back to the Great Hall and pointed around. "Look, *these* people need you."

Nalin blinked, wiped his eyes and gazed around the crowded hall at the throng of dust- covered bloody stonegrabes. "What can I do? Ellotte and Palimin are dead. What is the point of anything anymore?" It was then he saw a most beautiful thing before him, standing almost untouched by the carnage. The cave-crawler. Their means of escape. He walked over to it and swept a layer of dust from the plaque on the fuselage. He read aloud what was written there: *Palimin — the greatest inspiration rises from the smallest of things.*

Magthrum stepped up behind and placed a hand on his friend's shoulder. "Their spirits will live on in your machine. Don't let them perish in vain. They would want you to fight on."

It was in that moment that Nalin's despair turned to determination, then to anger and finally to an unquenchable desire for revenge.

He climbed into the cockpit of the cave-crawler and

summoned four remaining Kaltis. He pulled down on two levers and put the great machine in gear, spurring the giant cave-grabes to exert themselves.

"Forward, you diggods, and dig us out of this tomb," he cried. "We will not die here. No, *we* will become the dealers of death, and Cuscosa will rue the day they set foot on our mountain!"

"Death to Cuscosa," Magthrum yelled, and was joined by a chorus of bellowing stonegrabes falling into line behind the belching machine, following Nalin as he dug his way towards the light.

## 28

# BLOOD ON THE DRAGON
# TALON GATES

---

The Darastrix Vrevel Portam had protected the royal Dragonian palace at Wyverneth for the best part of five hundred sols. Since the erection of the initial fortification by Ralgemah the Pyre-Queen, successive matriarchs had extended the palace organically by the addition of a barbican, ornate machiolations and turrets. The entire edifice was constructed primarily from the dark ironwood that grew exclusively on the slopes of the Dragon Vale. Each tree took about one hundred and fifty sols to mature, so the fact that the massive construct was composed of the material meant that its value in wood alone exceeded five million gold pieces. Once one added the cost of labour to carve the intricate designs that adorned the monument, then it was plain to the most novice of accountants that its value was priceless.

Etezora stood before the Darastrix gateway, sweeping her gaze over it, then up to the spires and bell tower that seemed to reach skyward in sympathy with the dragons that once flew from their tops. She had to admit that its splendour dwarfed that of the crude stronghold that was Castle Cuscosa.

*These Dragonians surely earn their reputation as craftspeople,* she thought, *but now the fruits of their labour are mine.* The import of this notion helped sweep aside the fatigue that still clung to her from the monumental exertions on the battlefield barely forty-eight hours ago.

The gates had historically provided a solid defence against all but the most determined assault, yet now they stood open and unguarded.

"You are to be congratulated, Zeetor," she said finally to the squat, pig-nosed man who stood next to her. "Not only were the city and palace secured, but you accomplished this without significant damage to the buildings."

"Thank you, your Majesty," he replied. In truth, once the city walls were breached there was little resistance to his battalion's assault. The only thorn in his side had been the incursion of dragons, but these had inexplicably withdrawn in short order. The man hadn't believed his luck.

"Ensure that your men fill their stomachs with whatever food they find in the Dragonian cellars, and of course you have my permission to empty their ale casks."

Zeetor saluted. "Your Majesty," he replied, passing no further comment. The offer of food and drink was a mixed blessing as the Dragonians plant-based diet provided meagre sustenance. There wasn't even the prospect of pleasures to be had with the captured Dragonians. Most had fled into the northern forests leaving only the lame and sick.

Etezora strode through the open gate, stepping over the bodies of two Dragonian guards. "See that the corpses are disposed of quickly," she said to Dieol, who followed closely behind. Beyond the gates, the grand hall opened out before them. It existed as a vast chamber pervaded by an eerie emptiness, as if the spirits of long dead Donnephon still inhabited the palace. At the far end of the hall, a bachar wood staircase split into two, each side ascending to the upper chambers. A massive dragon statue had been carved out of the wall bisecting the staircase, its scales made of inlaid pearlwood that shone in the transmitted light shining through windows in the vaulted ceiling. The beast's vast wings spread wide across the wall, and it seemed to Etezora that it guarded the entrance to the upper levels with its imposing presence. Giant legs with feet bearing talons the size of a fully grown man formed archways on each side while the head arched over, gazing down and casting its terrible shadow upon anyone who sought to pass underneath.

Etezora saw Tuh-Ma shiver at the sight of this monstrosity. The poor blue-skin had a phobia for the wyrms, yet to her they were simply objects of contempt. She resolved to arrange for the pretentious carving to be removed at the earliest opportunity.

Etezora placed her hands on her hips and laughed out loud; a hearty, full-throated snort of derision. "So this is how you have been brought down, oh mighty Dragonia! You fall with barely a whimper to mark your passing."

"Where are they mistress?" Tuh-Ma asked.

"The cowards fled," declared Etezora, "and today my kingdom spreads further than ancient Cuscosa could ever have imagined. It is I who accomplished this — I!"

Dieol instructed the Royal Guard to ascend the stairs first. "We cannot be certain if the Dragonians left assassins waiting, or might seek an opportunity to exact revenge," he said.

"Then tell them to hurry," Etezora snapped, "I am impatient to take my seat on the Dragonian throne."

Five minutes later Dieol gave them the all-clear, and the entourage passed upwards through several antechambers before entering the Fyreclave chamber. The horseshoe cathedras stood before them, arranged with half empty wine glasses and broken crockery — testimony to the speed with which the Dragonians had departed.

Etezora stepped forward and sat herself on Tayem's throne, savouring the sweetness of her conquest. Despite the empty silence oozing throughout, nothing could diminish the inner satisfaction of her triumph.

The stillness did not last, however. It was disturbed by a rustling from behind huge window drapes bordering the leaded windows that lined the southern wall. Tuh-Ma moved forward cautiously, his club raised, and then swept aside the curtain with a flourish. He jumped back in shock. There, cowering behind was a small dragonette. How the Dragonians were careless enough to leave the creature behind was bewildering, but to Etezora, the pathetic little wyrm seemed to epitomise all she hated about the Dragonians.

She stood up and chuckled. "You fool. A beast of a man like you frightened by a cold-blood?"

"Tuh-Ma will catch," muttered the embarrassed troll.

"No," she replied, "this will be my pleasure." The roiling energy behind her eyes seemed to erupt with a fury that took even her by surprise, and although she had no sense of having learned or practised the gesture, she raised her hand. A bolt of unholy violet energy shot from her fingers and arced across the room, scattering her guards and striking the helpless dragon. It penetrated the dragonette's hide and did its diabolic work inside its chest. Within seconds the creature was aflame, ignited from within, the intense heat causing scales to curl and its pleading eyes to boil in their sockets. All the creature could do was twist and writhe as it collapsed to the floor, crying out its agony to merciless ears.

Still, Etezora did not relent. She continued to allow the purple fire to issue from her fingers, walking forward to observe the dragonette in its death throes. Tuh-Ma had stepped back, his face a picture of wonder and fear. "Burn it 'til it is no more, Mistress," he burbled.

Etezora remained wordless, a crooked leer on her face. The power seemed to have swelled in the reserves of her psyche during her period of recovery, and for minutes she continued to discharge the fire until the thing was little more than a pile of charred bone and hide. The smell of burned fat and meat filled the room, and pungent smoke billowed around like a dense blanket. Dieol and the other soldiers were compelled to cough their lungs out in irritation, yet she savoured the odour. The Hallows energy was a tempest within her, and in a moment of doubt she wondered if she could contain it. The energy seemed to possess a mind of its own. Then, like a psychic turning of a tap, she shut off the well-spring, and the crackling electrified arc disappeared.

The sudden quelling caused her to stagger backwards, and for a moment she stood bewildered yet thrilled at what had just issued from her.

"Well," she said after a moment, "that was exhilarating." She looked round at the shocked guards. "What are you staring at, you witless buffoons? Open the windows and clear up this mess."

A command from Dieol sent two guards scurrying away to carry out the Queen's orders. She gave further instructions to Dieol and Asselin, charging them with overseeing Wyverneth's occupation. Once they had gone, she was left alone with Tuh-Ma in the throne room.

After sitting on the former seat of Tayem's power, contemplating her victory, she realised there was something undermining her complete satisfaction. For many sols she had dreamt of taking Tayem's throne, having the dragon-schjek kneel before her. But although the first had been accomplished, the absence of the second gnawed at her with increasing irritation.

She ordered Tuh-Ma to retrieve Cuticous and bring her some cured dragon meat. Her appetite had increased exponentially since the battle, and it seemed she had to feed almost constantly. *Do you have your own appetites?* She spoke to the Hallows. But there was no answer save for the shifting sensation she felt within, like that of a swilling vat of dark ichor sloshing about in the vaults of her corrupt soul.

She was annoyed that Zeetor was the next to return. Her stomach was growling with hunger.

"Your Majesty," he said, "We completed a preliminary search of the immediate city and ordered a contingent of one hundred soldiers to patrol beyond the northern wall. We hope to pick up the Dragonian spoor within the hour."

"Do you indeed? I have little faith in your enterprise," she said. "The Dragonians are not called forest ghosts for nothing. They are uncannily adept at covering their trail. I think we shall need more esoteric means to search them out."

Zeetor shifted uncomfortably. "Then what do you want me to do, Your Majesty?"

"Secure the borders and continue your search of the city. See if any survivors yield information about the Dragonian's destination. In the meantime, send for the sorcerer. I am impatient to receive his counsel."

Zeetor saluted and left, clearly chagrined at his sudden fall from grace.

While she waited for Zodarin, Etezora took the time to peruse the full length of the upper chambers. Tuh-Ma did not delay in returning with Cuticous, and the creature's prickly attentions helped soothe her sense of frustration at not seeing the remaining Dragon Riders and their beasts at her mercy.

"It is only a matter of time," she said to the salyx as she walked casually from room to room. She continued like this for the remainder of the afternoon, rifling through drawers of jewellery and handling countless Dragonian ornaments, running her hands over them and delighting in their beauty as a child would in a den of toys. She spent a brief ten minutes speaking to her annoying brother, Tratis who had recently arrived despite her instructions for him to remain at Cuscosa. Still her wizard did not materialise.

In fact, Sol and Sol-Ar had sunk low on the horizon

before Zodarin made his appearance. This was dramatic — but not in an imposing sense. Four men brought him in on a dais-come-stretcher, his form propped up on numerous pillows. They laid him on the floor then left, deferentially bowing on their way out.

The wizard's appearance shocked Etezora. His usual pallor had turned deathly white since their last meeting, and the grey crescents under his eyes were now dark purple as if he had received a hefty blow to each.

"What happened to you?" She asked, more out of a perceived sense of impertinence on the wizard's part than concern.

Zodarin coughed, a rasping that rose from the depths of his lungs, and when he spoke it was in a husky tone that seemed to require great effort. Etezora sensed the wizard was embarrassed that she should see him in this state. "My undertakings in the Dreamworld that secured your victory exacted more from me than I anticipated, your Majesty," he said.

"I see," the Queen replied, not sure how to greet this state of affairs. His condition explained his tardiness, but should she be concerned about its implications? She mistrusted the sorcerer, but it could not be denied that he had proved his usefulness.

Etezora decided not to chide him. "I am truly grateful for your intervention with the dragons," she said, "although I had hoped more of them had fallen under the might of your assault."

"We all have our hopes," Zodarin said. "They cannot all be fulfilled despite one's best efforts."

It fell short of an apology, but Etezora let it pass. "I take it you will make a full recovery?"

"I ... believe so," he said, although the hacking cough that followed did little to convince Etezora.

"Well, I certainly hope that to be the case," she said, "I require your talents again. As you no doubt heard, Tayem and her dragons fled northward to the Whispering Mountains. If they pass over, then they will melt into the unknown lands. I desire their destruction, Zodarin, and I will not be denied."

"I can divine their route eventually, perhaps, but my mind is clouded at present, Majesty. The Dreamworld will yield answers, but for the present I am somewhat ... depleted."

Etezora regarded the sorcerer and sensed he was not obfuscating. *By Shio, his exertions have indeed taken their toll.* Her ire rose again, and she beat her fist on the arm of the throne. "How long before you are of use to me again, Wizard?"

Zodarin closed his eyes, whether from pain or simply holding back a retort, she could not tell. "Give me until morning," he said. "The journey here has been long and I need to rest."

Etezora scowled and made to remonstrate, then thought better of it. "Very well. I will arrange for a room to be prepared on this floor for your comfort."

"Thank you, Your Majesty. But I would not presume to take up one of the royal chambers. I already ordered my serfs to prepare the bell tower. It serves my needs more effectively."

Etezora frowned. *More likely you don't want your activities monitored,* she thought. "I will allow it — for the present," she said, seeking to re-establish her authority.

Zodarin nodded, and then rang a small bell. It summoned his bier carriers, and they soon had him whisked away to his quarters.

"Tuh-Ma still thinks you should let me crush his skull," he said.

Etezora waved her hand dismissively. "I have better use for your talents, Tuh-Ma. How are your tracking skills?"

"Here — in the land of dragons?" The troll said. "Tuh-Ma can follow the trail of any beast and man. But Dragon Riders do not leave a scent — at least one that Tuh-Ma recognises. The only thing I sense is the scent of fear, and that disappears quickly."

"Then do what you can!" Etezora shrieked. "Gods, have I surrounded myself with dullards?"

Tuh-Ma became the latest addition to those dispelled from Etezora's newly acquired throne room with their tails between their legs.

Later that evening, Tuh-Ma visited Etezora in her chamber with something that would send her to slumber in a decidedly lighter mood.

"Mistress, come quickly. Tuh-Ma has found something that may help us find the dragon people."

"Where?" she replied, tetchily. The Hallows within was seeking some form of release — a phenomenon that left her somewhat disquieted.

"In the dragon pens. Zeetor is there already. You should come and see."

"Don't leave me in suspense, Tuh-Ma. Out with it. What did you find?"

Tuh-Ma looked crestfallen. She knew he liked to surprise her, but her patience had worn to a thread this day.

"Two of Tayem's courtiers," he said. "Tuh-Ma told you he sensed fear. I followed the scent to the enclosures and braved the presence of a wounded dragon to find its source." He emphasised this last point in an effort to make up for his previous display in the throne room, no doubt.

Etezora wrapped herself in a shawl, summoned her guard and followed the troll to the enclosures. She had hoped to avoid the scene of her humiliation over a decade ago, but the prospect of Tuh-Ma's find overcame any reluctance.

The smell of dragon dung as they entered the Vrant dragon pens brought these memories back forcibly, but she brushed them off when she laid eyes on the pitiable forms of Disconsolin and his wife, Merdreth. She recognised them from her childhood and wondered at how the ravages of age afflicted any man or woman. They were dishevelled and frightened, two bundles of quaking wretchedness. The guardsmen dragged them across the straw-covered floor and pushed them down before a Queen who had grown from a precocious child into a daunting monarch.

Disconsolin looked upwards at Etezora, mustering his best statesman-like expression. "Your Majesty — "

Merdreth screamed as Etezora brought her hand down hard across the elderly statesman's face. "I did not give you permission to speak. Show proper respect, Dragonian."

It was part calculation and part Hallows-induced cruelty that motivated Etezora's show of power, but she had to play these two carefully if she was to extract the information she needed. "Your Queen and her court have fled," she said, "and you only remain. Why is this?"

Disconsolin wiped the blood from his mouth. "Tayem, our Queen is a mighty ruler. But she is impetuous, and I sought to speak with you. See if we could come to some accommodation."

Etezora strolled around the abject form of the statesman, playing with a beryl amulet she had acquired from Tayem's dressing table. "Accommodation? You speak as if you have something to trade. But, as you witnessed, we now hold the Dragonian palace and all of Wyverneth. It seems you miscalculated."

Disconsolin lifted his head higher, daring to look at the Cuscosian Queen. "With all due respect, your Majesty, there is much we can offer in terms of your adaptation to the new royal seat."

"What exactly do you mean?"

"You acquired a city dispossessed of its people. I have held the position of administrator for over twenty sols. I know where its resources are stored, how to run the carpentry workshops, the deals we negotiate with the surrounding locals — even how water and waste systems are managed. Let me help you with this."

Etezora stopped circling him and stood behind, an unnerving tactic she employed to the full. "So, you're essentially defecting? You seem to abandon your oaths all too quickly, Dragonian. How do I know you will not reverse your loyalties again when the occasion allows?"

"I ... I wouldn't do that, Your Majesty. My loyalty is to Wyverneth and not to the upstart monarch of the Dragon Riders. I would see it successfully ruled by one such as yourself, observe as it rises to greater prominence under your rule."

Etezora gave a pretence of considering his offer. "It is true there is quite a task ahead of us and having someone conversant with the city's workings would be an advantage. But what of your wife? What use is she?"

"She would be a condition of my service. I do not ask for much. Simply a small wing in the palace and a meagre wage."

Etezora couldn't help laughing at the man's presumptuousness. "Hah, Your employment could be extracted from you as the price paid for your continued existence. As for your wife — well, she may prove useful, we shall see."

The conversation was interrupted by a mournful bestial groaning from one of the pens. "What is that?" Etezora demanded.

Tuh-Ma crossed to the offending stall and looked over the stable door. He picked up a pitchfork and extended it, prodding something behind. "Quiet, hell-wyrm, or Tuh-Ma will skewer you and put you out of your misery."

Etezora approached the stall and gazed in. "Pitiable creature. I wonder why the Dragon Riders left such a beast behind." She took a closer look at its curled form and noticed the softened, black scales. "It looks sick. Kill it quickly, Tuh-Ma. I don't want it interrupting our conversation."

A look of fear crossed Tuh-Ma's face, quickly replaced by a determined look. The troll's eagerness to please easily supplanted his natural phobia. Etezora turned her back on the scene and heard the stable door open followed by the sound of Tuh-Ma's pitchfork puncturing the defenceless beast in its vitals. The blue-skin clearly had to repeat the lancing as the wyrm squealed in pain several times before it completely expired.

*So much for a quick death,* Etezora thought, without emotion.

She turned her attention to Disconsolin again, seeing

how his eyes were wide with fear. "I'll spare your life," she said to him, "provided you show me a sign of your loyalty."

"Of course, Your Majesty. Anything," he replied.

"I need information. Tayem's remnant of Dragonians — where do they intend to regroup?"

Disconsolin, his brow furrowed and pensive, looked as if he was battling with himself. "I do not know, Your Majesty. Your troops fell upon us so quickly there was no time for the Queen to discuss a destination. I only know they escaped from the northern gate."

Etezora leant over him and felt the crackle of energy in her forehead. Her eyes and ears had become increasingly hyper-sensitive during this latest resurgence and she could hear Disconsolin's heart beating in his chest, like that of a petrified mouse. It was a natural consequence of stress, but it had changed since her question about Tayem. The pulse seemed more erratic. *Lies.*

"We both know you are withholding information. Now tell me all. Your reluctance is irritating."

"I assure you that is everything I know. The Queen accepted my refusal to join the evacuation. She would not have told me, even if she had a fixed destination in mind at that time."

"Very well," Etezora said. "I can see you need to be persuaded. Guards, tie this woman to that post." She pointed at an upright supporting the stable roof. Merdreth screamed as the soldiers grabbed her roughly and bound her. At Etezora's instruction, they pulled her hair backwards, securing a rope around her neck, locking it in place so it was immobile.

"Let her go," pleaded Disconsolin. "Have mercy." Yet his words fell on seemingly deaf ears.

"Tuh-Ma," Etezora said. "Do you remember how to remove the fyre-drench gland from a dragon?"

The troll swallowed, and then nodded in the affirmative. "Tuh-Ma will need to be careful. Dragon spit is very dangerous."

"That's the whole point," Etezora said. "Now do it quickly before this woman faints on us.

Taking a knife from his belt, Tuh-Ma entered the stall and returned, carrying a sac dripping with blood, skewered on the end of his knife.

"Give it here," Etezora demanded.

"Be careful Mistress. See how the green fluid already eats into my weapon."

Etezora took the knife from the blue-skin and soaked up the viscous green liquid with a rag passed to her by a guard. All the while, Merdreth struggled against her bonds and shrieked her protests.

"Stuff a cloth in her mouth," Etezora said, "I can't stand to hear her pathetic crowing. Now, I need another rag." Tuh-Ma obliged by pulling a piece of loose material from his tunic. Etezora took the cloth and used it to soak up the dragon's bodily fluid. As she did so, the material began to smoulder gently.

Tuh-Ma looked on in wonderment, then nodded as he

understood what she was about to do. Etezora noticed his absorption and handed the cloth back to him. "Would you like to perform this part?" she said.

The troll nodded, and took the cloth from her, careful to handle it by an unsoaked portion.

"You need to hurry," Etezora said, "before it eats through the cloth.

Tuh-Ma approached the frightened prisoner. "Tuh Ma will ask, and your husband will answer," he said to her.

"What are you doing, beast?" cried Disconsolin.

"Tuh Ma does not ask you darastrix sthyr, and I am no beast." He emphasised the point by kicking the man in the belly. "Now, once more. Where is the Dragon Queen?"

There was silence, the prisoners glancing at each other.

"Proceed Tuh-Ma," instructed Etezora. "The man is stubborn. He needs convincing."

With surprising dexterity the hulking troll gently rubbed his fingers on Merdreth's eyelids, massaging them open and then closed.

"You enjoy your sight, darastrix aesthyr?"

Merdreth could not reply but closed her eyes. Tuh-Ma then rubbed his thumb nails with the cloth, smearing a layer of fyredrench across the pointed horn-like envelopes covering the tips of his fingers. The spit started to react with the tough keratin, and wisps of smoke rose as the finger nails dissolved. Tuh-Ma reached over the struggling Merdreth and pushed his finger nails into the corners of her eyes in a sadistic gouging motion.

Merdreth uttered a muffled scream, while Disconsolin begged the troll to stop. After what seemed like an eternity Tuh-Ma stepped back and Etezora spoke quietly as Merdreth whimpered in pain.

"Disconsolin, do you want Tuh-Ma to stop?"

The statesman had lost his powers of speech, it seemed. His mouth simply opened and closed like a carp. "Yes?" she continued, "then tell me where Tayem and her riders are."

"No, you don't understand. I can't. Please leave my wife alone, we are no threat to you."

"That's not what I asked." This time the voice was harsh. "Tuh-Ma, proceed."

The grotesque parody of a stunted man stepped forward and pushed his thumbs into the eye sockets of the wailing politician again, slowly pushing his nails under the eyeballs. With an accompanying shriek from Merdreth, they popped out of their sockets. Merdreth slumped in her bindings, unconscious from shock and pain. The experience was too much for Disconsolin. He heaved the contents of his guts onto the floor and sobbed uncontrollably.

"Well, Dragonian?" Etezora said. "Shall we awaken your wife, and let Tuh-Ma continue his ministrations?"

"No, no," the man spluttered. "Tayem invoked the Vicrac. They have retreated to the hills. There is a sanctuary amongst the Whispering Mountains. A place called Herethorn."

"Herethorn?" Etezora said. "The place is a myth, spoken of in legends told by the extinct Gigantes."

"They know the way," Disconsolin said. "Every Dragon Rider learns of the Vicrac by rote from the earliest of ages."

Etezora observed the man, attuned her hearing to his heart beat, and knew he told the truth.

"Shall we go after them right away?" Tuh-Ma asked.

"We will depart by first light. You," she spoke to one of the guards, "call for Graywood the physician and also the Royal Scribe. Order them to attend to this woman's wounds and take down Disconsolin's directions. Captain?" she turned to the other. "Make preparations for our journey. Choose one thousand of your best men. We will track down this rump of Tayem's army, destroy their remaining dragons and see if this place Disconsolin speaks of truly exists."

On the way back to her chamber, Etezora relished in the re-vitalisation that coursed through her veins. Only an hour ago she thought she was in for a restless night, but instead she looked forward to an ancient's sleep.

# 29

# TIR TI RINOV WURUNWA DI LOREATIS (DON'T EVER DREAM OF DYING)

———

Milissandia stirred from a restless sleep, her body feeling as if weighed down by heavy chains. Strange images still lingered in her mind, spectres and suggestions of events she could not explain. Not for the first time since the unexpected visit from her estranged father, she felt the need to spend the night alone. This might have meant an evening without the physical warmth of a companion, but it provided the opportunity to evaluate her *path* — painful though this was.

She had sat in front of her fire, staring at the flames for hours the previous evening, trying to make sense of the confused emotions that engulfed her since Wobas re-entered her life. Did she really hate her father as much as her response suggested? The question burned in the forefront of her mind, and she needed to understand why she felt it with such intensity. Yet after worrying away at the problem like a tongue passing over a sore tooth, she eventually tried to seek solace in slumber. She had prepared a calming herbal draught hoping to get much needed sleep — yet it still deserted her.

"Krut," she said out loud as the early morning light shone through a crack in the curtains. There was a busy day ahead, collecting herbs, fungi and seeds she needed to prepare the healing potions that were her stock-in-trade. Mundane foraging perhaps; but as it transpired, the activity was to provide a watershed moment in her life.

Milissandia possessed skills coveted by both Cuscosians and inhabitants of the Dragon Vale. She was known as the healer of the hills, a free spirit with knowledge and lore to administer various forest fruits. She used these carefully selected specimens to produce medicines, tinctures and unctions used to heal and sooth a vast range of ills. It had always been her belief that these talents were inherited from her mother, Carys. Yet now she had an increasing sense there was something running deeper in her blood. Although she shied away from such notions, it was as if a greater power guided her. Frequently she might be dressing a wound when a muse descended, and her hands gestured over the malady without volition, her lips uttering words she never read in any tome or grimoire.

With great effort, she kicked her feet out of bed, and pulled a lime-green wrap around her shoulders. She drew the curtains which let the morning sun stream into the room. Looking out beyond her small garden, she could see across a lake to the lowland woods of the Dragon Vale. It was in these woods that she collected the raw materials for her craft — natural ingredients that when cooked, blended or distilled, transformed into the potions she used to such great effect.

The sky burned with a violet glow, taking on a contused appearance. *Have you been betrayed, Sol-Ar — or are you the betrayer?* She thought. Her father perhaps knew more of this import, but she was hardly going to ask him.

She decided not to dwell on the foreboding, focusing instead on the day ahead. She needed to replenish her store of medicines that treated the mind. These required particular fungi and cacti. She would blend the pulp from these plants to help ease a patient's torment, though the medicine would never completely cure them — that was beyond even her capabilities.

After downing a bowl of ripe juju berries and grains, Milissandia picked up her bag and knife, then set off across the water meadow, following a route towards the Vale beyond. Once she reached the lake's edge, she untied the rope securing a small wicker boat and pushed off with a spoon-shaped paddle. Using strong purposeful strokes, she sped the little boat across the glistening water. A gentle refreshing breeze kissed the surface of the lake as she approached the northern margin, and the clear blue water turned a green-red colour as she glided over the first clump of fyrereeds signalling an end to this part of the journey.

She came to a stop on a small shingle beach, got out and pulled the boat clear of the water. Instead of taking her usual path into the woods, she followed the beach to its western edge until she reached a sheltered lagoon. It was here that the *skjall anduleso* lived.

Milissandia had nurtured the colony of small tree serpents for many sols now. The wriggling creatures could be extremely timid, but came to recognise she presented no threat to their sheltered existence. Spending most of their time in the higher reaches of the gnarlwood trees, they took to the ground at times to devour leafy plantains and reeds growing in the lagoon. Unlike most serpents, these diminutive creatures possessed sticky toe-pads and strengthened skeletal structures in their feet that helped them climb the smooth bark of the gnarlwoods. However, it was their ability to change colour that fascinated Milissandia. Quite by accident, she discovered that the chemical secreted when they camouflaged themselves was also a cure for skin sores and lesions suffered by the Dragonians. Far less serious than the incurable dragon blight, she referred to it as dragon rash.

She smeared some juju paste onto a mat of reeds, and then sat patiently, waiting for the sickly sweet odour of the juju paste bait to attract the anduleso. As she did so, her mind wandered back to Wobas's visit again.

It was true his quest for the secrets of the Dreamworld drove her from him when she was a young child, but now she felt a sense of guilt for rejecting his overtures of reconciliation.

Was it the images that flooded her mind the previous night that stirred these feelings? She wished she could remember their substance. Perhaps her desire to understand the dream images was the source of her torment and served to deprive her of precious sleep.

"Questions, questions, questions," she mused as the first of the tiny aduleso settled close by and started to feast. She reached out quickly and picked up the tiny creature, careful not to damage its delicate skin. The sticky pads clung to her hand as she stroked its back repeatedly with a juju catkin. The animal uttered a curious purring sound as its body secreted a photosensitive mucus that reflected the colour of its surroundings.

She removed the mucus with the absorbent flower spike, the catkin serving as a sponge. Once she had placed the saturated catkin in a small earthenware jar, she repeated the process until the jar was full.

The morning had all but passed before she completed the task. The lure of the lagoon tempted her to stay and rest a while longer, but she knew she should move on and renew her assortment of fungi. Not only were they needed for medicines, but they would act as her meal for the evening.

Bidding a fond yet unreciprocated farewell to the tree serpents, she retraced her steps along the beach and followed a well-trodden path to the tree line. After walking for a periarch or so, she stepped off the main route and traced a path using waymarkers left from a previous visit. They led to a shaded copse rich in mushrooms, toadstools and tree fungi. This was her special place, a place to dream, a place to harvest jewels of the forest.

She settled into the task of picking the ripe fungal blooms, taking in myriad colours that clothed the multitudinous fruiting bodies carpeting the pungent forest floor. Vibrant red shrooms gave way to speckled white-caps, while a rare variety of golden-yellow bracket fungus occupied niches in the soft bark of a mangor tree. This precious tree heterotrope was a much sought after culinary delicacy. She was particularly careful to segregate the edible fruiting structures from other pathogenic species. Elsewhere, she had to identify other mushrooms containing psychotropic compounds desired by many of her clients.

She laboured tirelessly through the afternoon and now settled under a shady tree to take refreshment. She leaned back against the trunk and took a deep draught from her skin of sweet juju-berry juice. It was like nectar to her parched lips. Such was the soporific effect, she wasn't aware she had dozed off until a stinging pain in her right hand wrenched her from slumber.

"Krut," she exclaimed. She hadn't noticed the thorn-infested vine of the wild cucumber plant. The acidic venom was already causing her hand to swell, and she rifled through her bag for an ointment, only to realise she hadn't brought it with her. The pain crescendoed from a sting to a nagging, aching throb. If she didn't get treatment within minutes, the venom would spread up her arm and then to her heart.

Panic began to grip her when she remembered the jar of anduleso mucus. She fumbled the lid open and took one of the saturated catkins, rubbing it on the back of hand.

"Ahhh!" The druid sighed with relief as the pain subsided, and without thinking, bit into a slice of the golden-yellow tree fungus she had prepared for her meal.

Waves of sleep started to submerge her as she leaned back against the tree again. Through bleary eyes she noticed the fungus change colour after reacting with the serpent mucus on her finger tips.

"Am I dreaming?" she murmured as she transcended through the kaleidoscope of colours pulsating in her mind. "What is this wonderment?" she asked the small skjall anduleso that crawled into her lap.

Although sleep enveloped her physical form, Milissandia was wide awake in another world. A world of vapours, mysterious scents and the suggestion of distant melodies played on spectral instruments. Remembrance flooded back as she recognised the atmosphere of the previous night's dreams.

She looked down at her feet and saw they were three-toed, lined underneath with sticky pads. It was the most natural of behaviours to climb the stem of a nearby chasquite bush. From the sanctuary of its prickly branches and dense leaves, Milissandia's dream-avatar blinked and regarded her wondrous surroundings. And it was as she became lost in the magnificence of the vista that she became aware of a figure materialising from the misty glade; part horse, part reptile, part bird.

The creature stepped forward on gently placed hooves and Milissandia didn't know if she should run or hide. It had seen her and approached as if curious of her presence. It seemed to sense her trepidation and lowered itself to the leaf litter, turning to preen its fur with an amber beak.

*You have come to me at last, Little One*, it sent. The voice sounded sonorous in her mind, and at the same time like falling water. *Don't be afraid, I have been waiting for you to find your way.*

Milissandia cocked her head and looked quizzically at the Spirit Guide.

*I am not sure I know what is happening*, she sent finally.

*Destiny beckons my child*, the Spirit Guide replied. *You have been drawn here to satisfy your inner craving.*

*It is true that I long for answers to my questions, but how do you know...?*

*Tell me your yearnings. Words that escaped you in the Near*

343

*To have found their wings here in the Far Beyond. Now you must express them in dream-speak.*

Milissandia feared exposing her thoughts to this unknown entity, but she feared not-knowing more.

After a moment's hesitation she said, *I am worried about my father, and that I have been neglectful of my daughterly duties.*

*I sense sincerity in your words, but you have succumbed to your physical cravings, seeking to submerge your hurts in the waters of sensuousness. It is time to recognise the futility of this. Darkness has fallen over both your world and mine. I rejoice that you have taken the first step of your mystical ascension. It could not have come too soon.*

The Spirit Guide's words penetrated her defences like purifying salve applied to a festering wound; and though she tried to deny the release, she couldn't help revealing herself to this wise creature.

*My father came asking for help and his words fell on deaf ears in our world; but now the feelings of guilt have opened my mind,* cried Milissandia, her voice racked with deep sobs of anguish.

*I have watched from afar as you rose above your earthly desires,* the Spirit Guide sent, *and I have guided your entry into this world.*

*But why?*

*To enlighten and educate. You are the future, my child. You must now focus on your dreams and make reparations. The very future of your people depends on it.*

*I'm not sure my father will listen to me now.*

The creature rose to its feet slowly and ambled to the chasquite bush, fixing her with eyes deeper than the fissures of the earth.

*He will listen to you. His love knows no bounds. Do not desert him in his hour of need for he has a great weight to shoulder. Only by combining your youth and vigour with his experience will you both prevail.*

*I'm not sure I fully understand.*

*You will know when the time comes my child. Now go, reflect and rest. Yet whatever happens — tir ti rinov wurunwa di loreatis.*

Although she had never learned the language, she understood the meaning: Don't Ever Dream Of Dying.

*What are you saying — ?*

But the Spirit Guide had already turned and walked as if he glided over the mist-covered floor of the glade.

Then, quicker than she could react, she found herself back in the Near To. She roused herself, pushing up from the bole of the tree, dislodging a wide-eyed, iridescent green anduleso as she did so.

She smiled at it and said, "Thank you." The creature let her stroke it under the chin and listened as she declared her gratitude with a solemnity that fell from her lips like a creed. "You and I have created a wonderful serendipity. I know where my path leads now."

## 30

# BENEVOLENT MALEVOLENCE

———

Zodarin didn't know what was more wearying; the drain of energy because of his exertions in the Dreamworld, or Tratis's incessant whining at his perceived woes.

"My sister leaves without even consulting me," he said, pacing up and down his chamber. "I only found out her intentions from the Captain of the Guard. Me — the heir designate. This is unacceptable, Zodarin."

The prince had roused the wizard from a slumber as deep as death, and through a brain fogged by the greatest fatigue he had ever known, Zodarin was trying to grasp his complaint.

"So, you say she left for the north?" he said.

"Yes," Tratis replied. "Chasing after the Dragonians. She treated me as a servile messenger, saying 'Rouse the wizard.' Tell him he must finish the work he started in the Dreamworld."

"Finish? What was she referring to?" The question was not posed to gain clarity, simply to ascertain the extent of the seventeen-sol old's knowledge.

"I don't know," stormed the prince. "She said you would understand what she meant. But she repeated the instruction, saying it was of the utmost importance."

*No doubt,* Zodarin thought. *It would be embarrassing to say the least if she was squashed under the feet of Tayem's dragons.*

"Thank you for delivering the message," he said at last.

"Is that all you have to say?"

"I have other matters to attend to," Zodarin replied, massaging his temple. *Not least of which — ridding me of this accursed headache.* "Have no fear, Your Majesty. Etezora must hold you in high esteem if she has entrusted the running of Wyverneth to you in her absence." He impressed the words with his customary mesmerism, but even this effort seemed to weary him.

"Well, I suppose so," Tratis considered for a moment, "But where do I start? I'm supposed to oversee the repairs of the city walls, secure our food supply and arrange the burial of our dead. Does she think I'm a royal undertaker?"

Zodarin groaned, eager to take to his bed again.

"And what of the two Fyreclave? Should I imprison or execute them? I can't think what use they will be."

"Fyreclave ... who?"

"I forget their names — Dysentry and Murderbroth ... or something like that."

Zodarin's mind became more clearly focused at this news. "Two of the Donnephon were taken alive?"

"You know Etezora doesn't like you using that word — says it gives them too much dignity."

"Yes ... but tell me. Where are they held?"

"In the Barbican. The woman isn't too well. You should see what Etezora's done to her eyes."

Zodarin stretched a crick out of his neck. "I can only imagine. Well, let me see to them. No doubt they can yield information that will help you carry out your ... important undertakings."

The wizard gave Tratis a series of suggestions for his priorities, including sampling of the Dragonian wine cellars. "It's important that Etezora returns to a celebration worthy of her endeavours," he said. "Separate off the finest vintages and leave the rest for the officers." *That should keep him busy for an afternoon.*

After taking his leave, Zodarin made his way to the Barbican. He steadied himself twice as he walked, frustrated at not being able to fully shake off his lethargy. As he leaned against an ornate ironwood post, he noticed the back of his hand. The skin was raised in tiny blackened flakes that itched. He scratched the lesion then dismissed the distraction, willing his feet forward.

A single guard watched Disconsolin's quarters, and he

admitted Zodarin without question. The wizard found Disconsolin bending over the form of his wife, bathing her eyes with a cotton cloth soaked in some kind of salve. She was lying on a large double bed.

*Not such bad treatment for prisoners of war*, Zodarin thought.

So preoccupied was Disconsolin that he didn't hear the wizard's entrance and jumped when Zodarin greeted him.

"Forgive me for startling you," the sorcerer began.

"Ah — mighty Zodarin," Disconsolin interrupted. "Help her, please help my wife." He approached the wizard, pulling at his arm. "If it's in your power to do something, then act."

Zodarin nodded and cast his eyes over Merdreth, who he recognised from the days when Cuscosia and Dragonia shared a table at the Shaptari feasts. The woman lay motionless, the remains of her eyes still lying on her cheeks like lumps of half-digested gristle. Such a sight would not have fazed him in the past, but inexplicably, he felt suddenly sick to his stomach, disgusted at what Etezora had done.

What was this — compassion? *What a strange feeling*, he thought. *Is this a consequence of my experience in the Dreamworld?*

He suppressed the emotion, concentrating on what he could exact from the situation. These two could be useful to him, yet how typical of Etezora to vent her depredations on them.

Again, his vision blurred, and vague images flashed through his mind: a seething wriggling mass of rapidly expiring life, tortuous anguish, and excruciating pain. The import of these images echoed from beyond the centuries, yet every time he tried to grasp them with the hand of mental enquiry, his fingers closed on ghosts.

He coughed and cleared his throat. "Ask the guard to accompany you and fetch a bowl of warm dragon-balm," he instructed Disconsolin. "I take it you have some in the palace?"

"Yes, yes. We have."

"At once."

Disconsolin didn't need telling again and pulled himself away from his wife's side.

In the meantime, Zodarin put his lips close to the unconscious Merdreth's ear. "Hear me Councillor, I will try to right this wrong but you must help me. I see you sleep, but try to dream that your vision has returned and believe nothing less."

By the time Disconsolin returned, Merdreth's breath came evenly and her expression seemed more relaxed. Disconsolin placed a pitcher of dragon balm and towels on the bedside table, after which Zodarin motioned for Disconsolin to leave the room. "I need to be alone," he said, and the statesman seemed to accept this, despite his trepidation.

Zodarin picked up the pitcher and soaked his hands in the sterilising dragon balm. Then, taking each eyeball in turn, he reset them in the gaping eye sockets. Following this, he soaked a piece of towelling in the balm, and wiped residual blood from the elderly woman's face. He then reached into his waist pouch and removed a piece of mouldy shrivelled fungus, placing it across her eyes. Using all the energy he could muster, the wizard entered the Dreamworld once more. Although he felt a tug on his energy reserves, he did not succumb, and instead experienced an augmentation from the resurgent Hallows within.

The wolf stood looking down on the body of an old woman, her eyes open wide. She reached up to embrace the animal's neck, and he accepted the show of gratitude, taken aback by the turn of events. A wave of weariness broke upon him again, and he slumped down next to the old woman. Although it was at odds with his assumed nature, he found himself gently licking her face, and as she accepted his attentions a contrary stirring occurred in his breast. *This feeling is so strange. It seems to suppress the dark energy within. Should I be yielding to it?*

It was almost dark when Zodarin awoke, lying on a soft cushion in the prisoner's room. Disconsolin approached at the sound of the wizard coughing, a look of concern on his face. "Thank Sesnath, the guard thought I had somehow subdued you, rendered you unconscious.

Zodarin was disoriented. "How long have I been asleep?"

"A few hours, Lord Zodarin. I entered the room again as I received no answer when I called. You had fallen to the floor and Merdreth slept."

"You did well to convince the guard."

"He surmised I wasn't responsible for your state — I was with him all the time in the hallway, and Merdreth was in no fit condition to overcome you."

"How is she?" Zodarin asked, rising and flexing his arms and legs.

"I have seen what you did to her eyes. She woke up for a time and spoke of mysterious images, recollections of another life she doesn't understand. Yet she sees — and for that we are forever in your debt."

"She should forget what she may have seen," the wizard said, "or she will be forever haunted."

There was a period of silence before Disconsolin spoke again. "What will you do? The Cuscosian party has left for the mountains following my divulging of Queen Tayem's destination." He finished this sentence hanging his head. The shame was clearly more than he could bear.

"I will return to Castle Cuscosa to consult with Eétor, but I fear I may be too weak for the journey south."

"Surely you will travel by horseback with an accompanying guard?"

Zodarin questioned why he was confiding in this man. He didn't need to explain himself to anyone. Yet here he was, trusting in Disconsolin's loyalty. "I don't want Tratis to hear of my departure. He would not sanction my journey given the work that needs to be done here."

"I can provide you with food and means of transport," Disconsolin said, eagerness lighting his eyes. "There remains a single pygmy darastrix in the pens that you can ride, but it will still take a day just to get beyond the Vale to the lowlands — and it is almost night."

"Fly by dragon? The beast will not allow it."

"Pygmy dragons are very docile, and they cannot fly. Even I have ridden one in the past. I am too old now, of course, but it would make for a swift and comfortable transit. Far less wearisome than on horseback."

Zodarin considered this while scratching the back of his hand. Disconsolin noticed the action, and then widened his eyes.

"Your hand," the councillor said, "when did you contract the dragon blight?"

Zodarin took a step backwards, distancing himself. "Dragon ... blight?" he said. "That is what you call this affliction?"

"Yes, it is highly contagious. The quarantined dragon that the troll slew was infected, but you have not been exposed to it, so how — ?"

Zodarin swallowed, remembering the final dragon he approached in the Dreamworld. "I do not know," he retorted. "But what is the remedy?"

It was Disconsolin's turn to look worried. "Lord Zodarin. There ... there is no cure."

"No cure? That cannot be. Tell me I am not doomed to scrape my skin for the rest of my life."

"It is worse than that." Disconsolin raised his fingers to his lips, unwilling to offend the wizard even more.

"Well man? Tell me your prognosis."

Disconsolin sighed and then continued. "I'm afraid the lesions will spread. This can be slowed by application of grevalin unction, but eventually the skin will scale further and blacken before degradation results in blisters and exploding boils. Your organs will finally break down. It is not a pleasant way to die."

Zodarin reeled at the news. He saw no guile in the man and had to accept he was telling the truth. *I will not allow this to happen,* he resolved. *Yet how can I find a remedy?* He realised Disconsolin was seeing him at his weakest. Such a situation would have normally warranted the man's immediate 'disappearance,' yet it would serve no purpose here. The man could be of much use to him, given his loyalty — and Etezora's willingness to keep him alive for now. There were others back at Cuscosa, however, who *did* demand his attention, who were also aware of his vulnerabilities, and could exploit them. This attack on the Dragon Riders had become more than an irritating distraction — it had possibly signed his death warrant!

"It is perhaps just as well I am taking my leave alone, then," Zodarin said. He looked over at the reposed form of

Merdreth. "It will be a cruel blow if, in saving her sight I have transmitted a far greater curse."

Disconsolin nodded. "It cannot be helped. In any case I will know if she has been stricken within twenty-four hours."

"It *is* incredibly fast acting, isn't it? You say you have some unction to arrest its spread?"

"Yes," Disconsolin said. "In my former quarters. I can get it if I have leave to."

"I will accompany you. Then you must help me saddle up this dragon." He paused for a moment. "You realise I am probably dooming the dragon too."

Disconsolin bowed his head again. "Giving it to serve your needs is not the greatest neglect I have committed these last days."

The wizard nodded, his concession at gratitude. "Come then, I would leave straight away."

"You will be safe?"

The Hallows roiled silently within Zodarin, and he was already feeling a resurgence of power, together with a concomitant weakening of his recent benevolence. "I have adequate defences should my way be hindered," he said.

Within the hour he was steering the dragon along the switch-back path that led down the Dragon Vale escarpment. He had summoned glow-motes to light his way — a trivial sorcery, yet one that proved a boon. The pygmy dragon was pleasingly compliant and responded to his persuasions without resistance. Disconsolin had been right. The ride was extremely comfortable on the creature's wide back, its cushioned soles absorbing all but the most severe potholes in the path. He chose a route that avoided two encampments of Cuscosians and rode through the night, eager to put as much distance between himself and Wyverneth as possible. The knowledge of his affliction made his journey all the more urgent. He needed access to his grimoires and apothecary at Cuscosa in order to discover some kind of remedy. He took out the vial that Disconsolin had given him, and poured a drop of oily liquid onto the back of his hand, rubbing it into the lesion that now measured a full finger across. Next to it, one had transformed into a putrescent boil and Zodarin did not dare touch it, fearing the prognosis Disconsolin had given. Still, the unction soothed the itching elsewhere and gave him temporary relief at least.

As Sol and Sol-Ar ascended higher in the sky, then passed their zenith, he emerged from the trees of the Dragon Forest. Far to the west he could see fires still burning from the battle on the plains. *They must be cremating the bodies*, he thought. *Etezora exacted a heavy toll, but also sustained great Cuscosian losses. The sooner this madwoman is deposed the better.* The initiation of war had been rash, and now she was bent on pursuing Tayem until she was ridden into the dust. He smiled to himself. *She expects me to slay the rest of the dragons in the Dreamworld. Well perhaps I may be tardy in my attention to this task. I am* still not recovered after all. It would be a great shame if she was to meet her end in the mountains, he mused.

*One can hope.*

# 31

# BEREFT OF A KINGDOM

---

A week had passed since the fall of Wyverneth, but the ravages of that brief and momentous battle could not outweigh the anguish of what came after. If it hadn't been for the ingrained sense of responsibility and royal duty that rested on Tayem's shoulders, she would have seriously considered the way of the damned.

Of the three thousand that committed themselves to the exodus, a further eight hundred joined them from the forests on the lower slopes of the Dragonian Vale. Once they were sure they had reached relative safety, Tayem considered it of paramount importance to take a census and establish the extent of their losses. The Dragonians were a proud and close-knit people. They also possessed a centuries old community structure that ensured every household and enclave could access a leader or *shayan*, who would look after them and secure resources from higher in the chain of command. It was all too clear that an arduous journey lay ahead. The battle for Wyverneth had concluded in a rout, a mass fleeing of thousands with barely a scrap of food or extra clothing to carry with them.

Initially, the Dragonians reconnoitered the foothills of the Whispering Mountains and found a sheltered valley where the emigrating population could rest and re-organise. Yet the rise in altitude came with a corresponding drop in temperature that claimed the lives of many elderly and infirm. Any surviving wounded that limped or were carried from the battlefield had a hard time of it. Most perished from lack of treatment or the onset of infection, and each family told a lamentable tale. Many a night passed exposed to freezing temperatures, where Tayem fell into an exhausted sleep to the sound of wails and heart-rending cries. She considered giving the order for such indulgences to be curtailed, but how could she deny her people the expression of grief? The risk of giving away their location to either pursuing Cuscosians or unknown marauding tribes was quickly dismissed in favour of allowing a period of lamentation.

They lost so much — friends, family and, of course, their noble dragons. Tayem shuddered at the thought of how Etezora would have treated the slain creatures. The

Queen's depraved tastes for dragon meat were well known, and the schjek had enough flesh to fill her cellars several times over now.

It was after the third day in the valley that, following the advice of Gemain, she consented to a day of collective mourning. It allowed the Dragonians a chance to lay to rest what dead there were, and to deliver eulogies and testimonies to those who passed across the great divide. The act did much to lay a blanket over the more hysterical expressions of grief, but it would never take away the taste of defeat and sheer hopelessness that pervaded amongst the people.

As if the losses suffered and the guilt Tayem felt over her mishandling of the Dragonian response wasn't enough, she fought a constant battle with the turbulent Hallows storm within. Sometimes it took every vestige of her will to suppress the urge to mount Quassu and descend upon the occupying Cuscosians at Wyverneth with vengeful wrath. She confided in Cistre, who soothed her troubled heart with soft words and gentle massaging hands; but despite this, Tayem wondered how long she could contain the raging hurricane within. Ascomb and Gemain were stalwart advisers, taking up their share of the burden of leadership vacated by Disconsolin, Merdreth and Darer. They rightly advised that any spontaneous retaliation might expose the dragons to the mysterious weapon that assailed them at Lyn Harath. It would also divert her from overseeing the emigration of her people.

There were many other priorities to face if they were to survive as a people, but paramount was establishing a solemn resolve and a kindling of hope amongst the populace — and it was down to Tayem to achieve this.

"You should speak to the people today, My Queen," Ascomb said. "Another ten perished last night from cold or illness, and they need their Queen to reassure them, to lay out a plan for the immediate future."

"And therein lies the vexing problem," Tayem replied, raising her hands in the air with a gesture of frustration. "What is the plan? The Vicrac laid out a route and means to forge a way to Herethorn, yet its actual location evades us. What news is there from our scouts today?"

She directed the question at Gemain, who had seated himself along with the other advisers in a crudely constructed approximation of the horseshoe Fyreclave housed within Tayem's shelter.

"They have just returned," Gemain said, his expression betraying the contents of what was to follow. "Alas, they became disoriented in the accursed mists once more, as if the very weather conspired to hide the way from them. We have lost two scouts already — one fallen into a chasm, the other simply swallowed up in the fog never to return. We cannot risk a mass movement of the people until the mists rise."

"Is there any sign of that happening?" Tayem asked.

"No," Gemain replied. "They seem to be a permanent feature of the landscape."

"It is true, My Queen," Beredere said. He had been promoted to the Fyreclave along with a fiery young woman named Frodha and proved a dependable choice of appointment. "Even my patrols on dragon back have revealed no sign of this fabled sanctuary. I see Mount Gigantes to the North-West and can trace the line of mountains to where Herethorn should be, but it lies between dense pillows of mist. I tried descending into them but only narrowly avoided steering Choghym into the side of a mountain. We were completely unsighted."

"Then, with no immediate hope of permanent sanctuary I can offer nothing to the people but platitudes," Tayem said.

Gemain leaned forward, his long, white beard almost touching the ground. "You possess the golden tongue of your father," he counselled. "Don't imagine that the people need a report or relaying of facts. They need to be stirred to resolute action. We can help you draft a speech. But I agree with Ascomb — it needs to be today."

Tayem winced as she quelled another flare of Hallows energy within. It was almost as if this entity resented any words or emotions that conveyed hope or reason.

*You shall not prevail, diggod demon. Return to your dark hole, I have had enough of you today.*

Cistre sensed the disturbance and placed a reassuring hand on her shoulder. In the past, Tayem might have found the gesture irritating, but increasingly she found Cistre's subtle interventions not just timely, but *necessary*.

"Very well," Tayem said. "Gemain, help me devise a speech that will serve its purpose. Ascomb and Frodha, send word to the people to gather in the Dell once this meeting is finished." The courtiers spoke their affirmation, and the Fyreclave proceeded to turn its attention to other pressing matters. Food and shelter were utmost in importance, and it had been with great reluctance that the Dragonians acquiesced to the sanctioning of taking animal life. Ground nuts and conifer seeds could only go so far in providing adequate nutrition for the ailing people, and the trees on the mountainous slopes provided meagre yields compared to what they enjoyed in the Dragon Vale. The Dragonians hunted and trapped mountain hare, together with deer and the occasional boar, yet these were inadequate for their needs. It wasn't until the Dragon Riders found and slayed a giant garbear that the possibility of larger offerings were recognised. Of course, these beasts put up a formidable defence, but they were no match for a dragon. Silver salmon existed in the Minafael stream, but the Dragonians were not greatly versed in the skills of angling or netting the fish. So Beredere arranged tuition of the more adroit amongst the people in order to learn and pass on their skills in turn. This was all too inadequate, however, and with meagre rations it was likely that malnutrition and ensuing disease could follow.

"What of the Cuscosians?" Tayem asked, after they

completed planning further weatherproof huts and shelters. "Have they picked up our trail yet?"

"Mahren was in charge of that," Cistre said.

There was a pause in the discussion. Mahren's absence was the cause of great consternation. Indeed her departure the previous day resulted in the bitterest exchange that the Queen had ever endured. Her sister declared she was to set off and search for her Cuscosian mate. It had been typical but nonetheless irresponsible. Tayem almost wished that Sashaim had not returned from Hallows Creek with his news of the dissidents' rounding up and summary execution. Her cynicism increased further when they were told Brethis was unaccounted for, giving Mahren hope he was still alive.

"This man has you tied in knots — at the expense of the dire need that you remain here," Tayem scolded. But Mahren was clearly besotted, and could not be gainsaid. Now, as Tayem remembered their unfortunate parting, her anger was replaced with genuine fear for Mahren's safety. She was venturing into the lands of a most capable enemy, and a lone patrolling dragon might draw the attention of their unseen antagonist. The fact that the dragons had suffered no malady since that day on the battlefield held no comfort for Tayem. She was under no illusion that what assailed the Donnephon before was in all likelihood biding its time.

Tayem put the thought from her mind and concentrated

on practicalities. "Then we need another report. Cistre, can you organise a patrol this afternoon?"

"Of course, my Queen," the bodyguard replied. "I will take Sashaim and home in on the Cuscosians' last location."

Tayem looked visibly worried, and the astute Beredere seemed to pick up on this. "Do not be overly concerned, my Queen. The Cuscosians have floundered in the Whispering Mountains thus far. They are a people of the plains and are even less prepared for these altitudes than we are."

"Still," Tayem said, "I would rest easier knowing they are still confounded. It is enough of a concern that they followed as far as they did. It seems they were able to extract enough from Disconsolin despite his promises."

The Fyreclave nodded gravely at this assessment. Disconsolin and his wife were the subject of great disappointment. Whether they lived or died, the disgrace they brought upon themselves would haunt their immediate family for the rest of their lives. Donnephon honour demanded it.

Tayem dismissed the Fyreclave, save for Gemain, and they discussed the content of the address she was to give the people. The courtier was a biddable man to work with, and Tayem was grateful that amidst the turmoil of the Dragonians' predicament, the steadfastness of the noble Donnephon and experience of her advisers had not let her down. In fact, as Gemain scripted the speech, it was this spirit that inspired Tayem to deliver what could be the most important address of her reign.

When Sol-Ar passed to the third quarter of the heavens, Tayem stepped onto the cut stump of a once giant rocospen, and looked at the multitude that gathered in the clearing. An early afternoon rain had soaked the forest floor and raindrops still fell from overhanging boughs, wetting the assembled Dragonians. It did not seem to dampen their expectation, however. It soon became apparent that the Dell was not large enough to accommodate such a large throng, and the crowd extended into the underbrush. Tayem suspected its limits lay well beyond the tree boundary. She would have to speak loud to make herself heard — a talent she possessed in great measure. She held the royal Dragonian sceptre at her side, saved from the sacking of Wyverneth by Cistre. Its gold-plated standard and the crown she wore for the occasion added to her authority, the remainder of inspiration provided by the sight of so many expectant faces. Children were held on the shoulders of parents, and the stalwart elderly supported by younger members of each family.

Tayem could see the grief written on each face, but also something else; an underlying resolve, a willingness to unite in this hardship. Ascomb and Gemain had been right — she needed to deliver a message of hope, not vacuous promises she couldn't substantiate.

She struck the tree stump under her feet with the

bottom of the sceptre, and the quiet susurration of the crowd settled to silence.

"Proud Dragonians, we stand today a people dispossessed and wracked with a sense of great loss," she began. "We have buried our dead, yet their memory lives on. The circumstances of their passing fills us with an irrepressible urge to strike out at the ones who perpetrated these foul acts.

"I share your grief, I share your anger. This is all the more grievous because it is compounded by the harsh conditions in which we now find ourselves. I promised you a sanctuary that has yet to materialise. For this I apologise. It has meant we renounce the dietary requirements of vs' shtak — never to eat the flesh of beasts. Our ordeal has resulted in the regretful death of many through exposure. These things lie heavy on my heart. Yet I see before me today a people unbowed; women, men and children who have refused to let themselves fall into the dust of defeat."

She paused for a few seconds, trying to weigh the mood of the crowd, but it was impossible. The resolute expressions could have been stares of disdain or solemn politeness, she could not tell. There was nothing else to do but strike up a message that would stir their hearts.

"The way ahead will be difficult. Etezora and her curs pursue us, and we have yet to find a way to the sanctuary. Many more will die, and hunger will gnaw at your stomachs for some time to come. But I would ask you, humbly, to hear my promise to you. I will not rest until I have brought you to safety. All I need is your continued trust. You placed your faith in my ancestors and in myself on the day of Gilfarin, when the Dragonian crown was placed on my head. Will you walk with me still?"

These words drew murmurs of assent from the crowd, together with an isolated shout of agreement, and Tayem felt the first stirrings of encouragement.

*I am getting through.*

"I would ask you to remember the legacy of Ralgemah the Pyre-Queen," she continued, not wanting to lose her momentum, "and the spirit that saw our ancestors emerge from the Marauder wars as a proud people; a race uncowed by their oppressors. They built the kingdom of Dragonia, and though it has been wrested from our grip, I promise you this — we shall claim it back!"

At this point there rose a loud cheer from all sectors of the crowd. Those who had remained dour up to this point raised their fists in salutation.

It was more than an expression of solidarity, an indefinable spirit of unity and purpose seemed to have taken hold, such that children, hoisted on numerous shoulders, broke out in smiles of wonder and wordless cries of triumph. *What is this?* Tayem wondered, and as she took in the gravity of the occasion, she noticed with relish the malign whispers of the Hallows were at once silent. The entity was subdued, though not banished.

"I do not address you as subjects," Tayem continued,

"but as brothers and sisters. The Donnephon do not reign in the cruel manner of the Cuscosians. Their enmity and internal strife will be their undoing, and one day we will throw off their yoke once again. Therefore stand proud. Take this moment with you to your beds, and rise tomorrow morning with renewed hope and vigour.

"As my concluding words, I offer to you the tenet of Ralgemah: 'There is no shame in reaching for the Sun, even if you fall from the sky.'"

This last part was unscripted. Gemain did not write it, nor had they even discussed it. Yet as she looked at him, he nodded his reassurance.

By now, the multitude was roused to chanting in the ancient Dragonian tongue. She descended from the tree stump and retreated from the crowd with the cheers still ringing in her ears.

Cistre followed close behind, together with Gemain and Ascomb. They had not walked far when Frodha approached with two guards, holding a young girl attired in a dark-green, cowled tunic.

"My Queen," Frodha said. "Forgive me for the intrusion, but this woman has insisted on speaking with you. I would have dismissed her, only she has said things that convince me you should hear her out."

Tayem turned to the girl, surveying her strange angular features. "Who are you, outlander?" she asked.

The girl bowed in deference. "Queen of the

Donnephon, my name is Milissandia, and I have counsel that may save your people."

# 32

# SHADOW OF SHAME

---

The first beams of sunlight crossed the boundary between the shaman's mountain cave opening and the rock shelf outside, bringing with them a creeping sense of foreboding. There was a time when Sol led the heavenly arc, and Wobas used to welcome this infiltration of his domain. But now that Sol-Ar had become pre eminent, the indigo-hued insolation brought nothing but dread. The rays evaporated a jewellery of morning dew-drops hanging precariously on swaying emerald green grass blades as if Sol-Ar's baleful touch had banished them.

Wobas sat cross-legged on a hard stone floor, drawing the last of the warmth from a dying fire of smouldering coals. He raised his eyes again and looked beyond the cave mouth to the sun-drenched hills. It should have been a cheering sight but nothing could lift him from his melancholy.

If it hadn't been for his encounter with the augur-imposter in the Dreamworld, he might have succeeded in marshalling his thoughts and strategies, found a way out of the blind canyon that was his estrangement from Milissandia. As it was, the experience had made him dread entering a realm he had previously considered a haven. He had questions for Memek-Tal, if the Spirit Guide would grace him with its presence, that is. Yet every time he contemplated passing across to the Far Beyond, a choking fear paralysed him, rendering him incapable of coherent thought or decisive action — the same feelings an age-old acquaintance had once instilled in him.

*This is an affliction of the mind*, he told himself. But even this diagnosis could not stir him from his hermitage, and he did not possess the remedies to cure him in the cave. Perhaps there was one he could reach out to? But who might know about his predicament? He was, after all, Herethorn's shaman — and what value a sooth-sayer who cannot heal himself?

He closed his eyes and uttered a low moan of despair. Yet even closing himself off from the immediate world in this way held no release. With eyes closed, his mind conjured unforgettable images of writhing tentacles and oozing pustules. Vignettes of a deathly terror that haunted his dreams, left him sleepless and fatigued.

His eyes snapped open again, and he allowed the next hour to pass staring at the glowing embers as they dulled to black, leaving only inert powder. He felt terrible; he had no energy and pain ate away at his joints. Adding to this were the incessant headaches that tormented his waking hours.

*Please give me deliverance from this malaise.*

There was no relief for him, however. His inner nervousness now began to manifest itself as a restless itching in his joints and an aching of his muscles. Eventually he had no choice but to rise to his feet, resting one hand on the wall, wincing as pain wracked his stooped back.

*You old fool. What use are you to anyone? And that you should choose this time to wallow in self pity while cataclysmic events loom for the Gigantes?*

Then, through the woollen margins of his perception, he detected an approaching figure; large, looming, and threat-filled. His eyes scanned the immediate vicinity but could make nothing out.

*Am I under attack? Who has penetrated my magical defences?*

Nobody had ventured north of the treeline in many a sol-cycle; and even if they did, they would become confounded in the sorcerous snares he had laid about his cave. Again, Wobas thought he heard something but his eyes detected no movement. A panic gripped him.

*Is this how it ends? Death by an unknown assassin's hand?* He glanced at the ashes of the fire wondering if his own life flame was about to be snuffed out.

*Perhaps this is for the best.*

As he offered a prayer to the mountain gods, a voice carried across to him on the wind.

"Wobas," it said, "Wobas, are you there?"

Out of the heat-haze a familiar silhouette emerged, and for the first time in weeks, Wobas' mouth curled with the hint of a smile. "Ebar, is that you?"

Wobas watched in disbelief as the giant came lolloping over a ridge and along the path towards the cave.

*Bless his heart — the Cyclopes has found a way through my enhanced Dastarthes perimeter!*

He willed his weary legs forward out of the cave, holding a hand up to shield his eyes. This was no apparition. The Gigantes statesman's signature presence could not be denied. "Why are you here?" Wobas stammered.

Ebar approached his reclusive friend and looked down on him with kindness, his large central eye blinking as he gathered his breath. "There is much to discuss my friend, and time is against us," he said, looking at the dishevelled being before him. "When did you last eat and sleep?"

Wobas rubbed his eyes with one hand. "I forget. The desire for food has abandoned me and my sleep is filled with dream phantoms."

"Here, taste this," Ebar said, thrusting a skin into the

shaman's hand. "Fresh fig berry juice. Drink deeply, it will refresh you."

Wobas accepted the giant's offer and took a deep draught from the skin. The juice sent a re-vitalising energy through him as soon as it hit his stomach.

The two friends settled on the comfortable weathered granite, letting silence speak while one gathered his breath, and the other his thoughts.

"So what is so important to bring you beyond the tree line?" Wobas said after a time.

"Worry."

"The burdens of leadership?"

Ebar blinked at him earnestly. "Concern for *you*, my friend."

"I did not want to be sought out," Wobas replied.

"Which is a very good reason why I *should*," the Cyclopes said. "I have never known you withdraw for this long without telling me."

Wobas hung his head. "A great malaise afflicts me."

"I can tell that," Ebar said, "which makes me wonder why you didn't reach out for help."

"I fear no one can help me."

Ebar placed a gigantic hand on the shaman's shoulder. "Tell me," he said, "and hold nothing back."

Wobas saw the compassion on Ebar's face and understood he had to expose his vulnerability — it was either that or die. And so he related the Dreamworld encounter, and how a sickness borne of fear had descended upon him.

When he had finished, Ebar looked east and took in the sight of the Hallows rupture; a gash in the mountainside that even in this strong sunlight spewed forth an effluvium of purple energy. "I think you have spent too long in the presence of that baleful source."

"You know that I never succumbed to its temptation," Wobas said, defensively.

"I'm sure you didn't," Ebar said. "But the Hallows waxes strong. See how Sol-Ar's beams reach down to the earthly rupture. It is as if they conspire and strengthen each other. The very air has changed. Reports reached us from outlying hamlets lying close to yonder Hallows. They speak of people growing restless, arguing amongst each other. Husbands and wives quarrel over insignificant things and lifelong friendships are broken. If that is how the Hallows can affect things at that distance, think how you must suffer being *this* close.

The Cyclope's words rang true and Wobas felt he had been given a key to unlock his affliction.

"Blindness has overtaken me," he said, his voice reduced to a croak, "and my powers have deserted me."

"Nonsense, my friend. You see matters through eyes distorted by the Black Hallows malignancy. I know it is within your power to aid us. Emerge from this shadow of shame and help protect our people." Ebar paused wondering if his friend was listening to him.

"Our world faces a great threat from the plains," he continued. "A ghost from the past given life by the Hallows energy has emerged. The Cuscosians rise in anger once again and bring terror to the dragon-folk. Even as we speak, the Donnephon flee their ancestral home and make their way towards us."

Wobas looked down to the earth. "This is a disturbing turn of events. If the Donnephon should discover us, our people will be overwhelmed as they seek their own sanctuary. But surely they can't circumvent the Dastarthes mists?"

"So far our defences hold, but Tayem is a persistent monarch. The Council fear their incursion into our lands. History led to our isolation and it must remain so. The dragon-folk are not wanted."

"And you come to me for help?"

"Yes. Your powers can enhance the hanging mists — just as you bolstered your own peculiar defences here."

"*You* managed to breach them."

"Only thanks to a charm provided by Ginnie." He fingered a rusty looking amulet hanging from his neck.

"I did wonder," Wobas said. "But I'm not sure I possess enough reserves of strength to aid you yet. The attrition of this last few weeks has overwhelmed me."

Ebar gripped the shaman's wrist. "Let me take you from here. I beseech you — return with me to my home and spurn this hermit-like existence which is driving you mad."

Wobas looked hesitant. "I will disappoint you."

"You have never proved untrustworthy in any respect. All I ask is that you try. If the Donnephon reach our homes then who is to say if the Cuscosians are not far behind? Then what will become of us? Think of my family, your daughter. What will become of her under the tyranny of Cuscosia, if you don't at least try to aid me?"

At the mention of Milissandia, Wobas closed his eyes as the pain of their last encounter returned.

"Ah," Ebar said. "That brings me to another vexing subject."

The shaman opened his eyes again.

"Your daughter," the giant continued, "has not been seen this last week either. Vaedra had sent word for her to tend to his son's broken leg — a casualty from one of the Hallows' influenced family feuds. A string of messengers returned with no report of her whereabouts. She also missed her weekly clinic."

Wobas became weary beyond endurance at this news.

"I am sorry to be the bearer of further bad tidings, but I sent Brownbeak to search the lower hills. We can only hope that some misfortune has not overtaken her." He took another look at the Black Hallows. Another flare of energy escaped from the scar on the landscape. "Let us go before all your dreams turn into persistent nightmares, and peace of mind eludes you forever."

Wobas nodded his assent. "I will come," he said. "Your

words carry great wisdom. But tell me, is there anything else I should know?"

"Let us depart, and I will tell you as we walk." Ebar was clearly anxious to capitalise on Wobas's surrender to his offer before the shaman changed his mind.

Wobas gathered a few belongings in a sack and accompanied the giant away from his retreat. Ebar chose a route that skirted the Hallows rift as widely as possible, the Cyclopes stepping slowly to allow Wobas to keep up.

"I heard Kaldora Prime is no more," Ebar resumed his news-telling. "The stories are a little unclear, but travellers said the Cuscosians attacked Jennu Narod, causing a cataclysm that engulfed the valley. We are told no one survived."

"The Kaldorans too?" Wobas exclaimed. "The pain of Dragonia reached me in my dreams, but I received no omen of the stonegrabes' predicament. Perhaps if I had ventured back into the Far Beyond, I might have detected this, but I am afraid to re-enter the Dreamworld. It is inhabited by another of great power, something that has possessed or usurped the Augur there." He went on to describe in detail the monstrosity he had glimpsed, and the repercussions that manifested themselves through his dreams.

Ebar listened as Wobas described his encounter with the Augur, together with the pain and anguish arising from visions of a future violent death. After listening, the giant said, "There are myths that tell of beasts similar to the one of which you speak, but they were slaughtered many aeons ago."

"No," Wobas replied. "This was as real as you and I. It exists in a different form now, and walks the halls of Castle Cuscosa, I am sure. Yet its true identity still eludes me. It reminds me of one I once knew. But that ghost of violence is dead too."

"Are you sure?"

Wobas dredged his memories or a recollection of his last encounter with the one called Zodarin. There was some uncertainty over the circumstances ... "Perhaps ... I don't know," he muttered.

Ebar, seeing his friend was lost for words and tired, decided to hold his questions for now.

It seemed like an eternity before Wobas saw the shape of the Gigantes village emerging from the Dastarthes mist, and by now he had had to relent to Ebar's offer to carry him on his shoulders.

Shamfis came running from Ebar's house to greet them, beckoning the giant to bring the shaman inside. He was laid on a bed covered with garbeast blankets.

After furnishing him with a warm brinn-herb broth, Shamfis said, "Rest will be the best medicine. Now come and sit with the children. They have missed you."

It was two days before Wobas was well enough to leave his bed. Shamfis had tended to his needs and his appetite had returned. Now, sitting on the blackwood platform, he took pleasure from watching the children play, although their youthful energy tired him. Djabi, the youngest of Ebar's children crawled across the floor collecting wooden building blocks while Dshambi, the elder child followed. They stopped when they realised the shaman was watching.

The two children looked at the stranger momentarily, and then went back to their play, setting out blocks in the form of a Gigantes village. Their laughter was infectious, and Wobas felt the curtains of darkness part, allowing a ray of optimism to penetrate his tormented soul. He was so engrossed in watching the children play he didn't see Shamfis standing in the doorway. She paused for a moment before quietly going to fetch Ebar.

When they returned, they found the shaman on the floor with the children, telling them a tale based on the scene they had just constructed. Wobas's face was animated as he recounted the myth of the Cyclopes while the boys listened to their diminutive storyteller with wide-eyed wonder.

"It seems our shaman has undergone a healing of sorts," Ebar said to his wife.

"Just as well," she replied. "You both have much work to do before time runs out."

"Give him the remainder of this day," Ebar said. "He deserves that much."

# 33

# PATH OF THE GIGANTES

———

Mahren blinked twice. *Am I even allowed to think this is true, that it is not a dream?*

"Careful," Sashaim said, "I do not trust these humans."

Her small group of Dragon Riders stood at the top of an incline just south of Mount Gathan, having picked up the trail of a large band making their way through the coniferous forest earlier that morning. They looked down at some two hundred figures picking their way through the dense trees toward them. The man who led the way was uncharacteristically bearded, but boasted a crooked nose she remembered with great affection.

"These are not just any humans," she replied. "I would recognise Brethis anywhere."

Although these words were true, she had to admit the dishevelled staggering figure she saw leaning on a garbeach branch appeared to be weathered as if by a storm; beaten but hopefully not yet cowed. The flesh, exposed by holes in his ragged clothes, was scored by a dozen cuts and grazes, fragments of bramble leaf and twigs tangled his red hair. But the defiance in his eyes remained.

"Thank Sesnath for that," she whispered to herself.

"Brethis — is that you?" She called out to the man, forgetting Saishim's admonishment to refrain from any noise that would give away their location to Etezora's patrols.

The man she had thought dead looked at her in puzzlement, and then broke out in a broad smile. "Mahren? Gods, I cannot believe it. As the blood courses through my veins, can it be?"

The sound of his voice triggered Mahren into motion. She cast caution aside as she ran towards him. Her emotions goaded her to leap into his arms, but his obvious injury restrained her at the last minute. What a travesty it would be if her over-exuberance caused him to tumble down the steep hill and break his leg — or worse. Instead, she slowed her pace and held him in a tight embrace, half-holding him up.

"My love, I did not dare hope," she said, showering him with kisses.

He held her tight with one arm, clearly needing the other to support himself on the stave. "Word reached us of the Donnephon defeat," he said. "I too feared the worst for you."

"I may have survived, but the truth is we are a people on the run and defeated ... at least for now." She stepped back and took a closer look at him. "Are you hurt?"

He looked down at his right foot. "Stood on a chasquite-thorn spelk on the lower slopes. It's driven in deep."

Mahren sighed with relief, thankful that at least he hadn't been wounded by the Cuscosians. "Our surgeons can see to it," she said, then kissed him again, less urgently this time, but with a lingering borne of fear that this might be a fleeting moment of bliss. Sashaim approached behind, alternately scanning the trees and a gathering crowd of Cuscosians for signs of hostility.

"Who are these people?" Mahren asked Brethis.

"Refugees," Brethis said. "When Eétor's guard slaughtered our families, I fled with Oathair here. Others joined us. It was only a matter of time before Chalmon targeted them. There are many others still dwelling in Hallow's Creek sympathetic to our cause but unwilling to stand up to Etezora."

Mahren noted the pain on his face and stroked his grimy cheek. "I am sorry to hear of your family. None survived?"

"They butchered old and young alike. But their actions forged a blade of defiance that will have its revenge. I led these people through the forests seeking a place to regroup and build our resistance."

Mahren looked at the crowd of sullied humanity with a sense of pity. She had not seen a more unlikely group of revolutionaries. "They will not fare well if you lead them further toward the mountain. It is a cruel sentinel and its slopes are home to marauders and garbeasts. You are better joining us further to the west."

"Surely Tayem will not countenance this," he said.

Mahren fixed him with a resolute stare. "*I* will not countenance otherwise."

The remainder of that day was spent ferrying Brethis and the wounded via dragon to the Donnephon camp. Sashaim remained with the other humans — those who were reasonably fit — to act as guide and lead them back to the Dragonian camp on foot. The lieutenant was somewhat reluctant (Mahren could see it in his face,) but obedience elicited a dutiful response, and he promised to undertake the task to the best of his ability. Mahren estimated it would take another day at least for them to reach their destination. Time enough to prepare Tayem for their arrival, a task she did not relish but was determined to accomplish. It was also time enough for Etezora's troops to discover them if fortune conspired.

She circled Jaestrum in order to approach the Dragonian camp from the north, keeping him close to the treeline, ever fearful that at any moment an invisible assailant might strike him from the sky. She had named the unknown enemy 'Shadow Man,' although she could not be certain it was in fact a man who had perpetrated the atrocity. The only reassurance she had was that she would recognise the premonitions if they happened again. At Lyn-Harath, the malignant tremors she had perceived on the ether had only given her minutes warning, but it would be enough to perhaps execute evasive manoeuvres. It might be a vain hope to steer her dragon out of range from the hidden adversary, but she was prepared to try anything if it meant saving Jaestrum.

Brethis held on to her in the dragon harness, petrified at this most breathtaking of journeys. Mahren found it difficult to see things from his perspective as riding dragons was second nature to her, but she guessed it must be singularly unsettling. Once alighted safely in the makeshift draconest, she called for the dragon-hands to help Brethis to the physicker's quarters. The thorn would be removed there and give him much needed relief. In the meantime she mentally prepared herself for the inevitable meeting with her sister.

She found Tayem in her command hut, deep in conversation with Gemain, Frodha and a peculiar looking woman dressed in what seemed like druidic apparel. When Tayem laid eyes on her, Mahren thought she detected a hint of relieved warmth in her sister's demeanour. However, it was quickly replaced by a look of stern disapproval.

"I'm astounded you have the gall to show your face here

again," she said. "Did you decide to call off your fruitless search, sister?" Her curt response drew a calming hand on her shoulder from Cistre, who stood, as ever, behind her. Mahren had noticed Tayem tolerating this tactile comfort more readily in the last week. It might have raised her hackles before, but she saw how it seemed to help still the Hallows malignancy she knew resided in her.

Mahren decided not to rise to Tayem's scolding. "I bring heart-lifting news, My Queen. Brethis is alive, and he has led a surviving group of dissidents out of Cuscosia."

She waited for the outpouring of vitriol and was surprised when, instead, her sister cocked her head. "That is ... good news," she replied. Then, turning to the dusky-skinned woman said, "It would seem that your predictions are holding true so far."

"My hope is that it will be enough to convince you to accompany me along the path to Herethorn. I too have my own reparations to make with a family member — I understand all too well how hard this can be."

"Come join us," Tayem said to Mahren. "This is Milissandia, dweller in Herethorn and representative of the ancient Gigantes."

"Gigantes?" Mahren said, sitting on a roughly hewn tree segment, "but you're so ..."

"Small?" Milissandia replied, smiling. "You are thinking of the Cyclopes. They are the progenitors of our race, but mostly our kind are of shorter stature. The woman's accent was truly outlandish, with 'rs' pronounced like the sound 'ah,' but after a little adjustment, Mahren was just about able to make out her meaning.

"I would request something from you, my Queen," Mahren said, eager to get this next part over with.

"You wish us to give succour to the Cuscosian dissidents?"

Mahren bit her lip, "I know our resources are stretched, but — "

"It shall be done," Tayem said. "If we are to defeat Etezora then we need to recognise and welcome all who would lend us their aid."

*What has come over her?* Mahren thought. "You have no objection?"

A purple light flashed across Tayem's eyes. It did not go unnoticed by Milissandia. "Your Majesty," the Gigantes said, "I sense a great conflict in your soul. If I may make so bold; did you drink of the Hallows?"

Tayem looked at the soothsayer sharply. "You overstep your position of trust, wise-woman. I — "

Cistre rubbed her Queen's shoulder, distracting her, and it was Tayem's turn to be interrupted. "You have no need to conceal what lies inside your heart, or indeed to be ashamed of inviting something you thought would give your people hope," Milissandia said. "But understand this; the Black Hallows has nothing but chaos in its mind. If you hold on to its essence — it will surely destroy you and your people."

At her words, the Hallows light audibly crackled as its

energy seeped out of Tayem's eyes. This was to Mahren, the Hallows most overt expression she had witnessed since fighting by her sister's side on the battlefield. At the time, it had given her a perverse feeling of satisfaction as she saw how the power leant strength to her sister's assaults, reaping the Cuscosians by the dozen. But now it only filled her with dread.

No words passed between any of them until the fire subsided. When it did, Mahren saw a look of helplessness pass across Tayem's face.

"How can I be purged of this affliction?" she said, and Mahren recognised the significance of the confession. What she didn't understand was how this strange woman had drawn it from her proud sister.

Milissandia sighed. "Alas, it is not within my power to exorcise you of the Hallows' dread influence, but I know one who might achieve such a thing."

"Who?" Tayem said, her upper lip trembling.

"My father."

# 34

# AT WATER'S END

———

Zodarin had allowed himself to fall asleep in the dragon's saddle. The gentle sway of the dragon's gait induced a soporific effect, and although his eye kept partial watch on the immediate environment, his mind drifted towards the Dreamworld. This was an unprecedented occurrence as in the usual course of events he would consciously invoke the transition. But since the killing of the dragons he had found the border between the Near To and the Far Beyond increasingly blurred.

The wolf craved solitude. It was wounded, infected — legacy of its encounter with the darastrix. The harroc found it disquieting to have this sense of malaise in the Dreamworld. The disease affected not only his sense of wellbeing but also his vision. Images shimmered like mirages, and when they moved their edges became indistinct, blending with those that came before and after. Was that the winged night sentinel he saw? It seemed to watch him from its perch, eyes filled with dread, but also pathos. He could not remain under its gaze and broke into a run, distancing himself from a creature he suspected was a friend come enemy.

He ran over rolling downs until he reached the forest. *Perhaps I might find rest in the shadows,* he thought. But even here there was no solace. There, in the lower branches of a garbeech he spied a tree serpent. The sight of the creature would have been unusual in itself, as they were a retiring species, yet this one was immensely beautiful, with skin of iridescent greens and blues. Why had he not seen it before? Instinctively, he knew it was a *she.*

The anduleso watched him with a sense of animal caution mixed with a higher being's audacity, and although the creature was dazzling beyond measure, he had the desire to seize the thing in his jaws and relieve it of its life force. As these emotions rose within the wolf's breast he found his form changing, reverting to something more primitive. *What is this?* The wolf that was Zodarin grew, its outer skin sloughing off to reveal something altogether more slimy and warty. His last transition to this ultimate form had been ordered consciously, but this —

this was beyond his control. He felt the Black Hallows fuelling the change, but the direction and speed of the transformation were being interfered with by some other agency. Something he could neither predict nor control.

Events were transpiring at a rate that defied him. Before the change could complete itself, he sensed a force drawing him back to the Near To, a protective strand of magic warning him his presence was required there.

He came to his senses with a jolt, the dragon halting abruptly. There, rising out of the grass tussocks in front of him were three vile Kaldorans. The first was larger than the others, its skin encrusted with suppurating rocky scales. Two scrawnier individuals flanked this one, each encased in shabby stonegrabe armour. The tall one, obviously the leader, brought a slingshot to bear upon him, a wicked looking spiked sphere loaded in the launching pouch. The other two wielded spears with jagged, hooked tips, fashioned for melee and capable of tearing open a victim's innards when withdrawn.

"Stand down wizard," declared the leading stonegrabe. Its voice was the grating of two stones against each other.

"Stand down?" Zodarin replied, "but I am unarmed."

"Watch his hands, Gruford," muttered the one on his left through blubbery lips, "don't give him a chance to cast one of his cursed spells."

"I know!" Gruford replied, irritated by his henchman. "Wizard — raise your arms."

Zodarin smiled. "As you wish." He dropped the reins and slowly complied with the stonegrabe. It was amusing to him that the Kaldorans believed he required arm movements to exert his power, but he obeyed their wishes nonetheless. He cursed himself for not being more alert, but the fact they had not simply shot him from his saddle indicated they had other mischief in mind.

"Tie him to the tree, we need to know what he knows," commanded Grufrod.

"My noble Kaldoran friends," Zodarin said, "no need to be uncivilised. Tell me what you want and I'm sure we can come to some agreement without resorting to unpleasantness."

It was Gruford's turn to smile. "What — and do without our fun? Tarchon's blessing on that one, human. You *will* tell us what we want to know, but not before we've had our sport."

The two henchmen pulled Zodarin roughly from his saddle, and then made to slay the dragon.

"Your Fellchief will thank you for keeping the dragon alive, my friend," Zodarin said. "Fresh dragon meat is always more favourable than old, and you are far from your borders."

"We do not answer to Magthrum," a henchgrabe said.

"Quiet, fool," Gruford said, slapping the Kaldoran across the face.

Zodarin did not offer any resistance to his treatment and allowed the Kaldorans to pull him to a lone yarra tree where he was bound with thick witch-hemp ropes. He noted they refrained from killing his compliant steed, however.

*They aren't exactly the sharpest needles in the sewing kit,* he reflected.

He tried to engage the stonegrabes in further conversation, but Gruford commanded them to ignore him while they tied the dragon to a hammered-in stake. As they lit a fire the twin suns descended toward the horizon, and Zodarin surmised the Kaldorans would want to eat before starting their devilment.

*Always putting their stomachs first,* he thought. Despite their limited exchange, he had already gleaned useful information. They held no allegiance to Magthrum, and they understood the currency that dragon meat represented. This was not a typical preserve of Kaldorans — more of Cuscosians. *Hired hands then,* he thought.

He contemplated entering the Dreamworld to dispose of them, but that realm had proved unpredictable. He decided instead to employ subterfuge.

As they pulled out pieces of indeterminate meat that Zodarin suspected were human in origin, they muttered in their guttural mountain tongue. He was too far away to overhear their conversation, and if he was to learn anything before they carried out their threats, he would have to act soon.

"Are Kaldorans still partial to a sack of gold or two?" he shouted across to them.

Gruford looked up from his meal, scowled, then ambled over.

The wizard looked up at the stonegrabe and offered his friendliest of smiles. "Deliver me safely to Cuscosa and I will pay you twice that which Eétor offered you," he said.

"You can afford three hundred gold pieces?" Gruford said before realising his mistake. His fist extinguished Zodarin's smile as it slammed into his jaw. "You think you can weasel information from us, wizard?" He said. "It will do you no good, seeing as you won't survive this night."

Zodarin spat out a mouthful of blood and then met the Kaldoran's gaze. "Are you sure about that?" He sensed a growth emerging from his side and realised he had expended considerable energy restraining the transformation that now become undeniable. *Let it come, then.*

With a suddenness that took even Zodarin by surprise, the tentacle that had emerged from his back lashed out at the Kaldoran, snaking around his throat and constricting viciously. It took only three seconds for the stonegrabe's neck to snap, and so swift was the wizard's attack that the other stonegrabes did not even notice the execution of their leader.

Further tentacles emerged from the dissolving form of the wizard, and his body swelled like a bladder filling with water. This was not a pleasant experience for Zodarin. He felt as if his internals were exploding, and every nerve ending was afire with excruciating pain. The physical disruption to his body was traumatic enough, but more so was the total abandonment of control. A loud moan erupted from what had been his mouth, and the ropes about him snapped as easily as gossamer.

The commotion was enough to attract the attention of the remaining two stonegrabes, who rose to their feet, eyes wide in terror. One soiled itself, a sickly green effluvium dripping down its leg, while the other turned on its heels and ran.

Zodarin did not so much leap forward but *surged*. Now that the transformation fuelled by Hallows energy was complete, an inexplicable joy filled him, as if he had cast off centuries of imprisonment. He overwhelmed the transfixed stongrabe, only vaguely aware that he had snuffed the creature's life out, and then moved across the plain in pursuit of the last fleeing prey. As he closed in, seeing its terrified face looking over its shoulder, a faltering occurred within. The conflict that had caused his release now seemed to be absorbing his energy. He was slowing, and Zodarin faced the very real possibility that the Kaldoran might escape.

*No, this shall not be!*

Then the fates intervened. The stonegrabe was running headlong in the half-light and its rocky foot stumbled on a clump of reeds. It was brought to the ground, limbs tangled amongst themselves. Then Zodarin was upon it, his savagery unleashed, inflamed by a frustration and bewilderment at the phenomenon he experienced. This was not the sadistic gratification exhibited by one such as Etezora, but an archaic primal hierarchy expressing itself. Uncountable tentacles wrapped themselves around the stonegrabe, and although Zodarin's strength was on the wane, their constricting power was enough to burst the fragile Kaldoran shell. The stonegrabe's intestines were forced up through its gullet while every bone snapped under the irrepressible force.

As the rocky body went limp in his embrace, an extreme lethargy overcame Zodarin and he fell forward into blackness.

A sandpaper-like rasping on his raw cheek brought Zodarin to his senses. He was laid on his back, blinding sunlight piercing his eyelids. He forced them open and saw the dull visage of the pygmy dragon stooped over him, licking his face. He tried to raise his hand to ward it off but didn't have the strength, so he lay like that for another half hour.

*So I have reverted to human form again,* he thought.

The wyrm had imprinted itself upon him, somehow uprooting the stake that restrained it.

He was thirsty, a throat-parching insatiable dryness. More than this, it was a bodily yearning to be immersed in water. These feelings were strange yet somehow familiar, primal desires reaching out from an indistinct past.

He gathered his resolve, and with a little nudging from the dragon, managed to sit up. Around him was evidence of the previous night's carnage, the ruin that was the Kaldoran's bodies spread over the floor of the plain. He assumed the events had occurred the previous night, but now he wasn't so sure.

*Gods, how long have I been enveloped in blackness?*

He examined the back of his hands. The skin had now turned completely black and pustules covered them like a bubbling, pestilential carpet. Worse than this, the blight had started to spread up his wrists. A despairing moan escaped his lips as he contemplated how much time he might have lost.

*I need to access my pharmacy and grimoires. I also need to deal with Eétor.*

This recent encounter had taught him three things: Eétor had plotted against him, his primal nature was coming to the fore, and time was running out for dealing with the dragon blight.

## 35

# THE ANGER WITHIN

---

"You have lost the trail again, Captain?" screamed Etezora. The shriek echoed through the forests scattering a flock of ringed doves from a tree overhead.

The man winced. "Yes, Your Majesty, it's as if the dragon-folk vanished into the very trees."

It was the end of another arduous day, trekking almost aimlessly through the lower wooded slopes of the Whispering Mountains, and Etezora had reached the end of her patience. The Cuscosians were a people of the plains, and Etezora was tired, hot and irritable — the result of steering her horse around what seemed like an endless morass of vegetation.

---

"We know they headed for the mountains," Etezora said, the frustration and menace in her voice unconcealed. "Why do we not simply strike out for the nearest pass?"

A troop of Praetorian Guard had scouted ahead of the main Cuscosian caravan following what they believed was the route taken by the fleeing Donnephon. As the undergrowth had thickened, progress had slowed to a virtual standstill, and the Captain had called a halt, returning reluctantly to deliver his report — and face the wrath of his Queen.

"These are uncharted lands," the Captain replied, "and we are not equipped for higher altitudes. It is my guess the Dragon Riders aren't either. They are a people on the run, and would perish on those heights."

"So they cannot be far from us," yelled the Queen. "Tuh-Ma followed the trail with ease yesterday, why is it you can't, Captain?"

He blanched, trying to choose his words carefully. "With respect, my Queen, your troll ... I mean ... loyal consort possesses particular skills. But since he came down with the wyrmbite, he has been next to useless. His senses are dulled and — "

"Quiet, dolt. Do not give me your 'with respect' mord. You show me no respect whatsoever. You do not need to remind me of Tuh-Ma's predicament. What I need is competence and decisiveness — and you provide me with neither. Dismissed."

The man saluted, grimaced and guided his mount away

from the Queen, thankful she hadn't chosen to vent her rage on him in a more fatal manner. Two commanders had already had their employment terminated during a luckless foray into northern Dragonia already, and he clearly didn't want to join them.

It was the second piece of bad news Etezora had received that day. Why were circumstances conspiring against her and the pursuit of the dragon schjek?

Since the Cuscosian battalion had left Wyverneth, Tuh-Ma had led the scouting party, his well-honed tracking skills soon identifying the route of the fleeing Dragonians. The remaining bulk of the Cuscosian force had made good progress through the open woodland of the Dragonian Vale. Yet once they had reached the sub-tropical deciduous forests of the lower Imperious Crescent, progress slowed to the pace of a gar-slug. This came to the fore when they encountered the marshes and lagoons marking the transition from Vale flatlands to denser upland forests. They had subsequently spent days hacking through undergrowth that seemed to conspire against them, wandering in circles despite Tuh-Ma's tracking abilities.

"Tuh-Ma sees many trails leading off from each other," he had said. "But when Tuh-Ma follows one for a few hours, it circles back to where they all began." The blue-skin had been forced to follow each individual trail in turn until he happened on one that led away in a consistent direction. This success lifted them, and they believed they were closing in on the escaping Donnephon. That was until they had made camp the previous night. While the troops had rested, small blood-sucking insects living in the marsh grasses surrounding what they hoped was the last lagoon, feasted on their exposed skin. The insects' saliva transmitted virulence to their victims causing severe itching and a rash. It was only a matter of hours before the soldiers were writhing in the throes of wyrmbite. The infection affected the lungs, causing fits of wheezing and intense congestion of the nasal passages. Much of the Cuscosian battalion were reduced to a sneezing, spluttering mass of misery.

Tuh-Ma had been bitten repeatedly. Whether it was his exposed leathery skin, or something in his blood that attracted the insects, he had suffered more bites than the pale skinned Cuscosians. He had come down with a fever and rendered immobile as his limbs refused to support him.

Etezora understood these facts, but the Hallows madness was upon her, and it was difficult for any to turn aside her fury. Her second in command, a man called Heliot tried, nonetheless.

"Your Majesty," he ventured, pulling his steed closer to Etezora's. "We are unable to proceed in these circumstances. We have significant casualties as a result of the wyrmbite. Your men need treatment and it would behove us to fall back to the Vale and consider another strategy. I'm sure your exceptional mind will think more lucidly away from this miserable environment."

Heliot was better at choosing his words than the Captain, and Etezora deigned to listen. "Captain Nestra chose this campsite," she said, glaring at the retreating officer.

"In his defence, Your Majesty, the terrain is foreign to us, and we left Wyverneth without adequate preparation and limited supplies. We are not equipped to deal with this illness."

The man's assessment was reasonable, but the Hallows wasn't. Etezora felt it rise like bile within, consuming her rational mind and oozing out like a vile, irrational ichor. A tendril of energy snaked out towards Heliot's throat and he flinched from its approach, beads of sweat forming on his pallid face. Yet just before it wrapped itself around his neck, a vestige of restraint stayed Etezora's hand.

"I suspect a note of insubordination in your words, Heliot, but I will show mercy on this occasion. What do you recommend?" She said.

After a moment's pause the colonel sat up straight in his saddle and adjusted his tunic.

"My Queen, the Donnephon can wait. They — "

"Do not use that word in my presence," Etezora rasped, "It gives them too much respect."

"As you wish, Your Majesty," the man continued. "The Dragonians are hemmed in by the mountains too, and they are many in number, carrying sick and wounded. We have caught sight of their dragons occasionally in the distance, but always this side of the mountain range. It is my belief they have nowhere to run and no one to help them. I therefore beseech you to let us regroup and tend to our sick — *your* troops." He concluded his entreaty, closing his eyes and expecting no mercy.

Etezora bit her lower lip trying to dissipate the anger within. Perhaps Heliot was right, she thought. She *did* need Tuh-Ma, and there would be medicines at Wyverneth. Perhaps Zodarin's wizardry could help. In addition, his sorcery might be used to seek out the Dragonians' whereabouts. Hopefully he had already disposed of the bulk of Tayem's wyrms, although the presence of some above the mountains was still a concern.

"Very well," she said, slapping her skin to crush another offending insect, "prepare the men for departure. Carry the sick on biers, the able-bodied can take the burden."

"As you command, Your Majesty," Heliot said and left her with barely concealed relief.

~ ~ ~

Tratis was in conference with Disconsolin when he learned of Etezora's imminent return. The 'runner' had entered his offices advising of the Queen's aborted mission. He smiled to himself, secretly enjoying the misfortune that had befallen his manic sister.

Etezora strode briskly into the throne room five minutes

later, her troll and a small entourage following close behind.

Tratis smirked at her and was about to pass a snide comment when he noticed the thundercloud of her visage and thought better of it.

"Not a word from you, brother. I know what you think, but you do not rule Cuscosia yet; and it would be unfortunate if you were to fall foul of some misfortune before your accession to the throne," Etezora said with menace.

Tratis endeavoured to drop his smile, but only half succeeded. "What — you don't even veil your threats now, Sister? You speak of misfortune, but it appears you have enough of your own to contend with."

"That dragon schjek!" Etezora said, dropping herself onto Tayem's throne. "I swear to you I will slay the Dragon Queen before the month is out." She kneaded the arms of the throne as if trying to draw authority from it. "Now where is Zodarin? I need his council."

It was Tratis's turn to look uncomfortable. "I understand he has returned home."

"You ... understand? Either he has, or he hasn't. Which is it?"

Tratis took a seat in the horseshoe and clasped his hands together. "He left without notice. I do not know when. I suspect deception."

"You are a fool Tratis. That wizard follows his own agenda. I thought he was too unwell to travel."

"So did I. But the facts speak for themselves. I sent out a small search party, but they returned without finding any trace of him."

"I will send Tuh-Ma to summon Eétor — when he is well enough. Once he arrives back, we will discuss family matters, and how to deal with the wizard." She paused. "How are the repairs to the city walls progressing? Do we need to prepare for a counter attack?"

Relieved that the subject had changed, Tratis outlined the ongoing program of works and the growing inventory of supplies. "Our patrols report no sign of an incursion. It would appear the rout of the Dragonians is complete. They have only found isolated peasants and woods-people in the surrounding forest. Nothing to raise concern."

"Nothing indeed, other than a lack of a workforce to see to the rebuild program."

"Give it time, Sister. Already, an influx of three hundred builders and carpenters from Cuscosa has bolstered our workforce. There are more on their way. Our consolidation of power here is assured."

Etezora breathed in deeply. "Very well. I see there is much you have accomplished. Maybe you are ruler material after all. Now, what of the Kaldorans? Have they been kept at bay?"

Tratis gave his sister a calculated look. *How will she receive what I am about to tell her?* He cleared his throat. "There is good news and bad. A messenger from Cuscosa arrived just this morning. He reported that the stronghold of Regev is no more."

"Really?" Etezora exclaimed, sitting up straight. "What happened?"

Tratis conveyed the truncated report passed on from Eétor. It had taken over a week to discover what had befallen at Regev as Urrel the ambassador had not returned, nor had any of the battalion. What they knew had to be pieced together from the remains they found — and the bodies.

After he had finished, Etezora's face was unreadable. She said nothing to him, but called for Cuticous and a plate of dragon meat. Tratis knew better than to interrupt his sister's deliberations, especially when a purple glaze periodically passed over her eyes, accompanied by a barely susceptible electrification in the air. After a time she declared, "The sooner Eétor appears here in person, the better. The Kaldorans defeat looks auspicious on the surface, but where are the survivors? And what befell Captain Torell and our soldiers?"

"We don't know. But I agree with you," Tratis replied. "Understand that I have directed patrols and spies along all our borders, but we have yet to hear further news from Kaldora."

Etezora tore into a large piece of cured dragon meat, chewing on it like a raptor as she thought. Tratis's stomach turned at the sight, and he wondered how he could in all truth be related to this unstable monster. *Bide your time,* he told himself.

"I would talk of other matters," Etezora said after swallowing her meat. "The Dragonian traitor, Disconsolin. Where is he? I have a score to settle with him."

Tratis looked around. "He was here a minute ago. I suspect he may have retreated to the dragon pens, he spends time there when not caring for his pitiful wife."

"Then we will accost him there," Etezora replied, the purple aurora extending like a haze from her eyes. "Once I have washed away the stains of that accursed forest, that is. Tuh-Ma, pour my bath."

"Yes Mistress," the blue-skin replied, limping away, a continued weakness resulting from the wyrmbite.

"Meet me at the dragon pens in an hour," Etezora commanded Tratis, who bowed then returned to his quarters, glad to have escaped relatively unscathed from his audience.

~ ~ ~

Disconsolin stood at the edge of the ancient shale pit, watching over the Agnarim dragon. He had been present at the initial interchange between Etezora and Tratis and was relieved she hadn't questioned him about Zodarin's disappearance. Nonetheless, he had slipped away as soon as he could. Though he had proved his usefulness to

Tratis, he couldn't be sure the Cuscosian Queen would hold him in such high esteem. He remembered the torture his wife had endured, her screams at the pain inflicted upon her by the sadistic monarch. He shuddered at the memory then fixed his eyes again on the sleeping beast.

Oga had escaped the attention of the Cuscosians thus far. A minor miracle considering his size, but perhaps the almost instinctive enmity the humans harboured for these magnificent creatures dissuaded them from investigating the dark recesses of the draconest.

The massive clay-coloured dragon had spent more than a decade in the bosom of Sunnuth, and although Disconsolin was no rider, he knew enough from the lore that he was undergoing the great metamorphosis.

The sound of approaching footsteps startled him from his musings, setting his heart racing. At the sight of Etezora and her courtiers striding towards him, the elderly statesman tensed, dreading what mischief she had in store.

The Queen stood before him, imperious and haughty, her head inclined as if weighing him up afresh. "Tratis informs me I was right to spare you, Councillor, yet I am shall we say ... perturbed at recent turns of event."

Disconsolin remained silent, unsure if explanations or questions would serve his cause or not.

"What is in this pit, Dragonian?" asked Etezora looking down into the darkness. "Wait, don't tell me. That pathetic wyrm still sleeps after all these sols?" she laughed, the sound of it very much like that of a hyena to

Disconsolin's ears. "Typical male, dozing while his mate takes to the battlefield and dies."

Tratis, who had arrived with his sister, peered into the gloom then stepped back from the edge as if sensing danger. "I think it best we leave well alone, Sister — "

Etezora raised her hand to silence him, then stepped closer to Disconsolin. "What would he say if that wyrm knew his mate featured as main course on my dining table every night?" She accentuated the statement by licking her lips.

Disconsolin knew she was toying with him, yet he could not stop the rising tide of panic in his breast.

"What do you think Dragonian?" The Queen continued, "Should I slay this monster as he sleeps, just like we did his brethren on the battlefield?"

Shame and fear warred within Disconsolin, but in that watershed moment he decided that he would offer unquestioning subservience no more. He stepped between Etezora and the dragon. "Your Majesty, I have betrayed my people once, but there are limits to how far I will stoop. If you intend to put an end to this noble line, then you will have to do it over my dead body."

Etezora stared at him, the very air crackling with Hallows fire, and Disconsolin reckoned that his lifespan measured in seconds. Then, the Queen tilted her head back and expelled another hyena laugh to the cavern roof. "Hah! The courtier has some spine after all. I may spare you yet — just for amusement. It all depends how you respond to my questions."

Faster than Disconsolin's eyes could follow, a tendril of Hallows energy whipped out from Etezora, forming a lasso around the councillor's throat and constricting viciously.

Etezora stooped over Disconsolin as he fell to his knees. "How is it that the Dragon Riders manage to elude me Councillor? Did you tell the truth about the route to their sanctuary?"

Nothing but a gargling sound escaped from Disconsolin's throat.

"Ahem, Etezora," Tratis said. "The man cannot speak if he has no air supply."

The Queen sighed, as if denied a treat, and then relaxed her hold on the man a little. "Speak," she hissed.

Disconsolin cleared his throat with some effort then said, "I told you what I know, Your Majesty, but I cannot be accountable for our fleeing people's ability to hide their trail."

"Then perhaps you are no use to me after all."

"Wait Sister," interrupted Tratis. "I need this man alive. He has proved invaluable in the running of the city, not to mention his expertise in the rebuilding program."

"You weak fool Tratis. If you had more ambition, you would see through this man's deception," Etezora replied.

Tratis stared at his sister, as if appalled. *Even her brother fears her*, Disconsolin thought.

But Tratis was an expert diplomat and seemingly arrived

at a method to circumvent Etezora's rage. "Sister," he said, "I feel your anger at the Dragon Riders, and I sense that the power you hold needs its release, but do not vent it on this man. You are wiser than that." He nodded at the pit below in an unspoken suggestion.

Whether Etezora recognised Tratis's distraction for what it was became immaterial as the Queen could contain the Hallows no longer. She looked down at the slumbering dragon, leering in ecstasy as dark malignancy overcame her. She pointed at the defenceless beast, screaming as she discharged the full force of Hallows energy at it.

Disconsolin rose to his feet to witness the appalling spectacle of Etezora's bolt striking the dragon's back. There was a sound like that of a great ignition as a chunk of dragon scales and flesh erupted from the site of impact. As smoke from the charred flesh cleared, it was uncertain if the beast had reacted to the assault at all. Then a deep rumbling passed from the side of Oga's mouth. He rolled over and moaned in pain. First one rhomboid eye, then another opened, fixing their focus on the source of his torment.

Etezora screeched her annoyance at having achieved so little from her opening salvo and sent out another bolt of purple energy. The ethereal missile struck the dragon on its exposed belly, and this time the damage was much greater. Oga roared in agony, the wind of its breath reaching the figures above and blasting them with its odour. Etezora's courtiers screamed and fled from the cavern while Tratis took hold of his sister's arm. "You have barely scratched its hide!" he said. "The beast is too formidable. We must retreat from this place."

"Never," Etezora replied, and Disconsolin saw in her eyes the absence of sanity as the Hallows fire rose again. A bolt, twice as intense as the previous two, erupted from her fingertips and struck Oga's wing, raised protectively as the beast threw off the last vestiges of its long slumber. It rose on its back legs, the two rhomboid eyes set in its elongated head staring at the Cuscosian Queen. Measuring over one hundred spans from snout to tail, the gargantuan stretched its wings wide. The backdraft from its exertion caught them by surprise, knocking Tratis and Disconsolin to the floor.

By virtue of the Hallows' extraordinary invigoration, Etezora remained standing and let out a manic laugh, raising both hands to target two bolts of Hallows energy at the gargantuan beast. Her power was on the wane, however, and the dragon's more resilient frontal scales deflected them. This time, Etezora's shriek was that of frustration as she realised events were spinning out of her control. Oga bore down its wings, raising a wind that even Etezora could not stand against. It swept her back, her foot tripping over Tratis's prostrate form. The dragon rose to full height, climbing the rough-hewn walls of the pit and casting its huge shadow over the three bodies lying in the dust. It examined them through baleful orange eyes as if deciding how they should die, and for the second time that day Disconsolin showed his latent valour.

"Noble Oga," he said. "I beseech you. Fly from this place and go serve your Queen. Do not waste your might on us." He supposed they were words uttered in vain, yet the beast regarded him, moved its snout up and down as if nodding, then looked upwards. The cavern roof was a dome of shallow rock with a small aperture at its apex to admit the light, and Disconsolin understood that this king of dragons would not wait for him to open the great doors. It pulled itself onto the surrounding perimeter of the pit and rose, its back pushing at the fragile crust of rock above. The layer might be like tissue to the dragon, but the weight of material above would crush the life from the helpless figures below.

"Tratis," Disconsolin shouted. "To the adjoining chamber, before it's too late."

Oga strained against the ceiling and already chunks of rock began to rain down. One struck Disconsolin's shoulder, almost knocking it out of joint. He ignored the pain, pulling himself to his feet. Tratis had managed to stand too but Etezora lay motionless. They looked briefly at each other, an unspoken understanding transferred through the dusty air. Then another shower of rock fell.

"We must pull her away from danger," Disconsolin said.

"Er ... of course," Tratis said, but Disconsolin could see the reluctance in his eyes.

"Help me," Disconsolin said, "before we are buried in rubble."

And Disconsolin of Wyverneth would regret his decision later, but he took the lead in dragging Etezora's unconscious form from the cavern. With Tratis's aid they escaped the final deluge of rock that marked the rising of Oga from his ten sol repose. Unrestricted by the shattered dome of rock, the dragon unfurled its wings to their full extent and rose ponderously into the sky. He circled the palace once, growling in anger before turning and flying north.

# 36

# AMONGST THE MIST AND SHADOWS

———————

It was always a source of consternation for Tayem, deciding who she should entrust with the command of the Dragonian people in her absence. Mahren was the default choice, but in these circumstances it was necessary for her inclusion in the prospective journey to Herethorn. Beredere had proved more than capable recently, but he might have to make decisions required at a political level, and that was not his forte. He was a military man, and an accomplished Dragon Rider, so at least he could be trusted to defend the Dragonian remnant in this place. Tayem had her doubts about his ability to make more statesmanlike decisions.

Then there was Cistre. She had all the qualities of a leader yet was subservient and attentive to Tayem — particularly so of late. This diminished her in the sight of the Donnephon and the people in general. Sometimes she seemed so content to remain in the background. But then, her role as bodyguard necessitated this. Nonetheless, she would disapprove of leaving Beredere in charge. The two of them did not get on. Was it perhaps Beredere's barely concealed amorous overtures toward Tayem? Cistre could be so protective of her Queen — even claustrophobic. Why should it concern her if Beredere had romantic motives in mind?

In the end, it was a straightforward choice. She had to make decisions based on pragmatism, not by any notion of upsetting people's feelings.

"We depart for Herethorn in the morning," she declared at the conclusion of the Fyreclave meeting. "Mahren, Cistre, I need you to accompany me along with a retinue of the Royal Guard. If Milissandia can guide us to the sanctuary, then it is important we do not appear to pose a threat."

"Passing through the Dastarthes mists will not be difficult," Milissandia said. "But an audience with the Gigantes elders? That will be the harder task. You are wise not to travel with a large company of soldiers."

"We must succeed in this," Tayem said, her brow

furrowing as she concentrated on suppressing another Hallows flare-up. "Beredere, take command of the people. You know the priorities — guard the perimeter of our camp, secure our food supply and oversee the construction of sturdy shelters."

"As you command, my Queen," Beredere replied with a deferential bow. "At least we have some respite with these reports that Etezora is withdrawing her company from the lower slopes."

"Indeed," Tayem replied, "but be vigilant. The Cuscosian Queen is a cunning snake, and it could be a ruse."

"My Queen," Mahren interjected. "Can I suggest a liaison detail to ensure our dissident allies are integrated properly?"

The Hallows energy flared again at her sister's perceived impertinence, but Tayem recognised it for what it was, and quelled the irrational reflex to utter a retort. "Very well. Gemain, this will be your brief."

Gemain accepted the order, and with that, the council meeting finished leaving Tayem and her entourage to make preparations for the expedition.

Milissandia assured them the trek would take less than two days, and they should carry supplies accordingly. She also administered a soothing potion for Tayem, recognising the strain the Hallows was exerting on her. The herbal concoction induced sleep, rather than a purging of something that Tayem now recognised as spiritual cancer. As she drifted off into a drug-induced slumber, her last thoughts revolved around the conflicting motivations that led her to allow the dread influence in: a conclusion to her father's lifelong search to engage with the Hallows; the need to secure a source of power to aid the Dragonians; and a less than selfless desire to exert control.

As if reading her thoughts, the Gigantes druid spoke gently to her as consciousness left Tayem. "Learn to forgive yourself," she said. "It is a troublesome path, I have learned. But one we must all tread."

Twelve hours later, Cistre roused Tayem. "It is time to leave, my Queen. I left you sleeping as long as I could, but we need to take advantage of every daylight hour."

Tayem rose unsteadily, Milissandia's potion leaving her disposition groggy. But the anticipated resurgence of the Hallows was absent for now. *Unpredictability,* she mused, *isn't that the very nature of chaos?* It was the road that Etezora had chosen to follow — yet another reason for Tayem to reject it.

After half an hour of vigorous trekking up the steep wooded slopes of northern Dragonia, Tayem's head had cleared, but her thigh muscles were already feeling the strain.

"Our dragons would have eaten up these miles," she said to Mahren who had matched her stride. Cistre was taking the lead behind Milissandia, stating that she didn't quite trust the druid and wanted to keep her eye on the stranger.

"True," Mahren replied, "but you know they are confounded by the mists, not to mention the intimidation they would present to the Gigantes."

Tayem's lack of a reply indicated her acknowledgement, if not her total acceptance. They continued in silence for a time until Tayem could not contain her question any longer. "There is something on your mind, Sister. Speak. I cannot bear your prevarication."

"You don't make it easy for me to broach the subject," Mahren replied. "There are many things that weigh upon me, but I realise you have your own burdens, and I do not wish to add to them."

Tayem stopped to catch her breath, looked out over the valley they were skirting, then sighed. "Forgive me if I am short with you. It is not always I that speaks, but this wretched malignancy within."

Mahren looked at her with a sad smile. "How is it?" she asked.

"can tolerate it," Tayem replied, but her expression contradicted the statement.

"Do not see sharing your feelings as a sign of weakness. If the last month has taught us anything, it is that we cannot face the future in isolation. You need to trust us to help you. Perhaps part of this is confiding in those closest to you. Let me make it easy. I know my absences and impetuous actions have driven you to despair, and for this

I am sorry. I also understand your mistrust of the dissidents, and your disapproval of Brethis in particular. But our rules sometimes work against us, hem us in when we could co-operate with those of like mind — and our aims are the same as Brethis's movement. Anyway, this sounds like excuses, but it is my attempt at an apology. I know you need my loyalty and support. I offer that to you now."

Tayem looked at her sister, saw the sincerity in her eyes and nodded. "You speak the truth, Mahren. It is hard for me to let go, and for a time the Hallows seemed to offer a way of achieving our survival. But I see now that its agency came at an unacceptable price. Even now it stirs within, tempting me with the desire to lash out at any who would stand in my way. This manifests itself in my words, yet if I gave it free rein, I shudder to think what it might lead me to do."

"You would become like Etezora."

"That is why I must be cleansed of this terrible virulence."

"Milissandia seems confident her father can accomplish this."

"She does. But that does not mean her confidence is well placed. She has told me of the rift that exists between them. What if he refuses to help?"

Mahren placed a soothing hand on her sister's arm. "Do not think of it. We must live in hope."

Tayem locked eyes with her. "Yet if this proves to be

a disappointment, I must make provision for the stable leadership of the Donnephon."

"If that were to happen, and I don't believe it will, then there are others that can assume the mantle of leadership."

"That would be you, dear sister."

Mahren frowned. "You know that is not something I actively seek."

"But your duty to the kingdom would nevertheless require it of you."

Mahren lowered her gaze. "If that day should come, then I would reluctantly accept the rulership from you."

Tayem looked away from her at the wooded slopes stretched out beneath them again. "And what if the swelling malignancy of the Hallows did not allow it? You have seen how its unrestrained power can affect me. The Donnephon may have to act decisively ..."

"You don't mean?"

Before Tayem could reply, Cistre joined them, having back-tracked from the head of the party. "My Queen, is there something amiss? We were worried you were not keeping up."

Tayem looked knowingly at Mahren, and then replied, "We are fine. Come Sister, we should increase our pace."

With the conversation effectively terminated, Tayem concentrated on keeping up with Milissandia. She would resume the vexed subject she had raised with Mahren at a later time. For now, she wanted to question Milissandia further.

This proved to be more of a task than she expected. The girl was evasive, a trait Tayem should have recognised as one who was protective of her own thoughts and emotions. But, then again, might Cistre's suspicions be justified? She knew so little about this strange woman. Perhaps the timing was not right. She decided to let her be for the present.

The party took a short rest under a sheltered overhang of rock, a place where they remained concealed, yet could observe the surrounding area with the viewpoint of an eagle. From this elevated position, Tayem scanned the vista laid out before her. The lofty peaks to the north seemed to assert their nature as monoliths of the aeons. They did not need to declare their pre-eminence, their very nature demanded it. Further to the south, she traced a line from a distant ridge of garbeech known as the *Gar Skjalli* to where a rise in the tree line marked Wyverneth's position behind. These arbours too seemed to murmur their communion as one voice, and though the Hallows rebelled at the notion, she tuned into the wordless message of the million living sentinels that sent their roots into the sacred soil.

Never had she surveyed the kingdom of Dragonia from this perspective, and as she viewed its grandeur, her previous sense of ownership was displaced. She saw now that she and her people were not so much rulers of the land, more its custodians.

*I will be true to this charge,* she thought, *and I swear that things will change if you simply allow the spirit of vs' shtak to prevail.* Her thoughts were a prayer, and though her faith in Sesnath had dwindled in recent sols — she was, after all, a most reclusive of deities — Tayem needed something to hold on to.

They resumed their journey shortly after, and the terrain grew more rugged. Milissandia seemed able to pick out trails as if she shared a mountain goat's disposition. This meant that, although the route was arduous, they covered ground more swiftly than the previous scouting parties. As a reminder of what they faced upon their return from this quest, Sol-Ar beat down upon them as it reached its zenith, smothering the bright yellow of Sol with its violet glow. As Tayem absorbed its rays, she felt the long subdued Hallows rise in response. Her mind grew irritable, and the cacophony of conflicting desires and temptations swelled in sympathy with the malignant source.

By the time they had gained the summit of yet another peak, the storm within Tayem had reached unbearable proportions. Milissandia advised a halt to the day's journey saying, "We have made good progress. We can afford to make camp here and allow our Queen to rest."

This they did, and as the painted sunset sky shone like a great purple window at the end of a cathedral aisle of mountains, Tayem allowed her to administer another dose of sedative potion.

"I hate relying on this witchery," Tayem said tetchily, but drank the draught.

Milissandia looked taken aback for a second, but nodded in understanding. "It will not be for much longer. My remedy will not create a craving in you — unlike the influence that invades your body and mind. Now lie back and let sleep do its work."

The druid made to withdraw, but Tayem indicated for her to wait a moment longer. The girl could not be any older than Tayem, and the Dragonian Queen recognised a similar tempering of rebelliousness with the rapid maturing that comes with adversity. "Speak to me truly," Tayem said. "What are the chances of your father succeeding in this ... this driving out of the Hallows?"

Milissandia inclined her head, and then looked off into the distance, not saying anything. Her manner was such that Tayem thought she would shrink back again — as she had earlier that day. "My father and I are in conflict at present," she said, surprising Tayem.

"I believe you told us, yes."

"We have been estranged for many sols, and I do not know if the damage done is irreparable. But certain things have happened to me recently that mean I must seek reparation. I can only hope he is not too far gone to reach a meeting of minds." She looked back at Tayem, and the Queen tried to read what was behind the steel-grey eyes that regarded her — but it was impossible. "One thing I do know," she declared. "Wobas, Great Shaman of the

Gigantes has the ability to treat your condition. However, I do not know the full consequences of that treatment. There is always a cost to such undertakings."

Tayem nodded, her mind fogging over as Milissandia's potion took effect. "I have come to learn the truth you speak of in the mysterious tapestry of life," she said, slurring her words. "Yet anything is preferable to this torment."

"Rest now," Milissandia whispered, and as the curtain of sleep closed upon her, it was as if the druid's whispering became one with the breeze that gave the mountains their namesake.

By late morning of the next day, mists rolled down from a greater ridge of peaks that Milissandia identified as the borders of Herethorn. They extended at first like silver-grey tongues that licked at their feet, but once they had entered a denser canopy of garpine, the fog accentuated the trees making them appear as phantoms, monstrously magnified as if to convey an unspoken threat. The Royal Guard, though battle-hardened and bold, became jumpy, bringing their weapons to bear every minute. Such was their nervousness that Milissandia called a halt to speak with them all.

"The path will become increasingly treacherous from now on," she said. "You will allow me to lead. Step only where my feet tread. One misplaced footing could see any of you fall into the chasm ahead. The place is called Aichrach's Fall, and not without reason.

They all accepted the druid's instruction and fell in behind her. Yet even though Milissandia was confident in her ability to track a way through the mists, she became more hesitant as the minutes extended out.

"What is it?" Cistre said eventually, her patience wearing thin at the frequent pauses to their progress.

Milissandia exhaled deeply. "I came this way but three days ago, yet there is something that confounds the way. Someone has laid additional confusions in our path. Do you not hear the voices?"

Tayem strained her ears, and at first heard nothing. Then, faintly, a host of mournful wails came to her.

"Mountain ghosts," declared one of the Guard. "They will invade our minds. Drive us to madness."

"Still your cowardly tongue," Cistre scolded. "Phantoms cannot hurt you."

"No," Milissandia said, "but what they herald can."

"What do you mean?" Mahren said.

"They are often accompanied by illusions. Trust nothing you see. I suspect the hand of my father in this."

"Why would he seek to harm you?" Cistre said.

"The Gigantes will be aware of Etezora's presence on the lower slopes, and they will have strengthened our defences."

"Can't you ward them off?" Tayem asked.

"It is beyond my ability," the druid replied. "We can

only press on. But keep each other in sight and let nothing distract you."

Milissandia's usually inscrutable manner gave way to a worried expression that disturbed Tayem. However, she followed her into the mist, placing her trust in the girl. What choice did they have? The mists had closed in behind and there was no sure way out of this deathly place without her.

As they walked forward, the moaning grew in volume and floating apparitions assailed the party, brushing their faces and hands, eliciting shudders and the occasional scream.

"They are not real!" Milissandia said from up ahead, the sound of her voice muted by the fog. "Ignore them."

*Not easily accomplished,* Tayem thought.

As time elapsed (Tayem couldn't be sure whether it was seconds or minutes,) a sense of isolation fell on her. She had lost sight of Milissandia in front, and when she turned her head, there was no sign of Cistre behind. Devilish phantoms bearing the faces of those known to her, only distorted into grotesque parodies, loomed at her with increasing intensity. Such was their relentlessness that she found her own voice moaning in sympathy with the sounds they made. This was fear like she had never known.

Then, to her relief, Milissandia appeared out of the whiteness ahead. "Do not be afraid," she said, extending her hand. "Hold on to me, and I will guide you out of this madness." Tayem took it, and although the druid's touch felt like ice, she grasped it with a desperation born of extreme terror.

"Not much further," Milissandia said, and Tayem felt herself pulled forward, much faster than before, feet stepping recklessly, carried along by the panic of one who is truly lost.

She abandoned herself utterly until her foot stepped into nothingness, and she pitched forward into the emptiness. Milissandia was gone, and she let out a scream cut short by a rough tugging on her belt. She was hauled backwards into the embrace of Cistre.

"You followed a phantom," her bodyguard said. "It lured you into the abyss," and she pointed at where the mists were temporarily blown away. In front of her was a chasm that fell away into nothingness, its sides bearing jagged shards of rock pointing upward like daggers, taunting her to fall onto their cruel points.

She looked back at Cistre, and a sudden misgiving overcame her. "How do I know you are real?"

Cistre smiled at her reassuringly — a rare thing — and cupped her hands around Tayem's cheeks. "Do I feel like a phantom?"

Warmth emanated from the woman's hands, and Tayem understood this was someone who would always be there for her, unquestioning, loyal, steadfast; and she saw in her eyes something more. *Could it be ...*

"There you are!" It was Milissandia. "I told you not to trust anything you saw."

"A fine thing to say when these kruts can shapeshift to appear as yourself," Tayem retorted.

Milissandia sighed, holding her hands up in frustration. "Curse my father. If only he realised he has inadvertently brought about the end of those that might be his only hope of saving the Gigantes."

"You cannot lead us from this place, then?" Tayem said.

"I could make it on my own, as I recognise the subterfuges of Wobas, but I cannot watch over all of you."

"Did someone mention my name?" The voice came stridently from somewhere above them.

Milissandia looked up and narrowed her eyes. "Do not trust what you hear. It is another phantom."

"I am no phantom," declared the voice, and immediately a vast gust of wind blew down from the heights, dispelling the blankets of mist and allowing the blessed light of Sol to illuminate their surroundings.

Tayem steadied herself, and then gasped at what she saw. Towering over them were dozens of enormous figures, each the size of a young garbeech. Some were dressed in woollen robes, while others wore leather tunics. At their head stood a much smaller man leaning on a staff, his expression hooded.

"You keep suspicious company, Daughter," the man said.

"Father," Milissandia replied. "I have not come to seek a quarrel, and these people are no threat to you."

Wobas turned to the closest giant and made to speak, but before he could, the figure sternly signalled to the other giants who descended upon the Dragonians, seizing them in hands the size of shovels. Tayem could do nothing to resist, even though the Black Hallows coursed vigorously through her, increasing her strength tenfold. The giant raised her up, as did the others with the rest of her cohort. Then they transported the Dragonians away from that place to a land of wonder and impending peril.

## 37

# DREAMER DECEIVER

---

Zodarin drifted in and out of a restless sleep, waves of tiredness washing over him, yet the deep slumber he craved eluded him. Turning this way and that on his comfortable bed, he cursed the shifting images that surged through his mind; strange visions from an ancient past. Were they nightmares or memories of a different time and place? It was impossible to fathom.

Locked in a state he could neither wake from nor control, he was subjected to scenes that disturbed him in their alien nature, yet brought to mind a familiarity that had remained dormant for centuries. He saw his birther; the caring being that guided him through his early life and protected him from the barbarity of the past. She … it … had nurtured him, even sacrificed itself — of this he was sure. Now a great yearning and sense of loss assailed his psyche. The memories were so distant that he struggled to make sense of them, and they certainly didn't explain the entirety of his experience since contracting the cursed dragon disease. However, increasingly, he understood something of his origins, if not what his future held in this multiplicity of forms and consciousnesses.

He was finally wrenched to wakefulness by the memory of his birther's dying screams, and he reached for the skin at his bedside. It contained a potion he imbibed every three hours since returning to Castle Cuscosa. It soothed the internal itching he felt from the dragon blight, but hardly slowed the progress of the disease.

As he sighed in reaction to his misfortune, part of him longed for a time before the Dead Zone battle; when his fortunes were on the rise, and he was confident in his increasing power and apparent control over the Hallows influence. Now he was sure it conspired with the dragon blight to wreak an irrevocable change in him, a longing for his original state together with an irrational notion of benevolence towards others. What other explanation was there for his empathic actions towards Disconsolin and Merdreth?

Only yesterday, while stalking around the village as Oswald, he experienced an irresistible desire to immerse himself in the waters of Hallow's Creek. This was only arrested at the last minute by the aversion to water of his feline form. He wondered what that tentacled thing might have done if he had allowed it to usurp his feline body? Yet he did not dare give the thing that destroyed the Kaldorans unfettered reign, for he feared the longer he allowed himself to assume its shape, the lower the likelihood of returning.

So many questions that required answers, but now the urgency to deal with his treacherous former ally loomed close, and he must give his energy to it. Sol had not yet risen, and the potion was beginning to take effect. Perhaps he might gain an hour's sleep before he set about the day's unpleasant duties.

Sleep once again descended, and this time he dreamed of events a little more recent, a happier time when he enjoyed the hospitality of the Dragonians. In particular, he recalled his friendship with the hill shaman, Wobas.

The Dragonians had taken Zodarin in as an abandoned youngster many hundreds of sols ago, and during the course of his maturing years his ventures into the Dreamworld exerted a greater influence upon him. He soon learned that his longevity was far greater than those who surrounded him, and so as not to arouse suspicion he would disappear into distant lands once he reached a certain age. In this way he adopted a society for a lifetime, only to return once a new generation emerged in the intervening time. It was migratory behaviour born of the need for protection. He knew all too well how outsiders were treated. How much more so with an off-worlder?

Of course, it also meant he spent many sols infiltrating a community and establishing himself. No wonder it took him so long to find a sustainable position of power.

And so it came to pass some fifty sols ago that he once more arrived at the lush forests of Dragonia. He and the young man, Wobas, became friends, sharing spiritual desires and talking about their dreams often. Zodarin's knowledge of the Dreamworld took centuries to amass, yet here was one who seemed to float into that realm effortlessly.

When they explored the Far Beyond together, Wobas had an innate ability to commune with the avatars they encountered there. The wizard learned that he could trade his knowledge of natural magical lore for Wobas's insights into that most wondrous of realms.

Zodarin did not remember exactly when the divide between them sprang up, but he did recall the reason. He had assumed the form of a wolf more frequently, a transformation that disturbed his confidante, Wobas.

"Why would you want to assume the form of such a fearsome predator?" Wobas would say.

Zodarin could not reveal the entirety of his growth in power to the youthful Wobas; that he partook in the euphoria that accompanies an avatar's slaying. He was careful to only bring down his prey while on solitary prowls. But eventually Wobas had learned, witnessed the killing of a small mammal in the Dreamworld. Back in the Near To it resulted in the death of a Dragonian family's goat. The circumstances remained a mystery to the family, but Wobas knew.

This would not have been irreparable had it not been for the intervention of an arrogant, spiteful warrior called Atsa. The man went out of his way to humiliate Zodarin, taking every opportunity to insult and assault him. Eventually, the sorcerer could not take any more and tracked the man's avatar down in the Dreamworld. When the man's body was found in the Vale — having succumbed to mauling from a wild beast — Wobas confronted Zodarin, demanding he confess to the Fyreclave about the incident. When he refused, it was Wobas who took his suspicions to the council. As a result, the fearful people cast out the wizard. He wandered alone for many a sol until proving himself useful as a sorcerer to the House of Cuscosa.

These memories formed pastiches in Zodarin's half-sleep, each one eliciting different intensities of emotion. Most profound was his recollection of the report concerning Wobas's disappearance. He'd thought him dead, but now it was all too evident the shaman had simply bided his time with the Hill People. How did he feel about him now? He was certainly a threat, and he would never forget how he betrayed Zodarin to the Dragonian Council. Yet, he could not find it in himself to hate Wobas — especially now that Zodarin committed the most heinous of acts — the slaying of the dragons. His was the greater sin. Perhaps Wobas was right all along. He possessed a dark heart to match the Black Hallows that dwelt within.

He rose from his bed and poured himself a green-berry juice. It refreshed his dry throat, and he quickly poured another cup, walking to the window and staring out at the grasslands beyond.

"The scops," he said under his breath. *Strange how Wobas now assumes the form of a predator too. And what of the tree serpent? This is surely a being of great significance too. But what is its identity?*

Further deliberation was interrupted by a sound at the foot of his tower. He waited a short while until he heard the soft padding retreat, and then carefully opened the door to his upper chamber. He walked to the edge of the giant spiral staircase and looked down.

*Grizdoth snooping again. This must be curtailed.*

Returning to his chamber he sat down and made a decision.

*Within moments the wolf stalked the grasslands of the Dreamworld once again. It was a strain to prevent the easy slippage into his amioid form, but resist it he did. That path threatened to drain his energy too much.*

*He picked up a scent in the air; the smell of betrayal filling his nostrils as he followed the unsuspecting bear cub. The prey did not even detect his approach, and it was not long before he was standing over the kill, blood dripping from his mouth. Only it wasn't the same as before. No longer did he delight in the slaying. This accursed interaction between the blight and the Hallows had placed an alien entity in him — a conscience.*

But consciences could be suppressed; and this is exactly what Zodarin did as he emerged from the Near To.

A commotion in the courtyard outside brought him to the window. Grizdoth's lifeless body had been found with his throat torn out. Eétor would deduce who was responsible, and Zodarin found he was quashing his conscience further as he contemplated what he must do.

A short while later, he received the expected summons and entered the castle's Great Hall. Eétor stood in front of a mammoth fireplace staring at the rising red and orange flames.

"You sent for me Praetor?"

"Yes," Eétor said without turning, a slight that did not escape the wizard. "You have no doubt heard of the assassination?"

"Your adjutant? Yes. I never liked him."

"Indeed. But who would do this within our own walls?"

Zodarin paused for a second, "I warned of Kaldoran treachery M'lord."

"Is that what you believe happened in this case?" Eétor looked at him with a hint of contempt. "You are so dull. All the remaining stonegrabes are locked up or lying under a thousand tons of rock in Kaldora."

"And yet," Zodarin said, stepping closer, "Kaldorans

attacked me on my journey here from Dragonia." Eétor turned at this, and Zodarin caught the look of surprise on his face before he could completely hide it.

"That ... surprises me," Eétor said.

Zodarin smiled. "I'm sure it does — to some degree."

"What exactly do you mean?"

Zodarin took another step closer and Eétor flinched. "Secrets," the wizard said. "Everyone has them. You have yours and I have mine. Indeed, we share some confidences that — if they were known more widely — might undo both of us."

Eétor recovered some of his composure. "But we have always trusted each other, have we not?"

"We have — to a certain extent."

Eétor slowly raised a pewter goblet and sipped the thick fruity jarva juice. "Perhaps it is time for *total* truth between us — to ensure there are no further misunderstandings."

"Or... accidents?"

"Precisely."

"What do you wish to know, M'Lord?"

Eétor took another sip of jarva juice. "I have always allowed you freedom to access your dream state without question because I trusted you. Others don't know the extent of your power in this respect, but I understand completely how the Far Beyond provides a means to dispose of your enemies."

"You mean *our* enemies."

"Grizdoth was not my enemy! I recognise your

handprint in his demise, wizard, and it makes me think that if you silenced my trusted adjutant then what would you do to me?"

"What indeed?" Zodarin sensed the Hallows fire rising within. Gone was the voice of conscience. "What do you want of me my Lord? My death? Perhaps banishment? No — I think not. You need me if you are to claim the throne."

"And you need me to ensure your continued position in the Royal Council. One word from me and Etezora will have you removed or even executed. It is no secret she mistrusts you."

"So, we need each other."

"It would appear so. Yet I sense this balance of trust is skewed. Perhaps your Dreamworld prowess extends even further than I imagined? I would know more."

"Be careful what you wish for, M'Lord. Remember your previous passage to the Far Beyond. It was somewhat traumatic."

"I was but a stripling. I am made of much sterner mettle now."

Zodarin nodded, then said, "Those who do not possess the gift of passage can not easily cross the great divide."

"But there is a way, is there not? It has happened before."

"It has. If you drink the juice of the glistening cacti or *divine messenger*, as it is called."

Eétor could not conceal his glee. "Are there risks?"

The wizard paused, "Other than a powerful sleep, I do not know of any."

"Prepare your potion," ordered Eétor. "Do this for me, and you will have proved your loyalty."

"Very well. Give me your goblet." There was an uncomfortable silence as Zodarin took the vessel from him and opened a leather pouch on his belt. He extracted a small earthenware bottle with a cork stopper, and then poured a small amount of milky white powder into Eétor's drink.

"Sit down my Lord and drink this," he said, offering the goblet to Eétor. "Once it takes effect we will enter the Dreamworld together."

"How long does the effect last?"

"About six hours."

Eétor abandoned all caution and, at last, Zodarin understood how much the Praetor craved what only he could provide. "I am ready," Eétor said.

Zodarin sat down on the floor next to Eétor's chair and closed his eyes. The Cuscosian Lord lifted the goblet to his lips and drank the concoction.

On the first occasion he accessed the Dreamworld all that time ago, Eétor had been frightened more than anything. But what he perpetrated later that night with Zodarin's help replaced his fear with an intoxication that arose from exerting one's power over another — and he wielded it in the most potent expression possible. He understood why Zodarin resisted his overtures to access the Far Beyond since, but now the wizard had acceded his domination, he felt no fear at all.

That was a mistake.

At first, the Praetor experienced a strange sensation of calm as he seemed to float as an incorporeal entity through the room he and the wizard occupied in the Near To. He looked down and saw his soulless body slumped in the chair. Now that he had abandoned it, he allowed his new mind-self to fill with a kaleidoscope of colours. After a time exhilarating in this experience, the shifting patterns slowly cleared, and he saw a ginger-coloured calti beckoning him forward through dream mists into a dwelling of sorts.

Inside, the calti sat on its haunches atop a rough-hewn table in the centre of the room. It was a pleasant, comfortable chamber. A home. A nexus.

*This is my humble abode,* the calti said, *pray relax and tell me what it is you seek.*

Eétor scrutinised the calti, somewhat puzzled by the feline's presence. Where was Zodarin? What was it Grizdoth had reported? The knowledge escaped him, so he decided to engage with the creature.

*I seek enlightenment, Great Spirit, a view of the future. What is in store for me?*

*You wish the Hallows to bestow a prophecy? A vision of your destiny comes at a cost, it sent. Will you give yourself to the Hallows?*

---

Eétor abandoned all hesitation. The subjugation he endured at his sister's hands, her dismissal of his contributions and a sense of losing his place in the history of their emerging great nation. All of this urged him to seize this opportunity with both hands. *If that is what it takes, then I am sure.*

The cat lifted its paw and pushed a cup across the table. *Drink, and then tell me what you see in the looking glass.*

Eétor obeyed, drinking the glass of jarva juice dry. He looked into the small reflective surface.

*I see nothing but colours,* Eétor sent.

*Keep watching.*

Eétor looked again, and this time saw himself. He was searching, his eyes casting around the room. A creeping disquiet took hold as he looked for a door — but there was none. No matter how he searched he couldn't find a way out. He was trapped!

The Praetor wrenched his eyes away from the glass and saw that the calti was gone — so was the door. It was just as he had seen in the glass. The animal gave him a vision, true — a minute's foreshadowing of the future that was now a reality.

He tried to wake himself from the dream that was becoming a nightmare, but was unable to rouse his body from sleep. His ethereal body staggered around the dream-room, arms sweeping crockery and ornaments from the surfaces, looking for any way out of the place. With the door's disappearance, the only portal to the outside world was one small window. Yet there was no latch or opening mechanism. He took a large weight from a set of scales and threw it at the window glass, yet it bounced off as if it were made from steel. Three times more he tried, the last attempt resulting in the weight rebounding to strike his head.

*Krut you, Calti! What have you done to me?*

Then through the window he saw the animal, looked into its amber eyes and remembered Grizdoth's warnings of the shape-shifting wizard. It smiled at him — an expression of resolve, but also mixed with ... what ... regret? As he gazed at the creature, it transformed into something beyond even Eétor's darkest nightmare — the thing that had killed his father. He had blotted it from his mind, but now he saw it in its grotesquerie, swelling in size such that the window could not provide sufficient field of view to observe it all. It was a giant mass of thrashing tentacles, typhus-green slime oozing from reddened warts, and what he did see of its shrunken head — a myriad of blinking amber eyes.

From some place far in the distance he heard Phindrath's voice. It was tremulous, calling for a healer. He cried out to her until his throat was hoarse, but she could not hear. And all the time, the terror outside observed him until he could stand it no longer. A mind can only receive so much shock and trauma — and Eétor's was approaching an irrevocable unhinging. It did what every protective mechanism does under such circumstances and closed down into blackness.

~ ~ ~

After examining Eétor's body and sniffing the empty goblet on the table, the healer offered his diagnosis.

"Phindrath, your brother has entered a comatose state as a result of ingesting large quantities of *divine messenger*. Its influence can not be easily undone. His body is alive yet his mind is elsewhere. It may return in time but — "

"My brother was not taken to addictions," Phindrath said to the apothecary.

"And yet the evidence is plain to see."

The young princess was shocked at this development. She was perplexed at how Eétor had taken upon himself a solitary existence since Etezora's emigration to Wyverneth. Now, perhaps she knew the reason. Yet with his incapacitation, it fell upon her to take over rulership of Cuscosa — something she was unprepared for. She needed counsel, and there was only one she could turn to.

She instructed a guard to take Eétor's body to his bed chamber and make him comfortable. "Send for Zodarin," she instructed another. "We must get to the bottom of today's events. First, there was the murder of Grizdoth, and now *this*. Double the guard on the castle gates too."

Oswald watched what transpired from his hiding place behind one of the great drapes. Purring contentedly, the dreamer deceiver closed his eyes. He had disposed of a problem without resorting to actual murder. Eétor might yet prove to be useful, but until the wizard assumed command the Praetor would remain trapped in the Dreamworld. In the meantime, he could easily manipulate Phindrath.

*I ought to return to my tower,* he thought. *Phindrath's guard will be looking for me. Well, let her wait. I have exerted myself enough and Oswald, like any cat, wishes to sleep.*

He padded out of the room, unseen, and found a warm corner of a stable to curl up in. For the first time in many days he slept soundly.

# 38

# THE CULTURE OF HIDDEN MEANS

---

Tayem's instincts caused her to struggle against the giant's grip, but after a while she concluded it was useless. She might as well have tried to remove herself from a burial up to the neck in sand.

*At least I can breathe,* she thought, *even if this is so undignified.*

The Gigantes' strides ate up the distance, and with the mists now cleared Tayem could take in the wonder of the passage — and the enormity of peril they had just escaped from. The giants were carrying the Dragon Riders along a causeway of wrinkled, grey rock that formed the only route forward. It divided a chasm that sank to untold depths below. Tayem understood now why Milissandia had baulked at leading them along this treacherous route while still shrouded in mist.

Ahead, the causeway ended in a winding path that snaked over a rise layered with garpine and mountain spruce. She would have enjoyed the spectacle of the landscape more if her predicament did not demand she focused her attention on more urgent matters. *Perhaps appealing to this giant might help.*

"Giant! Do you know who it is you have affronted?" she said, unable to resist the Hallows' rising ire.

The giant looked at her with distaste. "I know you are Queen of the Donnephon," it said. "But there is something in you that denies your heritage."

*He means the Hallows,* Tayem thought.

"Save your entreaties for now," Milissandia said from below. She was jogging alongside the giant. "His name is Ebar, and he is Hill Warden of the Gigantes Council. He will not listen to you until you are safely ensconced in Herethorn. Just don't aggravate him."

Ebar regarded the druid and narrowed his eyes. Tayem looked up at his face and saw, drawn in its creased darkened surface, the wisdom of countless sols.

*Diplomacy,* she told herself. *That is the attire you must wear now. Perhaps Milissandia is right. I should be patient.*

Although that was the received counsel, she hoped she

would not be made to wait much longer. The giant's grip was becoming uncomfortable.

"At least," she said to the druid, "can you tell him to loosen his grasp. I can hardly breathe. There isn't any risk of me escaping — you know this."

"Ebar?" Milissandia said to the Gigantes.

He gave out a *haarumph,* and then placed the Queen on his shoulders. Although the perch was unsteady, it was much more preferable to her previous position. With her greater elevation she was able to look behind and see that the Gigantes, carrying their Dragonian passengers, were spaced about twenty strides apart with the one called Wobas bringing up the rear. As Ebar trod the causeway, the Dastarthes Mists closed behind him, veiling the route they had come with a dense blanket. Out of the depths, the sound of shrieks and moans emanated once again, protecting the sanctuary with their dread presence.

When Tayem turned once more, they were cresting the steep rise, and Ebar stopped a moment to let the rest of the train catch up. Tayem gasped as she took in what she saw.

*So this is the sanctuary we sought,* she said to herself. *Its beauty rivals that of Wyverneth itself.*

Below their vantage point, embosomed amongst a family of lofty mountains, she saw a beautiful valley, thickly wooded with cypresses and garpines. They covered the folded landscape, netting the defiles with emerald shadows. Here and there, in isolated clearings, cabins and dwellings were dotted, their inhabitants moving amongst them like crawling insects — some large, some small. The mountains on which they stood were composed of a white quartz-like rock. They extended round in a broken circle, magnificent and snow-wreathed precipices that reached for the deep blue sky.

*Blue,* Tayem thought. *Is it that this place is untouched by the Hallows?*

To the north she heard the distant roar of mountain cataracts tumbling over white-scar rocks. The water eventually formed a river, lying like a black ribbon in kinks and curls as it wound its way to the west and some unknown course.

Far to the east, a lake nestled in the lap of the great mountains, sunlight glinting off its surface; and beyond this, the prickly peaks gave way to a pass leading to lands that appeared baked by the Hallows purple that seemed to besiege this mysterious place on all sides.

The other Gigantes had joined them, and Ebar took this as his cue to descend along the path that zigzagged between wind-tossed crowns of great trees below.

Ebar's footfalls shook the ground, jarring Tayem's body. Yet his steps were sure-footed, and she began to relax as she gained confidence in his ability to navigate the slopes.

A half hour later, the land began to level out, and they emerged from the trees to behold a village, long worms of grey smoke billowing lazily amongst the rooves.

Although the temperature had risen upon their descent, Tayem kept her cloak wrapped around her. It seemed that ice inhabited her bones, as if the Hallows were retreating to her core and reacting to this place by instilling a deep chill. She shivered in response, and was glad when they emerged from the woods, beams of sunlight radiating her skin.

She ventured a question to Milissandia, who was just managing to keep up with the bounding Ebar. "Where will they take us?"

"To the Council Chamber, I would guess," she said.

"Are we their prisoners?"

"Not if I have anything to do with it," Milissandia replied.

Viewed from Tayem's lofty position, the druid's cowl hid her face, so Tayem could not judge how confident the woman was in her statement. "Would it be too much to ask your leader to set us down?" she said.

Before Milissandia could answer, Ebar picked her from his shoulders and placed her gently on the ground. "Follow me into the village," he said in a lazy tone, and paced off along a descending road that widened into a jumble of wooden buildings.

Their entry into the village drew a considerable crowd of onlookers, although all of them seemed to be of smaller stature. As they passed through, Tayem caught snippets of conversation in common-speak distinguished against a hum of talk related in a language which Tayem was only barely familiar with.

*Old-speak.*

"These Gigantes show no respect for the Royal House," Cistre said, drawing up alongside. The other giants had followed Ebar's lead in laying down their passengers, and gradually the Dragon Riders reformed themselves into a fast-moving huddle.

"The Gigantes respect *people*, rather than positions of power," Milissandia said in reply. "Would you rather they forced you to make your own way here? You'd still be half-way up the Whispering Mountains. Besides, it is *they* who stooped to transport *you*. Few can boast to have travelled on the shoulders of the Cyclopes."

"This place is wonderful," Mahren said. "How is it that both Donnephon and Gigantes claim it as sanctuary?"

"There are only so many questions I can answer," Milissandia said, "but I wouldn't make mention of claims too hastily. You are here as guests, but can easily be ejected as interlopers if you do not choose your words carefully."

"Daughter," said a breathy voice from behind. Wobas had struggled to keep up, but now hobbled along to join them. "It is wonderful that you returned to the village. We feared you had fallen foul of some treachery."

Milissandia looked at her father, and Tayem detected a deep-seated, unresolved hostility between them. If what the woman said was true regarding her relationship, then there was some significant bridge building ahead of them.

"We have much to relate, father," Milissandia said, "but it must wait until after the Donnephon speak with the Council. Suffice it to say these people need our help, and if you can aid in achieving co-operation between our peoples, then it may just prevent a great evil from advancing across the Imperious Crescent."

"Very well," Wobas said, "but we face an uphill task. The Cyclopes are hostile to any involvement in the outside world. Ever since the Decimation there has been a cloak of suspicion preventing any contact with other races."

"A great shame," Tayem said, "seeing how once the Gigantes were purveyors of much blessing in times gone by."

"The Cuscosians put paid to that," Mahren said.

"Indeed they did," Wobas said. "Yet it is not I you need to convince, but the Gigantes' Council. Now hold, we reach our destination."

The building they approached was constructed from blackwood and stood imposing above the remainder of the village. It lacked the grandeur of the Donnephon palace, but nonetheless conveyed a sense of authority. It was clearly designed to accommodate bodies far greater in size than Tayem's entourage. They scaled the gargantuan steps and walked through a tall open doorway into a cavernous but brightly illuminated room. There were scant adornments save for a large tapestry on the far wall illustrated with a multitude of pastiches depicting numerous dramas and legends of the Gigantes people.

Seated around a central fire were the Cyclopes who had

carried them here, along with a handful of others, none of them female as far as Tayem could tell.

"Enter," Ebar said, his single eye prominent against his sun-kissed skin. The appearance, besides being disconcerting, made it difficult to judge the giant's expression. At times it seemed he glowered at them; yet at others, a smile or a turn of phrase contradicted this. The Donnephon Queen decided not to make hasty judgements in this most delicate of discourses.

"You will have to make do with sitting on floor cushions," Ebar said. "I'm afraid our chairs are designed with more sizeable bodies in mind." At this, a few members of the Council let out chortles of laughter, but their tone did not seem mocking.

The Dragon Riders stepped cautiously into the ring of chairs and took positions where there was a gap in the seating. In this way they could all see each other without craning their necks.

Tayem was grateful for the warmth of the fire, although her companions did not seem to feel the chill as she did. "I thank you for receiving us into your midst, Great Chieftain of the Gigantes," Tayem said.

"No need for grand titles," Ebar said. "I am sorry for the manner of your entry into our sanctuary, but there is good reason to be wary of outsiders. You were lucky that Milissandia accompanied you, otherwise the outcome of our meeting might have been ... less friendly. But let us hold our words, your journey has been arduous and you must take refreshment."

He beckoned, and three Cyclopes women entered from a side door carrying trays bearing drinks and plates piled with pastries and roasted root vegetables for the unexpected guests. The Dragonians dug into the welcome victuals while Ebar and a number of the other Cyclopes lit up pipes of jarva-leaf. Tayem found the practice a little incongruent given they were about to discuss matters of great import, but she held her counsel, enjoying the taste of hearty kernel-bread and nut-roast slices.

"Your food is wonderfully prepared," Tayem said to the nearest serving woman. She responded with a kindly smile and a nod.

"They are not allowed to speak in the Council Chamber," Milissandia said to Tayem. "Do not take their silence as rudeness."

"Strange behaviour," Tayem said. "Does this mean you will not be able to speak either?"

"It will be frowned upon," Milissandia said, "but I'm not going to let that stop me."

Tayem smiled and drained her goblet of fig-berry juice, revelling in the warmth of the spicy drink.

Once they had finished their repast, Ebar rose and called the meeting to order. "Fellow Council members and esteemed people of the Donnephon, it is time to speak. Let me start by saying that, as visitors, you are welcome — and free to leave at any moment. We will extend our fullest hospitality to you, but it goes without saying we expect you to keep the location of this sacred sanctuary a secret from all others."

Ebar took his seat again, making it clear that the Dragon Riders had the floor. Tayem stood and searched for the right way to start. She knew nothing of the Cyclopes customs, but her instincts told her they were not ones to stand on great ceremony, despite their apparent disdain of women.

"Ebar, and all other distinguished members of the Gigantes Council," she began, "we come to you at a time of great need. Milissandia has told us you heard of the tragedy that befell us in your former home of Lyn-Harath."

At the mention of the place that marked their decimation, several council members murmured in what seemed like a prayer or warding invocation.

"There is now a doubly strong reason for us all to remember that place with great sorrow. You lost most of your brethren, as did we. In addition, our dragons were slain in a manner most heinous and terrible."

Once again, the Cyclopes murmured their empathy.

"As if this were not enough, the Cuscosians have driven us from our home at Wyverneth. The Dragon Palace has fallen, and we are a people dispossessed. Even now we exist on the slopes of the Whispering Mountains, exposed to the elements, our sick and wounded falling prey to harsh conditions." She scanned the faces of the assembled Cyclopes Council to judge how her words were being received. Some, she noticed, gazed at her with sympathetic expressions, but most were unreadable. True, they all listened attentively, but what were they actually thinking! *Nothing to do but continue.*

"We had hoped," she continued, "to gain sanctuary in this place. So it came as a great surprise to find that, not only did the Gigantes survive in considerable numbers, but you took up residence here."

Tayem tried not to make the words sound vindictive, but the Hallows was pushing at the edges of her consciousness again, and there was a sharp edge to her tone.

The Cyclopes remained silent, and Tayem didn't know whether she had offended them or if this was simply their way.

"They would hear more," Milissandia whispered in her ear, "but take care not to raise their ire." She had stood to offer her words of advice, a service Tayem was grateful for. "Remember, you exert no authority here. Appeal to their common decency — they possess that in great measure."

Tayem nodded in acknowledgement. "Forgive me if that sounded disrespectful. I simply wonder how this secret place was laid down in *both* our lores as a sanctuary to which our peoples could flee."

Ebar nodded at her, but did not say a word. *Is this a sign of acceptance or him just tolerating my speech?*

"To tell the truth, we are desperate. If we do not find

adequate shelter soon, it will only take one severe storm and we will suffer a heavy toll."

It was as she vocalised the Dragonian plight that a wave of sadness overcame her, and she faltered for a moment. But Cistre was there, as always, to bolster her. She appeared at her side and placed a hand on her shoulder.

"Why not pause for some time, let them consider what you have said, my Queen?" Cistre said.

"In a moment," Tayem said, recovering herself. She turned back to the Council leaders and spoke up once more.

"Therefore I come to you on behalf of my people — to request a place under your protection, noble Gigantes. We need time to recover and plan our next move against the Cuscosians. Without your aid, I fear the Donnephon will be scattered to the winds."

Tayem decided she had said enough and sat down on the floor once more.

Ebar puffed on his pipe, looking lost in thought. He turned to the other Cyclopes and watched as each of them nodded or gestured to him affirmatively. He took the pipe from his mouth, and then addressed Tayem. "We have heard your entreaty, Queen of the Donnephon and thank you for your words. Now the Council must talk. We invite you to retire to rooms we have prepared and rest. We will summon you when we have something to say."

Tayem and her party rose, understanding the audience was over for now, and followed one of the women who had served them lunch. She led them to a house located a stone's throw away from the Council Hall complete with washing facilities and freshly made beds. Most of the party threw themselves onto the cots and dropped off to sleep straight away. But Tayem could not rest. The Hallows raged within, almost as if it was offended by this place and sought revenge for bringing it here. In addition, she was anxious about the Cyclopes' impending response. She knew from ancient lore, and from what Milissandia had told her, that the Cyclopes were a proud and cautious people. They had good reason to mistrust any outsiders after what they had suffered at the Decimation.

She judged she had been wise to stop short with the request she had made. In truth, she had much more to ask of them. But that would have to wait for another time. At present, their fate was in the hands of this simple yet enigmatic people.

Milissandia seated herself next to Wobas on a wooden bench overlooking the village square. They were away from general observation (the villagers were gossip-mongers to a person,) yet close enough to the Council Hall to respond quickly when the Council recalled them.

She looked at her father and noted again how worn he looked. Yet he seemed to have lost some of the reticence he once possessed. *A good sign?*

"The Queen presented herself well," he said to her.

"She holds the wisdom of one twice her age," Milissandia said.

"Yet I sense an inner turmoil."

"You judge aright. She labours under the torment of the Hallows."

"Her wisdom clearly did not prevent her from succumbing to temptation, then?"

Milissandia felt a familiar prickling at her father's judgmental comment. *Stay your anger,* she admonished herself. "Neither of us are strangers to temptation," she replied. "It can come in many guises, and the most noble of persons might court evil in order to accomplish good."

Wobas stared ahead, as if meeting Milissandia's gaze might cause him to utter intemperate words. "You think this is why she invited the Black Hallows in?"

"I know this much," she said. "Tayem Fyreglance recognises the Hallows for what it is now and seeks release."

"It is a vexing problem to overcome."

"She cannot do it on her own."

Wobas turned to her, his eyes widening. "You think I can help her?"

"You possess the skill."

Wobas hung his head. "I do. But it requires that I enter the Dreamworld, and I have not dared venture into the Far Beyond for many weeks now."

It was Milissandia's turn to express surprise. "You haven't? Why not?"

And so it was that Wobas unburdened himself to one who he once thought was the least likely to share such a weight. He told her of his encounter with the false Augur, his fear that Zodarin — or the thing he represented — had returned, and of the spiritual malaise he had endured.

When he finished, Milissandia felt something melt inside. She knew from her own experience in the Dreamworld why Wobas had sought answers in that realm. It was not a selfish desire to draw worldly power from the place, but rather a quest to allow what it offered to bring good to the many — whether that be healing, reconciliation or comfort.

Without another word, she reached out to him and embraced her father for the first time in over ten sols. They held each other like that for many minutes until she felt her cheeks moist from the mingling of both their tears.

"There is much to tell you too, Father; and perhaps when I finish you will understand that all is not as bleak as you think."

She recounted her experience with the tree serpent, and how a happy mix of circumstances had allowed her to tread across the boundary existing between the Near To and the Far Beyond. It took some time to relate, and they could not help sharing their common adventures, and wonder at how the place left them both enraptured. In particular, it heartened her to learn that the Spirit Guide had sought them both and that, in this, they had an ally.

"Do you see, Father? If we can both tread the paths of

the Far Beyond, then we can support and strengthen each other. This evil creature you speak of is subject to the Dreamworld's environment as much as we are. We cannot let fear of this wizard's dread presence prevent us from helping Tayem.

Wobas looked at her with new eyes, and Milissandia understood in that moment they were conversing as equals. "You possess the bravery of your mother," he said. "If you are not daunted venturing across the border, then who am I to baulk at the challenge?"

"We need to act quickly, then," she said. "Tayem's torment grows by the day, and the Hallows works against everything she is trying to achieve."

"And what is that?" Wobas said. "I sensed she did not unburden herself fully in the Council chamber."

"You are perceptive as ever," she said. "But I will let her share the fullness of her entreaties once we hear the result of the Council's discussion."

"I think that will be sooner than you think," Wobas said, pointing at the messenger who approached them from the direction of the Council building. "They have reached a decision."

# 39

# TUNNEL OF TORMENT

---

After two whole days of digging under Nalin's instruction, the Kaldoran excavation team took a turn towards the valley. The collapse of Jennu Narod and structural weakness of the remaining frontage meant their escape tunnel had to run parallel to the cliff face for approximately a quarter periarch. Then they would need to plot a course that gradually curved a full ninety degrees. This meant they would exit the escarpment into the valley just south of Spidersnatch Cavern.

Nalin had meticulously planned the cave-crawler's route using the detailed geological maps the Kaldoran people had made over many sols living and mining beneath the surface. The initial fear of suffocation had passed when the stonegrabes had cleared some of the interconnecting tunnels linking the Great Hall and collapsed cave network. It was just a question of digging themselves out of a living grave before any further calamity.

Now, two days later, Nalin felt they were making real progress as the tunnel boring machine slowly turned towards the limestone valley. Drawing from his pipe of smouldering jarva-leaf, he inhaled the intoxicating fumes, allowing the potent cocktail to energise his nerve endings and muscles alike. He had worked continuously since the start of their perilous journey, impelled by a sense of guilt, duty and over-riding desire for revenge on those who had perpetrated this despicable act. Such was his nature, that he had supervised the dig at close quarters, carefully watching over the precious machine. Every hour he lubricated key bearings, every minute cajoled the driving Kaltis and every other second monitored levels of fyredrench in the spray tanks. There had been no stopping. Nor could he, because he accepted the doom that had befallen Kaldora was entirely his fault.

He steered the cave-crawler in a gentle arc and prepared to start the next stage of the dig. If his calculations were correct, they would break into a large cavern in the next couple of hours. Then he would allow himself time to rest before the final push to freedom.

However, the ensuing dig proved harder than

anticipated. The Kaldorans were experienced miners, their expertise spanning back thousands of sols yet they were up against extreme conditions. They might be physically adapted to their subterranean environment, but they also understood the dangers and rewards of the living rock that surrounded them. Indeed, many worshipped the mountains as gods, each stonegrabe clan giving prayers and offerings to their own particular deity.

As a practical consideration, the Kaldorans reinforced the tunnel roof and sides. They filled and levelled the floor behind the cutters to ensure smooth traversal for the wheels of the giant machine, and to allow safe passage for the following Kaldorans. The disc-shaped diamond cutters on the circular frontal shield showed little signs of wear as the revolutionary chemical agent weakened the rock integrity before they tore through tons of stone and dirt.

All went well, but Nalin still had concerns. Groundwater seepage was always a potential threat, although there had been little sign of leakage from the surrounding aquiferous rocks. There was also the risk of excavations destabilising ancient fault lines and causing massive slippage of the surrounding strata. *Plenty to keep a stonegrabe awake,* he thought.

A great cheer from up ahead broke Nalin out of his worried ponderings, and he stood up in the cave-crawler's seat to see what the commotion was. Four Kaltis were jumping up and down at the spectacle of the drilling machine breaking through the last layer of limestone that marked the transition into the cavern beyond.

*By Tarchon,* he thought, *I doubted we would ever make it.*

The machine crawled forward the last few strides, and Nalin disengaged the drive. The cave-crawler shuddered to a halt, and he reflexively reached for his pipe, re-ignited it and inhaled deeply of the aromatic smoke. He noted in a detached way how these days it took longer for the jarva-leaf to bring the solace he desired. Where once he could take one inhalation and enjoy an immediate hit of euphoria, it now required at least three puffs. This might become a problem if his intake of the leaf outstripped supply, but for the present his stock was plentiful. *Time to recharge the coffers once I access my plantation.* Now there was a hopeful thought.

His inner pain tormented every waking moment, and it was only the jarva-leaf that prevented him from sinking into a morass of despair. His gummy balls had run out many days ago, which was a shame as they gave him a more immediate hit.

*I am the one who brought calamity on my people.* The thoughts kept returning. Not only this, but he had also served as architect of his family's demise. He closed his eyes to shut out the pain of their memory, but was jolted back to reality when Magthrum slapped him hard on the back.

"I've ordered the stonegrabes to rest and make camp,"

bellowed the Fellchief. "You ought to take some time to rest too, my friend."

It was true that this had been Nalin's intention, but now he had to face the prospect of his wife and son's horrible deaths tormenting his dreams. "I'll rest when we're out of this hell hole," responded Nalin tetchily. It was the jarva-leaf talking, but Magthrum seemed to understand, despite his ebullient mood. "You are hurting," he said to his closest friend. "I know the pain you feel. It was the same when I lost Hetherin."

Nalin turned to Magthrum, his eyes questioning. "When will it go away?"

"Alas, it never does. But you learn to bear it better."

Magthrum meant well, but the words did little to assuage the raging storm in Nalin's breast. He paced away before the Fellchief could see the tears flooding from his eyes and checked over the cave-crawler once again. They streamed down his cheeks as he stroked the dusty nameplate on its side.

"I brought this upon you," he said to himself, "and I'm not sure how long I can live with the burden."

Another voice answered his lamentation. *Long enough to exact your revenge, surely?*

Before he could address the voice in his head, there was a sudden loud rumbling sound from the tunnel behind, followed by screams of anguish. Where once there had been the compacted rock of the tunnel floor, there was now only a yawning hole.

"Sink hole!" Nalin yelled and rushed back to where the limestone had collapsed into what seemed like an endless pit. On the far side of the chasm he could see a handful of grimy stonegrabes staring into the blackness.

"How many lost?" he shouted across to them.

"Two," replied a shocked Kaldoran.

Magthrum drew up alongside him and shook his head. "Bridge the void," he said after a second or two. "It is only a temporary setback isn't it?"

"Groundwater ingress," Nalin replied. "It's what I was afraid of. Sinkholes and tunnel collapses are common enough in this karstic limestone."

"I don't care about the technicalities," Magthrum said. Nalin noted the smell of ale on the Fellchief's breath and realised he would not be mourning the two stonegrabes.

After the drama died down, Nalin dozed off on the footplate of the cave-crawler. It was a tormented sleep littered with images of screaming stonegrabes fleeing the falling rocks of Jennu Narod. Ellotte and Palimin called to him for help as the weight of the mountain came down on them, yet try as he might he always arrived at the scene of devastation too late.

*No, no ...* he repeated until it became a mantra of despair.

The words were still on his lips as he woke suddenly, jarva-craving twisting his already tormented mind. He reached for his pipe, and when his hand closed on the bowl he thought to himself, *here comes another puff of temporary relief.*

In the morning Magthrum rallied his stonegrabes and the day's digging commenced. Nalin had refused to step down from the tunnelling machine despite his fatigue, and the Fellchief's protestations. Nalin had got the Kaldorans into this mess and he was going to get them out, he assured Magthrum.

The excavation work had slowed as the cutters were grinding through harder intrusions of granite in the limestone face. Fyredrench was less effective on the igneous rock, and Nalin had to reduce the cutting speed to avoid damaging the heads. Once past the intrusion, the machine hit limestone once more and the cave-crawler increased its pace. By now however, the reserves of fyredrench were rapidly diminishing, and Nalin had to face the prospect they might run out before reaching their destination.

As was true to their spirit, the stoic Kaldorans laboured on undaunted; making progress stride by stride while shoring up weak spots. These caused by the accelerated dissolution of soluble gypsum sediments by percolating groundwater. Just when the stonegrabes thought the wall of rock would never end, Nalin spotted a purple ring of light ahead. The rock softened, caving forward like a child's fist through a sandcastle, and the wheels lost traction.

If Nalin's navigation held true, they were on the brink of the valley he had set a course for. He ordered a troop of stonegrabes armed with picks and shovels to dig at the rockface. They toiled for several hours, enlarging the hole and reinforcing the opening in the cliff face. Soon, the portal they had enlarged was wide enough to admit two stonegrabes side by side, and a round of cheering cascaded back along the tunnel as word of their escape filtered down the chain. It had taken almost ten days but the revolutionary cave-crawler and its drug-fuelled inventor had prevailed.

Magthrum was ecstatic, slapping any and every stonegrabe on the back in jubilation.

"Fellchief come quick," cried Nutug Hillgrop, one of Nalin's aids.

"What is it?" bellowed Magthrum.

The Fellchief pushed his way through the crowd of Kaldorans and witnessed a dismal but not unexpected spectacle. Nalin lay on the deck of his cave-crawler, unconscious and totally limp with exhaustion. A healer was called, and pronounced Nalin comatose, the result of sleep deprivation and excessive use of his precious jarva-leaf.

"Make him comfortable," ordered Magthrum. "There is little we can do for him now except allow sleep to heal his soul. Call a meeting of the Rockclave too," he shouted at Nutug. "I would address my council."

In a matter of minutes the remnant Rockclave members were assembled, and Magthrum ordered that each should be provided with a cup of ale. Guzzling a large flagon himself, he called the meeting to order with a typical epithet.

"All hail, you stone-encrusted kruts I call brothers. I stand before you to celebrate our escape from the mountain. We have confounded the plans of the Cuscosian scum. Tonight in the purple light of Spidersnatch we drink and toast our saviour, Nalin. We pray to Tarchon for a speedy recovery — which I'm sure he will make. Now let us embrace the power of the Hallows and rise against our Cuscosian foe."

He paused to take a drink and felt the malevolence of the purple mist infect him. The Rockclave must have noticed its manifestation because looks of trepidation and fear were drawn on many a face. Those nearest even flinched backwards. As they observed their leader however, revelling in the intoxication of its power, the influence seemed to reach out to all of them. Magthrum was the conduit, but the Hallows was not satisfied in corrupting just one, it craved the infection of all — whether they be Dragonian, human or lowly Kaldoran.

"My loyal grabes, we must prepare to fight," Magthrum said at the top of his voice. "We will strike at the heart of Cuscosa, the mighty castle itself. Our engineer Nalin has shown us the way with his magnificent war machine. If we can tunnel out of this great crag, then we can also burrow our way under the castle."

One stonegrabe standing close raised his grimy hand. "A question, my Lord." The grabe was new to the council and did not yet understand the protocols of Magthrum's chamber. If he had, he would have held his tongue.

Magthrum's eyes flashed. "What is it?"

"Castle Cuscosa is over one hundred periarchs away. Surely we cannot tunnel our way from here?"

There was a time when Magthrum would have punished the stonegrabe's insolence with a swift hatchet to the head, but a leader's wisdom stayed his hand. The Kaldorans were but a vestige of their former selves and they needed every stonegrabe fit and healthy for their plans to succeed, however stupid the individual might be. "Have faith," Magthrum said instead. "We will build a transportation vehicle and hunt down another herd of rockbulls. It will take many days, perhaps weeks, but we will carry our machine over land by light of the moon until we are close to the heart of the Cuscosian Empire. They may have the numbers, but we have our stealth and cunning. We will elude them and strike at the centre of their kingdom. Nalin has shown us what is possible. Are you with me?"

The stonegrabes, spellbound by Magthrum's Hallows-induced rhetoric replied 'Yes, oh exalted Fellchief.' A loud chanting ensued with shouts of 'Tarchon's favour on Magthrum,' and 'Praise to Nalin.' When the ululation began to subside, Magthrum initiated a new chant: 'Death to Cuscosia!' The anthem had reached fever pitch, spreading beyond the Rockclave to the Kaldoran remnant at large. They were incensed, infiltrated by Hallows energy ejected from Magthrum and spilling from the fissure at Spidersnatch. Magthrum raised his arms and punched the air, leading his people in a litany of ancient Kaldoran battle cries and death chants.

The treaty with Cuscosia was effectively void. Tonight the stonegrabes would celebrate their survival, and tomorrow they would usher in a new era of Kaldoran expansion.

Next morning, Magthrum visited Nalin on his crudely constructed cot. The engineer remained unconscious, and in the indigo light of morning, with the chants of the stonegrabes but echoes from the night before, Magthrum felt a pinprick of doubt. The healer's prognosis regarding the coma offered little optimism.

"He may remain like this a time longer than I originally thought," the physicker said. "I fear the exhaustion and narcotic intake has been compounded with extreme grief."

"How long?" Magthrum replied.

"A few days, perhaps a week or more. Maybe even months."

The Fellchief furrowed his brow in concern. "Do what you can for him. But if he dies — I will hold you responsible."

The healer's lip trembled. "I'm sure his state is only temporary, Fellchief. Let me prepare another dose of willow essence. It will help cool the fever of his mind."

As the stonegrabe busied himself crushing herbs in a

mortar and pestle, Magthrum regarded his friend. *Mayhap it is best you sleep,* he thought. *You are carrying a weight of guilt, and only time will salve your conscience.*

The anger welled up inside him again. Eétor would pay dearly for the Cuscosian betrayal, and he, Magthrum, would personally pull the krut's larynx out with his bare hands.

He summoned Nutug.

"You have worked closely with Nalin, yes?

Nutug nodded.

"Then commence the construction of a transporter for the cave-crawler. I will lead the hunt for more rockbulls. I need the thrill of the hunt to invigorate my soul."

"Take care, Fellchief," Nutug warned, "the tribes of Gurunthi may have been emboldened by the fall of Jennu Narod and roam abroad in the mountains to the east."

Magthrum picked up his war-axe. "My hope is that they *do,*" he replied. "It is a long time since I have tasted human flesh, and my appetite is great."

Nalin was floating. He looked down at his body lying beneath and understood he was but a spectre, hovering over his corporeal self. Had he died? Perhaps he had started his journey to the lap of Tarchon. Then again, it could be the jarva-leaf. He saw Magthrum talking to the healer. Their figures were indistinct, dream-like and although their mouths moved, he heard nothing of what they said.

He wanted to call out, but his jaw seemed clamped shut, and as he pondered his predicament, he realised he was sojourning in the void between life and death. Although there was none to instruct him or direct events, he understood he had a choice. He could sever all ties with his body now, pass into the bosom of the gods and his suffering would end. But that would be a betrayal of the Kaldoran people. He might find peace, but at what cost?

His other choice? To return to a world of pain and mental anguish, the insufferable tonnage of guilt for the sins he had committed. As he floated on the wisps of the nether-world he concluded he really had no choice at all.

Nalin startled the healer as he sat upright with a gasp, eyes wide open.

"Lord Nalin," the healer said. "You are with us once more." The relief on the stonegrabe's face was all too apparent.

"Indeed I am," Nalin said, sweeping back his bed sheet and rising to his feet. "Revenge has brought me back from the nether-world."

Anger burned in his soul, and he knew he would not rest until he had tasted the juices of Cuscosian flesh cooked over a burning spit. The torment of his deeds had crystallised his resolve and, although he was still in the deep throes of jarva addiction, the Black Hallows that pervaded the air galvanised every sinew of his body.

For the first time in weeks he smiled, an expression the healer clearly didn't quite know how to interpret.

"You need more rest, Lord Nalin. Magthrum gave strict orders for you to — "

"I have no time for that," Nalin said. "I must be about my business. Now, where's my jarva-pipe?"

## 40

# A QUEEN'S MESSENGER

———————

It had been two long weeks since Etezora and the Cuscosian troops had returned to Wyverneth. Those affected by the forest fever recovered after Disconsolin had once again proved his worth by dispensing what, to the dragon folk, was a simple herbal potion distilled from the sap of the dragon willow.

Tuh-Ma had been the slowest to recover. The fever had exerted a much tighter grip on his great hulking body compared with the diminutive humans. It was fair to say that the blue-skin was not enjoying his enforced period of recuperation. He was fed up of being surrounded by the Cuscosian soldiers and courtiers. He craved the attention of his mistress, Queen Etezora, but she was preoccupied overseeing the construction of giant crossbows — machines to bring down the dragon squadrons should they return before Zodarin could deal with them.

Oh, how he worshipped his Queen. She was beautiful beyond measure, and he delighted in her strength, her decisiveness and the depths of her depravity. He longed for the day when they might take to the battlefield once again, or roam abroad on a predatory spree, despoiling and dispatching their victims in a partnership of sadistic glee.

But as he plodded wearily around Wyverneth, shaking off the remaining ravages of the wyrmbite, he sensed that affairs of state and military preparations distracted her. He tried to occupy himself with carving small figurines as presents for his Queen, but his hands still trembled from the ague, and the soft trappings of the Donnephon were not to his liking. Most of all, the lingering smell of the dragon pits turned his stomach.

*Why did Etezora not even visit him or allow him in her presence? Had she turned her back on him? Written him off as a casualty of war? No — he would not believe it!*

Then, on the fifteenth day after their ignominious return from the foothills of the Whispering Mountains, his Queen called for him.

"I have a task of great importance that I would entrust to you," she began with no word of greeting or enquiry regarding his health. Tuh-Ma did not mind. It was enough that he was in her presence again, feasting on her seductive beauty, and it seemed to him that she was even more glamorous than he remembered. He loved the way her mouth moved when she spoke, as if it snarled the words she formulated in her exquisitely twisted mind. The manner in which she stroked the salyx mesmerised him, and he wished he were that creature, sitting on her lap and enjoying her attentions.

*Perhaps one day*, he dreamed — the very idea that his misshapen form would be a comfortable fit on her royal knee irrelevant to his simple mind.

He had listened as the Queen told him of her frustration with her brother Eétor, about the rumours of Kaldora Prime's downfall and her anger at the Praetor for not telling her about his decision to commit troops to the mission. Most annoying of all was the patronising wizard, Zodarin's disappearance. She had now lost patience and charged Tuh-Ma with a fact-finding mission to Castle Cuscosa. He was to accost her brother, demand an explanation and update to his stewardly decisions and progress. "Do not be fearful to act on my full authority," she said to the blue-skin.

"You mean Tuh-Ma can ... use force to get the information?"

Etezora gave Tuh-Ma a crooked smile. "If need be," she said. "Give Eétor an opportunity to offer an explanation first. But if you are not satisfied then use your talents to impress upon him the need to ... comply."

"Tuh-Ma can crush?" he said with eagerness.

"By no means, you ignorant troll. I still need him to administrate at Cuscosa. My feeble sister, Phindrath is hardly up to the task."

Tuh-Ma received the scold with difficulty, but it was forgotten in a minute. He was back in her favour again — and she trusted him with an important mission. He could not be happier.

The North Road was a well maintained highway and the blue-skin's massive steed galloped up the miles in a matter of a day and a half. The route bustled with supply trains and mounted troops, and all those who saw him pass gave way to him. Everyone recognised the Queen's blue-skin servant and none would even consider delaying or waylaying him.

By the time he approached the gates of Castle Cuscosa, he had shaken off the last remnants of his malaise and once more regarded the battlements of the place he called home. He patted his saddlebags, checking they still contained the royal scrolls laying out Etezora's demands. They bore her seal and full written authority to act on her behalf.

He passed through the outer gate without challenge and tethered his exhausted mount. The beast was twenty spans tall — a battle charger. But the difference between carrying a soldier and the deformed mass of muscle that was Tuh-Ma could only be described as considerable.

He lumbered up to the guard post on all fours, adopting the gait of a large gorilla.

"Tuh-Ma here to see Lord Eétor," he grunted to the guard on duty. The man recognised the blue-skin, sneered at him but took care not to pass any derogatory comment. He understood what would happen if he did and bottled his reservations.

Tuh-Ma was directed to the Captain's quarters in the outer courtyard, and after waiting for his knock to be answered — with no response — nudged the door open, entering without further hesitation.

The Captain was engaged in a frantic conversation with his Sergeant at Arms and two others. Their voices were raised, and it was no wonder they had not heard him knock.

"What do you want?" said the Captain, turning to face the source of interruption. "Oh, it's you, troll." The man looked him up and down in a manner that filled Tuh-Ma with the urge to wring his neck. *Another time, Tuh-Ma,* he told himself.

"Queen has told Tuh-Ma to speak to Lord Eétor," he said, presenting the royal scroll.

The Captain took the document from his large, wart-covered hand, broke the seal and opened the manuscript.

"Scroll is for Lord Eétor," repeated the emissary. "Tuh-Ma must speak with Lord Eétor only. My Queen wants answers."

The concerned Captain looked at the two guards and turned back to regard the large figure before him. "The

Praetor is not here. We thought he had travelled to join the Queen at Wyverneth."

"No, Tuh-Ma not seen him. Eétor should be here."

"Princess Phindrath might know the answer to this puzzle, Emissary. Follow me."

The Captain led the way to the throne room, passing on what information he could to Tuh-Ma. His reading of Etezora's instructions had clearly put him in a less haughty frame of mind, and despite his apparent lack of perception, the blue-skin reckoned he would be glad to leave Phindrath with the task of apprising him. "Lord Eétor was here when the wizard returned, but is now nowhere to be found."

As they passed across the central courtyard Tuh-Ma spat in response to what he saw in an animal pen. "Krut," he cursed. Grazing at a trough of dried figs and grasses was a pygmy dragon. "Why wyrm here?" asked the blue-skin. "Disgusting serpent. It not belong."

"It is Lord Zodarin's ride," replied the Captain.

"Wizard rides dragons?" stammered Tuh-Ma. "He has betrayed us."

"I do not think it wise to speak thus," the man said. "The wizard's eyes and ears are everywhere."

"Tuh-Ma not afraid of that sorcerous krut."

The Captain snorted, but refrained from commenting on what he considered a troll's worthless slobbering.

Zodarin surveyed the courtyard from his lofty chamber

and witnessed the blue-skin's arrival. He cursed under his breath. "Another unnecessary complication," he muttered to himself.

Although he had recovered his magical strength after the assault on the dragons, the dragon blight had wearied him, and the spiritual leakage required to keep Eétor confined in the Dreamworld only tired him further. The Praetor's comatose body had been ensconced in the cellar basement of the wizard's tower at his instruction, and only the Princess, the royal apothecary and a handful of select guards knew of it. He intended to make sure Eétor's predicament remained a secret, even if it meant concealing the fact from Etezora.

*What she doesn't know won't hurt her,* he judged.

He needed to be present when the blue-skin met with the Princess. But before he left the chamber, he removed his gloves and applied another layer of ointment to his encrusted skin. The dragon blight had continued to spread across his body, and the gloves concealed the scaly degradation.

Gods only knew what he would do if and when the blight started to assault his face.

*None must hear of this weakness.*

A cure for the affliction still eluded him, and he was starting to wonder if he would find one before he succumbed to its grip.

After replacing the gloves he descended from his tower, frantically thinking how he would deal with the blue-skin.

He certainly didn't want the troll snooping around. Another disappearance would be very difficult to explain, and he doubted clever words would assuage or circumvent Etezora's wrath. Thus, he dismissed the idea of killing the beast. He had to find another way of getting rid of him.

He entered the throne room to find Phindrath already in conversation with the blue-skin. Zodarin wasn't sure if the Princess was aware how obvious her disgust of Tuh-Ma was, but the way she held her handkerchief to her nose when in his presence left nothing in doubt to anyone else.

It was not just Zodarin who understood that Phindrath did not have the wherewithal to sit on the royal throne. She was but a feeble shadow of her venomous sister. This was why he had strongly advised her not to reveal the truth of Eétor's incapacitation. The citizens would grow restless and even rebellious if they knew they were no longer under the iron hand of the Praetor.

The Captain had recounted the news from Wyverneth and shared the contents of the scrolls with Phindrath. She now re-read the scroll as if she'd missed something, but Zodarin could see by her expression that she was desperately trying to think of a way to distract the blue-skin from the subject at hand.

"So what would you have me say, troll?" she said at last. "I do not know where my brother is. He just up and left after the death of the lurking Grizdoth."

Tuh-Ma looked at her suspiciously. "What about fall of Kaldora? What has Princess heard about that?"

Before Phindrath could respond, Zodarin coughed and stepped forward, making his presence known. The look of relief on the Princess's face was impossible to conceal.

He bowed as he approached the throne.

"Ah Lord Zodarin," Phindrath said. "This is a timely intervention. I was just telling Etezora's emissary about my brother's puzzling disappearance."

Zodarin passed his amber eyes from the Princess to the blue-skin and back again. The blue-skin hissed as he stepped forward.

"Yes," the wizard said, "it is very perplexing. We sent out search parties to all points of the compass, but there has been no trace of him. I have my own theory, of course."

Tuh-Ma shambled across to him, looking at the sorcerer with contempt. "Tell Tuh-Ma. Do not hold anything back, Wizard. Etezora is not pleased with you either."

Despite the blue-skin's bulk, Zodarin still stood two spans taller, and he looked down at Tuh-Ma, amber eyes tinged with purple. "It is clear the Praetor incurred the Queen's displeasure, and with the murder of his agent he may have felt under threat. After all, if a man can be slaughtered in broad daylight in the royal courtyard, then who indeed would feel safe?"

"Why no one found the killer?" Tuh-Ma said.

"Another unsolved problem," the wizard said, "and it is not for the want of trying. Still, the guard has been trebled, and there have been no further incidents. I think perhaps the Praetor had taken up with some less than savoury characters. I don't imagine the Queen will mourn his disappearance."

Phindrath looked increasingly uncomfortable, her already pallid complexion had turned as white as a ghost's. "You must tell Etezora we are doing all we can," Phindrath said, but her response was met with a narrowing of the blue-skin's eyes.

"Let me see the Queen's scroll," Zodarin said, taking it from the Captain. He scanned the contents in seconds, and then rolled it back up. "Your Majesty," he said, addressing the Princess. "You are instructed to take charge of the castle. It seems the Queen had designs on removing the Praetor from command, anyway. Why don't you write a response, and I will stay with her emissary ... to answer any remaining questions he may have?"

Phindrath looked at the wizard's calm, nodding face and took her cue.

"Yes," she replied, "that is exactly what I will do. Captain, arrange refreshment for the Queen's emissary."

The Captain saluted his response, and Phindrath exited the throne room, lifting her dress clear of her feet and walking at a pace just less than a run.

Once the two of them were alone, Tuh-Ma turned to the wizard and squared up to him, his hooded eyes glowering, and saliva dropping from his jelly lips.

"Wizard, Tuh-Ma not trust you. Never has. My Queen has raged night and day because you have not dealt with the dragons yet. Now, Tuh-Ma sees you have taken one as your pet, riding it as your steed. Tuh-Ma thinks you are traitor!"

The blue-skin was now inches from Zodarin, his eyes flaring with anger. But as he looked into the wizard's face he faltered, as if seeing something there that gave him pause, reason to fear. Then it passed. But it was enough for the blue-skin to step back and adopt a less threatening pose.

"That is not so my friend," Zodarin said. "I returned to the castle because I uncovered treachery regarding Eétor. It would have been premature to voice my full suspicions in front of the Princess — she is a delicate soul after all. As I said before, I believe he has taken to hiding. It was my intention to return to our Queen, but my recovery from decimating the dragons in the Dreamworld is slow, and I fatigue quickly."

The blue-skin was not a quick thinker, and his loyalty was stronger than his intellect, yet even he could not accept such an explanation at face value. "Tuh-Ma not sure," he said. "Maybe wizard is play-acting. Why should Dreamworld make you tired?"

Zodarin's eyes flashed. "Come with me to the Far Beyond and experience its delights. Then you will understand the ebb and flow of the energies there."

Tuh-Ma shook his head vigorously. "Tuh-Ma not trust Dreamworld. He likes it even less than dragons. Why should Tuh-Ma bother? Tuh-Ma should just kill you."

*One more step closer, Zodarin thought, and you will see at last what you are dealing with, blue-skin!*

Once again the blue-skin caught a glimpse of the amioid and didn't press home the threat. "Our Queen needs me," Zodarin said, "and she will be angry if you harm me."

The blue-skin considered the wizard's reply, licked his lips, and then said, "You come back with Tuh-Ma to tell Queen."

At that moment two servants arrived and placed a tray of drinks in front of them. Zodarin used the interruption to defuse the situation and poured them both a goblet of wine each. He took a sip from one and handed the other to the blue-skin who sniffed it, suspiciously.

"You think it poisoned? Servant — taste the wine for our guest."

After the nearest had performed his duty, Tuh-Ma was somewhat pacified and risked a draught.

"I am ready to return to the Dreamworld to complete my task," Zodarin continued. "I believe I can also seek the Dragon Queen. But I am far too weak for a long journey." The promise of finding Tayem was a lie, but the blue-skin wasn't to know the laws that governed which peoples were found in the Dreamworld.

"Queen would not be happy if you killed the Dragon Queen. That is to be her pleasure."

"Quite," Zodarin said, his tone patronising. "So what can I do to convince you I hold the dragon folk and their wyrms in as much contempt as you do?"

He looked across the courtyard at the small pygmy dragon he had grown attached to, and a thought occurred to him. An uncomfortable notion for sure.

*Survival is more important than compassion.*

Tuh-Ma followed his gaze and hissed when he saw what Zodarin was staring at.

"You really don't like them, do you?" the wizard said.

The blue-skin smiled and nodded.

The sorcerer stood motionless and closed his eyes.

*In the Dreamworld the wolf moved in for the kill. The attack took the small wyrm by surprise and it collapsed without resistance.*

Tuh-Ma watched as the unsuspecting dragon rolled forward in its pen. A seizure had taken hold, and it dropped to the floor like a stone.

Zodarin opened his eyes and regarded the still body on the other side of the courtyard. Inexplicably, he found himself holding back tears.

*Curse this blight. Would that it had been you I had slain, troll.*

"Perhaps you prove something," the blue-skin said. He paused or a moment, slurped back a string of spittle then pronounced, "Tuh-Ma not kill you today. Will tell Queen that you still work for her. That you still kill dragons. Maybe she believe you, maybe she won't. You better pray, wizard. You are not off the hook."

"Thank you, Emissary, I'm grateful," replied the wizard.

"I will have the royal butcher skin the beast and prepare cuts of meat for the Queen. I'm sure she will enjoy them. Now, if that will be all?" He didn't wait for a reply, and took his leave, retiring back to the wizard tower. It had been a small foray into the Dreamworld, yet it still fatigued him.

*Time is running out. Gods preserve me if I don't find a cure soon.*

Next morning, Tuh-Ma ate a hearty breakfast and saddled up his horse with the best cuts of salted meat from the pygmy dragon. His mount was refreshed, and it wasn't long before he was travelling at a mighty pace back northward. He would miss the freedom of the castle but was glad to take back his position at the Queen's side.

The Captain had passed him Phindrath's scroll for Etezora's scrutiny, and he only hoped Etezora would be satisfied with the outcome of his mission. He sincerely wished he had been able to dispose of the magic man, but something had brought him up short, something in the wizard's eyes, something from beyond the Dreamworld.

"Maybe when dragons and their Queen are gone," he said out loud, "then Queen will let Tuh-Ma deal with wizard." And as the miles were eaten up, he imagined his misshapen hands closing round Zodarin's neck, squeezing, constricting. He heard the last rasps of the man in his mind and, last of all, saw the remains of a tentacled thing extinguished forever.

# 41

# FOR WANT OF A SOUL

---

"We grant you sanctuary in Herethorn."

They were the words that the Dragon Riders had wanted to hear, and despite her initial feelings of affront towards these people, Cistre savoured the relief and gratitude filling her like fresh water from a mountain spring. The re-convened meeting with the Cyclopes was brief, and it wasn't long before the tasks that now presented themselves began to form a long list of priorities. Tayem thanked Ebar, wisely avoiding questions and requests regarding what would be an inevitable conflict with the Cuscosians.

Mahren was keen to make the return journey to the

Dragonian encampment as soon as possible, not least because she wanted to be close to Brethis. Yet there was also a pressing need for the Dragonian populace to make the transition before harsh weather set in or — Sesnath forbid it — a raid by the Cuscosians. Ebar commissioned five Gigantes guides, although none were Cyclopes, and gave leave for them to set out by first light. Cistre's initial assessment of a people lethargic and indolent proved to be hasty. As she saw how the Gigantes rallied together and worked efficiently at accommodating the Dragon Riders, she became impressed at their cohesiveness and obedience.

"They survived the Decimation, and their roots extend back millennia," Tayem reminded her. "It is perhaps a lesson for us not to judge by appearances too readily. We have been naive regarding the Cuscosians — and similarly not recognised the faces of our true allies." They had retired to a single cabin reserved for the Queen, and it was only now that Tayem seemed to take down her guard and allow the possibility of a long rest to do its work. However, there was another consultation to engage in before she would permit herself this luxury.

A knock on the cabin door presaged the entry of Milissandia and her father. Cistre had extended a grudging respect towards the druid, but as yet did not fully trust her intentions. As for her father, she would have to apply the recent advice about prejudice from Tayem forcibly as he did not offer an immediate projection of acceptability. The man's matted, long grey hair hung over a semi-naked dark-skinned body, and the swamp pigment tattoos he wore only added to the appearance of strangeness. His eyes were searching yet held a kindly glint, and Cistre suspected they hid a troubled past. *At least there seems to be no malice there.*

"Forgive us for interrupting your rest," Milissandia said, "but we wanted to talk with you as soon as possible."

"Of course," Tayem said wearily. "Do sit."

Dark grey shadows formed crescents under Tayem's eyes and Cistre noticed she winced every few seconds as if she nursed a serious injury.

"My father has something to say," the druid said, looking at her father expectantly.

"Speak freely, then," Tayem replied.

Wobas inclined his head and did not speak for a few seconds. Tayem's patience was wearing thin, despite her royal sense of decorum straining to keep her from rudeness. "Well then?" she said. "Did you come merely to stare at me?"

Wobas smiled. "You maintain your noble bearing well, Queen Tayem, but I sense the tumult you harbour will not be gainsaid for much longer."

Tayem shifted uncomfortably. "What exactly do you mean, Shaman?"

"Let us not duel with words. It is crucial that you open up to us if you are to be rid of your torment."

"My torment?"

"It is written in your eyes. You cannot hold back the tide of what you invited in for much longer."

Tayem dropped her head, all pretence gone. "What am I to do?"

Wobas looked at Milissandia who nodded back at him. "There is a ritual I can perform for ones afflicted. It requires that I enter the Dreamworld and find their avatar."

Tayem lifted her head, eyes wide. "You could do this for me?"

"Do you truly want to released from its grip on your soul?"

Tayem hesitated, and then said, "Yes. With all my heart. The Hallows seeks to take over. Every hour of every day it offers the power to bring down my enemies, to fulfil my every dream. But I have seen how it corrupts, and keeping it in check drains my spirit."

Wobas nodded. "I understand the power of its persuasion. I too was enticed, when Sol-Ar entered the cycle of dominion."

"There is a Hallows site in Herethorn?" Cistre said.

"Close to my abode high in the mountains," Wobas said. "But its influence is contained, and up to now I have kept watch over it — to ensure none succumb to its temptation."

"I noticed how Sol-Ar's colour seems not to affect the skies over Herethorn," Tayem added.

"The Ancients have blessed this place," Wobas said.

"Their blessing rises from deep in the mountains, inhabits the very soil and air we breathe."

Tayem reached out and touched his arm. "When can you do this?"

Cistre saw the desperation on her Queen's face and a deep solicitude rose in response to her plight. *Oh how I wish I could have helped you more.*

Wobas frowned. "This is not an easy thing. First, the Donnephon do not have a counterpart in the Far Beyond as other races do. This has kept you safe from marauders in that realm, but it also means there is nothing for me to establish a connection with."

"Then it is impossible?" Tayem replied, her shoulders sagging.

"There is a way," Wobas said. "You will need to come with us into the Dreamworld by your own choice. The journey is not without risk, and you will need deep reserves of strength."

Tayem sighed. "I am exhausted tonight."

"Then you must rest, for we will attempt to accomplish this tomorrow," Wobas said. "I too need to make preparations of my own."

"My Queen," Cistre said. "Is this wise? We don't know what the dangers are. What if this journey proves too perilous? What if you never come back?"

Tayem turned back to Wobas. "These risks — what are they?"

"Your presence in the Dreamworld may attract others' attentions," Milissandia said to Tayem.

"What others?"

Wobas's brow furrowed. "Spiritual predators. There is one in particular I have reason to fear. I encountered him on my last sojourn there."

"Can we not combat it?" Tayem asked.

"Combat? I fear he is too powerful. But we might avoid his detection long enough to achieve what needs to be done."

"What is its name, this predator?" Tayem asked.

"In Old-speak it is called levethix di wurunwi. But its counterpart in the Near To is a wizard called Zodarin."

"The Cuscosian sorcerer?" Tayem said, eyes growing wider.

"He is not of Cuscosian blood," Wobas said. "In truth I don't know exactly who or what he is. I thought I knew him once, but that was many moons ago."

Tayem looked at her feet. "It seems I will be putting you in danger too, Shaman."

"Both I and my daughter, yes. Yet even if we were not to attempt this thing for you, our destiny is tied up in the Far Beyond. There are other matters we must attend to there."

"Then, we should proceed." She looked at Cistre, as if seeking permission. "I cannot bear this turmoil any longer, and I fear what I will become should I lose control."

"You speak aright," Milissandia said. "We only have to look to the Cuscosian Queen to see that."

"There is one more thing you should know," Wobas said. "The levethix di wurunwi. It is he who is responsible for the death of your dragons."

And that is all it took for the Hallows to rise in Tayem. She picked up a wooden ornament from the table next to her and crushed it in her white-knuckled fist.

Cistre gripped her arm. "My Queen — "

"Then maybe it is good that we should meet this Zodarin in the Dreamworld. I would crush him as I did this figure."

Wobas looked startled for the first time. "Queen Tayem. Its power is even greater than yours. In the Dreamworld you will be in his domain, and even your Hallows power will not prevail. He too is infested with its malevolence."

"Your Majesty," Milissandia said, "we have told you this, not so you can exact your revenge but so you understand who our foe is. The predator *will* be brought down, but not on this occasion. It will require spiritual weapons, and my father and I have much to discover and prepare before we are ready for that encounter."

Cistre kept hold of Tayem until the Hallows ire subsided. When it did, she posed another question to the shaman of the Gigantes. "What is your plan?"

"I will tell you," he replied. And so he did. The four of them discussed what they must do until Tayem could hold her eyes open no longer.

"The morning then?" Tayem said, her words slurring.

"The morning," Wobas repeated, and left with his druid daughter at his side.

~ ~ ~

When Sol-Ar's glow first appeared through the Eastern Ardesk pass, Mahren shouldered her pack and set off with the small accompaniment of Dragon Riders and Gigantes guides. Tayem watched them disappear into the Herethorn forests, confident they were in safe hands. She now had her own journey to make. Milissandia's potion had given her a reasonable night's sleep, but with morning's light the Hallows was back with a vengeance. *Almost as if it anticipates its expulsion,* she thought.

She turned to Wobas and said, "I am ready."

The shaman nodded. "Then let us be about our task."

The rite Wobas wanted to perform would be carried out in Tayem's cabin. It was as good a place as any. Entry to the Dreamworld did not require any artefact or sanctum. The power to transfer was innate for the shaman. Milissandia, on the other hand, required her anduleso paste and yellow mushroom.

The four of them, Cistre included, sat down and steeled themselves for what was to come. Milissandia had made it clear she and her father would carry out a brief preliminary sortie. If there was no danger, Wobas would return for Tayem who would also partake of Milissandia's concoction. Herein lay the risk: Milissandia had only ventured into the Dreamworld a handful of times; each of which was only for a short spell. She had yet to calculate the optimum dosage of ingredients, and there was no supposing these would be the same for Tayem. Too much and she might remain in the Dreamworld, and they would not be able to revive her. Who knew if they might have to make a hasty exit? *It would have been much easier if I had my own permanent avatar in the Dreamworld,* Tayem thought. *What peculiarity of Donnephon lore prevents this?*

Tayem was almost oblivious regarding the risks to herself, saying that as long as the two Gigantes were safe, they need not concern themselves with her. It didn't take much to see past her motivation, however. The chance to engage with Zodarin and bring an end to him overcame any sense of realism regarding her prospects, and she welcomed the opportunity to be rid of the Hallows — whatever the cost. If she should die in combat with this levethix di wurunwi, then so be it.

The Gigantes were all too aware of her desperate state of mind, telling her that if there was any sign of Zodarin on the other side, then they would abort the mission.

"Very well," Tayem sighed. "Let's get on with it."

"Watch carefully, father," Milissandia instructed Wobas. "You will need to administer these unctions to the Queen when we have completed our sortie."

"So many unknowns," he said.

Milissandia proceeded to apply a thin layer of anduleso paste to her wrist. "This site provides maximum absorption for minimum application," she said. Following this, she swallowed a small sample of the yellow mushroom, and before long had drifted into a trance. Wobas crossed his legs, closed his eyes and was transported straight away.

"So — we wait," Tayem said to Cistre.

Her bodyguard appeared particularly tense, and Tayem wondered what perturbed her so. The woman had served the Queen since her accession to the throne, and no doubt felt extreme loyalty and attachment to her. Perhaps it was the fact she was an orphan. Her father had accepted her into the royal household without hesitation, and apart from Mahren she had spent more hours with her than any other Dragonian. They had reached maturity together, fought side by side against the enemy, and ridden the skies in tandem. Yes, she could not hope for a better guard. Perhaps she was more than that, however.

"Why so anxious?" Tayem said to her. "This is for the best. These Gigantes hold the only hope for my release."

"But if something befalls you in the Dreamworld?" Cistre said with palpable emotion. "What will I ... what will *we* do?"

Tayem took both her bodyguard's hands. "If I cannot be released from the Hallows domination, then a far worse burden will remain. The Donnephon cannot have a queen possessed with the same evil as Etezora. Its strength grows, and with it a madness I cannot control."

Cistre looked at her Queen, a puzzled expression appearing on her face.

"What are you saying?"

"Cistre, if this does not work. I may need you to fulfil the utmost of your duty."

"You mean ... no I could not do that. My loyalty is to you, my Queen."

"Your loyalty is actually to Dragonia and to the Donnephon. They must take precedence over any monarch."

"Please do not ask this of me. I — "

"It is your duty," Tayem said, holding her hands more tightly. "Say you will not falter. Mahren cannot do this, it is forbidden for Royal Family to perform the kutri."

"No, I will not — "

"Promise me!"

It was too much for Cistre, and tears formed in the corners of her eyes. Yet she did not get the opportunity to swear the oath because at that moment, Wobas's eyes opened.

"The realm appears safe," he said. "Now quickly, let me apply the unction. Milissandia waits for us on the other side."

Wobas carried out the application swiftly, and then invited Tayem to sit cross-legged in front of him. "You must relax totally. Here, swallow the mushroom."

Tayem took the fungus and bit into it. It tasted spicy and not altogether unpleasant. She closed her eyes and did her best to relax every muscle and allow her mind to clear. The Hallows protested at this orchestration, but Tayem was rested, and quashed its impertinence. After only a few seconds, she found her thoughts were not her own, and an ethereal apparition came to her, fluttering closer like a feathered ghost.

The night bird, for that is what it was, flapped over her head and spoke to her. *Follow me*, it said, *we may not have much time.*

Tayem looked down at her body, wondering if it had changed too, but it was her own. The wurunwa ith flitted between the branches of the overhead trees, but always remained in sight. Tayem followed, her steps damped by leaf litter, the sensation in her soles almost non-existent. *This is like floating,* she thought. The surrounding trees were similar to garpines, yet did not have the spiky offshoots she normally associated with the species. Her field of vision extended only a few strides as a frosted mist billowed all around. *This is like the Dastarthes that surrounds Herethorn,* she mused. *Wobas has produced a recreation of the Dreamworld environment around the sanctuary.*

Time slipped away, and she wondered if anything was amiss. *Wobas,* she sent. *Where is Milissandia?*

*Where the trees border on a meadow. Up ahead,* the scops replied in thought-speak. *But beware using our names. These utterances echo across the Far Beyond and others may hear our conversation above the dream static.*

Tayem submitted to the nightbird's admonishment and continued forward into the trees.

~ ~ ~

Zodarin dropped the flask he was holding. It contained his latest attempt at an elixir to combat the dragon blight, yet he deduced its contents were impotent. It shattered on the stone floor of his chamber, but he did not care.

*The shaman has returned to the Dreamworld!*

The means by which he knew this were beyond him, yet he heard the wurunwa ith's name mentioned by another, an alien signature he could not identify.

*I must investigate. But what if I find them? Do I offer Wobas a partnership once again? And if he refuses — do I have the strength or will to overcome him?*

These were unanswerable questions, but he was resolved to act. He couldn't let this opportunity pass him by. Time was running out.

~ ~ ~

The tree line appeared ahead, backdropped against a lighter glow. Tayem noted the arbour had changed in composition to a deciduous mix made up from swampland trees. As she stepped forward cautiously, the scops came to rest on a thick, moss-covered branch next to an iridescent tree-serpent.

*I see you,* she sent, remembering Wobas's instruction not to invoke names. *What happens now?*

The dream creatures looked at each other, then the serpent scurried in front of the bird and coiled itself up. The bird spread its wings in what appeared to be an arcane posture.

*Step closer and raise your arms,* the night bird sent. *You need do nothing except open yourself. The power of wurunwa is strong here and it will be upon us to effect the ritual. But do not think your task can be accomplished without a great application of will. The malignancy within is unlikely to relinquish its grasp easily, and you must resist its every overture.*

The scops' words were true. Already, Tayem could feel it stirring in her belly. *Please start,* she sent, *it knows that something is afoot.*

Without further word, the wurunwa ith opened its beak and uttered a low, sweet train of sound while the anduleso swayed its head from side to side with the rhythm.

~ ~ ~

Zodarin was levethix di wurunwi, wizard of dreams, existing in his human form. He had dispensed with the calti embodiment — Wobas would not entertain the one that had impersonated the Augur. He had also shunned the wolvern's body — too fearsome, and as for the harroc di wurunwi — that would not be conducive at all. He ran across the meadow towards the tree line, following the sound of the invocations, knowing they signaled a healing process. *But what?* He needed to know. Then he would deal with the shaman and his new confederate.

~ ~ ~

*It has its hooks in me,* Tayem sent.

*They are not hooks,* the anduleso said, *simply excuses you make to yourself. Let them go!*

Tayem tried, or at least she thought she did. She saw the hooks in her mind's eye, and the thing they were attached to. It was beyond abhorrent, beyond description and her mind recoiled in horror.

The scops did not contribute to their conversation, and Tayem surmised Wobas's energies were taken up effecting the ritual.

*Look at the hooks in a different way,* the anduleso sent. *Not as a device of the Hallows, but a construct of your own making.*

Tayem regarded the image, so real it encompassed everything she saw; yet she had the power to change it. But what did she hold as most precious? Was it something she should have relinquished long ago? *Maybe ...*

She exerted her will and replaced the hooks with an image of the carved dragon figurine her father had carved for her. Seeing it appear as this powerful image, she felt a longing for him and for all she had lost. *No, I cannot let it go.*

*You must,* the anduleso sent, *and you must do it quickly. The Harroc di wurunwi comes.*

Tayem focused on the figurine. She held on to one wing, while the malignancy held the other. She knew what to do — but it was so hard.

*Too late,* the anduleso sent. *Disaster is upon us.*

~ ~ ~

Zodarin climbed the hill toward the treeline. They were close, but his lungs burned with the exertion.

*Even here the blight afflicts me,* he moaned.

Now that he was close, his dream sense identified the three entities: Wobas, his daughter and ... could this be ... Tayem Fyreglance, Queen of the Donnephon?

He had come intent on a last negotiation, but with this discovery, he knew he had no choice. To gain Etezora's trust back he must strike down the Cuscosian's enemy. The blight contradicted him, showing an image of Tayem as a youngster, playing with Etezora — a time of innocence, a time of relative peace.

*No time for conscience. I must call upon my greatest strength.*

And just as Tayem was battling a reluctance to let go mere strides ahead of him, Zodarin did what came easy — he released the harroc di wurunwi. Tentacles replaced arms, eyes multiplied across his skin, and his form expanded two-fold.

With renewed vigour he surged up the hill.

Then another appeared, drifting in from the mists. One

he had met only once before and had existed for even longer than he.

*Stay your hand, Harroc di wurunwi*, it said. *Think of the consequences.*

*You are Memek-Tal*, Zodarin said. *Stand aside, you have no power over me.*

*You are correct, Zodarin, amioid of ancient times.*

*You know who I am?*

*That is my strength — knowledge. Would you not wish to know the nature of that which afflicts you? Discover how to rid yourself of the torment?*

*You would give me this knowledge?*

*It comes at a price*, the Spirit Guide sent, turning its bird head to indicate the three figures engrossed in the ritual behind him.

*Anything — tell me!*

*Promise you will not harm them.*

Zodarin, the harroc di wurunwi, contemplated the Spirit Guide's words. *How can I trust you?*

*I am bound to tell the truth.*

Zodarin held centuries of magical lore and history, yet he had no way of knowing this entity's nature. However, he did know that spirit guides spoke in riddles. If it gave him what he needed, would he be able to interpret it?

*What to do?*

~ ~ ~

*The harroc di wurunwi holds off its attack,* the scops sent, breaking off its invocation. *I have completed my part, Tayem. It is now up to you. Do you truly want to expel this thing?*

Tayem's mind was a storm. She had let in what she thought was the means of her people's salvation, tasted the fruits of its possession. These were gifts of immense gravity. Then she saw the death throes of her dragons, her railing against those close to her, the loss of Darer, and the slaughter she had dealt. Was this what she wanted?

*No!*

She let go of the dragon figurine's wing and its image recoiled into the dark violet mass that was the Hallows. Straight away she felt the uprooting of something deep-seated, something akin to a dark foetus within. It rose through her throat, its passage causing immeasurable pain, yet she could not cry out.

*I will surely die.*

*Hold on,* the anduleso sent, its voice indistinct, distant; and just as she thought her soul would be ripped from her body, the Hallows was expelled and Tayem breathed in the fresh soul energy of the Dreamworld.

*It is done,* the scops sent, its dream tone a mixture of triumph and panic. *We must away. Run.*

Tayem reached for the anduleso, picked it up and willed her feet forward. Once more, time elapsed with no sense of its pace. Would she make it to the border of the Near To? She looked over her shoulder. Nothing followed. *Why did the harroc di wurunwi stop?*

There was no time for conjecture. She swept after the scops, following its ghostly form through the trees, until at last they reached the point of transition. She did not hesitate but plunged forward, feeling the weirdness and exhilaration of transition.

Then she was in her body once more, and Cistre was shaking her. "Tayem, speak to me," she cried.

The Queen opened her eyes, saw the concerned expressions on Wobas's and Cistre's faces and beamed a smile born of release. "Why, Cistre? What has overcome you that you should use my first name?"

Cistre blushed. "Forgive me, My Queen. You were screaming. I thought — "

"It is done," Tayem said. "Now unhand me. We have much to do."

~ ~ ~

*You tricked me!* Zodarin sent.

*I did not,* the Spirit Guide replied. *You simply took your time deciding.*

*You caused me to miss my opportunity, and now they are gone. Do you think I will spare you for this?*

The Spirit Guide laughed. Not a mocking sound, but an expression of mirth that one makes when a child throws a tantrum. *Can a man destroy the wind?*

Zodarin lunged with four tentacles, yet they closed around nothing.

*You are testing my patience,* the Spirit Guide said. *Don't you want to hear what I have to say?*

*I was not able to fulfil my part of the bargain,* Zodarin sent, and shrank back to his human form. He couldn't stand the thought that his amioid avatar should be on the receiving end of this humiliation.

*No — except by default. Yet I would impart some wisdom to you. The blight spreads and, although magical means might yield a cure, you will not find one in time.*

*That is your wisdom — to gloat over my doom?*

*There is another way. Return to your origins, you have a final transition you can make.*

*What transition do you speak of? I have many forms. Which one should I adopt?*

The Spirit Guide lifted its head, as if responding to a call only it could hear. *I have already crossed lines that have dire consequences for me,* it said. *I too will pay a price for this degree of intervention today.*

With that, it turned on its hooves and broke into a gallop.

*No, come back,* Zodarin cried, *you must give me more.*

But the Spirit Guide was gone, and Zodarin did not have the strength to pursue. The affront he had endured caused the Hallows to stir within. It joined with his anger to produce a raging hot spout of fury.

*Very well,* he said to the unresponsive mists, *if you are simply going to hold out hope of salvation and cruelly withdraw it, then I will resort to what I know best. Wobas and his daughter will die, the Dragonians will be destroyed and I will reign over all.*

And the Black Hallows having lost one of its hosts responded within, infiltrating his cells to their deepest level. Zodarin felt the blight retreat, slowed down in its contagion. Not gone, but delayed long enough to see the harroc di wurunwi wreak its revenge.

# 42

# SOJOURN IN THE SANCTUARY

---

Cistre released the retaining strap on Muthorus's saddle and passed it to Sheldar who took it dutifully.

"It really needs a complete oiling," she said, "it's starting to crack in places and I think it's chafing Muthorus's back."

"I'll see to it," Sheldar replied, his expression serious and pragmatic. She hadn't seen his jovial side for many a week now, which was small wonder, considering the trials that had beset them all. Still, she missed the childish banter and even his inept romantic passes.

"There isn't any ground nut oil. What will you use?"

"The Gigantes have a shop that sells basic tack and goods. I believe they use an extract from the mallowpurse plant."

"Will it do? If it should irritate the dragon's scales ..."

Sheldar smiled. "It'll take a lot more than saddle oil to penetrate a dragon's armour. I'm sure it won't cause a problem."

"Thank you," she said. "How are the other dragons faring?"

Sheldar shrugged. "As far as I can tell they are adapting to this climate well, and they seem to like their new pens. These Cyclopes are speedy builders and their skill at joinery rivals our own. In these few short weeks they have built a draconest that gives substantial accommodation for our remaining squadrons. Mahren is concerned, though."

"She is?" The mention of Mahren's name didn't raise the same irritation it once did. Since the exodus from Wyverneth, the ordeal of survival had broken down barriers throughout the surviving population. Traditional distinctions between royalty and lower classes had all but dissolved as the Dragonians had sought to pull together in the aftermath of the plains battle. This dissolution had touched Mahren and Cistre's relationship as they adopted clearer roles.

"She says they are flighty and restless," Sheldar continued. "They still mourn their family's loss."

Cistre nodded, feeling a familiar bitterness towards the

Cuscosians cloud her mind again. "It is to be expected. Their slaying is not something any of us will forget, although avenging it will help salve the mental wounds." As she said the words, she became aware of her fists clenched so tight her nails drew blood from the palms.

"I hope that is true," Sheldar said, taking up a pitchfork to transfer some loose switchgrass-straw to Muthorus's bed. "It vexes me, seeing this Brethis and his dissidents mingling with our people, though. Why does Tayem tolerate their presence?"

"They are cast out of their homeland as we are, Sheldar. And Tayem knows if we are to defeat the Cuscosians, then we will need to forge a strong alliance."

"Ever leaping to her defence," Sheldar said. "That is to be expected too."

"It is my duty as royal bodyguard."

Sheldar eyed her in a manner she hadn't observed in him before. "Hmm, there are duties of office," he said, "and there are duties of the heart."

Cistre flashed him a reproachful glance, but couldn't hide the blush that reddened her cheeks. "I do not know what you mean," she said.

Sheldar dumped a forkful of straw into the dragon pen and looked down in embarrassment. "Forgive me, Cistre. I didn't know what I was saying."

The bodyguard glowered at him a moment longer, then changed the subject. "Maybe we can ease the sorrow of the Pygris. It has been a long time since they wrestled.

Come, you can match Hyvol and I will face Ymith. We can supervise each other's bouts — what do you say?"

"Mahren will scold us for it. There is a long list of tasks to get through this morning."

"Ten minutes a bout won't dent much of the schedule, and we need something to distract us."

Sheldar smiled. "Very well. Quickest time to hold their opponent for a count of five wins."

Half an hour later, they were covered in dust and laughing with abandon. It had been a draw — to the second.

"You grow more wily in your attack strategy," she said to him.

"Hah, more the case that Ymith has grown more stupid."

At the sound of his name, Ymith uttered a hurt groan, which set the two Dragonians laughing again.

"Finding time to waste?" A voice cut through their mirth.

"Mahren," Cistre said. "I didn't hear you approach."

"While everyone could hear you as far as the end of the village," Mahren said with a smile.

"You're not angry?" Sheldar said.

"There are more dire things to stoke my rage these days," Mahren replied, and Cistre reflected that the Queen's sister was more prone to mellower moods since being reunited with her Brethis. "Which brings me to why

I came. Tayem has called a meeting of the Fyreclave. She has an answer from the Cyclopes Council."

"About a possible alliance? What did they say?"

"I don't know," Mahren replied. "She will tell us at the meeting."

Cistre dusted herself down and left Sheldar in charge of the dragon's regime for the rest of the day. Mahren's responsibility lay in organising exercise sorties and training of new Dragon Riders, so she accepted Cistre's issuing of orders regarding feeding and pen construction without chagrin.

The Dragonian enclave lay only a few hundred strides away. It bordered the southern side of the Gigantes village, and consisted of six hundred basic ironwood huts housing the three thousand eight hundred Dragonian survivors. The conditions were cramped, and living together required significant sharing of provisions; but the people were grateful for the shelter, especially as they had only just completed the transit to Herethorn when a severe mountain storm hit the Gigantes village. Fortunately it only lasted a day or so and resulted in no further loss of life.

The influx of the Dragonian population and Cuscosian dissidents had been completed in just two days following the Cyclopes Council. It was a testament to the Hill People's hospitality that they accepted the disruption as well as they did. It rang true in Cistre's mind as she remembered the legends concerning this remarkable race from the time they dwelt in Lyn-Harath. They were a benevolent people, sharing provisions, medicine and expertise without reserve. As a result, the mortality rate amongst the Dragonian wounded plummeted once they were established in their new abode.

Mahren and Cistre were amongst the first to arrive at the Fyreclave, and Cistre took the opportunity to check on Tayem's needs and refreshment while opportunity allowed.

"Do not fuss," Tayem said to her, although it was without vehemence. "Sometimes I think you are becoming more maid than bodyguard. Cistre smiled, grateful that Tayem was much lighter in spirit since her exorcism. It also meant that the spectre of Tayem's implied request had been driven from the horizon — hopefully forever. Cistre was relieved to see Tayem had lost the greyness under her eyes and gone were the piques of rage that had characterised her rule prior to Wobas and Milissandia's intervention. Did this lightness of mood mean she had received a favourable outcome from the Cyclopes? She didn't push the question, deciding to wait until all had arrived.

It didn't take long, and within five minutes all seven were assembled. Cistre also noted that Wobas, Milissandia and Brethis had been invited to the meeting. Once all were seated, Tayem's expression grew sombre.

"I regret to inform you that the Cyclopes were less than

forthcoming," she announced without any preamble. "They are reluctant to lend arms to our struggle."

"That is disappointing to say the least," Ascomb said, "so where does that leave us?"

"It means we must assemble and prepare our army using what we have."

"Will the Gigantes not aid us in any form at all?" Frodha said. "Do they not realise that Etezora will not stop at the borders of Dragonia in her lust for conquest?"

Tayem held up her hand. "All is not lost. Ebar has committed to gathering intelligence on Cuscosian troop movements using his flock of raptors. He will also organise supplies and provide scouts for a future incursion. These are not insignificant resources."

The Fyreclave were divided in their response, some nodding their heads in recognition of the allied support, others scowling in frustration that they had not been offered additional help.

"There is more," Tayem added. "I invited Wobas and Milissandia to our meeting to share what they gleaned from the Dreamworld."

There was a murmuring amongst the Fyreclave when she mentioned the two Gigantes' magical influence, while Wobas himself looked reserved. Cistre wondered if his demeanour simply reflected a respect for the Dragonians or something else.

"Please share what you discovered," Tayem said and smiled her welcome at the pair.

Wobas looked at Milissandia and spoke up, leading the exchange. "I understand your disappointment at our response regarding a commitment to providing an armed force," he began. "But perhaps we can provide a means to confront the greatest threat to your army — namely that of the scourge that assaulted your dragons."

"You identified the origin of this malign sorcery?" Gemain said, unable to contain his surprise.

Wobas continued after a moment of considering his reply. "I do not know if the Fyreclave are fully aware of the existence of what the Gigantes call the Far Beyond. Some call it the Dreamworld, and I have dedicated my life to pursuing its secrets." The shaman looked at his daughter after uttering these words as if exchanging a message of regret. Milissandia nodded back at him, her expression calm and reassuring. "It was during recent sojourns there," he continued, "that I discovered the one who caused such devastation to your dragons. I believe it was Zodarin, wizard of the Cuscosians."

Ascomb held up her hand. "Pardon my interruption, but how could a mere man have wrought such destruction?"

"It is my belief that the wizard has drunk deeply from the Black Hallows and become extremely powerful in the warcraft known as wurunwa vargachic — this means dream battle. It has long been the practice of maladepts to take down those who stood in their way, often by slaying their avatars in the Dreamworld. But up to now, the

519

presence of the noble dragons has remained undisclosed, known only to an entity called The Augur. Zodarin slew this Augur and discovered the dragon avatar's signature. During the battle in the Dead Zone he used his knowledge and arcane power to bring down your dragons. But something must have prevented him from accomplishing their complete annihilation."

"Was it not you?" Ascomb asked.

"I wish that I had been present to prevent anything from befalling your noble beasts, but alas I was severely ... incapacitated. No, there was something else that stopped him, perhaps the same thing that continues to prevent him pursuing their complete extinction."

"If Zodarin is disabled, then there is hope," Gemain said. "It is the dragons that give us our strength. Not daring to take them into battle is a severe disadvantage."

"Hope, yes," Wobas continued, "but not a guarantee. The wurunwa vargachic requires the expenditure of great energy, but we know that the Black Hallows increases its influence by the day. It may be that this adversary simply awaits a time when he can unleash unprecedented power at a strategic time."

"You sound unsure," Frodha said. "Can you not enter the Dreamworld and discover these facts with more certainty?"

"I wish it was that easy," Milissandia spoke up, "and we *have* explored the Far Beyond repeatedly. But so far Zodarin has not reappeared. In this we are somewhat relieved — he wields great power there and, even if he is weakened he is still formidable."

Frodha raised her hand again. "Then what use is this ability to us?"

Milissandia looked at her resolutely. "There is another we seek there, a Spirit Guide. It was he who reached out to me, completed the bridge that enabled me to traverse the Far Beyond. I believe he holds the key to many things that could save all our peoples."

"Wobas and Milissandia work constantly on our behalf in the Dreamworld," Tayem put in. "They perform this at great risk to themselves. Once they speak to the Spirit Guide, I'm sure he will reveal the knowledge we seek."

"I don't know," Frodha said. "This talk of dreamworlds and spirit guides sounds like a bard's fantastical tale to me."

"Believe me," Tayem said. "I know the Dreamworld is real — I ventured there myself."

This remark impressed the Fyreclave, but did little to assuage their doubts.

"My Queen," Gemain said. "This may all be true, but it does not offer much regarding our plans to re-take Wyverneth. Even if the safety of our dragons is guaranteed, the Cuscosians outnumber us almost ten to one. Without the help of the Cyclopes on the battlefield it may take sols to build an army strong enough to bring them down."

Brethis spoke up. "I can offer some assistance here." He

had remained silent throughout the discussion, Cistre noted, possibly recognising his incongruous position as a Cuscosian contemplating the defeat of his own people. "As representative of our dissident group, I can formally pledge our allegiance to your cause. We too have good reason to see Etezora deposed."

Ascomb regarded the man with no little condescension. "We are thankful for your contribution, Brethis of the Cuscosians. But you number barely three hundred, and some of those are children."

"This is true," Brethis replied, "but I know many more living in the Cuscosian provinces that would support our cause if only they could be given hope."

"How could they be rallied?" Gemain said with scepticism evident in his tone.

"I propose a contingent of my people return to Hallow's Creek and carry on the work we began before our families were slaughtered or imprisoned."

Cistre already knew of Brethis's intentions having been privy to conversations between Brethis, Tayem and Mahren. She also knew Mahren was opposed to the idea. Having thought him once lost, the thought of putting him in danger again appalled her.

"Forgive my negativity," Gemain said, "but even if you could remain undetected in Cuscosia, what hope is there of bringing any significant number to our cause? Seems to me you will encounter an uphill struggle."

"It will be difficult," Brethis said, "but we are far less

naive now, and I still know key contacts amongst the townsfolk there. If they could be given a sign that the Dragonians can muster a formidable force then I'm sure we could convince them. My people cannot bear the cruel reign of Etezora any longer. This desperation breeds men and women who would sacrifice much for their overthrow. I sensed this before our routing. How much more must it be true given what we heard of Etezora's descent into madness?"

"A sign?" Ascomb said. "What more can we offer save our proud warriors and our dragons? We are so diminished in number that I doubt whether they would be convinced of that."

"There is one who might represent an ally to strike fear into the very heart of Cuscosa," Tayem said. "Mahren?"

The Queen's sister now spoke up, hesitation all too apparent. "This is what one might call a quest into the unknown, but there is reason to believe it is worth the risk and effort." She paused to gauge the Fyreclave's reaction, then seeing their curious expressions, continued. "I speak of enlisting one who once pledged their allegiance to our ancestors, one whose might on the battlefield devastated our foes in the battle of Marrowbane."

Gemain narrowed his eyes. "Surely you don't mean ..."

"Yes," Mahren replied. "Agathon."

The Fyreclave looked at each other, and it was Ascomb who eventually spoke for them all. "With all respect, the Agnarim have all but vanished from Varchal, Agathon being the only one to survive the age of forgetting. Yet no one knows her whereabouts."

"Even if you found Agathon, and even if she could be roused," Gemain added, "she would surely not involve herself in the affairs of the Donnephon again."

Milissandia looked puzzled. "Who is this Agathon?"

"She is the great dragon of Agnarim," Tayem replied. "She was Astronomotan, dwarfing even Ensutharr in size. What's more, she possessed the ability to drench her enemies with fire."

Milissandia's eyes widened. "It sounds like this dragon could turn the tide of any war."

"Indeed she could," Tayem said. "But Gemain is right in saying her lair is unknown, indeed she may even have passed from the world."

"Then what hope is there of even thinking about entreating her?" Frodha asked.

"Two things," Tayem replied. "First — what I discovered in Ebar's library, and second — Mahren's ability to speak to the dragons."

"Ebar's library?" Milissandia said. "I thought it only contained shamanic writings and recipes."

"There are also tomes relating to Gigantes and Dragonian history," Tayem said. "I spent many hours searching these volumes during my recovery and discovered one that held a clue to Agathon's location. The book I read told of Agathon's last flight and how she entrusted a message to Ralgemah, Queen of the

Donnephon. She said, 'my place of rest will lie in the Mountains of Onograve, in the vaults of a peak called Frostgaunt. I may well die there, and if I do, that is no matter for regret. You must remember it as a place you should avoid. I would not have your dragons seek me out, as they might. They would not be welcome.'"

Gemain pursed his lips. "A quest into the unknown indeed."

"More like a journey to one's death." Ascomb added. "It seems clear this Agathon does not wish to be disturbed under any circumstances."

"I believe we should try," Tayem said. "After all, who is to say that she herself might not be threatened by Zodarin's foul sorcery? I see it as my duty to warn her — if she still lives."

"So, who would go?" Frodha asked.

"Mahren and I," Tayem replied. "Mahren, because she has a way with dragons unprecedented amongst our people, and myself because one such as Agathon may only deem it fit to converse with the ruling Queen of the Donnephon."

"But we need you here to oversee the preparations for battle," Gemain said.

"Not so. I have full confidence in Beredere and Cistre to administrate the required tasks."

"No, my Queen," protested Cistre, "my place is at your side."

Tayem looked at her bodyguard kindly. "We shall speak of this later, Cistre."

There were many more questions and further discussions that extended well into late afternoon, but when the meeting drew to a close there was an agreement, albeit reluctantly from some quarters, regarding a plan of action. Sashaim and Aibrator would enable Brethis and Oathair to infiltrate Hallow's Creek. They would establish a suitable drop-off point using intelligence gleaned from Brownbeak's flock of raptors, and arrange a communication line so he could relay updates about his success — or otherwise. Wobas and Milissandia were to continue their forays into the Dreamworld in an effort to make contact with the mysteriously evasive Spirit Guide. The two of them seemed to have moved on in their relationship, and although they still bickered, they had a fruitful partnership. Finally, Tayem's journey with Mahren into the Onograve Mountains was approved. She had to force this decision through with the proviso that should they not locate Agathon within a fortnight then they would return forthwith.

It was this last decision that sat most uneasily with the Fyreclave, but it was to Cistre whom Tayem felt she owed a full explanation.

"I know your feelings on this matter," Tayem said to her, once they had retired to the royal cabin. Cistre was silent, unsure what words she could formulate to dissuade her Queen from this course of action.

"Speak to me," Tayem said, "I cannot stand your brooding silences."

"I — " Cistre began, but the words did not come. Instead, an outpouring of tears burst forth.

In living memory, Cistre could not recall an occasion when she had shown weakness of this sort. She tried to excuse herself, but Tayem gripped her arms and bade her sit down.

"Cistre, what is this?"

"I ... I do not know, My Queen. You must ignore me. It's just that, I thought I had lost you to the Hallows; and now your soul has returned from that dark place, am I to lose you again to the mountains or the great dragon?"

Tayem passed her a handkerchief and looked her in the eye. "The Queen of the Donnephon must not shrink from her duty, Cistre. It is clear only Mahren and I can accomplish this task. Agathon will only speak to one such as I."

"But why can I not accompany you? It is *my* duty to be at your side."

"Nothing would bring me greater comfort than for you to fly with me. But I need you to moderate Beredere's excesses. As a team, you accomplished much in the foothills of the Whispering Mountains. Thanks to your partnership you saved many lives. There is also the question of minimising risk. If we find Agathon and she should prove quick to anger, then not only will you be lost as well, but an additional dragon may fall. There is nothing to be gained from you coming — other than our comfort."

It was the first time that Cistre had heard Tayem refer to her as anything other than a loyal member of her Royal Guard. The fact that she derived solace from her company touched a place she had not dared hope existed.

"I must admit, my emotions are all asunder," Cistre said.

"It is so," Tayem replied and held her close.

They remained like that for a long time.

~ ~ ~

Next morning, dampened by a light rain, another couple had their own emotional parting.

"I won't tell you to take care," Mahren said.

"Neither of us take advice well," Brethis replied.

"At least we had one last night together."

"Don't make it sound so final. We will meet again — soon."

Mahren stroked Jaestrum's nose, a displacement activity to stop her crying. "It seems the fates conspire to keep us apart."

"You know I don't believe in fate."

"Then what *do* you believe in?"

"Our love," he said, "and that is more than enough."

They kissed one more time, then Brethis mounted Sashaim's dragon, riding in the pillion position. Tayem sat astride Quassu, and Oathair had taken his position behind Aibrator. Four dragons, two separate directions, one common purpose.

Tayem looked down at Cistre, who was holding her composure remarkably well. Beside her, Beredere saluted and uttered his parting words to them all in a suitably officious voice.

"May Sesnath be with you," Tayem said to them.

"Dixtrath semlessin," they all replied in unison. And with that, the dragons took to the skies, majestic wings beating against the rain-filled air, cries echoing across Herethorn as they disappeared into the distance.

# 43

# HOLY OUTLAW

---

It had been almost a week since the Dragonian queen and her sister had left Herethorn, and if one word could be used to describe the atmosphere that hung over the village, Wobas guessed it would be foreboding. He observed the orb of Sol-Ar, resting like a malignant violet spider's egg above the Ardesk Mountains and sensed its communion with the Black Hallows to the north. He imagined the purple cauldron roiling close to his cave in response to Sol-Ar's influence and sighed with relief that for now it was contained by the earth magic of Herethorn. But how long would it last?

He had taken to meeting with Milissandia on the seat

overlooking the village every morning. There they discussed how their Dreamworld peregrinations progressed. To the south, the business of the dragon folk could be heard as they built more shelters, forged weapons and trained for the battle that was sure to come. Up above, Cistre led a sortie of three dragons northwards, partly to investigate the unknown lands that existed there, partly to give the creatures their daily exercise and a chance to hunt.

"It is not the peaceful sanctuary it once was," reflected Milissandia.

"Nothing remains the same," Wobas replied. "We must accept it for what it is. Let us be thankful that the tribulations south of our borders have not yet breached our defences."

Milissandia grinned. "My father accepting change? Matters must be dire indeed!"

"Any word from the dragon folk regarding the Queen's expedition?"

"Nothing as of this morning."

"How are they taking to you?"

"The Dragonians? Beredere is accommodating, but Cistre mistrusts me."

Wobas nodded. "She is very protective. I sense a turbulent past."

"You saw Ebar earlier," Milissandia said, changing the subject. "Has Brownbeak returned from yesterday's ranging?"

"Yes. He reports further barracking of troops in and around Wyverneth, and his brothers confirm the complete destruction of the Kaldoran stronghold."

Milissandia took a draught from a small wooden water bottle she always carried with her, and then stoppered it again. "The Dragonian warriors are brave, but so small in number. They need allies."

"True. They might benefit from an alliance with the dissidents. Sashaim returned with news from Brethis. He and Oathair evade detection so far, and they've already met with leaders from the tribes of Midna, Amara and Quila. But he has much work to do in uniting them."

"I sense time running out for us. Etezora builds her defences stronger, and all the while there is the threat to the dragons from Zodarin."

"Sashaim said the wizard has not been heard from, and broods in his tower. I'm not sure what that means."

Milissandia looked at him as if weighing something up.

"There is something on your mind, Daughter. Speak up. I have not suffered our estrangement all these sols simply for your reproach to return."

"It is not reproach," she said. "Only that you do not speak much of this Zodarin. What is he to you?"

"Once a friend, now a mortal enemy." Wobas knew his tone was clipped, and he wanted to say more about his shared history with the sorcerer, but now was not the time. *Would there ever be a time?* He put his hand on hers. "Forgive me. The memories are painful."

"But if we must face this creature again, anything you know may be important."

"True. Let us talk after our completion of today's journey."

"The last five days have been little more than fruitless. There is no sign of Memek-Tal and the dragon avatars continue to be safe."

"We must maintain our vigil, protect the dragons and continue to seek the Spirit Guide."

"Very well," she said. "Let us perform this task. Shall we retire to your cabin?"

They made their way across the village, locked the door to Wobas's dwelling and settled themselves on a shaman seat each.

"Remember our plan for if things go awry in the Far Beyond?" Wobas said.

"Yes," she replied, rubbing the anduleso paste on her wrists and swallowing a yellow mushroom. "Face off the harroc di wurunwi in the first instance. Distract him, and then attack using the joint power of our vargachic weaponry."

"This we must practice. There are still vulnerabilities in our approach."

"Therefore let us traverse there," she said. "I am impatient to hone our skills."

Minutes later they were passing through the mists of the Dreamworld. Wobas kept his protective eye on Milissandia's anduleso avatar. He wished she could adopt a more mobile form, but multiple bodies were something beyond even his capabilities. Thus, he flitted and circled about her as she scuttled on her little feet upon the pine needles of the forest floor.

*Another periarch and we should find the dragon avatars,* he sent.

*I do not sense the harroc di wurunwi,* she replied.

*Neither do I, but there is a presence travelling from the northern moors. It might be a Spirit Guide, but it moves slowly — most unlike Memek-Tal.*

*Could it be a different threat?* The anduleso sent.

*If so, it is hiding its signature well.*

*We should await its appearance, make sure we have secured the dragon avatar's well-being.*

*Agreed.*

They travelled in this manner until they arrived at the once hidden grotto of the dragons. Wobas counted them, and apart from Oga's continued absence they appeared intact and content, albeit a little restless.

*Should it not concern us that the giant one has disappeared?* Milissandia sent.

*Perhaps,* Wobas replied. *Then again, he remained at Wyverneth — according to Tayem. Mayhap his absence here means he has escaped.*

Milissandia's anduleso form raised its head as if trying to count the dragon avatars.

*Do you feel some affinity for them?* Wobas sent.

*Strangely, yes.*

*It should not surprise you. The tree serpents trace a lineage branching off from the ancient dragon family trees.*

*I wish the tie was stronger. I can't seem to communicate with them, not even to warn of their vulnerability to the harroc di wurunwi.*

Wobas couldn't help a rise of mirth in his spirit.

*You find their plight amusing?* Milissandia sent.

*Not at all, simply that we give Zodarin that title and it elevates him in terms of our perception, instils fear. Yet I still think of him as 'Strip-Willow.'*

The anduleso cocked her head. *The spindly tree of the plains?*

*Yes,* he replied, a chuckle emerging from the scops's beak as a 'chirrup' sound. *You never met him in person, but he's rather tall, with pallid skin and sunken amber eyes. I common-named him Strip-Willow when I dwelt with him amongst the dragon folk. He never liked it.*

*All the more reason to call him that.*

*That we will do. We must see him as a being we can defeat. Humour helps diminish him in everyone's eyes.*

*He deserves to be diminished.*

Wobas turned his ear northwards as he perched on a branch and listened to the approach of the entity he had detected earlier.

*I hear it too,* Milissandia sent. *I sense no threatening aura.*

*No, but it appears ... wounded.*

As they watched the line of trees beyond the dragon avatars, the dream mists parted and revealed Memek-Tal.

Gone was his regal posture. Instead, he limped forward, favouring his left side. The scales on his flanks looked raised and flaky, while feathers stuck out at awkward angles from his eagle head. He skirted the herd of dragon avatars and slowly made his way toward them.

Wobas had the urge to approach the Spirit Guide, to prevent him having to travel further, but respect kept him on his perch. Eventually he stopped before them, and slumped to the grassy sward, taking a moment to lick a still-bleeding wound.

*Memek-Tal,* Wobas said, *What has befallen you? Did the Zodarin-beast inflict these wounds?*

*No,* the Spirit Guide sent. *It is the cost of intervention. It is not permitted for our kind to offer the kind of aid I extended to you.*

*Who withholds permission?* Milissandia said.

Memek-Tal paused, choosing his words carefully. *Those who hold the balance of power in this realm; those who are unseen.*

*But this is monstrous,* she continued. *Who are these beings to inflict such —*

*Hold, Daughter,* Wobas sent. *I sense he oversteps the mark even approaching us in this way.*

Memek-Tal nodded. *I paid a price, and I will pay another after this meeting. But I must convey a premonition of grave portent to you. Please listen, as I do not have much time. The one you once called friend is gathering his strength. He intends*

536

to strike soon, and when he does, the dragons will face complete destruction.

*He was strong before,* Wobas sent. *You say his might will be greater? Who can stand against him?*

*In this realm? Only the two of you. But now you are re-united, a new weapon is forged. Together you might yet prevail. An inner weakness afflicts the harroc di wurunwi, brought on by contracting the dragon-disease. You must use this to undo him.*

*How?* Milissandia pressed.

Memek-Tal looked over his shoulder towards the woods. *I will suffer much for this.* He paused for a moment longer, and then continued. *Only by entering into wurunwa vargachic will this be revealed.*

Wobas considered what the Spirit Guide had said, trying his best to suppress the rising frustration within. *Then we cannot fully prepare.*

The Spirit Guide looked towards the trees again, and Wobas thought he felt a change in the direction of the wind. *There is more. If the dragons fall before the Donnephon retake Wyverneth they are doomed. The Dragon Riders must strike at the Cuscosians immediately.*

The Spirit Guide's counsel was disconcerting beyond measure. Wobas's thoughts were a maelstrom of confusion and panic. *There is no time. The Dragon Riders are not ready. How can they prevail?*

*They will find a way. But I have said too much. There is a cost to everything, and you, shaman, will face your own exactment. Now, when the harroc di wurunwi comes, I will call you.*

*From across the realms — is this possible?*

*Possible, and irrevocable.*

*What do you mean?*

Yet the Spirit Guide was already turning on his hooves. The rising wind ruffled his feathers, and as he retreated to the trees once more he seemed even more stooped in his gait than minutes before, as if resigned to some dreadful fate.

*Is this the last time we will meet?* Wobas called after it.

There was no reply. Whether the wind caught it, or whether Memek-Tal lacked the strength or will to speak further, he could not tell.

*Come, Daughter,* he sent. *We must call the councils together. Perhaps Memek-Tal has warned us early enough, but we must hurry.*

# 44

# HIDING FROM THE LIGHT

————

The Northern Wastes are an expanse like no other. Frozen plains of purest white, ringed by spines of white-fanged mountains, shining like pyramids that tower above the surrounding vastness.

As Tayem and Mahren soared on their beasts above yet another range, Tayem imagined these peaks belonging to another earth, inhabited by alien races. Yet not another living soul did they see, even after four days of travel in that desolate landscape. They stopped hourly to rest Quassu and Jaestrum. These pauses were uncomfortable as the sisters absorbed the cold more keenly when exposed on a lofty crag or next to a frozen lake. The dragons' inner burning seemed to generate a warmth that they clung to while in flight, and Tayem wondered how long they would have survived without their beasts as a source of warmth.

While Sol-Ar was at its highest, they had halted on the slopes of a peak crowned with a headdress of glistening ice. The reflection of its rays blinded them, and they sat with backs to their beasts to avoid the glare. Tayem consulted the map she had procured from Ebar's library, while Mahren whispered softly in each of the dragon's ears, comforting them and throwing morsels of cured garbear meat into their expectant mouths.

During the first two days of their quest, the landscape had unfolded before them in mysterious splendour, and although it grew colder Tayem could yet marvel at the carpeting of conifers on the northern Herethorn Mountains. She regarded the beauty of crystal lakes and frozen waterfalls that appeared in glimpses as they soared the air currents circulating over what seemed like the roof of the world.

After spending a bitter night in a shallow cave at the end of their third day, the mood of the landscape changed. The trees, found only in isolated huddles appeared skeletal, shadow-like with icicles hanging from their branches like Death's fingers. Soon, even this hardy plant life disappeared and a blizzard falling from dark skies beset them. The snow beat against their faces, harsh and biting until they were blinded by a frantic wall of swirling white. The wind, brutal and unforgiving cut through their leather gauntlets and furs such that Tayem's skin became as constantly lumped as the mountain range they traversed, and her muscles quivered uncontrollably. It was a tempestuous onslaught of nature, wild and untamed.

As they attempted to fight their way through the blinding sea of white, Tayem thought of home, Wyverneth, curled up in front of a roaring fire in her private palace nook. She tried to remember the soothing caress of Cistre's hands as they massaged her neck and shoulders, easing out the tensions that wracked her aching muscles. But the memory seemed indistinct and lost in the fog that had become her every waking minute.

Eventually they were compelled to hunker down in a pothole gouged out in the rock and wait for the storm to pass by. Minutes turned to hours while the wind howled around them, piling up snow in drifts and blinding the night with ice-white dust. As they huddled together, resigned to spending the night, they talked of their hopes, fears and dreams; and it seemed to Tayem that every last prickle of sensitivity was withdrawn through their discourse. Mahren dreaded the loss of Brethis, just as Tayem feared the loss of the Kingdom and extermination of her people. Such being the stakes, how could she hold any animosity towards Mahren anymore? It was through this kind of union with a Cuscosian that the Dragonians might yet sow the seeds of their people's future.

They had spoken like this for many hours until the

travel weariness overtook them, and they fell asleep to the backdrop of snoring dragons.

Once morning broke, the storm had abated, and they pushed a hole through the snow bank that had accumulated during the night. Before them, beyond the flatness of a frozen waste, a distant range of mountains lay like a sleeping leviathan of granite bones. Mahren likened it to a mighty titan, slumbering since before time began. "Perhaps the beast fell into an enchanted sleep," she said. These words led Tayem to imagine Agathon, entombed in those compacted icy layers, slumbering away the centuries until she became one with the stone that surrounded her.

*Perhaps, even if we find her, she might not be woken,* she thought. *Turned to rock, her furnace heart doused by the ravages of time.*

And so, on the fifth day, after passing over an icy waste that appeared as a sea frozen in mid-swell, they found themselves on this magnificent mountain; a snow-wreathed precipice reaching into the purpling sky.

"Please tell me we near the end of our journey," Mahren said as Tayem traced her finger along what she thought was the range of mountains they now found themselves upon.

"If it is not," Tayem said, "we will have to turn back. We were lucky to find shelter last night, and I'm not sure we could survive another storm out in the open."

Mahren sighed. "Much as I hate giving up, I fear you are

right. There is no food for the dragons in these wastes and our own supply runs short."

"This mountain," Tayem said, pointing to a pyramid shape on her map. "Ebar described it as made of black glass. Does it not seem to you that this rock surrounding us has such a resemblance?"

Mahren ran her hand over the smooth obsidian surface of the boulder next to her. "It does, but surely all the surrounding mountains must be made of the same stuff."

"True, but as we approached this peak did you notice how its top was split in two, something like — "

"Like a woodsman had cleaved it with an axe?" Mahren interrupted.

"Yes!"

"Could it be ... ?" Mahren removed her hand from the boulder, as if her touch affronted the possible resting place of what might sleep beneath. She looked at the signature mark of the peak shown on the map in Tayem's hand. The resemblance was too close for co-incidence.

"Ebar's tome said the entrance to Agathon's lair lay on the north side."

"That would be down below," Mahren said, her eyes widening expectantly.

Tayem exhaled deeply. "If we find the entrance, then that is but the start of the challenge. We must find Agathon if she dwells there, wake her and try to convince her of our cause's worth." It was when she vocalised what they were up against, that the immensity of the obstacles threatened to overwhelm her.

*No, I will not think of failure.*

"We haven't really thought about how to approach this," Mahren said.

"From what we know; as an Agnarim, Agathon will only speak to a queen of Dragonia. So I think I should address her first. After that, I will rely on your skills as *Kirith-A* to guide us."

Mahren looked at her sceptically. "It doesn't seem like much of a plan, but I suppose it's all we've got."

Tayem noted there was no accusation in her sister's tone, another sign that their relationship had moved on. "Let us sweep the dragons across the cliff face, and see if there is any obvious entrance."

"Did Ebar's book give any clue about what to look for?"

"None, but I'm sure Agathon will not have placed a sign in front of it."

Mahren smiled at Tayem's attempt at humour and mounted Jaestrum. Tayem followed suit and drew her riding cowl over her head. The wind was sharp and nipped at her skin as Quassu dived over the precipice.

Sol-Ar's face was hidden on this side of the mountain, and shadows wreathed the edifice, making the task of picking out irregularities in the rock difficult. After half an hour flying back and forth in this manner, they were no further forward in their quest. Tayem signalled for them to rest on a small shelf of rock and pulled out the map again.

After perusal of the scant details for the hundredth time, Tayem screwed up the map in frustration.

"It is impossible," she said. "We could spend the rest of our lives traversing this mountain and never find the entrance. It is ever more certain that Agathon does not want to be found."

"Perhaps we are using the wrong method," Mahren said. "If Agathon will only speak to a true Donnephon, then perhaps she laid it in store that a seeker should use the kirith-a."

Tayem snorted. "If we cannot see the dragon, how can we entreat it?"

"The kirith-a is not only a tool of conversation, it is a spiritual connection," Mahren said. "I didn't dare suggest it before, but if you let me listen in silence, I might detect the signature of the Agnarim."

"Can you do that?"

"I heard the anguish of the dragons when they were assaulted from within the Dreamworld. Events of great magnitude leave a loud signature."

"A sleeping dragon does not seem to be such a momentous event."

"A *gigantic* sleeping dragon," Mahren corrected. "Let me at least try."

"It cannot harm," Tayem replied.

"You need to keep completely silent and keep our dragons from shifting about."

Tayem nodded and Mahren dismounted Jaestrum,

stepping over to the rock face. She placed her hand on the slick surface of the rock and turned her head until her ear was pressed up against it.

Minutes passed, during which Mahren moved along the rock wearing a pensive look and frowning every so often. Tayem wanted to ask how she was doing, but held herself back. Then, following a minute's concentrated listening, Mahren lowered herself down to a lower lip of rock.

"Take care," Tayem said, unable to contain herself any longer.

"It is necessary," Mahren replied, "I think I heard something."

She scrambled over the narrow ledge and once again adopted her listening posture. It only took another few seconds, and she lifted her face to Tayem, a broad beam spread over it. "We have the right mountain. I hear the breathing of a mighty dragon, deep down below."

"Are you sure?"

"It is faint but undeniable. We have found Agathon."

"But how do we reach her?"

"A dragon of her size would require a significant ingress. Now I know what to listen for, I can narrow down our search radius."

Tayem couldn't help a smile spreading. Even if they faced death below, it would be a fitting way to end her reign having at least confronted this great beast. "Lead the way, Sister."

Mahren indicated to steer the dragons toward a point

roughly half-way down the great mountain. Here, a small cleft afforded them another resting position.

"The sound of the dragon is stronger," Mahren said.

"I see no sign of an entrance," Tayem said.

"Let me try lower," Mahren replied. "Stay here while I investigate."

She took to the air once again, perching Jaestrum on a column of rock some five hundred spans below. Tayem saw her dismount and disappear behind the obsidian block. She emerged a few minutes later and waved to Tayem. The Queen didn't require further encouragement, and leapt onto Quassu's back, urging him downwards.

She had trouble finding a secondary landing point at the column, but eventually she chose a shelf to the east of Mahren. After dismounting, she took to scrambling across the cliff face. It was somewhat different to climbing garbeeches, but Tayem was sure-footed enough, taking care to gain secure purchase on the slick surface.

As she rounded a shoulder of rock, she discovered Mahren's hidden position in front of a black hole, obscured by the column that rose in front of it. The cave was some forty spans tall and perhaps thirty spans wide.

"Could an Agnarim fit through this space?" she asked.

"A dragon can squeeze into very small confines," Mahren said, "or so I've heard. Anyway, I could not be more certain that Agathon lies below. Her presence is like the call from your battle horn."

"I cannot hear anything," Tayem said.

Mahren curled the corner of her mouth. "Trust me," she said.

"Well at least our dragons can gain entrance," Tayem said.

"No," Mahren cautioned. "Agathon may see them as a threat. They should stay here. But we can get them into the shelter of the pinnacle."

Tayem agreed, and once they had settled Quassu and Jaestrum they lit torches to illuminate their way into the blackness.

"Our dragons were slow to settle," Tayem observed.

"They sense Agathon's presence," Mahren replied.

"Which makes me think the great dragon may detect ours."

"For the moment, she rests," Mahren said.

"I wonder for how long."

"Come, we should press forward. Our torches only have an hour's life in them."

"How far do you think she is?"

"Not far, but we don't know what obstacles we face, or indeed if there are any snares."

"Can dragons lay traps?"

"Our own dragon species? No. But one as wise and old as Agathon — who knows? We should be careful."

Mahren led the way into the cavern, the roof lowering somewhat once they were a few paces in. Once around a tight curl in the emerging passageway, the sound of the wind outside was silenced like a slain wolf, and all around

Tayem felt the oppressive weight of the mountain above. The floor was uneven and littered with boulders and fragments of rock. After traversing a hundred paces a wall of rock confronted them. As they looked upwards, they saw that at its top, the cavern extended to reveal another aperture.

"More climbing," Mahren said.

"With torches to hold," Tayem replied.

Mahren took to the rock face without another word, and Tayem understood that her sister was pushing forward without hesitation to avoid a procrastination that might paralyse them with indecision and fear.

*The time for caution is past.*

The climb was difficult holding the torches, but mercifully short. Once they crested the top however, they were faced with a more daunting spectacle. The black hole plunged downwards in an almost sheer drop.

"By Sesnath," Tayem whispered. "How did such a great wyrm traverse down that passage?"

Mahren sighed. "By squeezing its way. We, however, will have to descend hand over foot."

"Perhaps not," Tayem said. "I have some rope."

"How much?"

"One hundred spans."

"I hope it is enough. Secure it to this jutting rock here, it seems secure enough."

By the time they descended into the abyssal depths their

torches were half-burned, but Tayem chose not to think about what they would do when they finally died.

After five minutes of traversing into the black at a snail's pace, Mahren's footing slipped, and she slammed into the rock face, dropping her torch. Tayem saw it plunge end over end until it stopped abruptly about thirty spans below. It flickered for a few seconds and then snuffed out.

"Mahren," Tayem cried, "are you hurt?"

"Mmmf!" Came the reply, followed by a spitting sound. "I think I've lost a tooth," Mahren said, "but I'm otherwise all right."

Tayem directed the halo of her torch below, suspending herself by one hand on the rope. Mahren had regained her footing and peered up at her, a mask of blood covering her face.

"Can you hang on?" Tayem asked.

"Of course," Mahren replied. "It's only a busted nose and a split lip. I'll survive."

"Good. I think there's another thirty spans to go judging by how far your torch fell."

Mahren's brow furrowed. "Then our rope is fifteen spans short. We'll either have to climb or drop."

"Let's lower ourselves as far as we can go, then. My arms are starting to shake, hanging like a spider."

Mahren took her cue and covered the remaining rope's length without mishap. She then stopped.

"Can we climb the rock face from now on?" Tayem said.

"Alas, no," Mahren replied. "I've reached an overhang

and there is no footing." Tayem detected a touch of panic in her voice.

"We could climb back up," Tayem said.

"I don't think I have any strength left in my arms," Mahren said, "I'm going to risk the drop."

"I don't know how even the floor is below," Tayem said, "or if the torch simply came to rest on a ledge. You could fall to your death."

"I shall fall in the next minute, anyway," she said. "If I should not survive, then make your way out."

"Wait, Mahren. There might be another — " But Tayem's words were cut short as she detected the sound of an impact below followed by silence.

"Mahren! Are you — ?"

"In one piece, Sister," came the reply. "There is a tunnel ahead. Come, join me."

After a brief scramble followed by a controlled drop, Tayem joined Mahren at the foot of the rock funnel, and they held each other with a sense of relief.

"Don't do that again," Tayem said.

"Say that to my arms," Mahren replied. "Here, let me relight my torch from yours."

Once done, Tayem looked into the tunnel ahead, and now she felt like even she could detect the presence of something magnificent, gargantuan and ancient.

"Agathon lies just ahead," Mahren said.

"Does she sleep?"

"I do not know."

"Then all we can do is proceed." Tayem lifted her torch high and stepped forward. The tunnel snaked along a gradual curve for a hundred paces, then opened out into what Tayem could only assume was a vast cavern as the heights of it were lost in darkness. Every step they took echoed from walls of black glass. As they drew closer, the flickering light of her torch illuminated a wall of granular, stone-like material. She stopped and played the torch light left and right. "The rock ahead," she said. "It moves."

"That is no rock wall," Mahren replied.

They looked at each other and drew forward until they were standing some ten paces from the flank of what appeared to be a swelling hill of sepia coloured stone. The mound rose to their left, and then fell serpent-like to a craggy snout that curled round to face them. Tayem stood stock still as she was confronted with two yellow orbs staring back at her, and before she could even form words, the ancient dragon spoke to her.

"I see you, Donnephon Queen," it said, and its utterance was the moving of great vaults of rock to Tayem's ears. "I sensed you from afar and know why you have come."

"I ... I greet you, great Agathon," Tayem said. "Please forgive our intrusion on your domain, but we — "

"I would not waste words," Agathon said. "For I have to disappoint you. What you desire of me is impossible." And as the ancient Agnarim delivered her statement,

Tayem's heart sunk into an abyss far deeper than that which surrounded her.

# 45

# CHOICES OF THE DAMNED

---

Beredere gravely listened to the news he had been presented with. He had no doubt the shaman and the druid were sincere — even truthful — but the consequences of their report were far-reaching, and to say he felt out of his depth was an understatement.

"The Cuscosian wizard plans to strike soon, you say? How soon?"

Wobas and Milissandia were seated together with the Fyreclave at the centre of the Gigantes Council. They looked at each other, and then Wobas continued. "The Spirit Guide could not predict, save that we needed to act imminently."

"But there is no time," Beredere said. "We are vastly outnumbered, barely trained and with no definite plan to re-take Wyverneth."

"What's more," Gemain said. "Tayem has not returned, so there is no guarantee of the great dragon's help."

"I think we are being hasty," Cistre said. She would not have dared to speak previously, but Tayem had given her leave to take decisions jointly with Beredere and no doubt felt justified. "How do we know the dream worlders are not mistaken? This Spirit Guide seems vague in his predictions. If he is truly for us, why does he speak in riddles?"

"It is as we explained," Milissandia replied, "Memek-Tal is bound by laws that are beyond us. There is no reason to mistrust him. He was right about the Zodarin-wizard and predicted my transcendence to the Dreamworld. Without it, we would never have released Tayem from the curse of the Black Hallows."

"But are we to think the attack on our dragons will happen in hours or days?" Beredere asked.

"All we know is that the Spirit Guide will warn us. In addition, my father and I will double the frequency of our sorties into the Far Beyond," Milissandia said.

"Perhaps you should maintain your vigil there on a continuous basis," put in Frodha.

"We have our own battle to prepare for," Wobas said, "and a sojourn in the Dreamworld taxes us greatly. If we are depleted of energy before confronting Zodarin, then all will be lost before it has begun."

Throughout the exchange, the Cyclopes listened attentively. Ebar looked particularly solemn, and Beredere wondered if he would contribute anything to the meeting at all.

After a time, in which no one was able to add anything to the confusion of information that abounded, Ebar stood, his loftiness imposing on the gathering. "These are grievous times," he said, "and it seems the threat that faces the Dragonians sends waves that affect all peoples of the Imperious Crescent. We have heard about the fall of Kaldora, seen the tragedy of what befell Dragonia, and it seems clear that the Gigantes cannot hope to avoid a similar fate forever." He took a moment to draw on his jarva-leaf pipe, and then continued. "I spoke with the Gigantes Council, and it seems we can no longer remain neutral on-lookers." He cast his eyes around the seated members, receiving acknowledging nods from most. "I hereby declare that the Gigantes are once more prepared to take up arms with our allies as they did long ago."

Beredere heard Ebar's words, but hardly dared believe his ears. "This ... this is wondrous news, indeed." He searched for suitably dignified words of thanks, but his diplomatic skills were not fully matured. "We thank you, Great Ebar. Dare I ask what strength you can offer?"

Ebar turned to one of his Council members. "Taumahg, perhaps this is your domain?"

A long-bearded, gruff giant took to his feet and spoke. "It is long since we took to the battlefield, but the Gigantes do not forget their prowess and skills. Our fighting warriors number five hundred Cyclopes and one thousand of the Minutae."

"That is considerable," Gemain said, "but it does not even approach the force needed to re-take Wyverneth." He looked round at Cistre. "What of the Cuscosian dissidents?"

Cistre shook her head. "Brownbeak has nothing new to report. It could take weeks for Brethis to muster anything noteworthy. Even then, such a disorganised force would move slowly to join us in Dragonia — they would need to avoid the imperial troops that patrol northern Cuscosia."

Taumahg held up his hand. "What cannot be accomplished by force can sometimes be achieved by cunning and subterfuge. Etezora will not be expecting an attack on Wyverneth so soon, and her army do not know the forests of Dragonia as you do. Your dragons will be a formidable asset If Zodarin has not yet risen to full strength. You told us yourselves how they laid waste to great tracts of Cuscosians at Lyn-Harath."

"That may be true," Cistre said, "but your own spies reported Etezora building giant machines to shoot down our dragons. We might be exposing them to a grave threat, and we cannot afford to lose any more of them."

Ebar stood once more. "There are many challenges to

this conflict, but are we agreed that we should act upon the Spirit Guide's warning?"

The Fyreclave looked to Beredere and Cistre, as it was they who held the authority to make a decision, and the time for talking had passed. In actuality, Beredere deferred to Cistre. He might be a tactically gifted commander, but Cistre understood the wider implications of an impending war.

"The price of inaction outweighs that of taking this situation by the scruff of its neck," she said. "I say we pool our resources, set up a war council immediately and plan our attack. If we are to stand a hope, we must make our move tomorrow — before it's too late."

"Then we are of one mind," Ebar said. "Order your warriors to make ready, for tomorrow we go to war."

~ ~ ~

Zodarin brooded in his tower and gathered his strength. He had long given up hope of finding a medicinal cure for the blight and instead looked to the Hallows for an answer. In this there was great risk. Although he had seen one Hallows cycle come and go, there was still a vast cloud of mystery surrounding the phenomenon.

He had sat in the same position on his meditation dais for two full days, taking pause only to drink. His appetite had disappeared long ago, and he found that as he opened increasing numbers of doors to the Hallows, its energy seemed to sustain him in a way that simple nutrition could not.

The affairs of state passed him by, despite Phindrath's entreaties to him. He had increased the enchantments on his tower such that any who attempted to enter his abode were thrown into confusion. As the Hallows increased its hold on him, he lost interest in what he saw as the petty affairs of Cuscosa. His prime motivation now was survival, and he had to allow this other-worldly force to have its way, even if the cost was incalculable. He would rid Etezora of the dragon threat, if only to appease her. He would take no pleasure in destroying them. However, Wobas — the Gigantes he had once called friend — was a different matter. He had been humiliated in the Dreamworld and the shaman, along with his pitiable daughter and the Dragonian Queen would pay for their affront. Even an amioid was not above revenge, and their removal would mean he could inhabit the Far Beyond without threat. The Hallows would allow him to rise to greater heights of power such that even the Spirit Guide would not stand against him.

He took a deep breath and sensed Sol-Ar rising to its zenith, shining malign beams through his window and infusing him with its light. His power grew by the minute, and he was tempted to enter the Dreamworld right away, before the blight-confusion took hold again and caused him to take pity on his foes.

*Gorram this misplaced morality!*

Another deep breath dispelled his impatience. Tonight he would decamp to the Edenbract Hallows and drink deeply of its depths. Perhaps then he would be ready.

*So much to accomplish in such a short time.*

Yet the prize was in sight, and once he had conquered his foes and the blight driven out, he could resume his ambition to rule the kingdoms of the Imperious Crescent.

As he bathed in the violet rays, these thoughts permeated deeper into his consciousness and his confidence rose, accompanied by a satisfied smile to rival that of his feline familiar, Oswald.

# 46

# KEEPER OF EVIL

---

As Tuh-Ma passed through the Dragon Talon Gate of Wyverneth, an involuntary shudder passed through him. He wished these irrational fears did not afflict him so and looked forward to the day when Tayem's wyrms — epitomised in the architecture — would be no more.

The return journey from Cuscosa had passed without incident, and one thing he could be thankful for was the passing of his forest fever. The lumbering grotesque felt his inherent blue-skin vitality energising him once again, and the prospect of attending his Queen added a spring to his gait.

There was a lingering doubt, however. Etezora's recent

manic outbursts filled him with a sense of trepidation. He'd delighted in the outpouring of cruelty he had witnessed since her drinking from the Edenbract Hallows, but her more erratic outbursts unsettled him. Might he be the subject of her wrath in the future? It seemed she had shunned him while he suffered from the wyrmbite, and he had thought himself abandoned. No, she had entrusted him with the mission to Cuscosa. Surely he was back in her favour.

As he climbed the stairs leading from the entrance hall, he noted with satisfaction that the ornate dragon effigy had been replaced by a less extravagant design depicting Cuscosian ancestry and tableaus of their legends. He paused for a moment to take in the detail, finding himself enraptured with what he saw.

*The Cuscosian artisans have been busy*, he thought. *Perhaps Tuh-Ma might feature in these pictures one day.*

He had carried the royal seal of the Queen's emissary with pride and had relished the responsibility thrust upon him. The tormenting of the wizard and witnessing the death of the pygmy dragon were additional boons.

He focused once more on concluding the mission and patted his knapsack containing the royal scroll bearing Phindrath's words. One of Etezora's courtiers greeted him with a sniff as he entered the large chamber and announced his arrival.

His Queen was seated on the Dragonian throne, and to Tuh-Ma she seemed more beautiful than ever.

"What news, Tuh-Ma?" she said without any formal greeting. "Has Eétor or my wizard returned with you?"

The troll hesitated before speaking. "Tuh-Ma alone, Mistress. Princess Phindrath has sent scroll. Tuh-Ma met with wizard but Praetor not there." He handed the scrolls to Etezora who waved him to a seat. She broke the royal seal and scrutinised the papers before her.

"Tuh-Ma," Etezora said once she had finished. "This concerns news regarding my brother. If there was no sign of him, did you speak with that wretched spy, Grizdoth?"

The large head shook from side to side. "Grizdoth dead. Wizard said Praetor fled. Princess Phindrath has no knowledge."

"Eétor's actions speak to me of guilt. This confirms I was right to place my sister in authority. Does she seem to have things under control?"

The blue-skin wiped a string of snot from his nose. "Tuh-Ma thinks wizard in charge. Princess weak."

Etezora's eyes flashed, and Tuh-Ma winced. "What game does this magic man play?" she retorted. "Did he have any excuse for not dealing with the dragons?"

"Wizard showed Tuh-Ma he hates dragons. He killed the pygmy. Said he was still weak from slaying other dragons before this."

"So, should I trust the wizard anymore?"

"Trust him to kill rest of dragons — but no further. Sooner he is dead, the better."

"Very well, I will trust your judgement. You have been

faithful, Tuh-Ma. Once this is over, I will let you deal with Zodarin personally."

The blue-skin smiled at the Queen's judgement. *This is good reward for Tuh-Ma.*

Etezora summoned a guard. "Soldier, tell Captain Domart to dispatch a message to Castle Cuscosa. Phindrath is to ensure Lord Zodarin does not leave before my return."

"Yes, your Majesty," the man replied and left hastily.

"Tuh-Ma, walk with me," commanded Etezora.


The odd couple, accompanied by royal escort, toured the surrounding city observing the rebuilding work and how the city's growing population were making the place their own.

"Tratis is doing well building our defences," the Queen said, "though I doubt he would succeed without that treacherous Dragonian courtier Disconsolin's help."

Tuh-Ma nodded.

"Well you can dispose of him when the works are completed. I find his treachery sickening. If he has betrayed Tayem, then one can only wonder what he might perpetrate against our House. I don't care what Tratis says, if Tayem had not been so weak she would have executed him for abandoning her people."

"Will Dragon Queen return, Mistress?"

"The dragon folk may have fled for now, but Tayem will not give this place up easily, and I must be ready. Tell me all that happened at the castle. Leave nothing out so I can make sense of it all."

Etezora stepped closer to the battlements they now stood atop and looked out over the Dragon Vale while Tuh-Ma recounted his dealings with Zodarin at Castle Cuscosa.

Etezora reflected on the calmness that had now descended on her. She was rested, and most importantly in control of the mighty Hallows energy coursing through her veins. She listened intently to the blue-skin's words, and once he had finished, determined that Zodarin and Eétor were better off out of the way. Her anxiety would be more settled if she knew where Eétor had fled to and locking him up was certainly a much better option than having him roam free. It would be a step too far perhaps to have him executed, but then again, who was to gainsay her? The power within grew day by day, and perhaps the time had come to make her own decrees.

A thoughtful silence descended while Tuh-Ma waited patiently by her side. The blue-skin was indeed a disgusting creature, but as it transpired had proved to be the most loyal of her subjects. "You know, Tuh-Ma, I believe you may be the only one I can truly trust."

"Mistress?" The blue-skin replied, his expression softening further.

"It is true. In your absence I have realised that. Above all else, loyalty is to be most valued. Can I share something with you?"

"Tell Tuh-Ma anything, Majesty — your wishes, your secrets. Tuh-Ma will never betray them."

She looked at him, judged that he was sincere, and continued. "I've finally realised who I am."

Tuh-Ma looked puzzled. "You are Etezora — Queen of Cuscosa," he replied dutifully.

Etezora smiled, patient with his bemused response. "Tell me, have you heard the stories of our Cuscosian deities and the revered Pentacle of Gods?"

"No, Majesty, Tuh-Ma would love for you to tell him a story."

She scanned the cityscape below, the activity still frenetic even though Sol-Ar was about to set. "I have never taken much interest myself, but with the gift of the Hallows I understand my calling at last."

Etezora seated herself on an ironwood bench and beckoned for the troll to join her. "Siksta is our most important God," she continued. "He is god of the bright sun, Sol. They say my family are descendants of Siksta. He married Charir, goddess of the dark sun Sol-Ar, and together they guide the peoples of the Cuscosian plains along with Wkar, goddess of the celestral realm, and bringer of balance."

Etezora held Tuh-Ma spellbound with her story, and she realised he was hanging on every word she said. *The simple creature is besotted,* she thought absently, and while she relished the attentions of any number of human stallions as her royal prerogative, there was something particularly arresting about Tuh-Ma's devotion.

"Edar is the goddess of Varchal," she said, picking up the story again. "She is responsible for our climate, harvest and prosperity. The fifth of this pentacle of gods is Shio the supreme ruler of all creation."

"These gods," Tuh-Ma said, "are a strange family. Tuh-Ma not understand all you have said, Mistress, but I will think about these things.

Etezora patted the blue-skin on the head and carried on. "I never believed these fantastical stories and always thought gods were for the weak-minded. But now the Hallows has revealed to me another; a deity never spoken of before now, because of the fear she brings. I thought the idea of this god was just my imagination, but then I consulted ancient scrolls in Tayem's library and discovered the legends of Nurti, goddess of the *Neverworld*. Nurti was the twin sister of Charir, and as young girls they fought for control of Sol-Ar.

"Oh, how they fought. It was a delicious conflict by all accounts. The skies bled as they tore at each other. Charir pulled her sister's limbs from their sockets while Nurti gouged out Charir's eyes. Yet their constant battles offended the Pentacle, and there wasn't a place for both of the warring siblings. Eventually Charir prevailed with assistance from her lover, Siksta. Nurti was banished, cast out from her home in the heavens — that is until Sol-Ar assumes ascendency in the skies once again. And that time is now."

The blue-skin put his hands to his head. It was all too much to take in. Did Etezora mean ..?

Etezora understood the blue-skin found it hard to understand. Perhaps a more dramatic demonstration was in order. She stood, took a deep breath and held her hands to the sky. Jagged bolts of purple shot from her fingertips, and she shouted, "I am Nurti reincarnate, goddess of the Neverworld."

The sudden outburst of energy sent a number of the accompanying soldiers scurrying for the lower battlements in fear, but Tuh-Ma sank to his knees and bowed his warty head.

"My loyal servant, do not be afraid," Etezora said, holding out a hand to the deferential blue-skin. "I sense it inside," she continued, "just as the scriptures predicted: when Sol-Ar reaches its azimuth Nurti will be reborn, and her servant will transcend with her."

"But your body has all its limbs, Majesty. You are not broken like Tuh-Ma. Tuh-Ma could never be a god."

"Hah!" Etezora chuckled, "there is yet more to the myth. Nurti was served by Chullashico — a faithful servant, carrier of soul and mind, *vessel di sepa vur ricin*. The writings describe the servant as short and ugly with one leg shorter than the other — a great persuader and protector of Nurti."

"Tuh-Ma is this servant?"

"Who else can it be? From this moment forth you will always stand by my side as protector. I pronounce you Lord Ma of Cuscosa, the Queen's emissary, servant of Nurti!"

Tuh-Ma was swept away in the euphoria of the moment, not noticing the madness behind the purple eyes of his deranged sovereign. No longer could Etezora conceal the extent of her derangement, and the announcement of her ambition now took complete control of her psyche.

Tuh-Ma sunk to his knees, covering his face.

The silence that followed was broken suddenly by a guard rushing up the steps from below.

"What is this intrusion?" Etezora scolded.

"Forgive me, your Majesty," the man replied between gasps, "but there are dragons bearing down on the castle, and the woods are alive with our enemies. We are under attack!"

She smiled, looking down at the blue-skin and the few cowering soldiers who had remained. "At last," she said, "our enemy returns, and now she will experience the full venting of my power."

## 47

# A GATHERING STORM

———

It had been two days' hard march, over one hundred periarchs — firstly along mountain paths, then foothills and finally the lush forests of the Dragonian plateau. They had encountered pockets of Cuscosian exploratory parties but swiftly dispatched them — vicious justice that presaged a bloodbath to come. The disparate factions making up the allied advance were already fatigued to the extreme, and Cistre wondered whether twenty-four hours' rest and preparation would be enough to even stand a fleeting chance in the coming conflict. Beredere had been put in charge of the dragon cohort and directed his host to shelter in the original Dragonian refugee encampment. They would not declare their presence until battle commenced, not unless the Advance Guard were prematurely discovered.

Cistre had trudged with the foot soldiers, leaving Muthorus in the hands of her lieutenant. They were a ragbag of disciplined Dragonian remnants, hastily trained Cuscosian dissidents and mysteriously wandering Gigantes. Amongst them all, the Cyclopes made for the most incongruous warriors. She wondered how figures so large could move with such stealth through the larger leafy giants whose roots hugged the loamy earth. At one moment she thought they had dissolved into the undergrowth, but when she looked hard, she made out shifting forms amongst the dark shadows of voluminous trees that stood as passive protectors of this ancient place.

A downpour lasting hours had hampered their progress still further and, despite mapping a way through the secret paths of the forest, the sheer drenching left them wretched and morose. Cistre was not one for uplifting speeches or supportive cajoling, so she trod relentlessly on, leaving her constant companion, Sheldar, to provide what limited light relief he could. Tayem would have rallied them more effectively, but she was not here, and Cistre wondered if her Queen still lived, or if the frozen north had claimed her and her sister — never again to light her life.

When they finally made camp, twenty periarchs north of Wyverneth, in a secret moss-swathed valley, she was thankful that they made it thus far without detection.

"This downpour is a black rain," Sheldar observed as they sat around a camp-fire, obscured from sight amongst a set of dreary ruins — a long-abandoned site of worship to an unknown god.

"It is as if the Black Hallows greets us with a curse from the heavens," she replied.

"We need it to break by morning if we are to take up positions in readiness to attack." He had taken his sword and was sharpening it with a whetstone, the rasping sound echoing amongst the incubus darkness of the ruins.

"We will march whatever the conditions," she said. "Every hour spent in delay allows the Cuscosian sorcerer to increase his strength and destroy our dragons in a moment." It was as she said this that she understood fully the nature of the fear that gnawed away at her stomach. She did not shrink from the prospect of terrible battle, nor even from a ghastly, bloody death — she had faced it often enough in the past. No, it was the ever hovering dread that their precious beasts might fall at one stroke. Brownbeak and his minions gave them hourly reports of reserves status in the northern foothills, together with advance notice of Cuscosian deployments and troop movements. Yet even with this early warning system, the dreadful anticipation weighed heavy.

"An army of less than three thousand against who knows how many of the enemy," Sheldar said. "They are not good odds."

Cistre stared at him. "Then you must fight as if you were three men."

Sheldar nodded and smiled. "It's a far cry from wrestling a pygris, isn't it?"

She grinned back. "At least there will be no restraint. There are neither rules nor chivalry on the battlefield we tread."

"Those are conditions I like."

"You should sleep," she said, "rest that sword arm of yours."

"What about you?"

"I will ensure the sentries are doing their job properly, then I might rest a little easier."

She left the dragon hand covering himself with a blanket and snuggling down while she paced the perimeter of their encampment. She passed by tent after tent of soaked humanity, and the sounds emanating from beneath the canvas were common: hushed conversation, the sound of weapons being sharpened and the occasional snore. In truth, Cistre knew she would hardly sleep at all tonight and welcomed the opportunity of solitude, although it did leave her alone with her thoughts.

She stepped into a clearing where the canopy opened out onto a laden sky and looked up into the blackness. Raindrops hit her face like a punishment from the gods, but she held her pose nonetheless. *Are you still out there, my Queen? Perhaps you too are sheltering from the elements. Dare I hope to occupy a small place in your thoughts tonight?*

If she imagined a reply might carry on the storm clouds, then surely she had lost her mind. Yet hope she did. It was the only thing that kept her standing strong.

~ ~ ~

*What have I committed our people to?* Ebar thought as he looked out over the hunched figures camped under a grove of giant colossus pines. The Cyclopes mixed with the Minutae for there was no distinction in terms of status or respect — not here where they prepared for war. Shamfis had ever chided him for his doubtfulness. He often deferred decisions in the council to a vote; which made him wonder why the Cyclopes had ever elected him Warden. *They must have seen other qualities.* Taumahg was certainly more decisive, but the bearded one had often cited Ebar's ability to unite as his defining strength. *But united in what?*

As he mused over his people's fate, he caught movement as a Cyclopes emerged from around the pine bole. It was Hanar, largest of the Cyclopes, twenty spans tall and fearsome to behold — if one did not know him better.

"I see you, Hanar," he said. "Sit with me a while and perhaps I can bring a smile to your grim face."

"I doubt that," said the giant, "but a share of your jarva-leaf will."

Ebar chuckled. "I don't mind if you do. It may be the

last of my stash but it will give me pleasure if it brings you peace."

Hanar settled himself down, took out his clay pipe and accepted Ebar's jarva-leaf gratefully. "This is very welcome," he said, "all things considered."

"War is a grim thing for any Gigantes to contemplate."

"All the grimmer knowing you won't survive it."

Ebar looked at him, a deep melancholy descending. "You too? I was not aware."

Hanar took a flint and lit the leaf in his pipe, puffing deeply. "Third moon in the month of Adis was the date foretold on my twentieth natum day."

"Gandris mortallun," Ebar said, offering the traditional condolence at the receiving of such news. There were no more words to say. The Cyclopes accepted the fate of knowing the date of their death with stoicism. It did not make it any easier a burden to bear, however. Hanar would have made arrangements with his family and everything would be in place. Ebar hoped they would be able to bring his body home.

"To die on the battlefield is a noble end," Ebar said.

"It is — but I might choke on my breakfast or get bitten by a tree scorpion yet!"

Ebar laughed. He would miss Hanar's sense of humour.

"You have refrained from taking a census," the giant said, his face becoming solemn.

"Yes," Ebar said. "It would be an affront. A Cyclopes' death is a private matter."

"Not if the information might inform the outcome of a battle."

"Knowing how many will die cannot help us determine strategy."

"No, but it might give hope."

"What hope would there be in knowing every last Cyclopes is to perish?"

"Is that what you predict?"

"It is what I fear."

"Yet such a foreknowing might cause you to reconsider committing the Gigantes."

"Again — that is what I fear. This curse we shoulder afflicts us in so many ways. Sometimes it is better not to know. The council's decision is based on what is right. If we do not fight now, we might never fight at all."

Hanar nodded, accepting his leader's words.

"Let us not argue on your last night," Ebar said.

"Agreed," Hanar replied and placed a gigantic paw on Ebar's shoulder. "I know as a people we do not harbour thoughts of revenge, but I will not mourn taking as many Cuscosians with me as I can."

"No one would condemn you for such a thought," Ebar said and blew three smoke rings in succession. The inhaled heady vapours soothed his inner turmoil to a degree, and he leaned back against the bole of the pine. Soon, Hanar was snoring beside him, and as Ebar's eyes grew heavy, he pondered his own mortality. He would survive this battle, but was not sure he deserved to. *If only one could know the circumstances of one's demise,* he thought. Yet even this did not yield any comfort, simply opened more doors of torment.

*It is beyond me,* he finally declared to himself and shifted his position. Just before sleep claimed him, he saw Shamfis's face together with those of his children.

*Tomorrow I fight for you,* he declared.

~ ~ ~

Next morning the rain abated, although the ground was sodden and a damp mist settled in the valley where the allies camped. All about, the sound of people eating hastily prepared breakfasts and the bustle of disassembling tents could be heard. Cistre washed quickly in the nearby stream and then made her way to Ebar's encampment. She found him conversing with Brownbeak in an indecipherable language. She had only seen the raptor a handful of times before, but soon recognised the nobility of the winged creature. Although it was not related to dragon lineage, its sharp eyes held the wisdom of an ancient race, and she extended her full respect accordingly.

"Greetings, Ebar," she said.

"I see you, Cistre of the Dragonians," Ebar replied.

"What word from our feathered ally?"

Ebar pursed his lips. "Mixed news. There are five

battalions of Cuscosians between our camp and Wyverneth, fully armed and alert."

"Are they in communication with each other?"

Ebar unrolled a map and placed it on a tree stump. "They are positioned here," he said, pointing to five locations.

Cistre considered the positions for a moment, and then smiled. "They have gaps in their formations of one periarch, enough for us to slip through unnoticed."

"Yes," Ebar said, "although, when we attack, they will pose a threat to our rearguard."

"We will let the dragons take care of them," she replied. "What else?"

"Brownbeak says he has finally met with Brethis."

"That is welcome news!"

Ebar shook his head. "He has barely mustered five hundred more dissidents, all poorly armed. There was a promise of more from the southern plains, but they were not forthcoming."

Cistre sighed. "And Tayem?"

"Alas, nothing. Not even a whisper on the horizon. Brownbeak's son ventured three days into the Northern Wastes. Even if Tayem and Mahren still lived, they are too far away to lend us any aid."

"I refuse to believe they have perished!" Cistre snapped.

Ebar looked at her patiently.

"Sorry," she said. "It's just that I could do with some good news."

"I understand. But we can't count on them returning to help. We must play our strategy as planned, and hope that the spirit gods are with us."

Cistre nodded. "You are right. We should break camp in the next half an hour and split into smaller squads. The Dragonians will guide our Cuscosian allies, stop them from making too much noise as we pass through the enemy lines. I will entrust the command of your troops to you, Ebar."

Ebar chuckled. "Command? That is not our way, but rest assured, we will do our part."

"Then we will see you on the Maidwin hills. Dixtrath semlessin."

And so the Dragonian alliance returned once more through the borders of Wyverneth. For all their military might, the Cuscosians were not adept at detecting the approach of an adversary so skilled in concealment and stealth. The Dragonian scouts picked out sentries and clumsily camouflaged outposts with ease, and so they succeeded in bypassing the Cuscosian northern defence. They held the dragons back, awaiting Brownbeak's signal, and the allied troops congregated on the wooded slopes of the Maidwin hills just as Sol-Ar began to set. They were tired, but ready to do battle.

Cistre stood with Ebar, Wobas and Milissandia surveying a multitude of lights illuminating the battlements of Wyverneth. The invading allied forces were dispersing, as ordered, along the shrouded valleys formed by numerous tributaries that converged on the Halivern River's upper reaches.

"Brownbeak will have delivered his message to Beredere by now," Ebar said. "I still would advise patience and attack in the still of the night, when the defenders will be at their lowest ebb. It will also give a chance for Brethis to take up position."

"We have already lost too much time," Cistre said, "and Zodarin might make his move at any moment. Once we see the dragons approach, I will sound the horn." She itched with anticipation, all the time longing to be mounted on Muthorus, her beloved dragon. The royal host could not arrive too soon as far as she was concerned. With such air power, they might not need to scale the walls of the city.

"Will Aibrator be in place?" Wobas asked.

"I await his signal," Cistre replied, "but he has only been gone half an hour and he needs to navigate the dragon claw sluice."

The dragon claw sluice was a secret gate at the bottom of Wyverneth's fortifications which acted as an outlet for waste water from the palace. Aibrator's task was not a dignified one, but it was essential for the Dragonians' chances of victory.

"So many things to go wrong," Milissandia said.

"Or," Wobas replied, "so many opportunities."

The others didn't share the shaman's optimism, even if they did understand the motivation.

"The time for speculation is past," Cistre said. "Look!"

She pointed to the horizon behind, to where what looked like a flock of birds approached, appearing as pinpricks against the violet sky. "Soon the Cuscosians will identify them for what they are," Cistre said.

Sashaim ran towards them to confirm what they had all witnessed. "Our dragons have passed over the Cuscosian's northern contingent, they are already lighting signal fires," he said.

"Then let battle commence," Cistre said. She raised the battle horn to her lips and let out one long blast. Down below, they saw individual battalions of their warriors moving towards the battlements, bows and slings at the ready. Cistre hoped they had listened to their instructions regarding staying out of range of the Cuscosian crossbows until the last minute. She turned her head northwards again and judged the dragons were still five minutes away. Although she was impatient for their arrival, she still knew they would have the element of surprise.

Then, a low moan caught her attention amidst the commotion of activity all around. It was Milissandia. She held her temples as if in pain. Wobas too had a distant look in his eyes. *Cursed dreamworlders, why can they not contain their emotions?*

"What is it?" Cistre said tersely.

"It is Memek-Tal," Milissandia gasped. "He has summoned us."

# 48

# THE EARTHSHAKER'S GIFT

---

Tayem had faced adversaries and potential allies in negotiations many times before. She thought herself a seasoned diplomat, yet this stark pronouncement by the great dragon left her speechless. The thrill of finding one of the last surviving matriarchs of the Agnarim was wiped out with the numbing finality of the dragon's first words.

The dragon's head alone matched the size of Quassu, and Agathon lifted it now, causing the sisters to reflexively step back. "I know your cause is just," she said, "as I too have sensed the rise of the Black Hallows once more — although I am protected from its influence here under the mountain."

"Then you know how grave the threat to our people is," Tayem said, finding her words at last.

"I have witnessed the rise and fall of six Black Hallows cycles," Agathon replied, "and each brought over a hundred sols of misery. I know not how the evil manifests itself this time, but I am entirely sure I cannot expose myself to its influence again. Can you imagine what it is like to be possessed by an evil deeper than time itself?"

"I don't need to imagine," Tayem said, her voice barely a whisper.

Agathon extended her head further forward such that her breath was a breeze over the Dragon Riders, redolent of earth and parchment. "Yes, I can see in your eyes the scars of the Hallows. You escaped its grip? That is an achievement indeed. But for one such as I, the temptation would be too great."

"You fear your own choices?" Tayem said, an anger starting to rise within, despite her predicament. "You are wise beyond measure, your knowledge spans millennia, yet you cannot stir the resolve to resist the Hallows' enticements?"

"Dragons are wise. Dragons are mighty. Dragons are also vain. The prospect of unparalleled power draws us more than any human. That is why I now dwell in this mountain. If I emerged from my lair to aid you in your battle, Sol-Ar's rays would bathe me once again in their baleful glow. I would seek the nearest Hallows shrine and drink in the energy I found there — and nothing would be able to stand in my way. I nearly succumbed during the last cycle, and it was only a supreme act of will that urged me to bury myself here.

"Age overtakes me too, and I near the end of my days. There comes a time when the earth will claim me once again, and this is as good a resting place as any."

Tayem heard the dragon's complaint, but she was not finished yet. "You talk of your own demise, but what of the complete annihilation of the dragons? Would you countenance their destruction?"

"What is this you speak of, child? The dragons will survive this cycle — as they always have."

"Then you have no knowledge of the harroc di wurunwi?"

"You speak in the language of the Dreamworld, child. What does that mean?"

"Hunter of dreams," Tayem said. "A great sorcerer of the Dreamworld has arisen. He has already slain many of our dragons and now gathers his strength again to complete the destruction."

"I know nothing of the Dreamworld. How is this possible?"

"Like most other species, the dragons have avatars in the Far Beyond. When this monster slays in the Dreamworld, it is enacted in the Near To. Noble Enthusarr was murdered in this way."

"Enthusarr? I knew her as a hatchling, watched her grow into a mighty force of vs' shtak. She is gone?"

"I'm surprised your far sense did not detect it."

"A dragon has its limitations. My heart grieves for her loss."

"You are vulnerable too. The sorcerer may not have found your avatar yet, but it is only a matter of time before he does. You may speak of dying with dignity at the end of your days, but what does it say of the greatest living dragon if you are brought down by this monster?"

This news clearly took Agathon aback, and she raised herself up, blinking rapidly. "I cannot let this pass. It is beyond possibility to join with you on the battlefield, but perhaps there is a way I can help." She turned her attention to Mahren, regarding her with a look of respect. "Kirith-A, you have remained silent during our discourse, yet I sense you may be the key to confronting this problem."

Mahren looked at Tayem in bewilderment, but the Queen encouraged her to step forward. "I am not sure how I can," she said. "I am simply here to accompany my sister."

"You are more than a companion," Agathon said, "I sense a great talent within you. Indeed, were it not for your presence I would have dismissed your Dragon Queen out of hand. I am curious. You talk to dragons, but can you listen to them as well?"

"I understand the ancient language of vs' shtak, if that's what you mean."

"It is. Now there are sacred words that a dragon must learn if they are to transcend to the Agnarim. They are words of power, and can only be retained by one who is worthy."

Mahren's eyes grew wider. "You speak of the pneuma fyre? But there are no dragons I could pass this on to. Enthusarr is dead, and there is no other to equal her in sols."

"There is one," Agathon said, and she leaned forward to impart her words to Mahren. Tayem braced herself, wondering how her sister might receive this rare gift. But Agathon imparted her words in a whisper only Mahren heard. The only sign anything had happened was when Mahren closed her eyes and thanked the dragon.

The sisters' passage out of the great dragon's lair was much easier than their ingress. Climbing up the intervening space between the cavern floor and the tip of the dangling rope was tricky but not insurmountable. They doused one torch, using the light of the remainder until it reached the end of its life. Just as it started to sputter, Mahren relit her torch, providing enough illumination to last until all but the final hundred paces.

Back in the open, they found Quassu and Jaestrum huddled against each other. They raised their heads in grateful greeting once they caught sight of their mistresses.

"It is good to drink in fresh air again," Tayem said.

"That is true," Mahren replied. "I would not be an

Agnarim — stagnating down there in the depths of a mountain."

"Sshh, we don't want to offend her," Tayem said, but smiled nonetheless.

"Could it be true? What she said about one who could receive the gift of pneuma fyre?"

"She senses the movements of her kindred over these northern wastes. I don't think she was mistaken."

"But it seems so unlikely he would seek us out, given the state we last saw him in. I had thought him lost."

"Come, Sister. We waste time here. Let us greet him."

They mounted their dragons, allowing the beasts to stretch their wings and rouse their sluggish circulation. Once accomplished, they rose from the side of the mountain and headed south.

They had only been aloft for half an hour, when Tayem pointed across the snowscape to a speck moving across the line of a distant range of mountains.

"Could it be?" Mahren said.

"That is no bird or raptor," Tayem said. "It is too large." They spurred their mounts onwards, and it seemed that even they sensed the presence of a long-lost brother.

The speck grew to the size of a pinhead until Tayem made out the movement of great wings on its flanks, and still it increased in size as they closed the distance.

Another fifteen minutes and Tayem could clearly see the features of one she had previously observed only as a mound of sleeping scales. The dragon she now beheld was magnificent, possessing a sleek reddish-black hide, and a crimson crest crowning its head to match fiery-red eyes that burned across the distance.

"Oga!" Tayem shouted across the skies. "Welcome back."

# 49

# SHOUT AT THE WIND

---

Vanya knew most of the idioms and folk tales told in the kingdoms of the Imperious Crescent. She had heard poetic turns of phrase from Dragonia, cynical witticisms from Hallow's Creek and even crude sayings from Kaldoran stonegrabes. All of these were picked up through ten sols of wandering as an itinerant bard. The one that came to mind as she witnessed the slaughter at Wyverneth on the tenth day of the sixth month of the sol Wishellen, was 'salamander in a saucepan.' She could not have felt more out of place if she had tried, yet Brethis's charismatic address had stirred her. She was gripped by something greater than herself and motivated by the need to contribute to a greater good than her own self-preservation.

She had joined Brethis's dissident faction knowing she was no warrior. Yet she had healing skills, and more than the usual woman's share of independence, courage and sheer pluckiness. If nothing else, she reasoned, her foolhardy volunteering might yield material for a dozen ballads; that was if she survived — a diminishing prospect given what she now witnessed.

From her vantage point at the edge of the Eastern forests, known to Dragonian locals as Ocdrund, she observed the initial advancement of dissident forces against the outlying Cuscosian troops. The full moon bathed the open ground with its pallid light, revealing an enemy dug in behind sharpened garbeech stakes. Vanya was not privy to the entire battle tactics of the allies she had sworn allegiance to, but she knew the dissidents were charged with overrunning these defences as a flanking attack. If successful, it would pave the way for a full frontal assault by Dragonians and Gigantes, coinciding with the fall of the Dragon Talon gates. Whether Cistre's covert force managed to breach the internal defences to achieve this was very much open to the fates.

Fates? Vanya had her own primitive beliefs; mainly devoted to earth gods and forest spirits, but she had long since abandoned any notion they had plans for her. She didn't like the idea that her life was pre-ordained anyway, and Brethis's bold speeches had cemented this philosophy. *Death holds no fear for me,* she told herself. But death and dying were two different things, and what she now witnessed swept aside her sense of a noble conflict, harrowing her to the core.

At first the dissidents had taken the unsuspecting Cuscosians by surprise, swarming over the outer defences and routing the defenders with minimal losses, but they had grown over-confident. They stormed the walls of Wyverneth with their make-shift ladders, constructed more from idealism than any joiner's skill. Scaling the battlements was supposed to be a last resort, only attempted if the gates did not fall. Only they had been impatient, not waiting for Aibrator's signal — and paid the price. No sooner had they placed the ladders against the walls than the Cuscosians poured cauldrons of corrosive fluid over the climbing soldiers. Vanya heard the screams of agony float across the killing fields and her heart faltered.

She ordered runners to retrieve what wounded there were, but after fifteen minutes, half of them returned with only a few dissidents that had the breath of life in them. The acidic liquid had corroded their heads and shoulders to the bone, bubbling flesh dissolving away as the casualties moaned in agony. She attempted to wash away the viscous fluid but only succeeded in getting it on her fingers, burning them and rendering her abilities useless.

"What is this stuff?" she said to one runner.

"Dragon spit," the woman replied.

*How could the Cuscosians have come by this weapon?*

Then she remembered the battle of Lyn-Harath and the harvesting of remaining dragons from Wyverneth's pens.

"We can do nothing for these," she said, "only retrieve casualties attacked by sword, arrow or spear. These we can treat."

"What do we do with these poor souls?" The woman said, gesturing toward the writhing victims of the fyredrench.

"Release them from their torment," Vanya replied and handed her a two-edged dagger.

"I have never — "

"Then it is time you learned," she said and thrust the hilt into her palm. There was no time to cajole her further, and she turned her attention to the stretchers that now returned. These were men and women bearing light wounds, most struck by crossbow bolts from the battlements. Her orders were to patch them up and send what she could back into the fray.

After a further half hour of treating these wounded, she realised her efforts were futile. They had sent two back to the battlefield only to see them struck down straight away in a rain of bolts from above.

"We are useless here," she said, looking at the twenty remaining physickers. "If we are to perish, it is better we take some of the enemy with us rather than comfort the dying."

She drew her sword and exhorted those around her.

"Take up arms, brave warriors. For that is what we have become. Tonight we go into battle in the cause of justice and freedom."

And despite the fear on every face that looked to her, she also sensed a grim determination to stand up to an enemy that had cowed them too long. They would lend their strength to the cause — or die trying.

~ ~ ~

Etezora ran to the east side of the battlements, pushing her way through the throng of soldiers. Tuh-Ma lumbered behind, eager to watch the carnage he no doubt anticipated would ensue.

When she reached the outer wall, the first contingent of dragons were swooping down from above. She had just enough time to witness her soldiers repelling a wave of attackers from the walls, and to observe giant crossbows being brought to bear.

"Now we shall see how your beasts fare against our weapons, dragon haujen," she cried.

The Captain issued his instructions to the ballista teams, urging them to wait until the dragons were within one hundred paces. Etezora held her breath until he ordered the men to fire in two volleys. She heard the click of the mechanisms release and saw three shafts, six spans long, shoot at the nearest wyrms. One flew wide of its target as the beast swerved, but two struck home, one piercing the thigh of a battle dragon, the other embedding itself in the soft throat tissue of an iridescent ayku. The magnificent creature recoiled with a roar and plummeted downwards, taking its rider with it in a death spiral.

Two more shafts flew from the second volley, both of which missed their targets.

*Why so few bolts?* Etezora thought. She looked back at the ballistas, noting that five of them lay broken on the flagstones. One seemed to have burst into dozens of pieces, a shard of one stave having sprung back and mashed the face of a crew-member to a pulp.

"What is wrong with the ballistas?" she screamed at the captain. "Did you not test them before use?"

"We have not had time," the Captain replied. "This is their first trial."

"The components," she said, "who made them?"

"Why, Nalin and his engineers," the Captain said.

"That krut!" Etezora hissed. "He has sabotaged them. Eétor warned that the stonegrabe could not be trusted."

"Shall we load them again?"

Etezora looked up at the circling dragons. "No. The wyrms are wary, and in any case I have another weapon at my disposal."

She stepped toward the battlement, feeling the Hallows rising like a deluge in her mind.

"Careful, Mistress, you are open to attack here," Tuh-Ma said.

"Out of my way, Ma. This moment is mine." She fixed

on the squadrons of dragons, looping like giant kites in the night sky. "Where are you, dragon haujen?"

It was impossible to follow an individual beast as the troupe swarmed back and forth. Instead, she picked on the closest. It was much further away from her than the forest-warriors she had targeted at the Dead Zone battle, but she was much more powerful now. She held up her hands and directed a bolt of purple energy at the beast and its rider. It struck the target, effortlessly wrapping around the dragon's neck like a lasso. The unleashing of this intensity of power filled Etezora with unprecedented ecstasy such that she laughed out loud. She gave herself fully to the Hallows, allowing energy to surge in pulses through the lasso. Each pulse constricted the ring of energy more tightly until it cut off the dragon's airway. It was now writhing mid air, having long since thrown its rider to the ground, hundreds of feet below. Still, this was not enough. She pulled on the cord of energy, drawing the beast toward her.

"I would see the fear of death in your eyes," she said.

She pulled the beast in like a fish on a line, not feeling any loss of power despite the creature's naturally superior strength. Then, when it was close enough for her to observe the anguish and shock on the beast's face, she squeezed one final time. The dragon went limp, suspended in space as if Etezora held it in her own grip.

"Hah! I am Nurti — slayer of dragons," she cried. With a final burst of energy, she threw the dragon down into the midst of the attacking Dragonian foot soldiers, pulverising them and breaking the beast's body in the process.

She stood atop the battlements, her chest heaving with a mixture of exertion and exhilaration, revelling in what she had just accomplished.

"Queen Etezora is supreme!" Tuh-Ma said, jumping up and down. "But beware, Mistress, Dragon Riders will single you out."

The blue-skin's perceptions were accurate, for as Etezora focused on another dragon, the riders who had witnessed the bizarre death of the beast swung their mounts around and descended en masse. It was clear they intended to swamp Etezora with their numbers.

"Your majesty," the ballista captain said, "we must take cover. We cannot hope to repel such an onslaught."

Etezora raised her arms again, felt the Hallows guttering forth, and shouted. "Let them come, I am more than a match for any dragon."

~ ~ ~

Through hate-filled eyes, Cistre led the attack on the battlements. A battle fury consumed her, having thrown away any sense of caution. She had seen Etezora and her soldiers bring down Rargorren and Ymre, together with their riders — Sayndriosse and Nyrris, and her anger knew no bounds. She recalled all the riders and their mounts by name, yet she did not know if any of those left flying the skies would survive to mourn their passing.

*This shall not be,* she thought, and fixed her ire on the figure now standing triumphantly on the battlements of their once proud palace with arms raised to the heavens. The distance closed, and still the Cuscosian Queen had not unleashed her Hallows-fire.

*Why does she wait?* Cistre thought. *Does her power need to re-energise?*

Then, with a detonation that split the night, Etezora unleashed her dreadfully familiar loop of energy. It crackled toward Cistre, and in that moment she knew she was defenceless, her dragon too much set on its course to change trajectory. She cried in anger and frustration, bracing herself for the impact, when from the corner of her eye she caught a flash of green and silver. A skeredith beast darted in front of her, taking the force of Etezora's bolt in the chest.

"Sheldar!" she cried.

Muthorus swerved to miss the stricken mount, sending him on a course that would drive him into the palace wall. Cistre pulled on the reins, urging the dragon upwards. It was enough to clear the wooden castellation, although Muthorus's feet grazed them, shooting splinters of wood into the air. He stalled at Cistre's command, flapping his leathern wings to arrest his flight and beating the Cuscosian guard backwards.

The dragon alighted on the battlements and Cistre

slipped out of the harness, drawing her sword in one fluid motion. Etezora was fully absorbed in strangling Sheldar's mount and would have been open for attack, only her troll stood between her and Cistre, wielding a wicked-looking club in two hands. Incredibly, Sheldar had maintained his position in the harness, but if his mount's twisting continued in the same manner, it was only a matter of time before he fell with it — just as Ymre had. She had to reach Etezora before that happened.

"Dragon-woman not pass Tuh-Ma," the troll said, spitting gobs of mucus at her.

"We'll see about that," Cistre said and lunged at the creature. For one so seemingly cumbersome, Tuh-Ma moved with a speed that defied his bulk and knocked the blade aside with his club. By the time Cistre had recovered, the blue-skin had stepped inside her guard and pummelled into her, driving her back with the force of his wart-covered body. The blow knocked Cistre off balance, but she was lithe enough not to fall over backwards. The blue-skin had not pressed home his charge, obviously not wanting to leave his Queen vulnerable. This was wise, as further dragons were now landing on the battlements and in the courtyard below.

Without taking her eyes off Sheldar, Etezora sent another purple bolt from her free hand at a dragon that had landed to her right. She now held two beasts captive, one still in mid-air and the other squirming on the flagstones just a few strides away from her.

Cistre swung at Tuh-Ma again, forcing him to take a step back as he parried the blow with his club. "Attack the Queen from all sides," she shouted at the rapidly swelling ranks of Dragon Riders who now joined her.

Etezora looked around, the nooses of electric energy loosening a little as she lost concentration, and Cistre thought she detected a look of panic on the Queen's face. She swung her weapon repeatedly at the blue-skin, her nimble points and jabs compensating for the imbalance in strength. Two of her blows found their way past Tuh-Ma's guard, one slicing into a leather pauldron, the other cutting into the bare flesh of his forearm. The wound was only slight, but Cistre had smeared her blade with one of Milissandia's poisons prior to the battle.

*How long will you remain standing once the toxin does its work?* She thought.

It was then that a loud cry issued from the foot of the battlements. "What transpires?" she enquired of the nearest Dragon Rider.

"The Dragon Talon gate has been opened," he replied, "Aibrator has succeeded."

The news lent strength to Cistre's arm, and she slashed at the troll, forcing him back until he jostled against his Queen, who now found it difficult to maintain her hold on the two struggling dragons.

"Etezora," Cistre cried. "Your gates are down and our warriors will soon have stormed your defences. Surrender now, and we may yet spare your lives."

"Never," Etezora replied. "My Dreadguard still outnumbers your forces ten to one."

"You cannot hope to prevail against our dragons. Give the command to stand down, now."

Etezora still had her Hallows grip on the two beasts, but only to hold them at bay. She looked at Cistre intently, and then smiled in such a way that the Dragon Rider thought her face would crack.

"Your dragons?" Etezora said. "You place your trust in those wyrms? Look to the skies, schjek, and see how they are faring."

Cistre followed the Queen's gaze to where she should have seen the remaining host of the Donnephon descending. Instead, dragon after dragon writhed in the air, two dropping like stones to the ground; yet more were close to death.

"No," she moaned, "it cannot be happening again."

# 50

# BUSTED SOULS

————————

Edenbract, a site of great antiquity, older than Zodarin; perhaps even older than the accumulated sols of the great dragons themselves. Sandstone columns stood like guardians, their decay acting as a measure of time in a place of uncounted days. Moonlight shone down, illuminating the relics and causing the surrounding scar birch to cast their own peculiar shadows on the scene.

The amioid had read somewhere that this ruined temple had been erected by the ancient ones in reverence to the gods of the Hallows. He had also heard that the simple ring of columns acted as a focus of power to summon the

Hallows — or to hold them at bay. The amioid had no doubt which purpose he had in mind tonight.

At the centre of the weathered blocks a cleft in the ground loomed, issuing forth purple vapours like the very breath of evil, and it seemed that the ichor that coursed through his vessels increased in speed at the sight of it. Deep within its bowels he swore he detected the very shifting of Varchal's foundations, the planet's unholy response to Sol-Ar's ineffable traversal of the heavens.

He did not possess the true gift of far-sight, but something in the ether told him the timing of his quest was apt, urgent even. His amioid form was now fully manifest, and he made no effort to shape-shift, his only attempt at concealment being to pass through Cuscosa in the still of the night. Those who beheld his true appearance either cowered in fear, or deluded themselves they had seen an apparition. The amioid knew they would wake next morning to the memory of an abomination passing them by, like a tornado leaving them out of its trail of destruction or a great monster ignoring them as it searched for more worthy prey.

*Ah, the sheer intoxication*, it thought, welcoming the tendrils of energy once again. They entered the pores in its skin, energising it and suppressing the peculiar benevolent emotions elicited by the blight.

*Tonight I shall be rid of you*, it thought. Yet there would be time to revel in that later.

It was time. It would do the Queen's bidding this one

last occasion, and then it would seek out Wobas and his daughter. It possessed the energy, the means and the desire.

Settling itself in a depression eroded out of a large, oblong monolith that seemed designed for this very purpose, it closed every one of its thirteen eyes.

The force with which it entered the Far Beyond exceeded anything it had experienced before, and its two hearts beat ever more vehemently in response to what seemed to be a calling. It drove itself through the Dreamworld forests at a speed that swallowed the breath in its body, and yet it wasn't fast enough.

*They are here, and they are intent on stopping me.*

The amioid passed across the woodland boundary, moving like the wind over plains where the grass parted before it, until it came to the place where the wyrms dwelt.

*For beasts so wise, why do you congregate in this way and make my task so easy?* It thought.

There they were, facsimile avatars of themselves, huddled together as if they knew their time was upon them. Even in this state, the amioid saw and felt their nobility. This recognition stirred the blight-curse within, setting its murmuring against his malign intent.

*Still your voice,* he commanded it.

*Your affliction speaks the only voice of reason left within you,* came a voice from across the dell, and the amioid beheld the Spirit Guide standing regally if somewhat diminished.

The monster could not resist a desire to crow. *You seem*

*a little malaised yourself, Memek-Tal. Let me ease you of your burden.*

The Spirit Guide smiled, albeit painfully, and the amioid wondered if it was pain or pity at its root. *Release? That would be welcome, Memek-Tal* sent, *but it is not for you to ordain. There are others who will weigh my deeds in their scales.*

*Then why are you here?*

*To entreat and to witness.*

*You would entreat me? I am too set on my course, and I have waited too long.*

The Spirit Guide hung its head as if sensing further words would be ineffectual. *I see that. Yet true choices should be made with as much foresight as possible.*

*I have seen the future, Memek-Tal,* the amioid sent, *and it is glorious.*

*You have seen what the Black Hallows wants you to see. But tell me, amioid, who exerts the control — you or it?*

As the Spirit Guide uttered these words, it raised a limb, conjuring an invisible sigil in the ether. Before the amioid's eyes it saw a vision, its body writhing in alternate paroxysms of pain and ecstasy, purple ectoplasm issuing from its mouth, its pores, indeed every orifice of its body.

*No,* the amioid screamed. *You lie, Memek-Tal. The Hallows has never inhabited one such as I, and I am its master. Begone, duplicitous vision.*

It pushed back with its mind and the Spirit Guide staggered backwards.

*No more delay,* the amioid stated. *I shall vanquish these beasts, and the Gigantes shaman and his daughter will be next.*

*Why not confront us first?* Another said.

The amioid spun round, angry that it had allowed itself to be distracted. *Wobas? You have saved me the bother of tracking you down. I see your subterfuge, and will stay my hand no longer.*

~ ~ ~

Wobas viewed the thing that Zodarin had become and understood he was witnessing his former friend in his true form. The harroc di wurunwi's appearance hurt his scops eyes, even though it was but a Dreamworld apparition.

*The sorcerer,* Milissandia sent, crouching in the grass next to him. *Is this his true nature? I can hardly bring myself to look at it.*

Wobas's heart quailed within his breast, for truly the thing was an abomination. What he had previously seen at the edge of his vision was but a whisper compared to this monstrosity. The thing stood — if standing was a word that could describe its posture — at a height to rival Ebar himself. There was no head crowning its torso of bubbling green. The eyes were too many to count, embedded as they were in the folded flesh. Where its multitudinous tentacles joined with the body, their points of attachment disappeared in the depths of undulating folds such that

Wobas was left with a sense that the whole thing was the very concept of ambulation.

And then it spoke. Not through its mouth, this seemed reserved for functions more terrible than Wobas could imagine. *You have humiliated me, Shaman, and I would see you suffer before you breathe your last.*

*Then do what you must, Strip-Willow,* Wobas sent.

*What? Do you seek to denigrate me with such childish epithets?*

*You denigrate yourself, Hallows-slave!*

*You will not distract me,* the amioid sent, and with the speed of thought itself, the creature's tentacles lashed out and wrapped around the necks of two unsuspecting dragon avatars. Unlike Etezora's lassos of Hallows energy in the Near To, the amioid required no slow process of strangulation. The constriction of its tentacles quenched the life from the dragons in an instant, and Wobas knew two of the ayku had met their end over Wyverneth.

*We must strike now,* Wobas sent to his daughter, *before he can unleash his power again.*

*I am ready, Father. Though I wonder how effectual we will be against this thing.*

*Have faith, Milissandia,* Wobas replied, and gathered his will to join with that of his daughter. They had practised this many times, yet not in anger, and as he felt the reassuring linkage established with Milissandia's consciousness, he felt the awesome weight of what he was about to commit.

*Now!* Came his spirit-shout, and a wave of silver energy erupted from their conjoined locus and surged toward the creature. It struck the amioid at the centre of its mass, causing it to recoil with the impact, screaming in a voice as shrill as a hellish banshee. The flesh seemed to crumple inward around a small blackened crater as it reeled back. Then it stopped, the tissue knitting together until the crater disappeared, leaving only the vestige of a scar.

*Is that all, Shaman? This is what you assault me with?* It said. *I had thought better of you.* And with this statement, the amioid's tentacles uncoiled like whips and flew across the hollow toward the Gigantes avatars. It was only as a matter of reflex that their defensive shield rose in response, deflecting them.

*Our soul-energy hardly grazed it,* Milissandia sent. *How can anyone stand against such a thing?*

*Do not lose heart,* sent Memek-Tal in response. *The harroc di wurunwi was affected by your attack. Take the initiative before it —*

Only it was too late. The monster's attack was not intended to wound but to distract. Two more tentacles shot out and grabbed another two dragon avatars, quenching their life force in an instant, and still the creature did not seem diminished from the assault.

*Run,* Milissandia cried out to them, but either they were deaf to her plea, or were somehow paralysed.

*The harroc di wurunwi holds them in place,* Memek-Tal sent. *Do not waste your time warning them. They will only listen to one of the Donnephon, and the Dragon Rider's avatars are not present in the Dreamworld.*

*He is right, Daughter,* Wobas said and gathered his strength again. He did not need to signal his intent this time, as his consciousness was one with Milissandia's. Another argent tsunami swept outwards, this time striking the creature's tentacles, causing one to be severed and fall to the ground, writhing like an emerald snake.

*It is wounded,* Milissandia sent.

*But far from dead,* Wobas replied. *Strike again before it is too late.*

~ ~ ~

The Gigantes' latest assault sent a shockwave of pain through the amioid, yet it sensed with its unleashing, that somehow its assailants had spent themselves dearly. Their attack had taken its own toll on the amioid, of course; and despite the weeks of gathering its power, it sensed a diminution with the slaying of the last two dragons. There was also another factor to consider now. It sensed a Dragon presence to the north of the dell. Three of them — one a gigantic wyrm.

*It is the Dragon Queen,* it said to itself. *They may yet be the greater prize. I must rid myself of these bothersome insects.*

It had lost a limb, but it would regenerate in time. Ignoring the pain, it drew on the Hallows with increased fervency, and allowed it to possess its body even more, understanding there was an additional price to pay. It was dimly aware of what the Spirit Guide had revealed but chose to ignore it again. *You are the father of lies, Memek-Tal and I will not be swayed from my purpose.*

This time, it unleashed all of its limbs at the Gigantes, moving forward with the attack to add momentum to it; and although two tentacles were deflected, the rest wrapped themselves around its opponents, sapping their life energy.

*Now you shall both die,* the amioid sent, unable to contain its glee.

~ ~ ~

The force of the amioid's attack stunned Milissandia with life-shaking intensity, and she cried out as she attempted to absorb its effect.

*Milissandia,* her father cried, and she knew in the utterance of her name that something had changed. He never called her anything but *Daughter.*

*Father,* she replied, *I cannot withstand this onslaught. I fear I have failed you.*

There was no reply from the shaman, and Milissandia wondered if he was not lost already.

*Milissandia, Wobas,* came the voice of Memek-Tal. *It is not enough. The pool of your energy is diminished in the face of the harroc di wurunwi's attack.*

*Then we are undone,* Milissandia sent.

*It does not have to be,* Memek-Tal replied, his voice sounding weaker with every statement. *There is a way to defeat this creature. But there is a consequence.*

*Name it,* Wobas sent, his own utterances little more than a gasp.

*The path of Inuur,* Memek-Tal sent. *One of you must invoke it.*

*Inuur?* Milissandia sent. *The ultimate sacrifice?* She pondered for a second, conscious that the amioid was gathering itself for a final surge of power as its tentacles constricted further. *Is there a guarantee?*

*No ... guarantees ... except both your lives at the hands of this creature if you do not ...*

*Then I shall commit to it,* Milissandia swore. *Prepare yourself, Father. You must strike as soon as you sense the passing of my spirit-energy.*

But before she could invoke the act, she knew she had prevaricated too long. Wobas uttered three words: *Milissandia, forgive me.* And with that, she sensed a release from him, together with a subsequent charging of her spirit.

The Inuur — an irrevocable shamanic cantrip transferring the life force of one to another. Wobas had taught Milissandia about its existence, and she knew it only required an act of will in the Dreamworld — he had invoked it before she could do so herself.

*Do not delay,* Memek-Tal sent, *otherwise your father's sacrifice will mean nothing.*

Milissandia looked at the crumpled form of the scops next to her, felt her anger rise, and channelled her energy into one final outrush of silver-white fury. During the creature's onslaught it had drawn close, pressing home the attack such that it towered over the diminutive form of the tree serpent. Milissandia directed her wave of energy as a blanket, spreading and enveloping the amioid, entering every aperture in the surface of its body.

*Strike ... at ... its ... hearts*, Memek-Tal sent from an indistinct place. Milissandia responded and infiltrated the harroc di wurunwi to its core, saw in her mind's eye the repulsive beating organs and surrounded them.

She was weakening, had only enough energy for a final burst, and she used it to the full. Just as the amioid attempted to squeeze the life from her with its tentacles, she constricted her argent fists around both hearts, feeling them burst and release their abhorrent ichor.

*Aahh*, it uttered, a gasp of defeat rather than an agonised shriek. Then it was silent.

She opened her spirit eyes and witnessed the creature cave in on itself where it stood until all that remained was a smouldering pile of darkened green tissue.

As the smoke cleared, she saw the Spirit Guide from across the dell. It was laid on its side, chest heaving and eyes blinking uncontrollably.

*Memek-Tal?* Milissandia sent.

*It is done*, the Spirit Guide replied.

*But you — what is to become of you?*

*There is ... a cost to everything,* came the reply. *Return to the Near To... your father holds onto life but cannot last much longer. He would speak with you.*

Memek-Tal's eyes closed and his chest rose and fell no more.

# 51

# 'TIL ALL IS GONE

———

Aibrator held his torch aloft in the confined space of the sluice tunnel and led the way through knee-high water. He dared not look down at the colour of the fluid that soaked his breeches and seeped through the gaps in his leather armour.

*Cuscosian pollution,* he thought, as if their effluent was any worse than other humanoid species in the Imperious Crescent. *Could be worse. We could be infiltrating the depths of a Kaldoran stronghold. Sesnath knows what we'd be wading through there!*

He had almost ordered his small warband to leave their glaives behind. The low roof forced them to hold the weapons horizontally — posing problems as their points poked the soldier in front periodically.

At least they had not been detected during their entry. They were at their most exposed where the Halivern flowed past the sluice-gate and the castle waste flowed sluggishly through a rusted grille. But, after a few vigorous tugs from Bostrom, a hulking Dragonian brute, they'd gained access without an arrow being fired.

*Were the Cuscosians so lax that they had not discovered this entry point?*

Aibrator certainly hoped so. It would be just his luck to meet a patrol down here, and for him to meet an ignominious end in the sewage.

After traversing the tunnel for some five hundred strides, the warband came to a junction in the waterways. A large vertical shaft emptied its contents through the roof of the tunnel, and several smaller branches found their confluence here too.

"Do we climb up?" Bostrom whispered from behind.

"No," Aibrator replied. "According to Gemain there is an easier access point up this right-hand branch. Follow me."

Twenty paces beyond the confluence, up a tunnel so narrow it forced them onto hands and knees, they found a grating in the ceiling. As Aibrator gazed upwards through it, he saw the moon, large as a millwheel shining down into what he knew was a pillar-lined concourse. In the distance he could hear the sounds of battle — the clash of steel on steel, men crying out in pain and ... what was that? *The roar of dragons.*

"Our beasts are dying," he said, panic rising. "Come, we must breach the gate and join the fray forthwith. We may already be too late."

Bostrom made short work of the grating and the twenty men exited the tunnel like the sewer rats they resembled. They had only run a short distance when they encountered resistance — ten Cuscosians, dashing across their path with pikes held high. They would have passed in a minute, but one glanced their way, saw the incongruous intruders standing in the shadows and raised the alarm. All ten turned, took in the situation and ran towards them in a tight formation.

"We can't afford to engage them in melee," Aibrator commanded. "Archers?"

He didn't need to say another word. Five of Dragonia's top marksmen pushed through, crouched and loosed two arrows each in quick succession. The shafts found their marks despite the moving targets, and ten Cuscosians hit the cobbles in a matter of seconds.

Aibrator didn't hesitate. "Make straight for the gates. We may still catch the defenders by surprise."

The warband sprinted towards Wyverneth's main gates, drawing closer to the sound of pitched battle. As they approached the Dragon Talon portal, its heavy heartwood gates standing proud and secure, the warriors found themselves amidst a criss-cross of soldiers, rushing to bolster the defences. Aibrator marvelled at how they bore the Dragonians no attention whatsoever, such was their assumption that no enemy could attack from behind.

It was not until they had accessed the portcullis chamber that the guards recognised they were beset. Aibrator led his men against the five Cuscosians who rained down arrows on the invading army from slots set in the turrets' machiolations. Although initially surprised, the defenders offered a spirited defence. Aibrator ran two of them through with his glaive, the weapon giving him an advantage against their shortswords. Yet one of them, clearly a veteran of many conflicts, slew two of the warband in short order.

"Open the gates," Aibrator commanded Bostrom. "I'll take this krut."

The Dragonian commander's tactic had its effect. The swordsman took his eyes off the gate, allowing Bostrom and two others to operate the machinery.

Aibrator manoeuvred himself around his opponent, jabbing unpredictably to keep him at bay. From back in the courtyard he heard the alarm sound, and the rush of armoured feet up the stairs.

"They will be upon us in seconds," he shouted at the gate operators. "Hurry."

Bostrom, sweat dripping from his grimy face turned to him and said, "It is done," just as a Cuscosian blade appeared in the middle of his chest from behind.

*Rest well, my friend,* Aibrator thought and turned back

to his opponent. The man threw his blade from hand to hand, trying to keep Aibrator off-guard. He tried to second-guess the Cuscosians next strike, but when it came, he could not have predicted it. Like a flash of lightning, the man's blade slashed at Abraitor's glaive-shaft, slicing it in two. The blade clattered to the floor leaving him holding the severed shaft. Behind him, his men were fighting a losing skirmish with the troops who now swarmed into the turret chamber.

*Krut,* Aibrator thought. *I hope they wash my body before cremating it.*

~ ~ ~

Ebar swung his giant club down on the skull of an opponent, crushing it despite the man wearing a helm made from laminated Erybus steel. As the blow struck home, something died inside the Gigantes. He had killed thirty five Cuscosians, wounded twice as many more, and he recalled every one of the slain. There was no battle-lust to consume him, no fear of death, only a grim determination to achieve the allies' goal.

His fellow Gigantes had accompanied him in a joint offensive in front of the main gates. They had been compelled to take the battle to the defenders early when the impetuous dissidents made their doomed assault on the city walls. Had the Cuscosians not been caught by surprise, these defenders would have safely ensconced themselves within the walls. But Siksta did not smile upon them this night, and instead they were caught in a scissor-move between Dragonian forest-warriors and the Gigantes. Through his single Cyclopean eye, Ebar saw the fear on these men's faces as they were confronted by combatants that dwarfed them in every respect. It was because of these unfortunates that the battlement defenders had refrained from firing down upon them or tipping cauldrons of fyredrench. But once their number diminished, they had no such qualms.

When the first arrows started to descend, Ebar urged his allies back. They stood no chance against these defences. Instead, they needed to exercise patience as Cistre's assault from above ran its course. He did not have long to wait.

He heard the familiar rasp of downward dragon-wing strokes and their battle-roar descend from the shroud of the night. Shrieks of agony from above were followed by a cessation of missile fire, and he knew they had to press home the attack straight away.

"Ladders to the walls," he said, signalling the remnant of dissidents to resume their assault. They were down to ten ladders, but without the defence being pressed home on the battlements, Brethis led his nimble Cuscosian rebels up and over the top, joining in the fray. To add to their good fortune, the gates in front slowly opened, revealing the horrified faces of unprepared Cuscosians.

*Perhaps the tide turns,* Ebar allowed himself to think as the allies let out a roar of triumph.

It was the night's second unfortunate presumption. The agonised cry of the first dragon reached his ears. He looked up and saw baleful purple energy seizing the beasts mid-flight.

"It is the possessed Queen," Hanar cried as he drew up to Ebar. He dropped a lifeless corpse and stood, mouth open. "And what new evil is this?"

"It is a doubly malign attack," Ebar replied. "See how more of the dragons writhe in mid-air without anything seeming to assail them. The sorcerer's hand is in this."

Ebar was so preoccupied he did not see the hurtling body of a mighty dragon falling from the skies.

"Ebar!" He heard Hanar cry, then felt himself lofted several metres to the side, his body hitting the ground with numbing force.

Only Hanar could have accomplished the fete; but the largest of all Cyclopes met the cost with his own life. The ayku buried him under its plummeting form, crushing the life from his sacrificial body.

The dragon's tail struck Ebar's legs, but not with enough force to fracture any bones. Nonetheless, it took him a moment or two to raise his stunned form back to its feet. All around was chaos and confusion. The dragons had halted their attack, and now a new dismaying threat surfaced. From the west came an advancing guard of countless Cuscosian soldiers. The Gigantes leader had wondered why they had not met with greater resistance. Now he knew the answer. The bulk of the Cuscosian defence had been garrisoned north of Wyverneth. Had the allies been given enough time to carry out an extensive reconnaissance, they would have known this. But time had been against them.

Now they would pay.

~ ~ ~

Tayem had never ridden a dragon so hard, but Quassu did not complain. It was as if Oga lent both Jaestrum and he an unbidden strength. Still, the journey back from the Northern Wastes was arduous, despite taking a more direct route unhindered by the need to scour the landscape for hidden dragon lairs.

They had made camp in a sheltered ice hollow on the evening of their encounter with Agathon. Mahren was eager to converse with Oga, if that were possible, and the discovery of such a shelter served their needs in all respects.

They had eaten the last of their food, and there was nothing to cheer them save the prospect of a fire. But although they had the means to light one, there was no fuel, and in the pitch black of this northern plain there was no prospect of finding such.

"The fyre-cauldrons of our dragons run low without

food," Tayem said. "I think this may be the coldest of nights."

"Not necessarily," Mahren replied, looking at the plum-coloured, heaving monolith that was Oga's resting body.

"Even *his* inner fires are low after searching these wastes for us," Tayem replied.

"Then perhaps it is time to stoke the furnace," Mahren said.

"What ... here? I thought we were going to wait until the return to Herethorn. Besides, we are all exhausted."

"I am eager to see if Agathon's words are true."

"And I am supposed to be the impatient one," Tayem said, smiling. "Very well. It can do no harm, except plunge us into disappointment should our quest prove a failure at this final hurdle."

"Have a little trust, Sister." Mahren stirred herself and stepped toward the dozing dragon, gathering her furs around her to ward off the biting cold. "Great Oga," she said, and watched her breath appear as a vapour at the words' utterance.

The beast opened one eye, and Tayem thought she saw a trace of belligerence there, but also a sense of loss.

*Is he aware of his sister's passing?* Tayem wondered.

Mahren's next words were in the language of vs' shtak, and Tayem followed only the gist of what her sister said. Mahren could not only speak fluently in the ancient language, but possessed a quality to her speech which dragons responded to with warmth.

"Amin caela y' tondoren ten'lle, Oga. Teena tuulo i' atara en' ilya vs' shtak," Mahren said. The beast let out a deep growl that Tayem recognised as one of acceptance and respect.

*Speak carefully*, Tayem thought. *Oga may not know what you offer him.*

Then her sister placed her lips next to Oga's ear and whispered the secret words that Agathon had conveyed to her. At their utterance, Oga lifted his snout, eyes wide.

"Stand back," Mahren said. "Something stirs within."

Tayem was no kirith-a, but even she detected the change in Oga. His breathing grew more rapid, and he shifted to his feet, gazing up at the night sky that was visible as a faint glow in the ice cleft above. He coughed, as if bringing something up from his belly, then snorted, a puff of smoke laced with tiny sparks emerging from his nostrils.

"If that is what the great dragon has imparted," Tayem said, "then I fear we have wasted our time."

"Now who is impatient?" Mahren said.

Oga drew himself up to full height, turning his head towards a section of the ice wall behind and exhaled with a force as strong as a hurricane.

What the two sisters beheld next left Tayem in no doubt that Agathon had been true to her word. A long gout of flame issued from Oga's mouth and struck the wall of ice. The glistening edifice turned first to slush then water as large chunks of it fell to the floor of the cleft. They moved to a higher shelf of ice out of harm's way, and Mahren settled Oga back down again before he could express his pneuma fyre again.

As they gazed at the pool of melted ice below, Tayem said, "Sleep well, Mahren. For tomorrow we fly at dawn."

By late afternoon, they had crested the ridge of peaks north of Herethorn. From this distance, Tayem could make out the hidden Gigantes village wreathed in mists. As they drew closer, she uttered the words that Wobas had passed on to them, and the mists cleared to allow them admittance. Yet as they took in the village, Tayem recognised something had transpired.

"It is too quiet," she shouted across to Mahren as they circled the huts.

An abrupt landing and hastily exchanged words with a relieved Shamfis revealed Tayem's greatest fear.

*It has begun already,* she thought, sensing that events were unfolding at a distance beyond which she could exert any control. She allowed the dragons to take only a few minute's refreshment and food. They themselves bolted down some energy-giving biscuits supplied by Ebar's wife.

"You look weary beyond words," Shamfis said to her. "Must you take flight again so soon?"

Tayem looked south. "In a few short hours, battle will commence. If we do not join our kindred, then fatigue will be of no consequence. We must be gone."

It seemed to take an eternity before they coaxed their mounts into the sky again, although in reality it was less than half an hour. If the journey from the wastes seemed epic, this last hundred periarchs saw the Fyreglance sisters ride the wind like no other Donnephon had done before.

Mahren now rode Oga, her minute form dwarfed in an ill-fitting harness strapped to his back. Jaestrum had remained, although Mahren was loath to leave him. The good bye was swift, their one consolation knowing that he would not face Etezora's weapons on the battlefield. Whether he could survive an attack by Zodarin in the Dreamworld was another matter.

Sol-Ar had already set in the sky as Tayem observed the distant fires of battle over Wyverneth. She goaded Quassu on, leading the dragon flight down towards an unknown and unprecedented storm.

~ ~ ~

Through a blood-red haze, Cistre could see circling dragons against a full moon.

*This must be the afterlife*, she thought absently. Then the searing pain from her forehead informed her she had yet to walk Sesnath's golden halls. Memories flooded back: the fall of the dragons, Etezora's cry of triumph and subsequent exit from the battlements, Tuh-Ma's surprise attack and a vicious strike to her head with his club. Then blackness.

"The dragons are still flying," she said to herself and sat up, her surprise and relief difficult to contain. The battlements were empty, save for a few groaning wounded and Muthorus standing over her, a look of sadness in his eyes.

"Less of your moping," she said to him. "Your mistress is not dead yet." Clearly, Etezora's troll had assumed so as the Queen had hastily joined the battle below, compelling the blue-skin to follow before ensuring he had finished his deadly work.

She took a deep breath and stood up, swaying on her feet and wiped the blood from her eyes. Her nose was no doubt broken as blood dripped down the back of her throat causing her to spit out gobbets of the stuff just to clear her airways. She staggered forward to the castellations, drawn by the cacophonous sounds of battle below and steadied herself on the woodwork. When her vision cleared sufficiently, she took in the scenes of immense chaos that unfolded below. They were akin to something out of a hellish nightmare. A vast sea of Cuscosians assaulted a diminishing circle of Dragonians and their allies. It was impossible to estimate their number, but even the presence of some twenty dragons could not hope to hold them back. Sashaim could be seen leading the ayku and skeredith squadrons in repeated swoops on the enemy, picking up talonfuls of them and pitching them from on high. But they lacked co-ordination and were hesitant in their attacks, knowing Etezora was still dealing death from hands that repeatedly rose to the sky.

There seemed to be no stopping the manic Cuscosian Queen. Where before, her power had ebbed, bolts of purple energy still shot out with unrelenting frequency, snaring allied warriors by the dozen. Her troll then dispatched them with his merciless club. Small wonder the dragons were giving her a wide berth.

*She needs to be dealt with,* Cistre swore, and called for Muthorus. The dragon limped towards her, an injury to his thigh from a Cuscosian spear slowing him down. After a brief inspection she saw that his wings were undamaged.

"Are you ready for what might be your last battle?" she said to him, stroking his snout. "We no doubt fly to our deaths, but we must try to dispose of the evil one. Can you be brave, dear Muthorus?"

The dragon inclined his head and uttered a warm growl, enough of a confirmation to communicate that he held true. Cistre mounted him, uttered a prayer to Sesnath and took to the skies again. She circled around the back of the palace, urging Muthorus up into the void. She would attack Etezora in such a way that the moon did not frame her. Even this might not conceal her approach, but it was her best hope. She climbed and climbed until the palace became a small square below, then signalled for Muthorus to stall and tilt downward. The obedient beast drew in its wings like a falcon and plummeted, centring its descent on the sparks of purple fire that lit the battlefield below.

*Three hundred ... two hundred ... one hundred ...* Cistre counted the fall unconsciously, focused instead on the object of her hatred. A second later, she pulled hard on the reins, urging her mount to veer dramatically to the side. This was not an attack she would complete, as ahead she saw the ponderous approach of a dragon so large it rivalled that of Enthusarr. As she steered out of its path, she craned her neck backwards to take in the leviathan sweeping over the Cuscosian troops. It opened its cavernous maw and out of it erupted an immense plume of orange fire, incinerating all in its path. Dozens of the enemy spontaneously ignited, their cries terrible to behold. There was a figure atop the great beast, but Cistre could not identify it.

*Could this be Agathon?*

Then she spied something less incredible, but infinitely more heartwarming. A blonde-haired rider atop a regal dragon swooped down and alighted close to the locus of Hallows-fire.

"No," she cried, "you are too close to her." However, the cry was a whispering in a storm, and would have required a siren call to be heard across the maelstrom. Realising the futility of words, she swung Muthorus around again, speeding him on to engage with the Cuscosian Queen, knowing that in all likelihood she would not cover the distance in time.

~ ~ ~

From Cistre's perspective, Tayem had landed next to Etezora, but in reality the foreshortening of distance was deceptive. Tayem did not intend to put Quassu in jeopardy — that was *her* risk to take. She landed on the battlefield one hundred paces from Etezora, dismounting her dragon and unsheathing the glaive from its scabbard. Etezora was distracted by Oga, and was already drawing on fresh reserves, raising hands to the sky as if coaxing the great dragon back into range.

*No you don't,* Tayem said and leapt into the fray, slashing and thrusting with her weapon, leaping over fallen bodies and bearing down on the object of her attention. She could see Mahren bringing Oga round for another attack, his form like a giant harbinger of doom over the battlefield. Yet if Etezora was to ensnare him, would even this mighty beast prevail? And what if the sorcerer was to choose this moment to strike?

No time for thought. Another Cuscosian fell before her flashing blade, his throat cut, bringing her within striking distance of the slayer of dragons.

~ ~ ~

Tuh-Ma had ridden high on waves of killing glee as his mistress cut a swathe through the enemy. Her onslaught killed most of her opponents instantly, but many others were delivered to his feet only to fall beneath the crushing might of *Headsplitter,* his club. His euphoria was not to last, however, as his vision grew inexplicably hazy. It was as if a great sleep descended on him and his limbs became as lead. He shook his head, and once his vision cleared, he made out a sprinting warrior with blonde hair, bearing down on his mistress. She could not see her attacker, and Tuh-Ma could not allow this Valkyrie to get through. Although he did not know it, Cistre's poison was slowing him. Yet a blue-skin's constitution is strong and already his rampant metabolism was ridding him of its effect. Still, his movements seemed like treacle as he put himself in the attacker's path. He lumbered towards her, club raised, ready to strike. But the blow never came. A sudden weight struck him from the side, sharp talons gouged into his side — and he was down.

~ ~ ~

Tayem bore down on Etezora, and not even Cistre's attack on the troll distracted her. The thought crossed her mind that she should warn the Queen, give her a chance to defend herself. Perhaps the one who had been her childhood friend deserved that. But that girl no longer existed. Tayem had seen the wasted dragon bodies on the battlefield and understood that the Hallows had completely consumed Etezora.

*No quarter*, she thought, and covered the last few strides just as the Cuscosian Queen loosed a bolt of energy at Oga. It was enough to deflect the attack of the great beast, but not enough to strike it down. Still, the attack enraged Tayem, and she shrieked a battle cry as she leaped into the air and thrust her glaive into the Queen's side.

Etezora gasped in pain, her lasso of energy immediately dissipated. She was cast to the ground as Oga swept overhead and disappeared once more into the night. Yet the Black Hallows was now in its ascendant within Etezora's body, and a blow that should have meant instant death was already being healed by something whose nature was from beyond the stars.

"You," Etezora exclaimed, and as her mouth opened to utter the words, purple fire emerged, bathing her whole head in its conflagration. "Siksta has delivered you into my hands after all."

"Etezora," Tayem said, raising the glaive once more to strike. "Your reign is over. Surrender now, or die by my blade."

The Cuscosian Queen opened her mouth to laugh, and the sound was as a nebula of evil, utterly inhuman and beyond redemption. "I am no longer Etezora," she said. "I am Nurti, Goddess of Death — and now I impart my gift to you!" She raised her hand to Tayem, and before the Dragon Rider could react, a bolt of energy leapt from Etezora's finger, ensnaring Tayem by the throat. At the Hallows' touch, the nightmare of its possession filled Tayem with a terror she had hoped would never return.

"That's right," Etezora said. "The Hallows recognises you as a long-lost friend. Welcome back, schjek!" The lasso tightened until Tayem could no longer draw breath. Etezora was enjoying this, and Tayem knew her death would be slow. She still held the glaive, and she tried to raise it, but Etezora simply willed her lasso to push her further away out of its reach. A flick of the wrist rotated the cord of energy sending Tayem crashing into the battlement wall .

"No, your cursed Dragonian blade will not taste my flesh again," Etezora said. "Any last words, Tayem? No, of course not, you cannot speak. No matter. This is where it ends."

Tayem gazed at Etezora across the intervening battleground as she gathered herself for a final assault. It was then that she glimpsed a gargantuan dark shadow approach on wings of death.

*Have you come to take me, Sesnath?* She thought, as blackness threatened to descend; but an incandescent eruption of fire jolted her from her stupor. The plume scorched the ground in a trail leading to Etezora's position, forcing her to release her grip of death on Tayem and turn to face the approaching scaled behemoth.

*Mahren. Oga.*

Tayem saw the instruments of her salvation, and her spirits lifted.

The gout of flame encompassed Etezora and would have incinerated her — had she been any other mortal. However, the rampant Hallows energy within the Cuscosian despot absorbed the inferno, allowing it to strengthen Etezora's resolve.

*Can nothing vanquish this shjek?* Tayem thought.

"Hah! Is that the best you can offer, wyrm?" Etezora

cried, but as the Cuscosian Queen raised her hands to respond, Oga breathed in and flames gushed from his cavernous throat in a second salvo.

Tayem watched, agog, as searing flames consumed Etezora again. A look of astonishment transformed Etezora's features, realisation dawning that the Hallows former bulwark of protection was exhausted. Her body flared up in an incandescent pillar of hate, and in a matter of seconds incinerated skin was peeling from her exposed flesh, blackening like barbecued meat. It crackled in the night, searing muscle, bone and sinew; consuming the insane monarch as with an unquenchable hunger. The wind of Oga's passing swept the stench of burning tissue over Tayem, and she heard an inhuman scream of agony as Etezora collapsed to the ground, dragon fire eating up every last vestige of purple malignancy.

The shadow passed overhead, and Tayem fell into unconsciousness, no longer aware of anything.

~ ~ ~

Cistre saw Oga's attack, witnessed Tayem fall — all too late for her to intervene.

*Gorram the troll,* she thought, jumping from Muthorus and sprinting to Tayem's side. She reached down and held her fingers to Tayem's neck.

*Her heart still beats!*

There was no time to administer treatment here. Battle

waged all around and she had to get Tayem to safety. She lifted her Queen's limp form, all the time her own head thumping with the damage Tuh-Ma had inflicted. "Don't make me pass out now," she said aloud and carried Tayem to her dragon. It took her some time, but she managed to secure Tayem in the passenger harness. A number of Cuscosian soldiers stumbled upon her, but took one look at Muthorus and thought better of pressing home an attack. Already, she could hear the sounds of battle diminishing as the sight and sound of a hundred bonfires wreaked their toll on the enemy hordes. She'd thought the agonised sounds of dying Cuscosians would salve the mental wounds inflicted by the dragon slayings, but now all she felt was emptiness.

Once more, faithful Muthorus took to the skies and headed towards a place where Cistre knew her Queen would be safe.

~ ~ ~

Tuh-Ma raised his head and watched the Dragon Queen's bodyguard carry her away. He had seen the great duggod-dragon carry out its attack and cried in anguish when the fire consumed his Queen.

He crawled forward, his side shrieking its agony, his progress that of a slug, until he reached what remained of his mistress. Her form was disfigured beyond recognition, nothing more than a blackened husk.

"No," he screamed, looking down at her contorted form, trying to make out her features in the charred mask that now confronted him. "Ma was to be your prince, sweet Nurti," he said, and a tear fell from his eye onto what was once the Queen's cheek. As it struck, it vaporised with a hiss.

"Loyal ... Ma," a voice emerged, and Tuh-Ma wasn't sure if it was his mind or if the dying Queen spoke to him. His head still swam with the remnants of poison and the effects of Cistre's dragon strike, so he had plenty of reasons to think he was deluded.

"Ma hears you, Goddess," he said, not daring hope it was Etezora who spoke. "Do you still live?"

"Not ... much ... longer. This body nears death," came the reply. "Draw closer, Chullashico."

Tuh-Ma obeyed, and as he did, a faint purple tendril of energy emerged from the blackened hole that was once Etezora's mouth. He breathed it in, recognising it for what it was, absorbing the essence of someone he dared not hope would ever share this degree of intimacy with him.

*Welcome, Nurti,* he said to the being that now inhabited his brain.

*I greet you too, noble Ma,* came the reply. *You thought our dreams had been brought to naught, yet this is only the beginning.*

## 52

# AFTERMATHS

---

The amioid reached a point in the river where the ocean's tide ebbed and flowed like day passing into night. It was no longer harroc di wirunwi, not even wizard of the Cuscosians. It was barely even alive.

The call of the ocean had grown stronger and stronger as the blight spread through what remained of his physical form. The dream avatar was dead, and its hold on that realm now removed.

*Oh to be free,* it thought.

Undulating pseudopods carried it weakly to a cliff edge overlooking a sweeping meander in the river course. Looking straight ahead for one last time, it gazed at the morning sky, taking in the glow of violet-tinged sunlight. The Hallows' traction seemed somehow diminished, and its influence withdrawn. Without it, there was nothing to stay the spread of the blight. Its malaise entered his deepest tissues. The time was short. Death would claim him … unless …

For a moment there was sorrow. A warm salty substance emerged from ten of his thirteen eyes, and where it trickled, the blight, if only for a moment was stayed.

*It is a confirmation — of what I must do.*

The amioid tilted forward until gravity took hold, and it fell from the sandy cliff into the estuary beneath. On contact with the water, the mental bind maintaining its physical form dissipated and the brackish mixture reacted with its diseased cells.

As its body floated downstream, billions of cells continued to allow salt water to percolate through their looser arrangement. Through it all, a greater awareness arose. Thoughts, feelings and a calling that had been repressed for many sols emerged in the collective consciousness of the independent blastocysts. An immense satisfaction permeated each of these cells, which now transformed into a conglomeration of semi-motile polyps, each capable of understanding and enacting this true purpose.

*I am the progenitor.*

When the cells met the ocean proper, they coalesced, sponge-like into a form resembling a super-organism. And as the retreating tide carried this complex globule further out to sea, deep into the bosom of the very place it was birthed those many cycles ago, the amioid sensed the final loss of the blight. Microorganisms that initiated and maintained the disease no longer recognised their host and were no more. The globule sought out deeper abyssal places in the ocean until it settled in a place where no light could reach, rendering Sol-Ar's influence void.

As a great curtain fell on the amioid's consciousness, it surrendered to its nature.

~ ~ ~

Phindrath scolded her royal physician with a tongue that had grown increasingly sharp over the last weeks. "You better have a good reason to rouse me at this hour, Jashkin."

"Your Excellency," Jashkin replied. "You told me to call you if there was ever a change in Eétor's state. Well, I think you will be pleased at this turn of events."

They passed through the main throne room and down to Eétor's quarters where his comatose form had lain lifeless for so long.

Phindrath gasped when she found her brother sat upright in bed. His emaciated form was wraith-like compared with the portly body he had once sported.

"Sister," Eétor greeted her with a smile. His voice was edged with a huskiness uncharacteristic of a once strong baritone. "Do not look so dismayed," he continued, "I thought you'd be glad to see me revived once more."

"I ... I am glad to see you conscious again, Brother. You don't know just *how* glad."

"Well, Jashkin, don't just stand there. I have a ravenous hunger. Fetch me dragon meat and fruit. I would sate my cravings."

Jashkin bowed and left as if he had just suffered a scourging.

Phindrath drew closer and examined her brother. "We feared you might never wake," she said. "What happened to you?"

An inscrutable smile passed across Eétor's face. "I have spent a long sojourn in a place where my captor thought I would wither away, go mad or just perish. But a short time ago, the bars on the windows of my prison disappeared, and I was free again."

"Oh, Eétor. I am so glad you are back with us. Etezora has placed me in command of Cuscosa, and I fear that I am not up to the task. With most of our troops in Dragonia, we have been left vulnerable, and now there is talk of monsters abroad within the citadel."

Eétor's smile broadened. "I do not think we need fear any monster now, Sister. Let me relieve you of your burden."

"But, Etezora — "

"I suspect she is not in a position to argue," Eétor

replied, and as he made his pronouncement, Phindrath could not help but think she saw a purple glint in his eye.

~ ~ ~

Magthrum stood next to a boulder the size of a brabagant just outside of Hallow's Creek. He awaited a report back from his two lieutenants.

Nalin and Bilespit appeared moments later, the engineer puffing on his jarva pipe with an enthusiasm reminiscent of his many machines. Magthrum noted the maniacal look in his eye and marvelled once more at the stonegrabe's remarkable recovery and newfound zeal he had acquired at Spidersnatch.

"So, Bilespit tells me we will press home the attack in the early hours," Nalin said.

"You heard aright, my friend. Is the cave-crawler ready?"

"It is, and the fyredrench I stored at my plantation has filled its tanks to the top. It will eat through the limestone bedrock of the castle swiftly."

"Bilespit," Magthrum turned to his lieutenant. " I trust you have motivated the troops?"

"Indeed I have, Fellchief," the stonegrabe said in his oily voice. "The taste of human flesh does wonders to raise the spirits of our clans, and the hamlets we invaded provided succulent cuts of meat."

"Then all is prepared," Magthrum said. "Let us sleep, for in six short hours our assault begins."

It had taken nearly a fortnight, but the stonegrabes had dismantled the cave-crawler and transported it to its new location. Now, here they were, a Kaldoran vanguard, hidden in a small limestone cave beneath the north-west buttress of Castle Cuscosa. *Within striking distance,* the Fellchief thought.

Despite his enthusiastic call to arms, Magthrum had experienced a sense of impotence this last day, as if the Hallows had released its touch on him. Still, the Kaldoran's reconnaissance across the northern plains of Cuscosia had revealed an enemy in disarray, their attention focused on an unseen threat in the north. Now, while they were distracted, Magthrum intended to press home his surprise attack. What an irony to think the Cuscosians would be overthrown by a people they thought were vanquished — and from a front where they had no defence.

*Yes. Hallows, or no Hallows, Kaldora will triumph. Of that I am sure.*

~ ~ ~

Dawn was still two hours away as Milissandia joined with her body once more on the slopes of Maidwin. She uncrossed her legs and crawled over to Wobas's slumped form.

She placed his head on her lap and searched for signs of

life. His chest rose almost imperceptibly and then fell in a manner that signalled it was one of its last graspings at life.

"Father," she said, "can you hear me?"

Wobas' eyes opened a fraction and the corners of his mouth curled in the vestige of a smile. "Daughter ... Milissandia."

"Do not speak. I have potions, medicines that will save you."

"No ..." he said weakly. "I am beyond that. Now listen, for my time is short. I go to join Memel-Tal, but before I do, he has shown me the truth."

"The truth?" she replied, "about what?"

"About you ... and the Cyclopes." He swallowed, painfully, and then continued. "When I leave, the mantle of shaman will pass to you, and with it the release of the Cyclopes curse."

"Shaman? Me? But I am not a man. The council will never accept it."

"Things change," he said, "and I think Ebar will not stand in the way of this."

"Indeed I will not," Ebar said. The giant had approached quietly, but was still out of breath. He had clearly run the whole distance from the battlefield.

"My friend," Wobas said. "It does me good to see you one last time."

Ebar smiled but came no closer. This time was for him and his daughter.

"I do not know if I can traverse the Dreamworld without your guidance," she said.

"Memek-Tal has appointed another, and it will lend you its aid."

A tear fell on her father's cheek as she bent over to kiss his forehead. "We did it, didn't we?"

"Defeated the harroc di wurunwi? Yes. When people work together, they can accomplish many things. But the Hallows will rise again, and you must be ready. Take heart, though. You are not ... alone."

And with that, Wobas closed his eyes for the last time and his spirit left to join those who had gone before. As it did so, Milissandia felt a movement in her soul, like a seed breaking its dormancy. As it sprouted, her inner eyes were opened, and she saw what she must do.

Yet the anguish that now gripped her soul eclipsed any sense of destiny. *Surely this cost is too much to bear,* she thought, and a deep moan rose from her throat, unbidden, uncontrollable and utterly desolate in its expression.

While Ebar watched, his head bowed, a stirring in the grass caught her attention, and a sleek nose emerged from between the blades, followed by the snaking body of a tree serpent. Had it followed her here, or stowed away in her pack?

"You are Ith di wurunwi," Ebar said, breaking his silence.

"Yes," Milissandia replied, picking up the anduleso and stepping toward the giant. "And I have the key to removing your curse." She wiped the tears from her eyes and placed the anduleso on her shoulder.

"We have lost many this night," Ebar said, "and each of the Cyclopes knew it was to happen. That is too much for any being to bear."

"I can give no guarantee regarding the consequences of invoking your release," she said.

"The gift was given for a reason. But let us bury our dead first. Tomorrow is a new day, and there will be time for all those who remain to receive that which Wobas sacrificed his life to gain."

Milissandia nodded and looked back at her father, lying so peacefully on the sward. The tears came like a torrent now, and she did not try to wipe them away.

~ ~ ~

Cistre guided Muthorus down onto the battlements once more and lifted Tayem down from his back, staggering with the effort. A wave of nausea rose, and her head threatened to split open.

*Gorram, I don't know if I possess the strength to carry her inside.*

She spun round at the sound of heavy wingbeats and saw a mottled-grey skeredith alight on the flagstones.

"Sheldar, is that you?"

Mounted on the dragon was a gore-soaked Dragon

Rider, his face obscured by a mask of blood. "Need a hand, Mistress?"

The voice was Sheldar's, but she had thought him lost.

"I can see by your face you thought me dead," he said, dismounting and walking toward her.

"Yes," she replied, "Qardys took the full force of Etezora's bolt and I saw you both fall to your deaths."

"Fall? Yes, and alas, poor Qardys perished. But Mother always said my bones were made from purest heartwood, and a pile of Cuscosian bodies does a lot to cushion a Dragon Rider's descent."

Cistre had never been more glad to see her erstwhile sparring partner. "Help me get Tayem inside. I fear she is mortally wounded."

A look of concern clouded Sheldar's unsightly features. He knew better than to ask questions and supported Tayem on the opposite side to Cistre, so that together they were able to lift her down the steps and into the Queen's chambers.

Once in Tayem's former bedroom, they made to lay her on the royal furs but Sheldar pulled up short. On a perch next to the bed was coiled a large centipede-like creature. It was devouring a spiced morsel which Cistre recognised as dragon meat.

"What is that abomination?" Cistre asked.

"A salyx," Sheldar said. "Stand back."

He drew his knife and threw it at the creature. The blade struck home through the creature's head, pinning it to the wall behind. It writhed on the skewer a few seconds then went limp.

"Etezora's pet," Sheldar said. "Now it joins her in the Vale of the Damned."

But Cistre already had her mind on other things. She listened to Tayem's breathing, checked her heartbeat, and then once satisfied she was stable, set about treating the angry weals on her neck. "Etezora had her in that cursed Hallows lasso. I don't know how much damage it's done."

"Do not worry so," Sheldar said. "Her breathing is regular, and she bears no other major wounds. Our Queen will survive."

Cistre pulled a lock of Tayem's hair away from her face and stroked her cheek.

"She means a lot to you, doesn't she?" Sheldar said.

"The world," Cistre replied. "Now, look in those drawers over there." She pointed at an ornate chest, still wreathed in Etezora's garish trinkets. "If it hasn't been moved, there should be a bottle of powerful narcotic in a brown bottle."

"This one?" Sheldar said, holding up a stoppered vial. "Careful how you administer it, you don't want to choke her and finish off Etezora's work."

"It's not for her, stupid," Cistre said with a smile. "I need something to get rid of this thumping headache."

After treating each other's wounds and tending to Tayem, the two dragon wrestlers were relieved to notice their Queen stirring. They provided her with water and urged her not to speak. It was while they were administering their care that a stirring in the outer chamber caused them to draw weapons.

"Stand down, it is only us," Mahren said as she marched in with Brethis and Sashaim, sword at the ready. "Sister. How are you?"

Tayem raised a hand and waved weakly.

"Don't make her speak," Cistre said. "Her throat is severely bruised."

"No," Tayem croaked, "I will be ... all right. Give me more water. I would speak with my sister."

Cistre looked sceptical but passed a goblet of fresh water to her.

"What news from the field?" Tayem asked.

"Etezora is no more," Mahren said, "and her troops are scattered in the forests."

"You let them go?" Tayem replied.

Mahren hung her head. "Sister, we have sustained great losses. The kingdom is ours again, but we are but a remnant. We certainly had no appetite for exacting further vengeance. In any case, they have lost their Queen. They won't be re-grouping in a long while."

"And what of the dragons?"

"We lost ten more," Sashaim spoke. "Slain by Etezora, the ballista shafts or Zodarin's cowardly manoeuvrings in the Dreamworld."

They shared a moment of silence, after which Tayem spoke the holy words of vs' shtak blessing on the departing dragon spirits. "They shall be remembered," she said, "and commemorated with the proper ceremonies. The Cuscosians shall not gorge themselves on their meat."

Mahren sat next to her sister and informed her of what little she knew regarding the aftermath of battle. The Gigantes had retired to the Maidwin Hills, but nothing was known about Wobas or Milissandia's fate, other than that they must have been successful at averting the threat posed by Zodarin in the Dreamworld.

"Come the morning," Mahren continued, "we will shore up our defences and call back the scattered remnants who remained in the forests after the massacre at Lyn-Harath. But there are two prisoners we discovered who insist on seeing you. Given your state, I would suggest they wait."

Tayem looked beyond Mahren and saw two familiar figures waiting in the doorway.

"Disconsolin, Merdreth? No, let them in. They need to make their peace."

The two renegade Fyreclave members entered penitently and went down on one knee. "Majesty," Disconsolin said, "I must crave your forgiveness. My protestations during the Vicrac were misguided. I sought to assuage Etezora, but it proved to be a travesty. My wife has suffered more than I, but we have both experienced first-hand how the influence of the Hallows cannot be negotiated with. I understand that my decision to appease is tantamount to treachery, and I must pay the ultimate price. But let me at least impart to you what I have learned before I die."

"Disconsolin, that can wait," Tayem said, her voice breaking up after every word. "I forgive you, and as my last act I absolve you from all guilt. The time for retribution is past. The time for reconciliation and rebuilding has come."

"Wait," Mahren said. "Your ... last act? What do you mean?"

"Dragonia needs to forge alliances under a new leader, one who can unite the people, one who doesn't bear the scars of Hallows possession."

"You're abdicating?" Mahren said. "Do not be hasty, Sister. You have been taxed beyond endurance and need time to think."

"That is true," Tayem replied. "Which is why, once I am better, I will retreat to Herethorn and seek the true healing I need. In the meantime I give you full authority to rule in Wyverneth. Your union with Brethis is what both our peoples need."

"Tayem, I — "

"My mind is made up. Now, let me rest. See to our wounded now — whether they be Gigantes, Dragonian or Cuscosian. Let this be a moment when we lead the way in building a new era."

And with that, she dismissed all present, leaving only Cistre at her side.

"My Queen," Cistre said. "You have made your will

clear, and my first duty as Royal Bodyguard is to the ruling Queen, but do not forbid me from remaining at your side. If you can relinquish your position, then so can I."

Tayem turned to her bodyguard, friend and — who knew — something more, saying, "I dared not hope either of us would survive this night of death, Cistre. If you desire to remain at my side, then who am I to dissuade you?" She took hold of Cistre's hand and looked into her eyes. "Now say you will stay with me tonight. I would not spend it alone."

~ FIN ~

# Oga

# Characters

Cuscosians

(Ambassador Urrel) – Eastern ambassador
Asselon – Cuscosian military
Captain Chalmon – Cuscosian military
Captain Domart – Cuscosian Military
Captain Heliot – Cuscosian military
Captain Nestra – Cuscosian military
Captain Torell – Cuscosian military
Charir – Pentacle of Cuscosian Gods
Chullashico – Bearer of Soul and Mind
Cotarth – Etezora's father
Cuticous – Pet salix
Edar – Pentacle of Cuscosian Gods
Eétor  Praetor – Etezora's brother
Etezora – Cuscosian Queen
General Dieol – Cuscosian military
Grizdoth – Cuscosian spy

Jashkin – Cuscosian physicker/apothecary
Nurti – Cuscosian god
Orolotl – Cuscosian general
Oswald – Cat – Zodarin alternative form
Phindrath – Etezora's younger sister
Setaeor – Etezora's nephew
Shio – Pentacle of Cuscosian gods
Siksta – Pentacle of Cuscosian gods
Tratis – Etezora's younger brother
Tuh-Ma – Blue-skin, Etezora's companion
Wkar – Pentacle of Cuscosian gods
Zeetor – Cuscosian battalion commander
Zodarin – Sorcerer/off-worlder/amioid

Dragonians

Aedrellipe – Dragon Rider
Agathon – Agnarim dragon
Aibrator – Dragon Rider
Ascomb – Mature matriarch
Atsa – Dragonian – humiliated Zodarin
Beredere – Donnephon Royal Guard captain
Bostrom – Dragonian warrior
Celemon – Dragonian/exactment
Choghym – Dragon
Cistre – Royal Guard
Coren – Dragon Queen's Guard

Darer – Tayem's trusted advisor

Qardys – Sheldar's Dragon

Disconsolin – Fyreclave member

Elohaim – Dragon Rider

Ensutharr – Old dragon (Oga's mate)

Frodha – Dragonian advisor/courtier

Gathel – Pygmy dragon (with dragon blight)

Gemain – Donnephon administrator

Gostrek – Donnephon Underguard

Gundin – Donnephon Royal Guard

Hyvol – Pygmy dragon (Wrestling)

Jaestrum – Mahren's dragon

Jezethorn – Donnephon Queen – Tayem's mother

Kutan – Dragon (wrestling)

Magister Reganum – Fyreclave advisor

Mahren – Sister of Tayem/kirith-a adept

Merdreth – Disconsolin's wife

Muthorus – Cistre's dragon

Nyrris – Dragon Rider

Oga – Old Dragon (Ensutharr's mate)

Quassu – Tayem's dragon

Ralgemah – Legendary Dragonian Pyre Queen

Rargorren – Sayndriosse's dragon

Rusior – Dragonian veterinary surgeon

Sashaim – Dragon Rider

Sayndriosse – Dragon Rider

Sesnath – Deity

Sheldar – Dragon-hand

Staithrop – Donnephon Royal Guard
Tayem – Donnephon Queen
Teshgazzadar – Dragon
Thorshil Fyreglance – Tayem's father
Uniro – Donnephon captain
Ymith – Pygmy dragon (Wrestling)
Ymre – Nyrris's dragon


Gigantes


Brownbeak – Sentinel raptor
Carys – Wobas's estranged wife
Dshambi – Ebar's oldest child
Dyabi – Ebar's Baby Son
Ebar – Cyclopes Hill-warden
Ginnie – Minutus wise woman
Hanar – A Cyclopes
Milissandia – Wobas's daughter
Narchen – Cyclopes council member
Scorfleet – Cyclopes council member
Shamfis – Ebar's wife
Taumahg – A Cyclopes
Torthen – Gigantes council member
Vaedra – Minutus villager
Wobas – Shaman / hermit

Kaldorans

Belthraim – Kaldoran deity
Bilespit – Kaldoran stonegrabe
Buzmith Oakstone – Kaldoran foreman
Ellotte – Nalin's wife
Gorespike – Kaldoran soldier
Gribthore – Kaldoran stonegrabe
Grubet Bloodgut – Kaldoran healer
Grufrod – Kaldoran mercenary leader
Hakrish – Kaldoran stonegrabe
Hetherin – Magthrum's deceased wife
Kalor – Kalti leader
Kartasia Silverfox – Friend of Ellotte
Magthrum – Fellchief/Kaldoran Leader
Nalin Ironhand – Kaldoran Chief Engineer
Nutug Hillgrop – Nalin's cavecrawler mechanic
Palimin – Nalin's Son
Pandar Kaldoran – God of sleep
Pitchbass – Kaldoran stonegrabe
Ropetail – Kaldoran stonegrabe
Speedwill – Messenger bird
Tarchon – Kaldoran deity

Dream Entities

Memek-Tal – Spirit Guide
Swamp Augur – Dreamworld Augur

Townsfolk (Cuscosian Peasants)

Brethis – Blacksmith's Son/Mahren's lover
Eryx – Brethis's sibling
Jeramin – Brethis's sibling
Oathair – Townsfolk/Brethis's right hand man.
Petter Proudson – Townsfolk Inn Keeper
Ragonthorp – Townsfolk
Rawkin – Cart driver townsfolk
Singarin – Townsfolk
Vanya – Wandering bard

# About Tom Adams

Tom Adams is an imaginer drifting between lands of speculative fantasy, horror and bizarro. When he strays back into the realm called reality he finds himself in

Middleland; a geologically beautiful gamut of scenery in the north west of England. The forces that drive him shift their shapes with sharp needles of inspiration, but at present include the art of Zdzislaw Beksinski, the music and words of Ronnie James Dio and a frankenstein amalgam of word-scriptors such as Vonnegut, Tolkien, Clevenger, Leonard, King and Bradbury.

Tom is also an audio-narrator and has many titles on release from Audible, including 'Dark Gods and Tainted Souls – Books I , II and III' authored by Julius Schenk/ Arthur King, 'Lies and Retribution' authored by A.P. Bateman and 'The Psychonaut' authored by himself.

He occupies niches in cyberspace at http://tomghadams.com and https://www.facebook.com/ tomghadams/

# About Andrew Naisbitt

Andrew Naisbitt is a product of the innovative 1960s. An impressionable child, he was influenced by many of the iconic TV shows of the period: the creativity of Gerry

Anderson's "Stingray" and "Thunderbirds", TV classics such as "The Avengers", "Doctor Who" and "Star Trek" and later his imagination was stirred by the literary works of Fleming, Gardner and, more recently, Horowitz.

Having retired from a successful career in Public Service, he now has time to diversify into his family business as a hobby shop owner and follow his dream of being a writer.

Andrew is no stranger to the publishing world, having previously written articles for the "Continental Modeller" as an experienced model maker.

He has now put pen to paper to create the fantasy world and mythos of "The Black Hallows" which brings a multitude of characters to life, not only in book form, but also as source materials for fantasy role-play and wargaming.

Cyber links – andrew.naisbitt@lineone.net or Sales@hadrianshobbies.com

# Can't get enough of the Black Hallows?

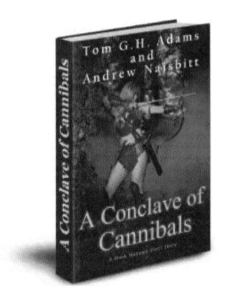

The second book in the Black Hallows trilogy is scheduled for release at the end of 2020; but if you can't wait until then there's another tale you can immerse yourself in straight away.

'A Conclave of Cannibals' is a short story from Tayem Fyreglance's past. She and Cistre have been charged with leading a small sortie of Dragon Riders into the far reaches of Dragonia in order to track down a murderous warband of Kaldorans. Tayem must prove herself as leader of the Dragon Riders and root out the marauding stonegrabes that assail their border, and ensure that no more Dragonians fall foul of the Kaldoran's cannibalistic appetites.

Featuring characters from 'Cradle of Darkness', you will experience a chapter from the Donnephon Queen's early life that helped shape who she is in later life.

To get hold of this short story, simply go to https://dl.bookfunnel.com/olj11dg3iy and sign up to the Black Hallows newsletter. You'll receive this FREE story and also get regular updates on all that is happening in the world of Black Hallows.

One more thing: If you enjoyed 'Black Hallows: Cradle of Darkness,' then please hop over to Amazon and leave a review. Andy and Tom would very much like to hear your feedback, and it also helps raise the profile of this book with other readers.

Many thanks.

Facebook page: https://www.facebook.com/Black-Hallows-Cradle-of-Darkness-112211593524934/

Printed in Poland
by Amazon Fulfillment
Poland Sp. z o.o., Wrocław

51380356R00399